Hang John Brown

by Donald Mann

First Edition, July 1, 2010
Copyright © 2008 by Donald F. Mann, Rose & Mann, LLC

Registration # TXu 1-644-948

Hang John Brown
Rose & Mann ISBN #978-0-615-38167

www.HangJohnBrown.com

Townley Rose & Donald Mann
Publishers
Rose & Mann, LLC
PO 981
Bentonville, AR 72712

www.RoseMannLLC.com

Printed in the United States of America

Book Design Phillip Unetic, UneticDesign.com
Cover Art Created by Mark Swift
Rendering of John Brown James McCarron
Authors photo courtesy of Donald F. Mann

...though a white gentleman, (he) is in sympathy a black man and so deeply interested in our cause as though his own soul had been pierced with the iron of slavery.

FREDERICK DOUGLAS

...and someday the black man will rise from bondage, even as high as President....

ANONYMOUS

Foreword

Writing a book is a personal process which once published becomes a very public experience. As in all creative efforts the exhibition of it while daunting and sometimes dispiriting is nonetheless a reason for joy. First of all it is completed, that alone is reason to celebrate. But the idea that someone else may find your effort valuable is a hope motivating beyond all criticism. I hope you can find enough value in this book that you can at least classify it as worthwhile. My hope is to bring to life not only the tone of the historical period and the character of the players, but also evoke the underlying messages of the time. My effort is but a snapshot of the complexity of events that conspired unknowingly to bring about the future we now inhabit.

This is a work of fiction based on historical events. The entire Zephaniah Jacobs story is fictional. Any resemblance to actual persons, living or dead, events or locales is entirely coincidental.

The portion of the book based on John Brown's life is only partly historical. John Brown, his family, mercenaries and contacts within the Secret Six are historical figures, among others, are fully fictionalized for purposes of the story. The character John Brown is partly based on available information but much of his speech, attitudes, and psychology are conjecture. It is hard enough to extrapolate on a current figure let alone a person from one hundred and fifty odd years ago. All other characters noted in relation to the John Brown story are real in name only; they have been created as characters of fiction to fill in gaps in what is known about them.

A work of historical fiction fictionalizes fact and adds factual textures to fiction; creative conjecture intermingles with documented events. There are major portions of this book that are completely fictional, others are loosely related to history, a few, most notably John Brown's raid on Harpers Ferry, are drawn as accurately as possible from historical information available; however, even the raid and the feelings and flow of events are by nature fictionalized once dramatization is added. Also some dialogue and speeches are fictional while some are drawn directly from the record.

In cases of the speeches of Charles Sumner, the words of Preston Brooks, John Brown's trial speech, Thoreau's speech on Brown, as well as information on the Underground Railway, the Fugitive Slave Act, Dred Scott, Jesse James, the background data on geography, flora, fauna, riverboats, and finally and importantly slavery, Wikipedia served as my primary research source.

In researching John Brown, I visited the actual site of Harper's Ferry, West Virginia. It is fully restored and extremely informative. I recommend it to any who need to experience the place to get a sense of the flow of events. There are many interesting exhibits, interpretive displays, not to mention helpful guides. It is a wonderful spot.

Two books instructed me greatly. First I highly recommend, *John Brown, Abolitionist* by David S. Reynolds. I learned from Mr. Reynolds many fine details surrounding Brown's life. It especially outlined Brown's meaning to history and his translation and transformation in the public eye by the likes of Thoreau and Emerson. The chapter in *Hang John Brown* called "The Raid" which depicts the Harpers Ferry action is a blend of information from Reynold's, the Harpers Ferry Site and Wikipedia, as well as fictionalization. As noted before, since this is work of historical fiction, it is not appropriate to note specific references on each page; however, Reynolds's book was the source for some actual quotes attached to Brown regarding his feelings on slavery and the meaning of his raids. There are also quotes or near quotes added in for the slaves Brown freed in the chapter 'John Brown Returns.'

Also please make note of *"Bleeding Kansas"* by Nicole Etcheson. In this work I learned much about the tenor of the times surrounding the border wars between Missouri and Kansas and the building tensions between north and south.

It is also important to note that Bible verses are from Wikipedia as well as *The Revised Standard Edition*. These are chosen due to their clearly intelligible English. The *King James Version* was the dominant text of the day but I have made the substitution for reasons of accessibility and intelligibility.

In dedication I would like to acknowledge my wonderful wife Cordelia Rust Mann, whose love and understanding have helped me in unmeasured ways to be able to complete this book.

My children Scott Francis Mann, Michael Donald Mann, and Catherine Ellen Mann have taught me as much, if not more then I could ever teach them. I hope reading this will unfold a desire in them to seek greater things within themselves and with God. They are growing into fine adults and I look forward to seeing what they will become, though fully satisfied with who they already are.

My recently deceased mother, Joan Grace Mann, and my father, William Leisenring Mann, as well as my brother William Hiram Mann, were seminal in my upbringing in the world at large. They helped me greatly to search for meaning in life, in the Bible, and in everyday events. They prove with their lives that love is indeed the greatest of all. This too is for them.

Townley Rose, my partner and friend, has devoted himself to bringing this book to publication, as well as the future film plans which are in the process at the time of publication.

I also want to mention my good friends John Naughton and Mark Swift both of whom have not only been most excellent friends for many years, but also have been part of many a deep discussion on matters religious, political, artistic and general. They both have a hand in this work, whether they want to admit it or not. Mark Swift also performed a service with his most excellent artistic interpretation for the original cover art of the book. Alice Roher spent time editing and critiquing the book and was much help, as she encouraged me with her comments to keep going. Amy Casey, likewise, spent time editing and critiquing and brought much value and insight to the process. Phil Unetic of Unetic Design, I thank for his efforts at layout and design of the interior of the book. James McCarron, who has done drawings of key events from the book, brought his own inspiration and art to the process and to him I am grateful as well.

Mostly however I feel at all times and in all places I should be thanking God for all the blessings in my life.

Prologue

Richmond, Virginia, May 25, 1900

Sunlight slants and captures itinerant dust in its lonely prism. I sit in my office on this cobbled side street and watch wandering particles float and drift. The smell of mildew and hints of summer swelter mingle in the air as I think of my life. The slow cadence of weary horse steps count out the seconds in an irregular beat, pock marking time, scarring like disease my last season. I am ready finally to set the record to paper. I know this is the day I have waited for. I don't know why it has taken me so long. But it is time for the retelling, for a final reckoning.

About my office are collections of mementos on dusty shelves, buried in drawers; they are all that is left of my life. They help me to remember, to make it all seem real. These papers and books and baubles are keys to gated pathways of memory that have gone overgrown. They remind me daily why I am here, how I ended up finally in Richmond, this city aging and feeble, this convalescing patient along the banks of the James.

Once capital of the South, Richmond was the axis of our law, code and honor, a midwife of slavery now infertile and barren, its dark child stillborn, this tired place revives—but barely—after years of neglect and slow bleeding abscesses, the tumors of lost war. The old Capital is consumptive, it coughs and sputters along, functional, but a mere shadow of itself in the glorious days. This broken place like the ruins of Greece which once stood for something far off in our memories is now lifeless and empty and cannot be rekindled.

We know in our souls we will never rise to our former vigor; hidden beneath our coats the weeping wounds from the four year fray leak our pride to our clothing which we cover in shame. These war wounds fester as we remember the pain and the loss with only past victories to muster our strength.

The soldier's infirmary where I found Zephaniah is haunted by ghosts anguished by their forgotten sacrifices. The beloved Stars and Bars no longer waves, it is folded in attics; it covers walls, a flag for decoration in memory of a time, a spirit, a myth. But we still hold it dear as we rebel the boot of stiff reconstruction—the indignity, and humilities of institutionalized subjugation.

I say to you now, I swear as God is my witness, that these things of which

I write happened. I know they were neither dreams nor visions though much of life often seems so. Before I am so old I cannot put order to events, when others will say my words are boiled in a brain mad with age, it is important that I record this story so it will not be forgotten as I most assuredly will be. An ancient relic of days gone by, I am resignedly aware I approach my final days. And so I write this, so all will know what really occurred back then.

⬥

The smelting furnace that was Kansas Territory in 1856 wrought iron clad ideas, crystallized by the heat of opposition. It was Dodge where I was born and came to manhood, my frontier awareness of the greater world growing with each bit of news of incursions by Missouri folk and slavery's southern sympathizers trying to keep us free to own our chattel. They stared down the abolitionist settlers backed by the north. Our border was the final dividing line between the north and the south. We circled and parried while the crowd took bets. We debated the issues in pulpits, parlors and editorial pages. But then, on came John Brown. Once he arrived on our soil, his deeds were the death sentence to our way of life. He was the hangman as the nations focus was drawn to Kansas like a noon hanging in the town square. He begat the last days of what we called the South. He started the Great War; he broke the first link of the Negro's chains.

Those days in Kansas and my journey to Manassas, before the great slaughter of blue and gray, was a time when legend and life wound together like twine. I felt surely baptized with a holy water of preordained events, washing scales of doubt from my eyes forever. I knew finally there was a hidden power behind such great turns in history. What happened on that trail before the 'War between the States'—while Brown still lived—no living man can attest to but I. I saw it. I swear it happened.

I learned then that time changes all, but a true story lives on forever. It has a soul that shines through time, translations, retelling, revisions; through wars, floods, plagues, pogroms, invasions, genocide. People cannot, nay will not, forget a true story once told.

I witnessed that thing called Truth; it is neither an illusion nor a thing clear to all. Truth is a rare bird, beautiful to see, not to be captured. It cannot live in caves but needs freedom. Light. Once seen it flies away, fleeting, only to be heard of in stories. Like a starved ache for love lost, it finds its way into heartfelt words to let others know it was real, entombed in the granite of nouns and verbs. Lifelong yearning for one more glimpse of Truth makes the telling of it the only salve. And so I write.

The witness to Truth will ever feel in a certain danger, compromised, unable to express oneself fully for fear of seeming odd. I did not speak of these things for many years. Speaking of it revives a kind of chaos to the mind, committing to it sheds the skin of predictability we wear so comfortably. We would rather shelter ourselves in the common fixed places of a spurious universe then venture like a tottering preacher to a pulpit unsure of our voice and footing.

I became a lawyer after my wandering days, after we lost the war. I settled here in Richmond, my final home. I retreated to the safety of Law. I studied the legal interactions of men. I sought solace in the set rules of life at the bar of justice and learned my profession well. I suppose I knew most of the laws that men live by; those created to establish a representative government, to protect property, promote jurisprudence and preserve habeas corpus; those which established the common conventions of life. I cling to those laws today, like a drowning man grasps a lifeline, I survive by their judgments. I am preserved in their patterns, secured with their insincere promise of order, always remembering those days when the Law could neither bind nor arbitrate, when our world's orbit was interrupted, its rotation reversed and our crooked path was made straight by a prophet sent to trod with men, sent to doom those who could not divine his vision, whose name was simply Brown.

Many nights have I thought on those times, books closed, arguments written, when my mind could rove again the trails in the wilderness, where I watched the collision of worlds whose physical patterns were torn asunder, when I rode one of them to the brink. Those days taught me what a slim thread of hope the law provides, when one man can cut the tether, can change an entire world, can pile stones on a nation and proclaim it a monument that will ever be a holy place to mankind. Those days taught me the power of Truth, that great experiences seed the stories of the world, a recounting for the generations, straight standing, staring time eye to eye, inspired by God. They start in the actual, may grow, molt, change, but I can be sure now they are begat from real things, from the Truth, from God. We should not forget that.

Twenty two years old in June of 56, days prior now seem so distant, no longer real, cavernous time away. In those early years I dwelled in a kind of subterranean world, shielded in a dusky veil of diversions, desires, doubt, hidden from the truth, still an unbeliever; then suddenly, distant presages of lightening flashed opposition to my God-given freedom to own property, both human and inanimate. Gray clouds rolled in, clouds of dissent against the spread of slavery into the territories. These angry, roiling billows of hate for us formed in Washington and darkened our sky, looming, dangerous. They collided with the thunderheads of our will rising over the sacred expanse of Kansas.

Brown started the downpour. He brought the deluge, the Biblical flood we sensed but could not foresee. Brown ripped a bloody gash with his sword along the Pottawotomie Creek near Lawrence, Kansas. His deed foretold our future as the news galloped across the land like an avenging angel. He threw salt in fresh wounds with his raid on Harpers Ferry, West Virginia. This was the start of the war of all wars; Kansas was the place where the great feud began. My freedom to own slaves as God decreed in the Bible opposed the self evident equality of all men as endowed by the creator in our Declaration; that was the barb that tore the flag. Brown's act near Lawrence drew men like flies to a bloated corpse. I was one so drawn; a journey that changed my life forever and led me here finally, to Richmond, so long ago. Angered, inspired, vengeful, I rode to the bleeding place of my Kansas, to find him, to hang him.

Kansas Territory

May 24, 1856

John Brown sat on his haunches looking blankly into the fire. He was a man of average height, yet even squatting so he seemed large. People always said he looked somehow taller than he actually was; something about him filled a room, breathing the very air of inspiration into others who came to be with him. His saber sharp blue gray eyes, hued as the blended dye of the dead soldiers uniforms from north and south, gazed mesmerized by the shiver of struggling coals to something beyond, something only he knew, to the battles he foresaw. He looked like this often and some wondered if he was speaking to angels, listening to God. He was calm countenanced, thoughtful, lean from spare living, from Calvinistic discipline and ritual self denial of common indulgence. But at the mention of slavery his slow fuse met the powder of his nature and he would boom with a rage he could not contain. His unkempt hair, pushed back, wavy, stunning in its volume and mane, rose like a promontory above a thin crooked mouth, a square jaw, large ears and a full prominent hooked nose of a size congruous to the other large features that populated his ridged face. He stared at the embers, one eye squinting. He was 56 years old, weathered, worn by a hard life, stooped but not broken, and driven. As he stirred the embers with a poker, he sang beneath his breath a version of his favorite hymn, *Blow Ye Trumpet Blow:*

> *Ye slaves of sin and hell,*
> *Your liberty receive,*
> *And safe in Jesus dwell,*
> *And blest in Jesus live:*

> *Blow ye the trumpet, blow!*
> *The gladly solemn sound*
> *Let all the nations know,*
> *To earth's remotest bound:*

> *Ye who have sold for naught*
> *Your heritage above*
> *Shall have it back unbought,*
> *The gift of Jesus' love:*

Brown's hand, calloused, large, strong gripped as a vise, held the wrought iron tool tenderly. He wore a soiled brown wool coat and a black tattered tie, as if off to a church meeting or a wake. His crumbled straw hat hung on a peg wedged in an empty knot. The building, a simple lean-to of rough cut wood, had a patchwork of skins and sewn fabrics covering the open wall.

His mind was set; there was neither doubt nor fear, guilt nor compromise clouding his thoughts. The world had drained his soul of hesitation, wrung it from his being like a wine press. There was one way to go now, forward; there was one thing to do now, murder. He was like a sick man whose medicine was ritual sacrifice, a dreamer whose final vision was cataclysm.

His sons sat around the fire lit room. John Jr. sat on a crooked cane chair, Owen on a broken rocker, Watson on a hewn bench near one wall, Oliver on the dirt floor near the fire, Salmon on a pile of firewood. His boys—men now—born of two mothers were only part of his brood. They were skinny, sickly, unkempt. They had struggled to survive these past two years as settlers, land staked. Disciples of their father, a militia of blood related abolitionists, ready to fight for their cause, they waited on his words.

Outside seated on the wagon was James Townsley, a painter, and Thomas Weiner, a Jewish book merchant, a large powerful man. Brown had ridden through in that same wagon from Nebraska, laden as it was with surveying tools which disguised the true gist of his journey. Hidden beneath the stakes, measures and plum lines were the implements of war—Sharps Rifles, pistols, ammunition—unseen by the grizzled border guards who stopped this slow talking laborer, whose dress, speech and actions were those of a commoner. Both Townsley and Weiner, mercenaries joined with a family of mercenaries, waited for their chance to engage again. Whittling and spitting they lingered while their leaders met in war conference.

Henry Thompson, John Brown's son-in-law, wandered off in the distance whistling a lonesome tune. He unbuttoned his trousers near a cottonwood tree. Relieving himself he looked at his stream as it ran on down and spread on the clay. The ritual complete he looked up with unspoken questions for a time at the moon rising through the scrubby branches, then went back to the wagon and sat down to his work at the grinding wheel. He pumped the pedal until the stone spun fast enough to grind. Heavy, it creaked as it rubbed on its axle. He lifted a two sided broadsword, held it even to the spinning stone and honed it, in search of perfect sharpness, as sparks roiled out in small universes in the air. Circling like flaming hot insects they expired quickly.

John Brown Sr. had been in Kansas some time now. He had attended long wordy meetings where they debated the border wars between Missouri and Kansas. The Missouri men had come in, burned the abolitionist presses, illegally stuffed ballot boxes with their votes, forcing their version of Freedom on free men. In Lawrence just a month before, John Brown stood and spoke publicly for the first time, denouncing the position of Reverend Martin White, an effusive, overweight, balding preacher, the grand equivocator, who comfortably straddled the fence between slavery's expansion and a free state, using legal terms to justify compliance with immoral laws.

White said, "It is now territory law, regardless of how it was voted in. We must obey it regardless of our opinion. It is now the law of the land. Law is Law".

The gathering was beginning to be swayed until a rumpled, poorly dressed man with clear blue eyes and a stern voice walked to the front of the assembly. As his sons watched from the rear of the room, Brown stepped up on a chair and replied, "Immoral law remains immoral. Negroes are our equals, sir, protected by the Constitution, endowed by their Creator with rights, included as human beings in our Golden Rule. Do unto others, sir, as ye would have them do unto you. I would rather see our country destroyed; have disunion, than our perfect God-given document interpreted so, by tawdry laws passed by fools. It is better that a whole generation should pass off the face of the earth, all men, women, and children by a violent death, then for one jot of our constitution or the Golden rule to fail so. I mean it, sir." And John Brown stepped down and raised the chair, swinging it to the floor, splintering it into many pieces and walked out followed by his sons. The audience was left in stunned silence.

Around the rustic lean-to were scattered John Brown's books, *The Sermons of Jonathan Edwards*, with a well read section, "Sinners In The Hands Of An Angry God." Beside it was *The Life of Oliver Cromwell*, Brown's Hercules, the revolutionary leader of England's church, who cleansed the Augean stables of idolatry, imprisoning many, burning Tyndale at the stake and beheading a monarch's religion. Cromwell massacred the Irish for their papist ways, establishing the primacy of the Bible, the Word as the law. Next to that was Brown's favorite book, *The Life of Field Marshall the Duke of Wellington*, which retold the story of resistance to the power of Napoleon. He saw in that work a model of leadership against great odds and superior force. Another well read book told of the revolt of Nat Turner, a slave who escaped and went roving the countryside freeing other slaves. They hid in the mountains and returned again to terrorize slave holders until he was caught, tied to a stake, eaten by hungry dogs then burned alive. Turner's rebellious followers were dragged from the hills, nailed to poles, and used for target practice.

And of course there was another well read book, Brown's Bible, never far off; it was as worn as his face, as creased as his soul.

John Brown Jr., his loyal but unstable son, sat red eyed from searing headaches which brought on bouts of near madness yet unexplained. He and his brothers had come to Kansas almost two years before to get ready while their father attended to his business affairs, failures, lawsuits, and burdens. His father had never amounted to much. He'd had big ideas, failed ventures in the wool business exporting fleece to Scotland. But it was a disaster. He had tried to dwell in both the real world and his land of visions for human equality, but without success. So now he had discarded the real world, left his family's fate to God, and had finally set out to establish the vision God had planted in his mind.

John Jr. thought of the predawn Bible sessions. Every morning of his stark life had begun with the Word without fail. After a night's sleep in quilt covered beds shared five children to one, sick or no, he'd rise to readings of Hebrew wars and destruction, of incest, of lust, of Sodom and Gomorrah. But also he heard of the love of God, the words of Jesus, of Paul, the decree to love your neighbor, to free the oppressed.

John Jr. remembered, too, the slaves from the Underground Railway sheltered in their barn beneath the floor. He remembered stern lessons on the great sin that was slavery, of his duty to free the oppressed as Jesus preached, as proverbs commanded. His father had nurtured them, trained them all their lives for this cause. And now finally they were ready to act.

Twenty-two children fathered with two wives were raised this way. His younger siblings died as infants from whooping cough, measles, or the ague, until one birth finally killed his poor mother. Dianthe. Dianthe was her name.

And Mary Day Brown, his step mother, lived alone in the mountains of New York, bearing up but barely existing with many mouths to feed and little children at her skirts while her husband roamed planning battles to free poor slaves.

John Jr. looked on his aging father and thought back to the time when he, John Jr., was forced to whip him in punishment. He was made to strike his father's bare back with a hickory switch over and over, hurting him deeply for what he, John Jr., had done. The problem was the dream John Jr. had dreamed as a boy, which he could still envision. He'd dreamed colorfully, vividly, thrillingly. He awoke full of wonder and grand ideas, full of amazing images he felt he must tell his parents about. He ran from his crowded bed to the table where his father sat eating bread before heading out to work their sparse farm and told them of his incredible dream. He could still hear his voice as he told his father, "The dream is real. My dream was real."

There was a long silence; he remembered an ominous stillness hovered darkly.

Father Brown's anger rose as his booming voice was unleashed with conviction too hard for a boy, "No son of mine dreams and believes."

He was filled with fear. He had seen his father's rages before and felt the beatings.

His father's world was filled with illusions, tricks of the devil that he fought to subdue and conquer. He saw the mind's night journeys as visions from the evil one, to entice us, to fool us that powers be where only human frailties exist, permitting us to think we can know things God does not intend. But this father would not simply punish the child for believing a dream. John Brown made his son whip him. This was young John's punishment: to apply firmly to his father what he should have received. John Jr. whipped him hard then harder as commanded by his father. John Brown wanted his son to see, as God sees, the pain he had caused with his sin.

John Jr. remembered still the switch swiping the air, wisping like a broken bellows, and his father counting out loud, "One, two, three, four, five, six", on and on, thirty stern lashes. Thirty. It had taught John Jr. his lesson in a way he'd never forgotten.

His father said, "We all punish God in the same way, all the time, everyday."

But John Jr. sometimes wondered why his father's visions were not subject to the same scrutiny of source, God or the Devil, as his. It was these thoughts perhaps which brought on his headaches, and he tried to suppress them because he knew the man who sat before him was more than a father; Father Brown was their leader in a cause. He remained unquestioned. He was followed now; a man chosen, he could not abandon his charge to free the slaves for mere thoughts, ephemeral and suspect.

His father looked into the fire and spoke slowly, deliberately.

"I have been here better than one year. When I first came you were all a sight, living in tents, scraping by."

John Jr. explained, "It was bad Father, we were sick, we had nothing, no money. I tried to get organized, got on a Free State committee, riding to Lawrence every week, trying to get it started."

John Brown said, "I have no contentment left in me, the time to plan is over. We are a weak, arrogant race, vile in the face of God. We sit in the warmth of this fire with the world splitting from injustice. It is time to act. It must be done to end this slavery outrage. It must be done to show these border ruffians we will not live under their tyranny and become slaves ourselves, let alone see our Negro brothers and sisters in Christ remain the same. Governor Robinson, the perfect old woman, does nothing. Nothing. He is more talk than cider. These politicians would rather pass resolutions then act."

John Brown went back to tending the coals for a little while.

"I have considered at great length my plan for Virginia. I have told you so, yet I have not resolved it, there are yet complications. It will come in God's good time, the final great storm that will end this greed. But it is God's plan, not mine. I am his actor only, unworthy as I am. But it is not ready yet, so it is here we will begin. It is time for the first skirmish. These few willing souls will have to do. Great odds did not deter our fathers. We will use what God has given for this task. It will suffice, it is His will."

He threw the newspaper in the fire, watched it smolder then continued, "Five thousand rode in, five thousand to vote, to use our democracy against us. They rode in force, took over the polling stations, jailed some, hanged any man who spoke or wrote against their God hated slavery. They voted in their own pro-

slave legislators who wrote laws, passed them, and we did not so much as squeak.
They sacked Lawrence, arrested Deitzler and Brown and Jenkins for the truth
they wrote. It was their God given freedom of speech, and they silenced it. With
a hatchet they hacked to death Reed Brown who tried to free a 12 year old boy.
They left his body on his doorstep for his wife to find. His blood dripped through
the porch boards to the free soil below seeding this night. And Sheriff Jones, he'll
be punished too. He said that night was his happiest, said he'd make the fanatics
bow down before him in the dust and kiss the territorial laws. I bow to no man,
to no law but God's. I tell you now they seek to control all government, to steal
the rights of all men, not just the Negro and not just here in these territories. No
one will threaten my flesh, my land, my country."

He rose and walked to the wall. He stood and looked straight into the
wooden fibers.

"We rode hard to join the fight, but no fight was had, all simply sat around
the fire waiting for reinforcements that never came. So nothing happened. And
it was that night we heard about Senator Brooks beating Charles Sumner. It was
that one last measure and my rage overflowed."

The United States Congress

May 20, 1856

Charles Sumner looked over the chamber filled with Senators, Congressman, judges, who listened raptly to his speech as it carried across the smoky space. The upper gallery was filled with reporters, pads in hand, whose attentive eyes were a collage of pensive expressions. He looked to the sleepy pages huddled in corners with fear wakened in their eyes after hearing his words. They awaited his next utterances. These were bold words, fighting words; words cracking the porcelain baked with regional compromise.

There had been many speeches here on the subject of slavery, the first made by Sumner himself, but none in such stark terms. None which sidestepped the niceties, the diplomatic rephrasing of what was actually happening, what each side knew was under the rug, swept there by a desire for peace, pushed back in view and spread anew by Sumner, soiling the Senate floor with the incongruence of slaves in the land of life and liberty.

Sumner had been committed to speak the truth as he saw it, as God saw it, from his first days in the Senate in 1850. But he had bided his time, observed the politics of trading human freedom for power. His first major speech broke all convention. He uttered words no one wanted to hear, which fell on deaf ears and brought no one to action. There were long sessions and heated debates, attempts to reconcile strongly held moral views against human bondage with respect for the property rights of the south. Both parties had fought hard and compromised on the Fugitive Slave Act. The Act redefined the Constitution with a basic tenet: runaway slaves needed to be returned, one state could not steal the property of another. Sumner had thrown the logic of this unholy truce to the wind in a few phrases.

He was from Massachusetts, a stubborn, clannish bunch who held their liberty close. After all, they had started the fight to begin with. They sat on their rocky coastline bearing up to frigid weather and slicing winds, scraping out a life on poor soil. With a good port, sure winds to London and a history of law and university, they were independent, dogged, educated, well connected, men of thought and commerce. Sumner could not let the law of the material, the rule of chattel and quit claim, stifle the supreme and the moral.

Sumner rationalized that this nation was based on philosophies espoused in the Declaration of Independence, of the divine rights of all men, not simply property rights and legal theories, inherited and applied. England had owned this land by charter, deed, and proclamation. But, regardless of the legal documentation, this place was ours. Our revolution wrote in blood that we were free men first, British second. The United States was a people with God given rights, superseding those conventions of men. The highest ground is the best ground in a battle. Sumner took it.

Supreme Court Chief Justice Taney sat like a goblin in a back row, remote, sunken, pale and sly as a card shark. Preston Brooks, esteemed congressman from South Carolina, sat with his hands white around the gold head of his thick gutta-percha cane. The cane, a bold style from the old country with a golden handle poured molten hot into the form of an American eagle, twin arrows in talons clenched tightly, stared fiercely to one side awaiting any threat. The eagle's look of foreboding anger crossed, too, the face of Brooks.

Stephan Douglas filled another seat. Thick framed, stubby, with a bulldog's bearing but diminutive stature, he sat in brooding silence; a deft walker of the tightrope stretched along the Mason Dixon line. As he listened, he could see the high wire he tread unraveling with each flourish of Sumner's delicately poised hand.

"You," Sumner said, and as with sword in hand he pointed to the gallery, then pulled back his arm and threw the verbal stab again at each section of the chamber, "You and you and you, are now called to redress a great transgression. Seldom in the history of nations has such a question been presented. Take down your map, sir, you will find that the Territory of Kansas, more than any other region occupies the middle spot of North America. A few short months have passed since this spacious country was open only to the savage, who ran wild in its woods and prairies. Now it has already drawn to its bosom a population of freemen larger than Athens."

Sumner then bowed his head in pause, leaving the impression he prayed to God for continued strength. A spellbound chamber awaited his next words. He savored the silence, the tension, the dramatic false calm until he leapt to his toes with an inspired vigor, surprising his audience so clearly now in his rhetorical power.

"Against this Territory, fortunate in position and population, a crime has been committed which is without example in the records of the past. It is the rape of a virgin territory."

Brooks pounded his cane in response to this phrase. Others grumbled and booed.

Sumner went on saying, "Compelling it to the hateful embrace of slavery. It may be clearly traced to a depraved longing for a new slave state, the hideous offspring of such a crime, in the hope of adding slavery's proponents in these very seats of this Senate Chamber, to take over the National Government. Even now while I speak, portents hang on all the arches of the horizon threatening to darken the broad land which already yawns with the mutterings of civil war. The fury of these propagandists of slavery spreads across the whole country."

He pointed directly at Justice Taney who glared with rheumy, corrupt eyes.

"A madness for slavery which would disregard the Constitution and our supremely inspired laws, and all great examples of our history."

He pointed to the galleries and newsmen, "A control of public opinion through venal pens and a prostituted press. A madness for slavery, there sir, stands the criminal, all unmasked before you—heartless- grasping- tyrannical."

He wiped his brow and waited for his words to settle then went on.

"But I must say something of a general character particularly in response to some Senators who have raised themselves to eminence on this floor in championship of human wrongs. I mean the Senator from South Carolina, Mr. Butler and the Senator from Illinois, Mr. Douglas. Senator Butler, the Senator from South Carolina, believes himself a shi-shi-shi-shi-shi-chivalrous knight (mimicking Senator Butler's stuttered speech), with sentiments of honor and courage. Of course he has chosen a mistress, who is lovely to him though ugly to others, though polluted in the sight of the world she is chaste in his sight. I mean the harlot Slavery."

Sumner stopped to wipe the sweat from his brow and the spittle from his chin. The clerk to his side wiped as well his desk, flecked by the spray of Sumner's fierce enunciations. Brooks sat rubbing his white hot temples, trying to contain himself.

"For her, his tongue is always profuse in words. Let her be impeached in character, or let any proposition be made to shut his whore out of the Territories, and no extravagance, no vigorous assertion is too great for this senator. The Frenzy of Don Quixote in behalf of his wench Dulcinea del Toboso is surpassed. The asserted rights of Slavery, which shocks the notion of equality, are cloaked by a fantastic claim of what, Equality itself? This is a mockery of the great fathers of this Republic."

"If slave states cannot enjoy full power to compel fellowmen to unpaid toil, to separate husband and wife, to sell little children at the auction block in these national territories, then sir, the chivalric Senator will conduct the State of South Carolina out of the Union! Heroic Knight!"

Sumner took a bow, a gesture of southern gentility, and then cast a deriding glance.

"Exalted Senator! A second Moses come for a second exodus. The Senator in the unrestrained chivalry of his nature has undertaken to apply vile words to those who differ from him on this floor. He calls them 'sectional and fanatical.' He denounces the opposition to the usurpation of Kansas as uncalculating fanaticism. Yet he is the uncompromising, unblushing representative on this floor of a flagrant sectionalism, which now domineers over the Republic, yet with a ludicrous ignorance of his own position unable to see himself as others see him. He applies to those here who resist sectionalism the very epithet which denigrates himself."

Brooks, Douglas, Taney shifted in their seats taking deep restorative breaths, trying to drop the pressure of the blood bulging in their veins. Brooks rested his chin on his cane's eagle head. He then looked down and rested his forehead on it, the eagle emblem was imprinted on his skin when he quickly looked up at the ever more inflammatory references, and he pounded his cane on the dented wooden boards beneath his desk.

Sumner then pointed to Douglas, dramatically then dismissively.

"The Senator from Illinois, a noise-some, squat, and nameless animal, not a proper model for an American Senator, Mr. Douglas is the Squire of Slavery, it's very Sancho Panza, ready to do all its humiliating offices. Standing on this floor, the Senator issued his ultimatum, requiring submission to the Usurped Power of Kansas. This was accompanied by a manner all his own, such as befits the tyrannical threat. Very well. Let the Senator try. I tell him now that he cannot enforce any such submission. The Senator with the slave power at his back is strong, but he is not strong enough for this purpose."

A pause and then, "There shall be no slaves here but slaves to principal."

There was great silence, and then a third of the chamber erupted in applause. Another third sank into grumbles and boos, while the remainder simply sat in confused, concerned silence. The gavel rapped urging order. But the call was not to be heard for many years to come.

The United States Congress

May 22, 1856

I n the near silent Senate chamber, Senator Charles Sumner sat at his desk writing. A few remaining Senators talked in echoing corners of the gallery. Congressman of South Carolina Preston Brooks, cane in hand, strode up to Sumner. He was followed by two other congressmen, one from South Carolina and one Virginia.

Brooks said firmly but with all southern courtesy, "Mr. Sumner, I have read your speech twice over. It is a libel on South Carolina and on Mr. Butler who is a relative of mine."

That said, Sumner started to rise but before he could stand straight, Brooks raised his arm and caned the Senator on the forehead, branding his pate with the cane's eagle knob, punching a welt that quickly poured forth blood. The sickening sound and Sumner's cry echoed around the chamber. Stunned eyes turned to the source of this distress, sounds so strange to these august environs. Sumner fell limply to his chair like a marionette with no master. He slumped forward and his face hit the desk as another blow struck the back of his head, then still another fell on the top of his head which caused him to slump back in his chair in a careless recline, his face ashen, as another blow then another were dealt with methodical power and the blood ran down his face, staining his shirt, dripping from his nose and forming a puddle on his desk soaking his papers. The ink of his written words, insulting, injurious and refined to a sharp political edge, mingled with a dark redness that flowed over the desks ornate wooden corners and spotted the floor below. He slid flaccidly beneath the table holding his head. All the while Brooks swung away as Sumner sought protection from the assault and crawled about blindly on the United States Senate floor. Trying to find a route of escape, Sumner crawled into chair legs and bumped against the desktop above, toppling spit buckets to the floor as he tried. At each turn he was kept from safe exit. He looked like an injured dog in a death match.

The desk, bolted firmly to the wooden floor, held Brooks at bay. It acted as both prison and shield, confining but protecting Sumner from the onslaught of his attacker. He could neither rise nor flee but crawled about dodging errant blows. Brooks could not land deadly strikes with it in the way, yet he swung his cane with a steady rhythm, striking anything that became exposed. He swung his eagle headed cane over and over and over again, pounding, bruising, tearing at any exposed part of Sumner. Brooks struck at his legs while Sumner crawled about trying to find an outlet. He smashed the Senators delicate fingers when they grasped a chair, a desk, Brooks' pant leg. The sound of Sumner's fingers cracking could be heard with each blow. Then frustrated at his inability to land the cane soundly, Brooks grabbed the desk and with a strength borne of great rage tore the shield away, ripping the bolts from the floor, splintering the floor boards. He tossed it aside as if opening a vault filled with gold, his eyes fixed and widening at the sight, his mouth drawn tight in concentration. The discarded desk flew into the legs of the blank faced congressmen standing transfixed nearby, injuring them but waking them from their shock.

Brooks continued to drive blow after blow on a crouching, helpless Sumner who now lay with arms raised in protection. The flabbergasted congressmen hit by the desk tested their bruised knees and continued to look on the bloody scene gone too far. Finally they moved to subdue Brooks, to control his cane. But his rage was so embodied in his steady motion, as if he was a printing press stamping out page after page, that he shook them off and delivered still more blows until his cane finally broke, its gilded eagle head flying across the aisle.

At this point the battered and frantic Sumner had enough strength only to crawl away trailing much blood, until in blurred vision he saw the safety of the chamber doors. This drove him to his feet in a half standing position and he stumbled along dragging one leg, cradling his broken arm, and calling out wildly. This last great effort and his grave injuries overtook him and he fell in a silent pile, unconscious.

A sweaty, heaving Brooks, still restrained by his peers, looked up to see the gory tableau of the fallen Senator against the lamplight in the open chamber door, bordered by a lone American flag.

The knob of the cane, its eagle head crowned in red Senatorial blood, lay on the floor, a testament to sectional slander, its consequences, and the new way to deal with opposing ideas.

Trampled Vintage

John Brown continued to gaze into the fire and spoke in hushed tones.

"This violence, these threats to our freedom, is unending. They test us at every turn. But in truth, I am glad they do not cease their aggression. It justifies, it justifies. Their foot shall slide in due time."

He paused, stared into the fire longer. Its red yellow glow lit his face, erasing the lines and giving him a younger look, illuminating his steady staring eyes.

John Brown continued calmly saying, "The battle begins here. It begins now." And he brought his large hand down on his knee with a force that sent dust from his trousers. Then he rose to his feet, still speaking calmly but gaining, gaining.

"President Pearce supports this proslavery legislature, voted in on a lie. Stephen Douglas of Illinois, the northern compromiser, compromiser on freedom, compromiser on liberty, compromiser on God given rights with that dog from South Carolina, Butler, they wrote the act and bartered the votes to get it passed. They will burn in hell fire, damned for all eternity. Slave power is what we witness here. Slave power passed the Fugitive Slave Act and the God forsaken Kansas Nebraska Act, slave power burned the Free State Hotel, slave power raised the cane of Brooks to batter Sumner, slave power started this. We do not start this. We act only in response to their aggression. It must stop here."

Owen said, "We're ready, Father. Been ready all our lives."

Brown looked at the fire for a while longer and reached down to churn it with the poker.

"I thank God for your letter; I thank you for that, for calling me here, for telling me the truth of how it is here, for asking my help. It has given me a purpose while my plans hatch for Virginia. I am here to save you, to save them, the oppressed dark people. My life has been disappointing, a failure to speak truth in all I tried, my wool ventures, my farms. But it was God's will; it is why I am here in the end. I have always felt myself an empty vessel waiting to be filled. Not yet called but soon to be. This cause, this truth, has filled me."

He paused and looked out to the men waiting near the wagon and said, "I think on the time when I was a boy, on the cattle drive with my father riding to Chicago to sell beef to the army during the war of 1812. I saw it then for the first time, the raw cruelty of bondage, the beating of a slave boy. I'll never forget it. I was so young but I pledged to dedicate my life to stop it, to stop it dead. And now I am old, I have waited long enough. Enough of talk."

And he picked up his sword.

"The rifles and broad swords I brought are gifts from kindred spirits who cannot act but want action. We are their hands, their arms, their muscles, their sinews. Our swords cleanse consciences. They will cleanse this land by stopping the spread of the evil of Slavery to this territory."

"Right now, right now, an army is building of pro-slavery fighters from Missouri. They are coming here to claim our land stake as theirs, to outnumber us and turn democracy asunder. They ride against God's will, for expanding slavery and human misery, for casting more illegal votes. They ride to kill us. The truth is they mean to butcher us, burn us out. We must show that our side can act. This has been a one sided war, them with guns, us with words. No…it all starts now. We will start the war to end slavery tonight. Tonight we act. Make your peace, prepare for a sacred expedition."

John Jr. spoke, "Don't be starting nothing yet. The militia is small, we have not fought together. We can't win a fight now. Let it play out. Let it roll downhill a bit. Don't do anything rash. Tar and feather, a good whipping will do, but killing will get us killed before we can do any good. Take caution."

"Caution, I am eternally tired of that word. It is nothing but a word of cowardice. No, we will use their own tactics on them, they will suffer now. You stay here, John, speak not to me about waiting any longer. I have waited my whole life for this. I have thought on this long. It is so clear but all they do is talk, talk, talk. No one will act, tangled in such a rope, we are. This knot must be untied. Someone must act. I will stand before my judge and plead my case, some must die so others may live as God intended. I forsake one commandment, Thou Shalt Not Kill, to live fully the words of our Lord Jesus to love all men as our brothers. I give myself to the great judge to determine my punishment or reward. Killing is the only way to straighten the crooked path they walk; they are pulling all of us down. This old earth is cleansed from time to time. When man disobeys God just sweeps it all up, starts anew. I am the broom. I am His instrument. I know it. You know it too. It is God's will. It is God's will that slavery be slain. This night was predestined when God made the earth. You stay here, John. We will buckle on our armor, tonight we will kill for the love of God."

And he stuck a pistol in his trousers, put on his weathered straw hat and, with his broad sword in hand, Brown led the others out through the patchwork of skins and rags into the moonlit night.

In silence John Brown walked, stooped shouldered and steady, down the California road, his sons Frederick, Salmon, Oliver and Owen tramped behind, eyes full and glittering. Following behind walked Thompson, Townsley, and Weiner, their eyes fixed on the moon dead ahead. It was a solemn mystery of men from a distance, featureless until they moved arms, legs, torsos, heads, swords, rifles against the moonlight; a strange silver hunting party stalking human prey who enslave men. Hypnotic crickets scratched their early summer song, growing louder, sensing death.

John Brown led the men along the bank of the creek hidden by clumps of river birch, then up along a drainage ravine. Waist deep they waded across a creek called Mosquito. They approached the door of the first cabin they came upon, a small squat structure. Mud and hay daubing sealed rough hewn logs, with an uneven roof and a door hung crooked on leather hinges. Sitting too close to the creek, it was built lazy for fetching water, not in consideration of overflows.

It was well past midnight and those inside, the Doyle's, were asleep, lanterns doused, embers glowing in the fireplace. New May mosquitoes buzzed past sleeper's ears. They owned little, it was a sparse life. But they'd sided with slavery after moving to Kansas from Tennessee, farm failure driving them west for a better future, seeking salvation in land stakes and a fresh start, a mighty gamble. They hated abolitionists, did not own any slaves, yet they supported the slavery cause.

John Brown held up his hand halting the stalkers and pounded on the flimsy door. There was a scuffle inside, muffled voices with urgent fear in their tones. They hushed. Then there was silence and only crickets.

"Who's knocking there?" Doyle called out.

"We are seeking the Wilkinson cabin?" said John Brown.

"This is not it, they are further down east of here," called his wife Mahala.

"Can you give me directions, I must get there tonight?" said Brown raising his arm to signal his men to wait.

Then Brown motioned the men to go. When James Doyle pulled aside the door they rushed into the cabin, swords drawn and rifles cocked, knocking down Doyle. Thompson lit a lantern outside and followed. The family slept all in a section of the cabin, separated by a low plank wall. The man's three sons, a boy and two older, now nearly men, sat protectively by their mother smothered by her fat arms wrapped tight in solace.

John Brown walked up, put his pistol square in the face of the man of the house still sprawled on the floor and said, "James Doyle, you, a member of the Law and Order Party, seeking to break God's law and destroy His order, you are my prisoner. I command you and your boys to come with me."

The man looked at his sons and his woman. Fear filled his wife, and she pleaded, "Leave them, please go on your way and leave us. We will do you no harm. We will move out, we will leave this place. Give it to you. You have won. You are in the right. It is the Sabbath; you cannot kill on the Sabbath."

Brown said, "It is better to do the Lord's work on the Lord's Day. Now out with you." And he motioned to the men to lead them out.

The mother held on to the youngest who was about fifteen or sixteen. She cried, "Leave him, leave him, my John is just a boy."

Brown warned, "Keep your child, woman, he knows not why you are here.

Teach him well to live by his own labor. Do not buy the children of other mothers to do his chores."

The three men walked out as the stunned woman cried in the darkness behind the door, hugging, almost choking, her youngest. Doyle and his sons, Drury and William, aged 20 and 22, walked ahead of the armed men in silence. Afraid and dressed only in their long britches, they were walked out beside the creek, told to kneel.

Then John Brown said, "Now pray to God to forgive your sins. Slaves to greed, slaves to sin, enslavers of men."

The swords shined in the waning moonlight and came down swift and flashing on William first. They hacked at a forearm and severed fingers held up for protection. Then a bold downward plunge split his head almost down the middle, off to the side a bit but not all the way through, about half way between the nose and the eye socket. Blue moonlit brains spilled out, a look of shock plastered his face, his mouth twitched on one side like he was trying to smile. Blood spilling, he fell over gracefully, slowly, almost peacefully.

An odd wail rose from his father. His brother Drury was shocked silent. As he moaned in anguish for his son, their father was pierced in the belly by the swords, gutting him, leaving him curled in agony with intestines leaking out, crying in pain.

Drury tried to run, but fell. The swinging swords shone again and three fingers from one hand scattered on the ground and an arm was severed with a grunting hack. Young Drury was stabbed in the side and the face. He tried to run away but, wild and crazed to escape his death; he tripped into a dark ravine he walked past one hundred times. One arm missing, he lay there as all expired and he bled to death.

The mother screamed in the cabin at the noises from her slaughtered family. She was mad with fear, wounded as deeply, as mortally, as her offspring and their father.

John Brown took his pistol from his belt and looked down, his steel blue eyes fixed on the writhing father, he stared, not crazy, not angry, just matter of fact. He then shot him in the forehead.

Owen Brown let out a whoop of excitement at what they had done. Brown, his sons, the others, looked at each other from face to face and wiped the gore from their weapons and clothes. They knew they had started something now and were ready for more. They walked away in silence except for the pounding force of their hearts echoing in their heads, the swelling sensation of great righteousness filling their chests.

Mother Mahala's screams and cries rose in pitch to a breathless whinny as she ran to her dead men's bodies. She rocked over them, moaned and let out a wail.

The young boy, John, followed slower, crying. He cried hard but soundlessly then screamed like a girl upon seeing the horror. He fell to his knees and pounded the ground, then yelled, "You'll hang John Brown! You'll hang! You'll hang!" Then with all his young boy might he yelled, "You'll hang!" And as his strength trailed off he cried softly, "Hang you Brown. Hang you..."

Brown's band looked to the darkness ahead, seeking the paths between the shadows, looking straight forward or down but not again at each other. Alone in their thoughts of what they had done, they walked along to their next target, stepping over ruts and washouts, the clank of swords on guns the only noise.

They stopped at the home of Allen and Louisa Wilkinson, a few hundred yards from the Doyle's, their cabin the local Post Office. Wilkinson had served in the bogus legislature voted in by fraud. He was said to be a mean man, a drunk wife beater.

A barking dog had already awakened them from sleep when Brown knocked on the door. Louisa heard the dog first, then some whispering outside, then the knock, and another knock. It could only mean more trouble in an already troubled life.

Brown called, "Is this Dutch Henry Sherman's home?" There was no answer.

Brown asked, "Are you a Pro Slavery man?"

"I am", answered Wilkinson, though his wife was afraid and begged him to be quiet.

John Brown said, "You are my prisoner. Open this door or I will open it for you."

His wife, now frantic with fear, tried to block the door. But Wilkinson roughly pushed her aside; she was not to rule him. He opened it to Brown, who with his men rushed in and scanned around for weapons, searching under beds, turning over baskets, pulling out and breaking the drawers of a cherished highboy, as they rifled through the room.

Brown asked, "What is your position on slavery?"

Wilkinson answered, "I am against the Free State Party."

Brown exclaimed, "Then you are my prisoner. Do you surrender?"

"I do", said Wilkinson.

"Then dress and come with us", commanded Brown.

"My wife is ill, she's had the measles. Can I find her some help first, before I go?" asked Wilkinson, concerned for the woman he beat regularly.

Seeing her bruises Brown said, "It matters not. Dress."

Wilkinson struggled to pull on his trousers. He fumbled nervously with the buttons.

Impatiently Brown said, "Forget your shoes. March."

They marched him outside, his sickly wife crying in the cabin. They walked away perhaps 100 yards, far enough so his wife could not find him this night. They did not want to hear her scream; Mahala Doyle's moans still rang in their ears.

Brown told Wilkinson, "Kneel down."

And as before, the swords came down hacking forearms held up for protection, one blade slashed across his neck severing the jugular, freeing his blood to pour forth, soaking his nightshirt. He grunted and fell over. They stabbed him again in the body, in his head, in his side. He lay on the ground near a stump he had been digging out, much work yet to be done on that stubborn old tree. And yet another emancipated woman's cries rose in the darkness mourning her bloodied and lifeless future.

The last cabin, owned by one James Harris, had several guests sleeping over.

Brown knocked on the door and said, "I am looking for Dutch Henry Sherman."

Then they barged in before any answer came. But while James Harris was not there, William, his brother, was. He too was marched outside. Then he was hung by the neck from a large willow limb where he struggled greatly trying to get air through his crushed wind pipe as swords were driven through his gut. But each stab took time. The body was slow to stop swinging and the killers wanted to take aim, to ram the sword to the hilt and pull it out cleanly, spinning the body round with the force of the blades removal, the rope twisting and creaking in rhythmic time between the piercings. The swords stabbed and stabbed repeatedly. The blades thrust through the lifeless body, exited the back, then withdrew with dripping disembowelment spurting forth. Then with one swing of a sword his hand was severed, another and the rope was cut. He fell hard to the ground.

The thrusting steel could not be debated or equivocated upon. It brought politics and morals to the intended collision. The awful truth was made clear as the news spread across the nation. Slave holders and their supporters were immoral and might be punished with death. John Brown said so.

Visitation

A Campsite, Kansas Territory

Zephaniah Jacobs sat by the slow burning fire reading his Bible. Eyes blurred from age, he wore spectacles, still the small print was a hard read by firelight. Each night he sought brief solace from the book of aged wisdom to carry him to sleep. When his eyes tired and he could read no more, he could drift off finally. But until he slept, he searched God's word for a message, a signal, a beacon he could follow in his life. His full white beard, furrowed brow and lined face were deceiving. He was an old man but still strong, fast, willful, filled with the spirit. He hunched over reading a proverb by the measured dance of the firelight. He turned the onion skin pages slowly and rubbed his chin whiskers in thought. He read from Chronicles 14:8.

When the Philistines heard that David had been anointed King over all Israel;
all the Philistines went up in search of David;
and David heard of it and went out against them.
Now the Philistines had come and made a raid to the valley of Rephaim.
And David inquired of God,
"Shall I go up against the Philistines? Wilt thou give them into my hand?"
And the Lord said to him,
"Go up, and I will give them into your hand."
And he went up to Baalperazim, and David defeated them there, and David said,
"God has broken through my enemies by my hand like a bursting flood."
Therefore the name of that place is Baal-perazim.
And they left their Gods there and they were burned.

And the Philistines yet again made a raid in the valley.
And when David again inquired of God, God said to him,
"You shall not go up after them, go around and come upon them opposite the balsam trees. And when you hear the sound of marching in the tops of the balsam trees, then go out to battle: for God has gone out before you to smite the army of

the Philistines."
And David did as God commanded him,
and they smote the Philistine army from Gibeon to Gezer.
And the fame of David went out into all the lands,
and the Lord brought the fear of him upon all nations.

Zephaniah removed his spectacles, rubbed his eyes, and then lay down. He put his head on a rock and looked up to the heavens. The stars were covered by clouds, hidden as behind windblown gossamer garments. They glinted in secret until a wind blew and revealed the familiar and luminous heavenly sparks Zephaniah followed as his earthly guides. The clouds proceeded to slide along, unveiling a brilliant ashen full moon. He looked on this glorious show and thought about his situation. He was frustrated. He had ridden hard but could not find John Brown. He had joined up with a group of angry men, a mounted mob led by Pate, but to no avail. Brown had disappeared like a phantom. Zephaniah wanted to finish him, make quick business of it, lance the wound, sever the sinning limb. But he had failed.

So he prayed for God to aid him in this battle. He prayed that, if it be God's will, He strengthen his arm as in the story of David. He asked God to give him the power to protect God's way of life which he had always followed devoutly, to protect this land for the riches of slavery, as it was in the Bible.

He looked up as he heard a rustle in the grass, louder than the wind rushing through it. He grabbed his Bowie knife but it sat on a rock too near the fire. The hot bone grip blistered a brand on his palm and he dropped it as an Indian stepped into the ring of light. The Indian walked into his campsite as if calmly passing through.

The Indian looked straight ahead, grinning, but carried no weapons. He seemed neither angry, nor deranged, nor drunk. It was strange, this curious Indian visitation. He looked to be in a trance. Zephaniah knew of Pawnee, Comanche, Kiowa, Sioux, Apache from down Mexico way. His wives were Apache and he had lived among them for a time to win them. Indians went far back into his memory as a boy. He knew them from stories his father and grandfather told. But this Indian, of an unclear tribe, dressed like a farmer and stood like a ghost in the night. His presence, his silence threatened Zephaniah.

Zephaniah asked, "Who be you?"

No answer.

"What is it you want?"

Silence.

"You'll answer or you'll die," he said in a flat tone of threat as he rose to a knee and looked to his pistol some distance off by his saddle. They stared, Zephaniah at the Indian, the Indian into the night.

Once a sure aim with a rock, Zephaniah picked up a fist sized stone and threw it square at the Indians head. The Indian moved with great speed avoiding the blow. But while this attack removed his grin, it did not anger this mysterious savage. Before Zephaniah could leap for the gun, the Indian dove across open space, grabbed the gun and threw it in the brush about twenty feet distant.

Zephaniah leaped at the Indian, grabbed his hand and twisted it backward. He pulled him to his back, rolled on top and reached as he did for another rock to strike him dead. This gave the Indian enough leverage to throw Zephaniah over and rise to a dominant position.

He pinned Zephaniah to the ground and said, "Why do you try to hurt me with a rock? Because I do not answer you? Do you own this land that no one can be on it?"

Zephaniah said, "You should speak your intentions and not scare a man."

The Indian answered with derision, "I do not have a weapon. I did not try to steal from you. You insult me. All white men are an insult to me."

"Get off me," sneered Zephaniah.

"I will get off when you pledge," said the Indian enjoying his power.

"I ain't pledging to a savage, a mixed breed, Kiowa or whatever you be," he answered.

"You are right. I do not know what I am. You have taken that from me. You have divided my family, shed my blood, infected us with your disease. I should kill you, but I am too sorry for you," said the Indian.

"Why sorry for me?" asked Zephaniah, "You are the one beaten, you flee to towns for our whiskey. You go into the wilderness for visions that do not come."

The Indian spit to the side and said, "I am sorry for your kind. You speak with rifles but without them you are weak, like a slow witted new born dog."

"You are a heathen," cursed Zephaniah.

"Yet I sit atop you like your kings sit on a throne in their big houses," the Indian said.

"I have no king but Jesus," said Zephaniah scornfully.

"Yes, Jesus is your king. I heard that from the missionary, the same who brought us the spotted disease in the blankets. You have strayed from the teachings," replied the Indian.

"Get off me," Zephaniah yelled as he struggled to free himself.

The Indian said, "I will get off you but only with a pledge."

"Indians can't pledge, it is not in their blood," said Zephaniah.

"It is white men who cannot pledge. You need paper and ink to seal your word. Words that are lies, paper that burns to ash. Your pledge blows in the wind."

"What pledge do you seek?" asked Zephaniah, still fighting and angry but giving in a bit.

"Pledge you will fight me until one of us wins. No guns, no knives, no rocks, just our hands."

"I can pledge you that. Now get off."

And the Indian jumped back as if thrown by a bent sapling. Gathering himself, Zephaniah stood and dusted himself off, then he began to circle for a fight, fists rolled, knuckles ribbed, at the ready to punch. The wind blew stronger raising a whirlwind of dust; the clouds rushed overhead covering the last remnants of the moon. The men circled, circled, faces lit by the wind flared fire. Zephaniah looked for the chance to strike or grasp, to find the lever to throw the Indian to the ground. Zephaniah felt alive, dizzy, dreaming.

He asked, "Where are you from?"

"Nowhere," said the Indian.

He asked, "Where you heading?"

"Nowhere," said the Indian.

"You got a name?"

"Indian or white?"

"Either?"

They circled and circled.

The Indian said, "Some will say I am Moroni, you are called Zephaniah Jacobs."

"How do you know my name?"

The Indian answered, "Tirawa-atius told me."

"Who is he?"

"He is the Great Father."

The Indian dove forward tackling Zephaniah, driving the blunt ball of his shoulder into his hip joint, dislocating it. The pain was excruciating and Zephaniah cried out, but fear and the rush of competition kept him rolling and wrestling. His aching hip popped back into place and he pushed away from the Indian and awkwardly rose, stumbling from the discharge of pain. He limped about.

"Look what you've done, I am lame now with miles to travel. I am on a journey, a mission of God. Why did you come into my firelight?"

"I came to see you, great Christian. I heard you were here. People talk of you, living as you do by the word of the false book. I wanted to see your great power first hand. But you are a weak man," said the Indian rising to his feet.

"I have God's strength in me," winced Zephaniah.

The Indian said, "But it leaves you now, just when you need it. With no guns or steel you are weak, the strength flew away just as it left the Jesuits who came with the black book for us, who pushed us underwater so we could be new born. But who died with us when the fevers rose. The pus poured from their sores the same as ours. Your God does not protect you from this world.

Zephaniah answered, "Do you carry the pox?"

"I do not know," the Indian said, and he laughed but then became serious, "I came to tell you I have seen John Brown."

"Where? How do you know I seek Brown?" Zephaniah asked in confused pain.

"I have come also to tell you I have given you a new name. You are to be called Coyote," the Indian said as he stepped backward, fading into the darkness, half in the light.

Zephaniah asked, "What does that mean?"

"Evening Star, Morning Star had a son and a daughter. Humans were born, but the son stole the storms, turned them loose on the world. Coyote is the thief of the storms. You and Brown are the same, you both claim God is on your side and you set loose the storm? How can God be on two sides?" the Indian said just before he ran away into the night.

Zephaniah tried to run after him but the pain was too great, he called out for him to stop, grabbed the gun, fired it into the air. But the Indian was fast, gone like a fleeing spirit, only the crickets could be heard in the shrouded silence of the night.

Zephaniah's hip ached; with each movement his hip felt as if it was being scraped over coarse gravel. He was filthy, sweating, and confused. All he could do was lie down on his back, head on a rock, as the fire died down and think of the mysterious encounter. The injury to his hip pulsed and throbbed as he reached for a canteen, drank of it, lay back down and looked at the moon. He watched the bats flitting, gliding with sudden jerks, darting shadows arching in new directions, like quick minnows on a shallow river bottom, swerving upside down then rolling and switching back.

In his head the word Coyote was said over and over. He did not understand it, the Indian's strange visit. Was it a dream? The pain in his hip was real enough. Evening star, morning star, the name, Coyote, the Indian had said. A wild dog, Brown and he the same, went through his mind over, over, over. The repetition of these words took on a speed of its own making, ran on with no effort, slowed then raced, louder then softer, rushed so it made him dizzy. The words sought some escape from his mind like a sparrow caught in a barn. The bird soon found a way out and settled on a branch, ruffling its wings to rest. Zephaniah's mind now sat beside this bird and he looked down on the world from his sleep.

He then witnessed something incredible. He slept deeply and had a powerful dream, a startling violent vision. He wrenched and tossed, talking and mumbling, sweating, until finally he started awake, his eyes detonated open and the dawn-streaked sky bled into his dire vision, so real, so present. Zephaniah knew it was sent to him for a great reason. A reason he needed to discover immediately. He had crafted his life to honor the Lord, to follow the Bible, so he knew when God spoke. He knew he was called.

He waited no longer than it took for the thought to enter his mind. So despite great pain in his hip he packed up quickly and saddled his horse, Beersheba, mounted her stiffly, and set off west, homeward, to see his wives, his sons, to consult with Joseph.

Journey to Manasas

Kansas Territory between Dodge and Lawrence, June 1856

My story begins here. I'd heard about Brooks righteous caning of Sumner, felt the hot wind from Brown's murderous slashing broadsword. As Captain of the local militia, I tried to get men to follow me so we could join up with the Missouri men who had come across our border to keep abolitionist scum out, to keep Kansas from freeing niggers; from breaking the back of Missouri farms. These Missouri bands, formed to protect our God given rights so we can own property free from government intervention, to vote as we pleased, to live as we willed and be free men, needed us to join them, to stand up and hold our ground. But my militia would not follow; too many concerns sapped those men. Conviction lacking, they scurried back to their farms and left cleaned rifles hung over the mantle, believing the murders to the east would not spread west. So I left Dodge on my own, bid it goodbye, not knowing if I would ever return. And I never did.

I rode for a few days, wearied, tired. My horse led me after a time and we wandered on a road through fluffy seed heads on the spring prairie; she carried me to Zephaniah's land in the Chautaqua Hills. I did not know whither Sagebrush took me. I did not direct her so. I was bone tired, not thinking. I could barely hold the reins in my hand.

I'd had several sleepless nights since I left, one unsettled blanket-tossed night with thoughts running through my brain about what lay ahead of me; one with prodding rocks as I lay beneath an oilcloth out of the rain and one with something evil prowling beyond the light of my fire, sounding like an Indian or a big cat. So I left in the dark, rode all night and watched the sun leak orange stains on the morning sky ahead of me.

The horse followed the wagon path like a sleepwalker with a sack of corn on its back. I was half dreaming, half speaking and I mumbled to myself, drooled on myself, held a conversation with my momma who was some days and many miles behind me.

She was telling me not to go, saying, 'Hiram you're a damned fool. Hiram don't get killed in another's fight. Don't waste your life on what amounts to a rich man's battle.'

I told her, 'Kansas needs to be free to own slaves, it is my duty, I am a man, men do this, who else will, called by something greater, God, heritage, country.'

She replied, 'We don't have slaves, we never will, ain't going to fight so some other gets rich.'

I said, 'The law was on our side, no abolitionists can tell us what to do, we were free, this is what it means to be free, this John Brown must be killed........' when Sagebrush stopped, almost toppled me off her back.

I wiped the drool from my mouth, lifted up my hat to look blurry eyed at the barrel of a shotgun pointed squarely at my nose, held by a boy of only thirteen or so.

He said, "Stop right where you be, do not move, not a flinch, not a reach for your gun or you'll be dead as Jesus on Good Friday."

He was serious and had a purpose. I sat very still, slowly raised my hands, noticed how remarkably awake I had become, how momma had just shut right up in my dream. I saw relief in his eyes that I was following his commands, then a hint of fear at what to do next. This was new to him, new to me having a prisoner, being a prisoner.

"Now you just walk that horse of yours ahead of me," he said, "You just walk a few steps, stand there, hands up, not a jiggle."

I did as he said. Nudging Sagebrush forward, I moved ahead blankly, hands in the air like a trick rider posed for a painting. He came up from behind my horse, reached to my holster and took my pistol, then pulled the rifle from my saddle. The weight of those instruments was a struggle for his small arms. I considered bolting, expected my horse to know what to do, to take off like my champion steed, to save me. But I did not know this boy's preciseness of shot and Sagebrush's finicky nature I knew all too well, so I sat pat.

I was much more comfortable with the gun pointed at my back than my face. I would much rather die from an unknown than a known. My fear trickled away some, since my whole life had felt this way, threatened from some force behind a curtain I could not see let alone parlay with. I was not afraid, even somewhat resigned to this small boy's whim. Quite strange being ready to die, I did not expect it to be so soon or in this manner; days away from home, killed and robbed by a near infant, rather than in the glory of a fight to save my rights.

I said, "I've got money, some valuables you could just have."

He said, "Shut up and get down off the horse."

Which I did.

Then he said, "Now lay down, face to the claypan."

Which I did.

Then he commanded, "Now put your hands behind you."

Which I did.

He snapped the leather leg straps off my holster with a neat clip of his knife, tied my hands like he was roping a calf, smartly done really. He put my rifle back in my saddle, pulled off my holster, put it on himself, rose on to my horse, lay his shotgun across his lap and said, "Get up."

And I did.

"Now walk," he ordered.

And we started to walk.

I was not sure where he was taking me but I was happy my brains were not a fine mist on the morning air, borne away by the clusters of spring gnats circling my head. So I stepped on. Eastward we went. The sun, straight ahead of us new morning bright, blinded me like I was snowbound, till I looked down, letting my eyes adjust. An eastward glance and I was blinded again. I heard the steps of the horse behind me. The boy sat on Sagebrush looking serious, riding carefully.

"What's your name?" I asked.

"Shut up," he said.

"Where we going?" I asked.

"Shut up," he said.

"What are you going to do with me?" I asked.

"Shut the hell up, just shut up," he said.

And he rode up and struck me with the gun butt on my shoulder, hitting the trigger by accident, causing the gun to fire. The explosion startled me and scared Sagebrush. But he controlled her well and I was sobered by the loud report, aware more finely of my precarious situation. He'd hit me hard, hurt me enough to show he wanted to finish the job with no trouble. We walked on in silence.

I expected a short walk to a homestead or a camp of thieves. But we just kept walking into hills of shale outcrops. After a few silent miles, I needed a rest. He didn't. In a few more I needed to pee.

"Pee on yourself," he said.

Then as we crested a small hill, he said, "Go in there, turn here."

There was a small path along a treed draw, no more than a footpath and I went in.

It was cooler in there, hidden from the spring sun, now well up. I still had my wool coat on, originally intending to take it off when the morning chill was gone but I'd ended up hog tied before that could be done. I was hungry as well as tired, wet with sweat, foot-sore in old boots that were holy as a Baptist, socks not on. I'd expected to be riding.

Around me was old scrub, shagbark hickory, red and white oak, older gnarled trees, crooked, useless for building. In a land of such wind, such expanse, this tract smelled ancient and damp, dew dripping and brooks running, then swirling, falling on down.

A water fall with a cool blast of air made me glad for my coat. It fell from a ledge rimmed by moss and paw-paw. Mists rose and soaked my face. We climbed a ways up, boot and hoof struggling for purchase, slipping on mossy mucked shale, to an alcove on a shelf with a view of the surrounding country. The place had the beauty of Eden, cool, clean, fresh. I asked if we could sit there, it was clear others had before us. I could see him hesitate. He was a boy with a boy's need to rest, to ponder and surely eat. I think he loved this place and had been here before, many times. His tough demeanor softened ever so much.

He asked, "You got food in here?"

"Yes, some corn cakes, jerky," I answered.

"OK then, sit over there," he said.

I sat on a rock, glad for the relief. He slid off Sagebrush, stirrups not yet adjusted, opened my saddle bags, took out the cloth wrapped food and laid the bundle on a rock before him. He then knelt and prayed silently. Then he opened up his voice. This was not a perky little grace like some folks might say particularly at the noon supper, said with more urgency to get at the food then to say thanks, not that. He knelt with cupped hands over the food like he was warming them over a fire, trying to suck some power out of it, trying to force some heat into it; I never saw anything like it.

He looked up to the heavens and said, "God, power behind the universe, knower of all things, greatest King, strongest warrior, Creator, you have blessed me, us, with this food and we gratefully......Get on your knees, I am praying to the One God," he said to me.

So I did.

He continued, "Thanks be to you, Oh Lord God, we gratefully and thankfully receive this blessing, our daily bread, we ask only for your continued blessing. Thank you, God."

I said trying to joke a bit, "It's just corncakes and jerky."

He looked at me as if I was a rodent and said, "You don't know God?"

I lied and said, "I do."

His voice lifted in suspicion as he asked, "You don't pray?"

I lied again, "I do."

"You're thinking I'm what?" he said rising, angry, "I'm a freak cause I prayed on my knees, raised my arms, said the words like it mattered?"

Trying to calm him I said, "No, no it was a good prayer, a real fine prayer. I'm just hungry, trying to get some food, God hears my prayers," I said.

He looked closely at me and said, "He does?'

"Yes he does," I lied again.

My hands were tied. He had the guns. I could not tell him of my doubts. Then I spoke another lie, "God speaks to me too."

He shook his head, "OK then," he said.

And he gave me some food, and we sat and ate. He fed me bits of crumbled corn cake from his dirty hand. He did not untie me. My wrists and shoulders ached, pain surged, skin raw. Our white faces, leaf shadowed through the wind swayed trees, were spotted with shade and looked like measles had set in. I stared glassy eyed on ribbons of water slipping over the broken ledge. It flowed as from an open vein, repelling off rocks, life draining away. Blue mists rose from an emerald pool, vapors fleeing, rising anew, escaping to heaven. I closed my eyes and felt liquid time slip by, washing over, falling over, over, over, sounds of slapping waters pattered randomly like guns in a battle.

A distant gunshot ripped through the water sounds and echoed off the stones.

The boy stood, walked off and listened. Then another shot vibrated past. His spirits rose considerably and he began to hurry.

"That's father. He's back," he said with inspiration.

He finished what food was in his hand, then forgetting my growling hunger stuffed the food parcel in the saddle bag, rose his skinny boy frame up on the saddle and said, "Get up and move." And we walked on.

The boy, whose name I later learned was Benjamin, was anxious. He moved with greater urgency, telling me to walk faster. He would not tell me why his father had gone away, I assumed on a hunt. We walked on a winding path through a wood, over a few small hillocks, across a field covered with wildflowers. I saw a tick on my sleeve crawling to find some grip on the fabric, testing for my skin, moving towards my neck. I flicked and blew at it, making quite a sight, but the boy looked ahead, did not notice my odd behavior. I lost track of the tick as I looked to where we were going, then tripped and fell, stepping in a gopher hole I did not expect.

I could see a homestead through the sunlight, a few small cabins strung together, added on over time, a sprawling configuration. Glass windows reflected the sun in flares and bursts as we moved. A small shed off to the side, a barn too, a slave cabin in the distance, away from the others. A large pot of boiling clothes steamed in the front yard stirred by a heavy woman, an Indian. She squinted from the smoke and steam and did not seem to notice us. Two nigger females worked. One slim, split wood near the fire, the other, heavy set, hung clothes on a line.

Two dogs ran toward us on a dog mission, barking raucously as we reached midway across the field. They ran at me, paws digging in, then leapt back keeping their distance circling in aggression. They yipped in challenge then growled a warning. One tried to bite my arm as the other bit me on the leg. I kicked it away, scuffled backward, crouched and stood in a standoff position growling back, arms still tied behind my back.

"Get, shoo," the boy yelled as he rode the horse at the bare fanged curs to chase them.

We walked past a small cemetery, the dogs trailed, growling a rumble to a bark, off on a playful trot, then serious and on the attack again. Four piles of stones with wooden crosses marked the dead, partitioned by a crude rail fence. The names on the crosses were not decipherable from that distance.

Sheep stood in clusters, chewing dully in three stalls, bleating, wooly, fat and separated by color—black with black, white with white, spotted with spotted.

Chickens wandered, necks jerking, scattering as we arrived. Their clawed feet scored the dirt, scuffing for a bug, a seed. A large peacock with a stunning fan tail, many colored, many eyes of God staring back from the spread feathers, strode regally, owning the turf. There was a good creek running near the site called Paradise Creek, no doubt the source for the waterfall, dammed to a small pond. Geese stood at the creek side, feathers ruffling, necks twisted straining to see the dogs. A large white swan glided soothingly across the pond, peacefully, looking inward.

By the water's edge a small pale boy fished with rod and cord for channel catfish trapped behind the jumbled stone dam. He had a crooked back and when he rose I saw he walked with a funny hitched step towards the fat woman as we came closer. His hair was straw colored. He had large deep blue eyes that penetrated. He was oddly handsome, striking.

Off beyond the home site, four older boys worked with horse and plow. One drove, one led, the others picked churned up rocks. A woman walked behind putting seed to furrow. They stopped their work as we approached and the boy captor on Sagebrush called, "Momma, I got me one. Is father back?"

The fat Indian by the pot turned, squinted in the steam, felt around her face to remove her spectacles, wiped them on her apron and put them back on to see better.

"What have you got there? He's a live one," she said.

The boy answered with pride, "Found him on the trail heading this way. Wasn't taking any chances just like father said. Where's father?"

"Still gone." She said rubbing her hands on her dress. "You're a good one, you listen better than the others, that's a sure thing. You sit down," she said to me, and I sat on a log she used for splitting wood.

The boy said, "I heard his gun."

"That was Simeon shooting that gopher in our garden. Got him too," she answered. A carcass was near the log pile.

The others walked over from the field. The boys were of varying ages. Some had the same curly hair and tanned complexion, the others were blonde or brown haired or had straight dark hair. They did not appear related, at least by appearance. The woman who was seeding walked over from the field with her basket. She removed her hat with a pull of the tie beneath her chin and, like yards of ebony silk, out fell her long black hair down to her waist. It bounced and swayed like a living creature, a thick, shining, serpentine abundance. As she walked closer, sweating and dirty from field work, her slender perfection came to dominate the scene, like a rippled pond gone smooth when the wind settles. She came on, clearer and clearer, beautiful in every way, though an Indian. She had fine bones in her face, eyes like a mare, full lips, a softness and strength about her. When she turned I could see she had a birthmark, a purple stain across her cheek and down her neck. I was stunned by her beauty, entranced by her birthmark.

They all walked up, stood around me, and looked on me like I was dinner.

"Well, will you look here," said one boy, the largest and the oldest. "Good work Ben, you done good."

Ben said proudly, "I bushwhacked him, we almost had a gun fight but I had the better of him, too quick I was. Bet your glad I was on guard today?"

When the beautiful woman spoke, her voice was round and pure. She asked, "Do you know who he is?"

"Don't matter, it is better if we lock him up for now," the middle sized son said as he swung a rusted shovel at my head. The metal started ringing in my ears before the pain splayed out, putting me down to the dirt, looking up at their faces. The beautiful woman yelled at the boy, the fat one squinted near the boiling pot; Ben jumped down from Sagebrush to join the fight, one boy looked on, the other held his brother back, the last stood off at a distance. All were quickly lost in a fog that came across everything, voices echoed as in a canyon as the bright sun made red parchment of my eye lids and all gave way to night.

———◆———

I awoke with a terrible headache, a constant ringing in my ears, a goose egg on the back of my head and sticky wet hair. The hay mixed with the congealed blood and formed a damp pillow. I rolled over and felt that my hands were freed; my wrists were red and sore. Curious of my situation, I tried to rise to my feet but a sea of nausea and weakness swept over me and kept me down. So I tried not to move, to hold at bay the waves of sickness.

The late day sun shone through open cracks in the shed wall, a fresh manure pile drew flies not far from my head. Something scuffled under the hay and ran out a gap in the foundation logs. I rose to my knees slowly, stayed on all fours as I collected my senses and settled my whirring dizziness. I tenderly crawled to the wall and sat by the largest gap where two crooked logs warped away from each other forming an oblong window the size of a hat.

Across the yard their horses were hobbled, saddles off, nibbling at a budding bush.

Sagebrush, bare back, drank from a trough. The two angry dogs slept in the shade of a briar bush and the family, with two older sons I had not seen before, stood in a circle. They were singing a hymn, I could not tell what. The beautiful Indian woman stood side by side with the fat woman; Ben, my captor, the boy with the shovel; the three other field boys; the crooked handsome boy; the two older brothers; the new ones and also a young girl who completed the circle. The girl was dressed in a manly way and appeared to be in her late teen years, womanly but not yet fully grown. She also looked to be Indian and was taking on fat like her mother, the stout spectacled Indian, I assumed.

They sang every verse by heart. Then when their last chorus disappeared on the breeze they all knelt, still in a circle. One of the sons said some words, it sounded like a prayer. They were too far off for me to hear anything. They prayed in unison then knelt in silence. A great long while they remained on their knees, painfully I thought. They did not flinch but stayed with straight backs, hands folded waist high, knees on pebbles and sticks, sun shining warm on a few and, as time passed, the shade grew until they were all removed from the sun.

I think I dozed leaning against the rough logs still in a daze from my ringing head. I woke up with bark stuck to my cheek, with deep imprints on my face from the logs surface. There was a rattle at the shed door, a chain was removed and in walked one of the older sons. He was a large dull witted kind of man, muscled, brawny, and he carried a gun. One of the other boys in his shadow carried a club, followed by the fat woman and the beautiful one. They carried a bowl of food and set it down on a milking stool.

The beautiful one spoke, "We were told by our husband to be careful. So until he comes back we'll keep you here. I'm sorry Simeon hit you on your head with the shovel."

"Father's off fighting the likes of you," the big one said haltingly, revealing his slow thought. "My brother Simeon was hoping to hang you right off, but we'll wait for our father to come home."

The ringing in my head gave way to a flash of panic and I said, "Hold on now. You don't know who I am or where I was heading. Had you asked I might not have this crack in my head."

The fat woman said, "We'll not be listening to you. You may be speaking truth or you may be a tool of the devil."

The beauty spoke, "Have some gopher stew. We'll share our food but if you try anything, try to hurt my family, you have to know we'll kill you." It was said with a feminine lilt that belied the seriousness of her words. She looked hard at me but her features were so perfect she might have told me she was going to cut off my hand and I would have agreed to get one moment longer to look on her.

The big son spoke again to show he was the cock of the walk, "My father will be back soon. He's off to kill your leader, John Brown. He'll be back and mete out what you deserve."

"My leader?" I said in disbelief. "I come to kill him myself. I am raised here in this territory, from Dodge City, a Law and Order man inside and out. These liars don't want nothing but to take away what I got. You have done me a great injustice, I am here to uphold our God given rights."

The boys and the women paused and looked at each other.

"You'll wait for our husband," said the beautiful one. And the women left.

The big son asked suspiciously, "What's your name?"

"Hiram. Hiram Hill. What's yours?" I asked.

"Reuben. You own slaves?" he asked looking closely in my eyes to see if I lied.

"No, but I would. Can't afford them yet. But I'm not going to let those apes in suits in Boston and Washington tell me what I can do with my land. And I am not going to let no wild men come in here and kill us because we live as we see fit," I said.

Reuben said, "You want John Brown dead?"

"Yes, I do. Dead as Lazarus," I answered looking straight in his eyes.

And he and his brother with the club left, locking my door, sealing me in once again.

Jacobs Stead, Kansas Territory

Day 2

T he next morning Reuben entered the barn carrying his gun, leading the fat Indian woman with the poor eyesight and followed by the beautiful Indian woman.

The one who hit me with the shovel, whose name I learned was Simeon, entered as well holding a Bowie knife the size of my forearm. He had little eyes and long curly black hair. Thin and wiry, he looked to have hidden strength in his limbs. He had a mean look about him and showed a childlike joy at the damage he'd caused me.

He came over, looked at me close up and said, "Whoooeeeeyy, that's a beautiful bump there. Must hurt still." And he touched my head.

I flinched and brushed him hand away. "Keep your hands off me,"

"Oh, he's one of those fighting abolitionist scum," he sneered.

"I ain't no abolitionist. I come here to defend my home from intruders."

"You're here to join up with John Brown," he said suspiciously.

"John Brown's got to die for what he done," I said.

They looked at me for a little while, trying to figure out if I was telling the truth.

"You a Christian?" Simeon, the mean one, asked as he squinted, looking at me through his tiny slit eyes.

"Yes, born and raised one, baptized in Cumberland creek," I responded.

"John Brown says he's a Christian too," Reuben added.

"I ain't his kind of Christian. I'm a Law and Order Christian."

"You read the Bible?" Simeon asked.

"Some," I answered.

"You read all the Proverbs?" he queried.

"Some," I answered.

"Know this one?" he said with a threat in his voice.

"A worthless person, a wicked man, goes about with crooked speech, winks with his eyes, scrapes with his feet, points with his finger, with perverted heart devises evil, continually sowing discord.

Therefore calamity will come upon him suddenly,
in a moment he will be broken beyond healing."

"Do you know that one?" he asked.

"No, I do not," I answered.

"That was Proverbs 6:12," he said, "I hope you are not that worthless person spoken of. Know any Psalms?" he asked.

"Some," I lied.

"Ever hear,

"Behold, how good and pleasant it is when brothers dwell in unity!
It is like the precious oil upon the head, running down the beard of Aaron,
running down his robes?"

"Ever hear that?" he asked.

"Yes," I lied.

"Well, which one is it?" He asked coming in close to my face.

"I don't know," I said.

"It's Psalm 133," he said.

"Know the Old Testament prophets?" Reuben asked.

"Some," I said.

Simeon said, "Hell, you ain't read half of it. How do you know what you are? You ain't even read the good book yet. God talks to you, you know, when you focus on his word. You ain't a Christian."

"I believe in God, in Jesus," I lied. "I don't need to prove myself to you. You've got no right to keep me here. There are laws."

Simeon came in close and strong whiffs of his stale breath went past my face as he said, "The only law here is my father and the Bible. My father ain't here. So right now there ain't no law except the Bible."

"Who is your father?" I asked.

He looked at me for some time, his small eyes revealing a brain. He answered as if with a weapon, "his name is Zephaniah."

"Your family name?"

"Jacobs, Zephaniah Jacobs."

"How long have you lived here?" I asked.

"Long time, my great grandpa was here first," he answered proudly.

"I have heard of you folks. I thought you were just a rumor."

He laughed, "Oh, we're more than a rumor. We're the original remnant. We're part of the plan. You see, that's why we have to be careful about you. You might be from the devil, you might be here to spoil the plan."

I argued, "I am not here for any other reason than to protect my momma and my homeland, same as you."

Reuben and Simeon looked at each other then Simeon said slowly, "You can tell it all when my father returns. But whether you're a killer or not you should be able to read the Word."

They left sealing my door and returned soon with a large old Bible. They left it near the door, just out of reach. Reuben said, "My mother told me to leave this right here."

I looked out on the Bible and wondered what game they were playing. The old book sat there for hours, the sunlight showed deep crevices on the cracked and curled leather, on the stained and faded binding. It was dog eared and well used. I stared at it for some time, broke away and paced, then stared some more, thinking about some of the stories it held, the things I did not understand, the good and bad preachers I knew. It was a slow ache to be so bored, so in need of something to do and to see a book to read, the good book, just out of reach. I never was much of a Bible man. Not really sure how much of it I believed. But the longer I looked at it, all that day, as it grew dim and afternoon roamed towards evening until the Bible was just a dark form in the growing haze of night, like a dead and forgotten man's name, the more I yearned to open it and read it. It is strange how a man wants what he can't reach; it becomes a goal even if it was not original to his own desires.

I slept sitting and looking out at the book and awoke as the night wore on. I imagined things that were not there, eyes dimmed from staring, closed, then blinking, then giving in to sleep again. I slept in this fitful way all that night.

The beautiful Indian returned in the morning carrying a bucket of water. "Here's water for your morning cleansing," she said in her soft female voice.

"Yes, ma'am," I said as I sat up, rubbed my eyes and touched the back of my head.

She put the bucket outside the door next to the Bible and walked away, looked back over her shoulder just once, as her long dress swept the dust like a china man's fan. I sat there in my jail looking out at the book and the water, something I needed to quench my thirst and wash, another thing I needed to sate my boredom.

I looked about at this new day and calculated the wealth this man had accumulated. He must have owned close to forty sheep. I counted seven horses, three cows, one bull, three calves, two female slaves. He owned a wagon, various farm tools, a plow, two large cook pots, fifteen or twenty chickens, the geese, a swan and peacock, a large spread of land, the cabins, and this large family. He was blessed beyond me, which raised my ire. And I knew I was not supposed to covet, but I did. I always did. I could not help it.

My anger rose as this day dragged on. I was in jail, barely fed, being taunted, thirsty, challenged, with my life threatened. This did not make sense and left me with desperate thoughts of what to do. I walked the inside walls on the small shed a hundred times, trying to keep my anger at bay, trying to keep crazy thoughts from my mind. I stared for a while at a wolf spider working on its web, spinning and scurrying about and I considered my plight. I did not want to try to fight my way out. There were always two armed men when they came to my prison, the large strong one Reuben and Simeon the mean one. Ben, my captor, was not seen again except in the prayer circle, but I knew him to be unafraid to fight. In truth I did not want to hurt the boy or anyone, but I was desperate. And the Indian women, I did not want to hurt them. Especially the beauty.

I felt some unease; there was something that did not seem right about this family. I could not think of exactly what it was that set them apart. The boys were all white, but had odd features. Some had straight black hair like Indians others had curly hair, all had dark complexions except for the small pale boy who was blonde and white as can be. Could these Indians be their mothers?

I wondered whether Zephaniah was an Indian himself, or whether the offspring were from others he'd impregnated, orphans, bastards, I could not say. With the age of the boys and the girl the fat one must have been giving birth once a year for many years. It was amazing she was still alive.

The graves I saw were family but I was not sure who. Children, parents, or grandparents, I could not be certain. But it did not matter. All I wanted was for their father to arrive, someone who could listen to me so I could prove my case and move on. I did not believe such a devout group could murder me. But times were tense from discord and fighting, from Brown's murders. My fate was up to the leader of this family, who if a man of the good book, could not, would not, be part of such an injustice. I hoped.

Not a person came near me that whole day. They did not feed me. They worked plowing the fields. The fat one with poor sight split wood. She used the axe handle at arm's length to take aim. She leaned the axe head on the log, measured the distance, tapped the strike point, then with one swift blow separated wood to halves, then reset the log to quarter it. She was amazingly accurate for one so at a loss for sight. She sweated like a horse through her dress made of simple cotton linen like her other one, but without the collar. The dogs slept most of the day while the horses grazed.

The pale boy with the crooked back I watched with interest. He acted oddly each time I saw him and he became something of a study for me. It was as if he was in a daze or saw something none of us could see. He seemed to hold conversations with people who were not there, mouth not moving, head tilting as if listening. But with all his oddness he was a handsome lad with beautiful yellow hair and wondering eyes. He was sorrowful to see walking along, hitched step, a look of amazement on his face as in a dream world. Sometimes he would just stop and stare, I was not sure what he saw. But he would just stop, as if hearing a secret song, then in a moment jump into his uneven gait to wherever he was going.

He liked to fish and I saw him catch two that day. He had a strange tendency to straddle the shade and the sun under a flowering dogwood, like a human sundial. He often stood still and watched his shadow. Sometimes he stood still so long I thought he was a statue, stiff and motionless. But if the sun reached his whole body he would move to the shade, preferring it. He was joyful. He would clap his hands when he caught a fish or when he said something in his mind he liked. But no one seemed to notice. It was part of their lives, his strange ways. He never spoke that I'd seen. The women clearly loved him, hugging him as he looked off to his distant visions. He was the only one they showed affection to.

The others worked and they did not talk much, just to answer a call or give an order.

There was no lack of respect; neither was there any fun, but they were one, no doubt. This was a family who had a deep abiding unity of purpose.

As dusk came on the whole family came back together, formed their circle and sang and prayed as they had the previous day. After the meeting, the beautiful one walked over to the shed and looked in on me.

"Thirsty?" she asked.

"Yes, oh yes, real thirsty," I said, and she handed me the Bible.

"Read it and I will give you some water."

"Can I have some first, I'm awfully dry?"

She smiled, a beautiful smile, like a warm blanket on a cold fireless night. For one so deprived it was a tonic. She handed me a ladle, full to the brim, spilling some, through the gap in the wall. I spilled more in my haste to take it and then drank deeply. She handed me another and another, and I drank savoring it. Then she handed me the Bible and left.

She returned shortly with another delicious though cold stew, I think it was squirrel or rabbit, but it did not matter. I needed more water but was glad for what I had got. She left me, and I read like I had drank, relishing the words, focusing on the chapters I had not ever read, some I never really noticed, hoping for her to return so we could speak.

It was a task reading like that. It is a big book with many stories. My head still hurt and my concentration was shallow, though hunger and thirst were slaked. I read until dark. When the black letters of the words lost all definition I put the book down. I listened a while to the sound of a bullfrog croaking its nighttime song. Then I slept.

The following morning she was standing at the crack in the wall looking over me as I slept.

She asked, "Who was Balaam going to see?"

"What?" I answered waking.

"Who was Balaam going to see?" she asked again.

"Who?" I asked rising up and sitting.

"Balaam in the Bible," she said.

"I don't know, I am sorry, I did not read that," I responded confused at her question, but glad to see her. I tried to gather myself, buttoning my pants, rubbing my face.

"Baalam, Balak and Baalam? It's a story in the old testament, Numbers," she said.

"Oh. Numbers. I did not read that," I answered, not sure what she was seeking.

So she sat down and said, "His jackass speaks to him after he sees an angel in their path."

This was an unusual story I thought. I had never heard of a Bible story of a talking ass. I answered with a mocking tone, "His mule speaks to him? I never heard of that." I'd heard of the parting of the Red Sea, the bread and the fish feeding the multitude, but never about a talking mule.

She looked at me perplexed. She was so beautiful. An angle of light crossed perfectly the diamond bones of her cheeks, a sight in the morning. She said with a hint of sternness, "Well that's what it says, and that's what it is. If you have questions you have to read it first." And she left.

So I read it hoping she'd return with food and water. And she did return with a bucket and some breakfast. I was getting used to this game.

"Well how did the writer of the story know what was in the mind of a jackass?

I mean, how could a mule tell a story?" I asked

"I am not sure," she said, brow furrowing.

I added, "Could it tell a whole story for someone to write down?"

She said matter of fact, "No Balaam must have told the story and someone wrote it down."

I pressed on, "Yes but who told Balaam."

She was getting confused and said, "I am not sure if it says that."

I continued in this line, "Did the jackass tell Balaam what happened? I know the jackass spoke and said 'why do you hit me,' but later did he also reveal that he had seen the angel before, so Balaam could write down the whole story?"

Then she said with finality, "It is the Bible, it just happened that way."

I surprised myself, spilling over like a one quart bucket with two quarts of milk, saying, "Yes but did the mule's mouth form words, did its tongue go between its teeth to form the letters, did it grow a voice? Did it join the church choir, or did he just go back to being a dumb jackass and never speak again?"

With a scolding tone she said, "Now that's enough. Don't be joking about the Bible. If it says it was so, it was so."

But I wanted to go on and asked, "But there must be some explanation, it seems so strange a story. I have not ever heard of it before."

Then she explained, "It's so simple a story, the children always loved it. You see, God told Balaam not to speak with Balak, who was a powerful man, and being a God fearing man Balaam obeyed. So Balak sent messengers who offered to give Balaam presents if they could meet. But old Balaam still obeyed

God. Then God changed his mind and told Balaam to go see Balak, and Balaam proceeded to go, of course. But God changed his mind again and an angel of the Lord with a blazing sword appeared in his way to stop him. But Balaam could not see the angel, only the jackass could, so the jackass ran away scared. Well, old Balaam is angry with this mule and starts whipping him and whipping him. So the mule turns and runs into a field and up along a rock wall, too narrow to turn around. The Angel appears again and the mule stops, crushing Balaam's leg against the rocks. So Balaam starts hitting the poor frightened mule. And the mule turned his head and said to Balaam, 'Why do you whip me so? I am your loyal mule. I have carried you forth all these years.' Then Balaam's eyes were opened and he saw the angel. See it's a simple enough story."

I asked, "But, why did God change his mind?"

She looked at me blankly and I decided it was better not to question this particular Bible story.

I said, "I read about Samson. He killed an entire army with the jawbone of an ass. Maybe it was the jawbone from Balaam's ass. It was probably a mighty big bone."

She looked at me with her gleaming brown eyes and smiled, knowing I was having fun with a sacred subject, but funny nonetheless. Then she looked straight in my eyes and said, "I think you're alright, but we are just listening to orders. You'll have to stay here until he's back."

"When will that be?" I said, my frustration coming through.

"Don't know. He left to find John Brown a few weeks ago, he swore to chase him down to avenge his murderous rampage," she answered.

"I hope he gets him and peels off his skin, he deserves it," I said trying to show my real intent.

"I think you mean that," she said still looking at me. "Well God is in charge and will be his judge, whether Zephaniah gets him or not."

"Yes, that true", I said. "Can I clean out the hay in here soon? It is getting ripe. I've been in here two days now," I pleaded.

She paused then said, "Yes, you'll wash in the river, clean out your mess today."

And she left.

Soon the boys, weapons in hand, walked me over to the pond and stood around me as I took off my clothes. The women waited farther off to get my clothes, to boil and clean them. I was embarrassed at my nakedness; my body was coated with filth. I walked on down to the brook's edge, it was spring cool, it shocked my skin numb but felt so good. I had not washed for a time since I had been on the trail. I needed it.

It was deep enough in some parts to swim a bit, especially by the dam. The young boy, the crooked one, sat on the other side fishing. He did not say a word to me, appeared not to notice me even as I went near his chosen site.

Simeon called to the boy, "Never mind him Joseph, don't give no mind at all."

I submerged and lay back looking at cauliflower clouds lumbering overhead, at the peaceful introspective swan, at the peacock striding, its tail contracted and trailing behind. I thought about running away but I had no clothes and nowhere to run to. I might get to my horse but with no saddle I could not get far; they would catch me. I might get shot.

They wrapped me in an itchy horse blanket while my clothes were hung to dry. They were going to lock me in the shed but I argued against it. I did not want to go back in and I tried to get them to let me stay outside, saying I could not run far with no shoes or clothes. So they took me to a tree near the pond where all could see me and let me read there wrapped in the itchy blanket.

I spent that day clean, refreshed, reading the Bible, scratching where the blanket touched me, until at mid-afternoon I was led back to my shed. The beautiful one came later bringing my clothes and some dinner, passing them through the gap gently. I was hungry, ready to dress, rubbed raw in places, skin scratched red from my long finger nails.

"What is your name?" I asked, "It would be easier to talk to you if I knew."

"Rachel. Rachel Jacobs," she said.

"Rachel, thank you for my food and clean clothes," I said sincerely.

"You are welcome, Hiram," she smiled.

"Are you a daughter or cousin?" I asked.

"I am neither. I am married to Zephaniah," she said smoothly.

"You are? I thought the other woman was."

"Esther, yes, she is too. We both are. She is my sister," she said with no hint of humor. "We follow the old ways."

Hearing that was like she'd slapped me across my face. I knew having several wives was practiced by some out in the monument country, but it was not common in these parts. It was not officially outlawed in the territory, you could do as you chose, but it was not considered right. This knowledge surprised me, made me wonder about the man soon to return who would decide my fate. Two wives, both sisters, what other ancient laws did he follow?

She said, "You look like you swallowed a pig. It's not so strange. It is a good life, we are a close family. We are blessed."

"So how many...whose children are they?" I stammered.

"Two are mine. Joseph, the blonde boy, and Ben, the boy who caught you. Reuben the oldest, the big one, Simeon the one who hit you, Levi, Judah, Isachar, Zebulan, and Diana are Esther's."

"That's only nine," I said.

"Yes," she said and looked down in thought for a moment. Pain crossed her face.

"Two were stillborn, one by Esther before Zephaniah had known me, one by me. I never named him. They are buried out yonder. The others, Gad, Asher, Dan, Naptali were carried to life by our slaves, Buela and Hannah. Esther and I were sick when it was time."

"The slaves are their mothers?" I asked in complete amazement.

"Yes, they carried our boys for us. It's alright, they are part of our clan. Their parents were owned by Zephaniah's parents. We are all one. Been together so long, one bone, one flesh. Zephaniah needed boys, did not want to wait, he never wants to wait. He did not know if we were to live, if God was to call us, he had a vision of what was needed. So Hanna and Buela carried the boys."

I stared at her some time unable to talk, unsure of what to say, of what I had just heard, unsure whether to speak aloud the questions that were springing in my head like grasshoppers. But I could not put thought to word.

She changed the subject, "Did you read much of the Bible?"

"Yes, all day, it was interesting. I had only heard parts of some books, a few verses here and there, there were many things I read today that were new. I'd never read this one before," I said as I handed her the open bible. "There were some powerful messages in this book."

"Let me see," she said reaching for the book. "Oh yes Ecclesiastes."

And she sat herself down and started to read, but then closed the book and spoke from memory. It was a moment I will always remember. While she recited to me my eyes wandered across the rough walls of my shed to the view beyond the space in the logs, and then, as drawn by a power I could not but stop, I gazed on her face, her wine colored birthmark, down her cheek, down her neck.

> *"The words of the Preacher, the son of David, King of Jerusalem.*
> *Vanities of vanities. All is vanity.*
> *What does man gain by all the toil at which he toils under the sun?*
> *A generation goes and a generation comes,*
> *but the earth remains the same forever.*
> *The sun rises and the sun goes down,*
> *and hastens to the place where it rises.*
> *The wind blows to the south,*
> *and goes round to the north;*
> *round and round goes the wind, and on its circuits the wind returns.*
> *All streams run to the sea,*
> *but the sea is not full,*
> *To the place where the streams flow,*
> *there they flow again.*
> *All things are full of weariness;*
> *a man cannot utter it;*
> *the eye is not satisfied with seeing,*
> *nor the ear filled with hearing.*

What has been is what will be,
and what has been done is what will be done;
and there is nothing new under the sun.
Is there a thing for which it is said,
"See, this is new?"
It has been already, in the ages before us.
There is no remembrance of former things,
nor will there be any remembrance of later things yet to happen
among those who come after.
I, the Preacher have been king over Israel in Jerusalem.
And I applied my mind to seek and to search out by wisdom all that is done under heaven;
it is an unhappy business that God has given the sons of men to be busy with.
I have seen everything that is done under the sun;
and behold,
all is vanity and a striving after the wind.

Engrossed in these words she said, "Here, listen, this is one of my favorites."

And she thumbed through the pages to a known spot, then put it aside, "I know this one by heart too," she smiled.

"The Psalm: 39.4
Lord, let me know my end and what is the measure of my days;
let me know how fleeting my life is!
Behold thou has made my life a few handbreadths,
and my lifetime is as nothing in thy sight.
Surely every man stands as a mere breath!
Surely man goes about as a shadow!
Surely for naught are they in turmoil;
Man heaps up, and knows not who will gather!"

"Or Psalm 22.9. I love this one," she said in a kind of reverie.

"*Yet thou art He who took me from the womb,*
Thou didst keep me safe upon my mother's breast.
Upon thee was I cast at birth and since my mother bore me thou hast been my God.
Be not far from me for trouble is near
and there is none to help.
I am poured out like water
and my bones are out of joint:
my heart is like wax,

it is melted within my breast:
my strength is dried up like potsherd,
and my tongue cleaves to my jaws;
thou dost lay me in the dust of death.
Yea, dogs are around me;
a company of evil doers encircle me;
they have pierced my hands and feet—
I can count all my bones—
they stare and gloat over me;
they divide my garments among them, and for my raiment they cast lots.
That's foretelling about Jesus," she said.

I took back the Bible and worked through the pages, trying to find the place with the verses that moved me to think of her. On first reading them I could think of no one else, as much as I tried to keep her from my thoughts. The passages were her words, were spoken in her voice. She was another man's wife, as unholy a marriage as it was to me, she was his still. I said to her, feeling insecure of my intentions, "Let me read something to you."

"I am very dark but comely, O Daughters of Jerusalem,
like the tents of Kedar, like the curtains of Solomon.
Do not gaze at me because I am swarthy
because the sun has scorched me.
My mother's sons were angry with me,
they made me keeper of the vineyard;
but, my own vineyard I have not kept.
Tell me, you whom my soul loves,
where do you pasture your flock,
where do you make it lie down at noon;
for why should I be like one who wanders
beside the flocks of your companions.
Your neck with strings of jewels.
My nard gave forth its fragrance.my beloved is to me a bag of myrrh.

The voice of my beloved!
Behold he comes leaping over the mountains,
bounding over the hills.
My beloved is like a gazelle,
or like a young stag.
Behold there he stands,
behind our wall,
gazing in at the windows,

looking through the lattice.
My beloved speaks and says to me:

Arise my love, my fair one,
and come away;
for lo the winter is past,
the rain is over and gone.
The flowers appear on the earth,
the time of singing has come, the voice of the turtledove
is heard in our land.
The fig tree puts forth its figs,
* and the vines are in blossom;*
they give forth fragrance.
Arise, my love, my fair one, and come away.
O my dove, in the clefts of the rock,
in the covert of the cliff,
let me see your face,
let me hear your voice,
for your voice is sweet,
and your face is comely.
Catch us the foxes,
the little foxes,
that spoil the vineyards,
For our vineyards are in blossom."

"That's The Song Of Solomon," I said, as I tried to force myself not to look at her, so as to hide the sin that was in my mind. But I had become so involved in reading this magical passage, I was as a sleep walker moving about the world but in a dream. I finally brought my eyes away from the words to look at her. I could sense she was moved. I could see some change, a rosier flush to her skin, a change in her posture, a silent sigh. Perhaps she missed her husband. Perhaps, I secretly hoped, she had grown in so short a time to think of me. Perhaps, the words had released some deep longing in her that had been left hidden in a secret nook of youth. Perhaps it struck in her a chord of departing love. She had no doubt married young. Who knows why, she married a man already with a wife who was her sister. Given or taken perhaps without choice, out of respect for custom, naturally drawn to this man, as if it was a meant to be, I did not know her well enough to say. All I can say is that she leaned against the logs, looked off into the distance, her beautiful eyes glazed over, as if in a memory of something sweet.

I looked on her with unblinking eyes until the pause, the silence startled her. She felt my eyes, became aware that she had let her thoughts cover her face like a wedding veil. She adjusted herself, rubbed her hands across her face shyly, laughed slightly, leaned a bit, looked straight into my eyes and said, "Those are some of the most beautiful words ever. They make me swoon."

I could not take my eyes off of her. It was a powerful moment after all that had happened, captured, knocked in the head, kept prisoner. To have time with this woman, a female as no other I had seen, to have reached her in some perceivable way was powerful for me. I was so drawn, so paralyzed by her; I could only stare in idiot silence. I was the happiest prisoner alive. I waited for her next words.

She said, "Well you've learned a lot about the Bible today. I hope you are who you say and Zephaniah does not kill you." And she walked off taking with her my sweet moment, throwing me back to lonely captivity. She left quickly I thought. She wielded her power over my life, severed the connection we'd made, used my fear as the remedy for the awkwardness together. She left me and I was alone again, as another day slid into dark night.

I was scared. I could only think of my life, of what would happen. A man would soon arrive unbeknownst to me. He would decide if I lived or died. He was to be my lone judge. I had ways to prove who I was, but I was not sure if he was a raging mad drunk or a religious zealot who would kill me without a hearing. I pictured a large hairy man riding in with the head of John Brown in a sack, ready for more revenge, driven by blood lust with an overpowering sense of right.

I laid there a long while thinking. The night crept like a June bug in the frost. I could not sleep. I was anguished for my life and confused by a rising lust as overwhelming and consuming as a plague of locusts. I was smitten with this beautiful woman, my captor, even though she was older than me, and nagged by a humming fear of what another day would bring.

Job

J ob was born in a corn crib in Danville, Virginia. The only greeting granted by his mother upon his arrival was her death. She'd always been a frail creature, small boned and slouching, but her lovely spirit had attracted her mate like honeysuckle in spring. His father was a third generation slave with a rumor of some African tribe still present in his demeanor. He acted proud among the other slaves, but among the white masters he showed the lowered gaze and timeworn subservience they expected. Job's mother and father were not properly married. It was frowned on by their master who felt those not fully human—only three fifths of a man and less of a woman—should not partake of the sacraments. So they eloped in private with only a blessing by the old mother to carry them into matrimony. Their stolen glances and secret encounters at night were the only joys they knew in their hard lives.

Since progeny was good business, the master was not disapproving of the pregnancy. 'Let the animals breed', he thought. He distained to some degree the idea of consorting with Negroes and since Job's mother was not a beautiful slave, she had large African features and was as black as tar, the idea never entered his mind to her. In truth, there were others he might consider on a cold winter night if his sap was running, but not her.

Job's mother was gone as fast as a summer rain and he never knew her. By the time he was old enough to comprehend her life the collective memory of her had been sold or died off, so he only learned her name and nothing else. He was raised by slave women, passed from one set of arms to another as they tired of him or were called to some duty. By the time he was three and walking about in torn homespun shirts, no pants or shoes, his father was counting his last days. He would never see his son rise to full slave-hood. A horse spooked and kicked his arm, breaking it nearly in half so it hung like a shank of new rope on a two way hinge. It was cut off with no whiskey to ease the tortured limb and he was sold with a beveled stump below his shoulder; one good arm and a pair of well muscled legs caught the veteran eye of a miller who needed a slave to walk his mules in circles crushing the wheat to flour. This task, like the labors of Prometheus, he did for the rest of his days; one monotonous circle after another, year in and year out. And he never set eyes on his baby son, Job, again.

So Job grew to a man without so much as a stiff reed to hold him up, leaving in him nothing but a faltering spirit of youthful vinegar and an uppity indignation which registered too quickly and far too threateningly on his black face. He'd been robbed of much in his life, of everything that comprises most people's lives, and he had absolutely no hope of recovery of anything like heritage or pride or family or love. In fact he never knew what it meant to be part of a real family, what it entailed or how he could ever reach a status that would allow him to responsibly father a small family of his own. How can one create what cannot be envisioned? A cloud was over him, a melancholy he could not fully understand but was visible to his white keepers. No course of action but rebellion ever seemed to make sense to him in his younger days.

The white overlords watched him like he was the whelp in the litter who would not survive. They knew from experience that he was the one who would need regular and consistent punishment to make him more manageable.

When he was sixteen he felt the bite of the lash for the first time. His back after forty strokes was a crisscross of bleeding stripes which pulsated with dodging pain and bleaching heat. But rather than drain his passion and bring on submission; the long period of healing and the tremors of fever that rattled him like a buckboard on a rocky road only elevated his rebelliousness.

He lay on his stomach for several weeks looking at the dusty feet of those who applied the poultice to his rare back. Whether by sigh or cough, every expansion of his rib cage ripped the nascent scabs and leaked his spirit down his back, which ran with a multitude of arterially latticed patterns and shone like trickles of scarlet sap on a tortured tree. And he was not broken, yet.

On the very first day he rose and limped about, stooped over, looking fifty years his own elder, he happened to look askance at his master, showing his displeasure with his painful chastisement. So they dragged him back to the pole and gave him thirty more deliberate lashes, crossing his back again and slicing open the tender, recently healed layers of skin, displaying a hue of pinkness in the spreading fissures, a colorful autumnal relief on his scabbed black back. The pulpy excrescences of his wounds were splattered about by the whip so the overseer directed it to Job's shoulders and ribs and legs and buttocks to keep the niggers bestial liquids from flinging about and staining his newly washed shirt.

He was cut down and left lying on the dirt which adhered to the wet ruffles of skin until a bloody muck formed on his back and exposed ribs and sliced hind end. In a tearful unconsciousness somewhere between a waking nightmare and a sleeping hell, Job cursed his life and cried like a child until he was carried back to his bed to once again look to the dusty feet of his caregivers for another set of months.

At the time Zephaniah knew him, Job had become an older and wizened slave. He shuffled as he walked, a habit from the shackles he always wore when he traveled; and he had a forward tilt, over and leaning, an attitude from forcing his spirit inward and his gaze downward. When he would think about it, which was not often, he would walk upright like a white man and look ahead appearing proud. But that had become an unnatural and secret trait. He was broken inside from those whippings, from losing his father and his mother, and from one final punishment that came his way.

Beside the shackles and whippings and spiritual malaise another cause for the lumbering plod of Job was the yoke. He had been locked in the heavy wooden necklace for one full year, from Easter of 35' to Easter of 36'. This brutal treatment has its intended effect. It finally and completely broke him.

The master was forever suspicious of his attitude and even when he was not glancing about with rebellion on his mind, he was perceived to be. So on Easter morning after the master returned from services and while a fine celebratory meal was being put on the table in honor of the risen Lord Jesus who walked from the tomb and escaped the finality of death, a fifty pound disk of oak was locked around Job's neck. The master simply and off handedly said Job looked angry and felt any simmering resentment was a problem that would surface soon enough and should be dealt with straight away. The master and the overseer dragged Job to the barn, with the help of a club and gun, and locked him in the wooden yoke. They left it on him for one full year and he learned in that time of leaning forward and sleeping upright how to control his anger and appear subservient. In time, Job's state of permanent slavery became true to who he was and he carried his inhumanness like a yoke he must bear all of his life. Its weight was far greater than the oak of a real tree because it was an eternal spiritual weight, an inescapable lifelong heaviness which he wore so he could survive and avoid the beatings.

Job could only find solace from listening to the Bible read by a slave girl who was of no small intellect for a beast of burden. Job learned to read from her, and in those moments when he could be alone he would revel in the words of the book which spoke of freedom from oppression and a new day coming.

Night, He cometh

Zephaniah Jacobs rode across the prairie onto his land. Hard from his trip to find and kill John Brown, hip still hurting greatly with each step of his horse, Beersheba and the words of the mysterious Indian circling his thoughts like a rabid dog on a rope.

Beersheba, a clean lined roan, fast and lean, strong for her size, stepped ahead knowing the destination was near. The familiar smells excited her. She was a fine horse who could run like a ray of sunshine, charge boldly, unflinching in a fight; pull a wagon full of grain or a plow to etch a dirt row. But she was too noble in bearing for mere work. That is why Zephaniah chose her for his horse. This horse strode as a queen wears her crown, she bore a regal spirit. Zephaniah sensed this when he saw her born. It was the strangest birthing of an animal he had ever witnessed.

Beersheba's mother was as skittish an animal as you can get, always was, but upon reaching the point of motherhood she calmed. It seemed she knew her time had come and she was ready for the sacrifice. She lay down to bring forth this foal and died doing so. She just bled out. Maybe her skittishness came of knowing she would die young, knowing she had one important role to play.

Everyone, Indian or white, ever to put clear eyes on Beersheba wanted that horse and tried to trade for her. Indians know horses like farmers know soil and weather. A horse is life, carrying them on the hunt or to the battle. Indians knew this horse, knew she could be trusted with the one life they had been given on this mother earth.

This horse was connected to something greater, something all men seek: purpose, spirit, vision. They wanted to own her, to absorb her. Indians had tried to steal her, a hobby they found more rewarding than drinking and begging. Even in a whiskey haze their equine desire rose, deep seated from their ancestors who lived and died by horses. They had to have this horse.

Normally, especially with horses, there is some complication birthing, the long legs of a foal can make birth difficult. But when the mother went to foal, Beersheba came out smoothly and cleanly and lay on the hay calmly, as if to say I am here now leave me be. When she did rise, it was right up, no bumbling and wobbliness, just up and proud, walking to her destiny. Unaware her mother would not rise again, she forged on determined.

Night fell, all were inside the cabins. Zephaniah had been away almost a month as best as I could tell. It was late May when John Brown's killings were done. It was now June 25th as I remembered it.

I knew he was coming. I knew he would soon arrive, sensed it before I'd heard or saw anything. Before, in the darkness, there was some motion. Before the horse steps pocked the grayness, or I heard the jangle of a bridle, I felt some change in the atmosphere, something like the clean air in a thunderstorm. He has there before he was. I sat up and listened for any sounds, but none came forth. I waited, ears perked, head swiveling like an owl. I had thought of him so much that night, I thought I had willed him there. He was coming, I was sure.

I needed to learn who this man was, what he was like, what were his intentions?

In that sleepless dark, knowing there was a fate for me coming in the night, I wanted to rise and yell, tell him to come on. I was ready. But I did not yell, I had my wits, this was no blood and thunder novel where heroic words mattered.

The silence was total and the air alive. The field rat or snake that jostled the hay in my nights in the shed knew something too, it was quiet and waiting. Even the crickets stopped scratching and the lightening bugs doused their candles. All was still as a corpse being measured by the undertaker, and he arrived.

He rode quietly to the hitching post near the front porch. Gingerly, with hip still hurting from his encounter with the Indian, he got off Beersheba and was greeted by the dogs with no great fuss of barking, just wagging and licking, submissive, low shouldered. They knew and loved their master and they nudged him. He touched their heads as if anointing them; he then limped into the house. The door closed and voices rose within.

He was not long inside when the cabin door opened spilling off kilter a widening triangle of candle light that reached midway to the pond, illuminating the night. He limped out onto the porch, boots on, clunking the boards, down the steps, scuffing the dirt, stepping in my direction. I sat up again, ready for the encounter I had thought so long on. He walked up in the dark and looked in. I could not see him but could hear him breathing. I did not want to speak first, move or get too close.

He said, "You awake?"

"Yes," I answered tentatively.

"What's your name," he asked, but he knew it already.

"Hiram Hill," I answered.

He asked, "Did you come to harm my family, Hiram Hill?"

"I most surely did not. As God is king, I come to harm John Brown," I said with conviction but not loudly.

"How do I know your words are true?"

I rose and came to the wall and answered, "Well, I can swear on your Bible. You can get a message to my home in Dodge, there's folks there who know my intentions. They know why I left, know my thoughts. Preacher Zed Altshuler, my momma Emma Carson Hill. They know me, they'll vouch."

Then I paused briefly and had to ask, "Did you kill Brown?"

He thought for a minute. "No. He got away. Ran away, a murdering thief in the night. I will hang him. Find him and hang him. But I am tired now, we'll talk in the morning. Do not speak again until I tell you. Do not speak to my sons, to my wives Rachel or Esther. Be silent. Do you understand?" he said.

I nodded in the dark, a pit growing to a watermelon in my stomach. And he left.

The candles burned late in the cabin that night. I thought of them all sitting around the hearth hearing the stories of the journey, talking about me, deciding what to do, how to kill me, or when to let me go. I did not know if they would pray on it or what the answer to their prayers would be. The rat scooted out through the hole. It was a rat I was now sure, I could hear its paws, my ears had grown so accustomed to the sounds of my confinement. I lay down and thought of the voice and the man. I slept and I dreamed of Zephaniah. He spoke words I could not interpret; he spoke in tongues.

Zephaniah Jacobs walked to the shed that was my prison before sun-up and opened the door. He stood and looked at me waking in the hay. He said, "I prayed about you last night and spoke to my son Joseph. He said you had good colors around you. He said you are our cousin. We are related. Your mother's name Carson is the name of my grandmother's sister's husband; your great grandfather no doubt. My great grandmother on my mother's side had three daughters, one married a Carson, and one named Sarah married a Jacobs, my grandfather Abraham Jacobs. The other died as a young girl and never married. So we are cousins twice removed. I know you are speaking true. I looked up your name in our family tree. You were born in Dodge, were you not?"

I nodded, 'Yes.'

Then he said to my great relief, "If I let you out will you swear to leave my sons and family alone, no revenge on Simeon?"

"I swear it," I answered quickly but honestly.

He said with a tone of apology, "You should have been welcomed but you were injured and jailed. I am sorry for the way you were treated."

I nodded, 'O.K.'

"This John Brown has made caution a byword. I told my family to be careful while I was gone, I did not want them to be the victims of these vermin," he explained as he pulled off the chain and lock on my door."

I nodded O.K. again.

"Please come in and join us for breakfast. You are kin," he said as he stepped back from the door.

I was stunned but was not about to argue my ancestry or question what the small crooked boy could possibly know about me. I stood up, brushed off and followed him to the cabin. He pointed me to the outhouse, where I spent some time counting the cobwebs. Then I went to the pond, filled a bucket with water and washed.

I went to the cabin after looking on Sagebrush. I thought about bolting, but there was something which drew me in. I don't know why I did not ride away then and there, but I patted my horse's snout, walked onto the porch, knocked lightly, opened the door and entered the dark smoky room.

The sun was not fully up. There was a rosy glow behind me that looked like a young girl's blush. The fire was down to coals and the hearth was the only source of interior light. I could see the entire family, slave women and all, sat at a long table in the dim room looking at me. As my eyes grew accustomed to the dark interior, I could make out Zephaniah at the head of the table, face featureless in the dark, standing over all.

He said, "Come in and sit there, next to Simeon. He will not hit you again."

They laughed.

"Hurry, sit. He may strike if he does not eat soon," he joked and he laughed again. "Come on now sit. We have been waiting for you."

Rachel walked in with a pile of biscuits. I nodded and wanted to say good morning but mouthed ma'am instead, remembering my warning not to speak to his wife.

"Morning Hiram," she said, knowing I could not answer.

I settled uncomfortably on a bench next to Simeon, who I did not like and did not trust. As I looked around the table I could see those gathered looked to their father. Zephaniah stood with arms raised like a saint in a cathedral. All there at the table folded their hands, bowed their heads, as did I. The words rose as from the depths of the earth, harmonically even, pitched perfect, in tone sincere and honest. I have never heard such music in a man's prayer before.

"Heavenly Father, God of the sun and stars, we know you are in everything, everything is of you, you hear every beat of our hearts, you know our thoughts, you have set the ship of our lives on a course following the north star of your love, we follow you, you are our north star, you are our north star. We thank you for all, all the gifts of this life. First we thank you Lord for our knowledge of you, brought to us by your Son, brought to us by your Son, we thank you for this greatest of all gifts, knowing God, knowing you. We thank you for our food and your gifts of life…"

The expression on the faces of those present, Negro and white, was one of complete peace, they all went to a new place, left the farm and the pond and the work. The entire room filled with warm pulsing air. The family, heads bowed and praying intently, was focused on one thing, one being only.

The cabin was simple, the same as most others I had seen in my life, but it had shelves all around filled with books; on each wall, on every surface, books were stored. I could see Bibles, histories, Shakespeare, Homer, Swift, Pope, on any level surface books were piled high. There were also about the walls hanging from pegs antlers, jaw bones, claws, a wolf's head mounted, grinning, dense eyed. A bearskin was draped across a chair near the fire. The hearth was large, well appointed with pots, a spit, utensils. There were doors on each of three walls leading to the other linked cabins, attached over time; these were the bedrooms I assumed.

Zephaniah continued to pray, "You have blessed us once again with a new day. The bounty of the earth you have so graciously spread before us. We pray Lord for the families of those mourning their dead, we ask your justice for John Brown and his band of murderers. Lord strengthen our arms, plant our feet firmly with your word. So we may carry on life as you commanded, with slaves and servants as in your book.

Thank you for Jesus, His bloody painful death on the cross for us, for us. Let us remember it and praise you every day. Amen," he finished.

And all said, "Amen."

Then he said, "Be there any in this room who have a prayer. Simeon?"

"Bless Hiram Hill, my dear relative. Let his head heal just fine, and let him not be too dizzy," Simeon said with a kidding tone making the others laugh.

Zephaniah said, "Rachel?"

And Rachel said, "Forgive me lord for my sinful thoughts, and my vanity."

"Esther?"

"Forgive me lord for my carelessness, my sloppiness," Esther said slumped over her bowl.

Zephaniah called out, "Boys, boys? Reuben?"

"I been lazy, thinking about food too much. I humbly ask your forgiveness," Reuben said slowly.

"Dan," said Zephaniah.

"Lord I been wanting things I can't have, forgive my covetousness," Dan said quickly.

"Naptali?" he called to his son.

"God I did not share my things with Zeb as I should have. Forgive me my greed," said Naptali.

And they went around and around for nearly an hour, my stomach empty and them praying and asking for forgiveness. It was a wonder they were not fainting they prayed so long. But finally Ben, my captor, asked for forgiveness for wishing harm on me, then they all looked to Joseph, the crooked boy, who had been passed by each time. I thought him dumb or unable to voice a prayer. His face stone fixed, the crooked boy stood, raised his arms, stood as straight as he could, his twisted spine pulling him over to one side. His voice was a child's, high, sweet, but his words rolled out slowly, deliberately, "God Almighty, I ask you to speak to me, show us the way, tonight."

And all said, "Amen."

They ate in complete silence. Through the window the early sun framed the irregular arching line of prairie mounds as it rose over the newly plowed field. A searching eagle sat on a branch, regal, fierce; looking for prey, lording over the crawling nearsighted creatures that were unaware this superior being watched them from on high.

After breakfast, all left the house and went to their work with no questions or talking, just silence and action. I was left there as Zephaniah ate his last bit of biscuit, rubbing up some gravy and dripping it in his beard. I waited aware of the warning to keep silent; discomfort ruminated with a still fear.

He finally asked, "Will you be leaving today?"

I waited.

"Speak, will you be leaving today," he asked?

"I will, yes. I want to leave as soon as I can saddle my horse," I said.

"Do you still seek Brown?" he asked as he sat back in his chair and belched out loud.

"I do. It was my reason for this journey," I said.

He tested me, "We have not changed your commitment, have we?"

"No you have not. This was unfortunate, but it will not deter me," I said making sure he could see my mettle.

He pulled his chair forward, leaned over closer and said, "I will be leaving as well. I will know where I am heading for sure tonight."

I was getting anxious to move on so I answered, "Perhaps we will meet again on the road." But my curious nature got the better of me and I asked, "Do you know where he is?"

He spoke as he walked to the window, "No. Do you?"

"I do not," I said rising and heading for the door.

"Then how will you start, where will you go," he said. "Brown has flown; his trail will be covered by those who protect him."

"I guess I don't know. But I am going try," I said and I started out the door.

He followed me out on the porch and said, "Why don't you wait, why don't you stay a while longer. You will join us. I saw the maps in your bag, you can be useful to us, we have a long journey ahead. You are a planner, a man of tactics. Brown was smart. He escaped our best men, held us off, killed some and captured others."

I stopped as I stepped to the dirt, "You fought him?"

"I did. I linked up with a group led by a General Pate but Brown got away. He is long gone. Down the river somewhere by now I am sure, traveling back to the sty he came from. We can find him out though, go after him. You have led men. I know that. You are needed. If we separate, you will be a leader. My boys are strong, solid, but they have never been in a fight of strategy."

How he knew I had served in a local militia, youngest Captain in the territory, chosen by a vote, is a mystery. But he did. I had never fought a military engagement except to chase down horse thieving Indians and kill them as they deserved. I had drilled, practiced, studied books of tactics, but never marched, never fought, never killed in a battle, though I'd thought on it much. I was by nature stubborn as a stump, determined as a brush fire in a wind once settled in my mind. I was set to get Brown, kill him, hang him, but I was going for Brown on my own.

"I don't think so," I said rubbing my head. "I will be on my way. He is gaining ground as we talk here."

"You are determined, I like that, but a wise captain prepares, learns what he can of his enemy before engaging him. There are things we can tell you, things that will help you. We will meet in ceremony tonight. You will discover something that will help you on your journey. Wait. Trust me," he said.

I paused, thought on it; saw the books, the claws, the skins, and then Rachel who was brushing her long hair, humming gently beyond the door. Perhaps he was right, I would wait.

The Foretelling

I spent the day reading the book of Job. How afflicted he was; tested by God as no other poor soul. The Devil challenged God that Job would not be faithful if his blessings were taken away. So God put him through many ordeals to prove the Devil wrong and Job's worth. I did not know God made wagers with the Devil or that the Devil was actually a fallen angel. And I did not know if I could ever hold true to God, with sores covering my body, my sheep scattered to the wind, losing all that I owned and loved. I hoped I would never be tested so.

That evening as the sun set orange and large, the family was busy gathering wood, piles of it. Arms full they trudged and brought in the fuel, some came in by the wagon load from the outer reaches. They stacked it in the field near the cemetery and built a bonfire to blaze high. As they worked, I read from the Book of Joel:

Then afterward I will pour out my spirit on all flesh;
your sons and your daughters shall prophesy,
your old men shall dream dreams,
and your young men shall see visions.
Even on the male and female slaves, in those days,
I will pour out my spirit.
I will show portents in the heavens and on the earth,
blood and fire and columns of smoke.
The sun shall be turned to darkness,
and the moon to blood,
before the great and terrible day of the Lord comes.
Then everyone who calls on the name of the Lord shall be saved,
for in Mount Zion and in Jerusalem
there shall be those who escape, as the Lord has said,
and among the survivors shall be those whom the Lord calls.

I looked up and Naptali walked a white calf from a pen and tied it to a tree by the cemetery. The metal ring in its nose and a rope secured it from wandering far. The pale boy, Joseph, sat in the shade looking up into the tree by the grave markers. He watched a squirrel shiver and jump about. He then seemed to speak to someone I could not see, got up and walked his hitch step around the graveyard holding his hand high in the air, as if leading an army ahead into battle. He marched onward, onward, seven times around the cemetery.

As the work day ended, each family member went to a different location at the edge of the field and sat alone, contemplating. Zephaniah brought the large bible, a small sack and a lit candle in a glass and sat them on a flat table rock near the graves. He walked up to me and told me to sit near the cemetery facing the setting sun. So I followed him, not feeling threatened, but curious about what was to happen.

As I sat and watched the sun, I could see motion from the corner of my eye and Reuben, the oldest, walked to the pond. He stripped naked and walked into the water. Zephaniah followed in his britches and spoke to him, easily, quietly, then dunked him under, saying more. I could hear the timbre of his voice but not his words, as he held his head beneath the surface, a long time, more than I felt comfortable with. Reuben arose from the water and hugged his father then walked out of the pond, dressed and returned to his place.

This was repeated by all members of the family. It took some time; each encounter was unique in some way. Some stepped right in and were prayed over; they listened head down and must have heard something special, something they wanted or needed to hear, because they lingered, waiting for more. Others waited by the shore and listened before going in, seeking permission it seemed.

As the sun reached its lowest point the shadows stretched. Those who crossed the ground appeared long legged on string bean bodies in shadow relief on the bluestem grass. Esther then rose and her girth appeared thin and lean in shadow as she crossed, following the voice of Zephaniah. When stripped, her large belly sagged to her thighs covering her woman parts; her flattened side-hanging breasts overlapped cascading layers of flesh. She bobbed as she was dunked then rose happy, sublime. She dressed, walked back peacefully to her spot.

Then Rachel stepped from behind a thick Black Jack Oak and walked to the pond. I had tried all of this time to only look towards the sun, averting my eyes out of respect. But they were pulled as tides by the moon to the edge of their sockets as I strained to avoid turning my head. She was magnetic, so attracting.

She undressed. Her naked body, slender and perfect, was stunning, soft, womanly, amazing. The purple stain ran down her neck and covered one breast. Zephaniah lingered with his beautiful wife, his demeanor signaled she was the favorite, the most precious. She was blessed and washed. She dressed then and walked gracefully back hair dripping to the tree. She sat in the shadows, a sweet female ghost in the shade.

Zephaniah called out, "HIRAM."

I was surprised. I thought my stolen look at naked Rachel had been caught. Alert now I listened.

"HIRAM, come to the pond," he called echoing across the landscape.

I rose and walked to the small pond by the dam, took off my clothes and stepped into the chilled water, surprised I had listened to him. Surprised that I was still there and had not left on my own. What world had I entered, where my will so easily submitted?

Zephaniah put his palm on my head and pushed me below. He held me down for a protracted time; his prayer, extended for my many sins, lasted longer than the air in my lungs. I struggled, reached to his arm, tried to move his firm hand, to push it away. But he held me down. I thought he was trying to drown me; that I was to be sacrificed as part of this ritual. I was scared, near panic, when he finally let me up.

As I wiped the water from my eyes, he leaned over and said to me, "Hiram your sins are forgiven."

I gasped, and coughed, "Thank God."

In the distance Joseph stood and blew on a cow's horn, a low, uneven sound. Eerie and dissonant yet beautiful, it echoed like an ancient call to arms, a primeval beckoning to gather. Seven times he blew it, seven times.

The family came from their places to the area near the waiting bonfire at the center of the field near the cemetery. I dressed and I too came over and stood in the circle near the woodpile, feeling strangely a part of this clan, having watched their practices from my jail and now called to join them. Zephaniah stripped, stepped in the water, cupped his hands full of water, reached up and let it run down on his head. He did this several times and said a prayer, speaking to the sky. He then walked out, dressed, and started toward the bonfire.

As he walked Zephaniah called out, "Let the ceremony begin. Let us pray to the one God for guidance. Ask for his blessing. Seek his wisdom."

With that Simeon walked over, untied the white calf and brought it over to Zephaniah who put his hands on its head and said a prayer. Zephaniah then went to the rock table, pulled from the sack a large knife, then returning he slid it artfully into the jugular of the calf. Crimson blood ran down Zephaniah's hands and wrists.

The animal stood looking dumbly at him. Its eyes rolled back and wobbly legged it stepped to recapture the balance swimming helplessly in the whirlpool in its head. It then went down on its front knees, tried to remain stable, fell on its side, bleeding a torrent out onto the ground. Zebulan ran up with a tin bowl catching some of the streaming blood, and poured it gently over the graves.

Simeon took the lit candle and set fire to the wood pile. A flame shot up ignited by something other, suddenly ablaze and rising toward heaven, licking and leaping, dancing and releasing its blistering joy. Simeon then grabbed the sack, took out twelve knives, handed one to each of us.

Zephaniah, with the largest knife, slit open the underbelly, letting yards of intestine ooze out. Dan dragged the bluish white guts over to the fire. Prayers were said and the entrails were dropped in the coals, hissing like a snake. Then

Zephaniah reached inside the red cavity, found the prize and cut out the steaming heart saying, "To you God we give our first rewards," and he threw the purple marbled heart into the fire. It sizzled in the new coals and sent up dark smoke in charred thanks.

Then we all set to carving up the animal, rear hips dislocated, two hind quarters freed with a cut of the tendons, a twist, a crack. Front legs off at the shoulder, cut, twist, crack. The head, removed with a butchers skill, three cuts around the circumference of the neck, a snap of the spinal cord, a wrenching of the vertebrae and a turn back and forth to unnatural positions. We were all blood covered. Levi and others wiped it on their faces like Indians on the warpath. At this point, spits were put in place and meat was cooked. Slices of the best sections were put in the fire in ritual sacrifice.

Once the work of separating the calf was done and the meat was on the fire, from the sack Zephaniah took out a large jug, pulled the cork and passed it around saying, "This is the finest whiskey I ever tasted. Met a man, a preacher with a boy this tall, near Kansas City last winter. Dan Call from Tennessee was his name and Jasper Newton Daniel was the boy. Jack he told me to call him. He was proud of his brew, sold me a jug from his wagon, sealed it was with wax.

We passed around the whiskey made by this preacher. It was without a doubt the smoothest I had ever had; tasted of good barrels and fresh limestone water. Each person had some, youngest to oldest, woman, children, slaves, all. Not too much but some to carve off the personal edge each person brought, to inspire something different from everyone.

I noticed just then, like she had been in hiding, the fine features of Hanna the slave. She was slim and fine boned in the face, with a quiet, sweet demeanor. She was a hard worker, building the fire, cutting the wood, cooking the slaughtered calf. Buela was broad and thick boned, happy in spirit with large laughing eyes, she was nurturing and had a voice for song. She was not attractive, her teeth were crooked, bucked and spaced, but she was motherly. She always sang the loudest when they gathered for a hymn.

Buela then led everyone in a song, singing out loud and clear in her full voice a field song about Jesus. The family followed in response to her. Sung questions. Sung answers. The jug of whiskey from Tennessee was passed around. This song led to hand clapping and a drum was pulled from the wagon by Isachar. This brought a constant beat and set everyone into motion, stepping, clapping, swinging, dancing. There was an increase in the beat and the voices raised, whiskey adding to the opening up. But there was about this a sense of freedom, not one of drunken revels.

I spoke briefly with Hanna. She said, "Lordy, Lordy, singing away like you mean it."

"I do mean it," I yelled over the drum.

"Keep your hands clapping; let the lord know you praise him. You praise him," she said.

This helped me to open up even more and I sang and sang, and danced about. All sound, drum and voice, increased in speed, rose in volume. Everyone was swirling and singing.

Buela was ringing out like a bell, shouting out, bellowing. The family responded and answered each call, "Jesus is my savior." "Jesus is my savior." "Do you love the Lord?" "Yes, I love the lord." On and on, around and around.

Then Zephaniah came into the circle holding a serpent. He stared at it sternly and slipped his tongue out in response to the serpent's, put it on the ground, and it coiled and shook its tail. He stepped proudly around it and over it, picked it up very fast, and strung it around his neck. From the field more snakes came to the fire spot; they crept out of the tall grass past the bare feet of the family into the circle of firelight. Zephaniah picked them up one by one and kissed them on the head. He put another around his neck and two more wrapped and squirming around each forearm. These he held high. Then Zephaniah started to babble ancient languages, speaking in tongues as on the day of Pentecost when the spirit entered the disciples.

Hanna fell to her knees and started to yell, "I see you Lord, I see you Lord, come to me, Lord, come to me. Thank you Lord, thank you Lord."

Buela sang out," Hallelujah. All praises to you Great God. Hallelujah."

Isachar beat on the drum, Dan, Gad danced wildly in circles, spinning, falling down to their backs on the ground, exhausted, looking up, arms reaching skyward, hands waving as if rubbing the air. Rachel cried and laughed, she wept open and joyous, as her blissful tears streamed over her birthmark.

From the darkness by the cemetery came the sound of Joseph on the cow's horn, blowing deep and sonorous, many times, many times. Suddenly, all stopped in place and stood still. For a time not a sound was heard except hearts beating and breath racing. And the horn's airy resonance enveloped us and hung like a solemn fog in the night. Out of the shadows by the graves came Joseph slowly moving forward blowing his horn, hitch stepped with a strange look in his eye, blowing and blowing. He walked to the outer edge of the ring of light and climbed up on the table rock. He stood there looking about with his odd expression.

In the sky there came a shower of shooting stars, thousands and thousands, like speeding torches rushing by, into and out of the column of smoke and off disappearing in night. Awe and wonder was in our glowing eyes, the cow's horn was bellowing in our ears, the lights flashing by, endless. Endless. And the moon turned a deep crimson red.

I stood in amazement at this sight, this portent, and then Zephaniah spoke, "Joseph, you are the blessed. You are the dream reader. I have dreamt a dream such as never before. I have seen a vision from the Lord, tell me what it means."

And he then told of the strange firelight meeting, the fight with the Indian in the night and the dream he'd had when the Indian disappeared.

"I was a bird sitting in a tree at the top of a hill, alone, content. Many, many birds, birds of countless colors and species flew from the heavens to the branches around this bird, the tree was filled with them, there was no more space. There was chattering and songs, grooming. It was a beautiful confused sound, loud and happy, full of life. Soon they all settled in the tree and at once grew silent, like at the command of some unheard rifle, instantly. There was complete peace and silence."

"Slowly, slowly, a star rose in the distance shedding a beautiful golden light across the land below the tree, showing a perfect farmland. There were farmers working alongside their slaves. The slaves were singing loudly, in unison, a song praising God."

"He is the amazing one, He is our God.
He is the amazing one, He is our God."

"Their voices rose in a negro chorus of praise. The females joined in; voices of women, soft and clear, rang out as they walked from their small cabins with little ones nursing at their breasts, children scattered and ran to the brook, splashing in the water, the laughter rising, ringing with the song."

"Then the clouds grew in size and gradually became darker until they blotted out the star and a noise spread out from them. The clouds then separated into thousands of parts until I could see they were formations of crows. Large black countless crows. The din from the wings, the calls of the evil army of black eyed birds became overwhelming. Fear filled the slaves and farmers. They started to run and scream, telling others to run, looking over their shoulders at the ocean of blackness descending on them, causing even greater panic."

"Innately the birds in the branches knew death was upon them and tried to fly away. But since they were many birds from many places they could not act as one flock, could not rise in a single formation. In their confusion they flew into each other, some falling. The hordes of black birds reached them attacking in mid flight. The crows dove at them spearing them with their beaks, throwing them off balance, rolling them over, spinning them around, feathers shedding, casting them to the ground below. The tiny birds were crushed with large powerful eagle talons; they grabbed them in flight, crushing then dropping them, then grabbing another. Then the crows landed on the injured birds, pecking at them, ripping them open. The people ran all in the same direction, away, away, away from this fearful specter toward the woods, to the safety of cover. But from the edge of the woods, from the gopher holes and the rock walls and logs piles slithered out huge blue fanged serpents, moving silently and fast on their rippled bellies, tongues darting, lethal killers seeking prey. Thousands of them writhed out from the forest edge turning the tide of fleeing slaves and farmers. They caught them and grappled, wrapping them, biting, ripping and sinking their teeth. The crows too landed on the besieged people, on anyone, one body after another, pecking, pecking, leaving only empty sockets and gaping mouths. Then a swarm of ants came from the earth devastating all that was there, felling trees, consuming them, leaving homes and crops heaps of dust, bodies went to bone. Even the sinews which held the bones together were chewed and severed. The ants carried the bones to different places. No burial was even possible, there were no bodies, just scattered bones, there was no one to dig the graves, no one to mourn."

Joseph listened, crooked and sallow, a look of patience on his face. The others sat around in pious awe as Zephaniah told his dream. They sat like wasted nomads wandering no more, worn out, spent, in rapt attention, eyes staring.

And Zephaniah prayed to the stars saying, "God tell him what this means."

All around said, "Yes, Lord."

Joseph, atop the table rock, raised his thin pale arms to the heavens, cow's horn hanging from his neck. He reached high, fingers straining, he straightened as best he could. His face pure, his expression intense with wisdom and wonder in his eyes. Joseph then slowly said in his small voice, "Life as we know it is over, war is near, war comes soon, burning, killing all in their way. Death, death everywhere, bones, skulls, children, mothers, all dead. Armies marching, shouldered guns, flags, explosions, blood. One will lead, one must die. John Brown starts it."

Zephaniah yelled, "Where is Brown? Can we stop his war? Can we stop it?"

Joseph said in a boy's voice, "Hang you Brown, hang you. Hang you Brown, hang you"

Then he sang,
"John Brown's body lies a-mouldering in the dust,
John Brown's rifle's red with blood-spots turned to rust,
John Brown's pike has made its last, unflinching thrust."

Zephaniah leapt to Joseph and said, "Can we stop him, do we have time?"
Joseph looked into the fire, "War is coming on sure as rain."
Lowering his voice Zephaniah asked, "Do I have time to stop him?"
Still staring Joseph said, "Yes, war is years away."
Zephaniah unable to contain himself yelled, "Tell me where can we find him?"
Joseph unflinching stared still and said the words, "War is north, war is south."
Zephaniah grabbing Joseph's arms said impatiently, "Where will the war begin, where?"
Joseph gasped quietly, like birth breathing. He pulled away from his father

and walked closer to the fire, wincing at his visions, face aglow. I waited in awe to hear what he would say, to see where this crooked boy's mind was taking us.

He turned and looked around at all of us, then fixed his stare on a distant place and he said in quiet childlike monotone, "Andersonville, Shiloh, Bull Run, Petersburg, Gettysburg, Seminary Ridge, Little Round Top, The Shooting Gallery, Chancellorsville, Vicksburg, Fredericksburg, explosions, craters, blood, death. A voice crying in the wilderness, I'm burning, I'm burning, save me, save me, my God. John Brown, John Brown, Harpers Ferry, Charles Town. Hang him, hang him, Manassas, Virginia, Manassas. The war begins at Manassas."

And he fell quiet and withdrew from us. Buela and Hanna went to him, wiping his brow, holding him.

Zephaniah cried out, "Brown will be found at Manassas. Joseph has said it. Here in the presence of our ancestors, our dead children. He has foretold, thank God. The harvests, the rain, the locusts, he has been right before. We will go to Manassas, kill John Brown, halt the devastation, protect God's way of life. Hiram, you will go with us. We will hang John Brown in Manassas. The Lord has spoken."

The Abolitionist Vision

The Nebraska Kansas Border, August 1856

John Brown and his men rode out of bleeding Kansas to Nebraska to safer ground; a place still part of the territories but not yet contested, not considered southern slave ground. He was sick with fever, after too many nights camping out in the elements, with little sleep and too many miles, Brown had come down with the ague. His fever burned. His face was flushed as he rode on thinking about Jerusalem, thinking about his triumph in Lawrence, thinking about his plan, of the little Negro children waiting for his arrival to free them. He thought he was still on the milky white mule, thought he rode triumphant into Lawrence, where people cheered him, crowded around him, listened to his every word. After a life in obscurity, of struggles in the world, against the world, victory was new to him. He felt like Jesus riding into Jerusalem before the Passover. He well knew what happened to Jesus. Yet he wanted to be like Jesus. He was ready to sacrifice himself for four million slaves, so they could be free. There would always be a Judas among them, those who would betray. But even that, deception, disloyalty, double dealing was part of God's plan, so he did not have any anxiousness about it.

They rode to a small cluster of log homes, a settlement, a haven he knew well owned by Quakers who supported him. Not violent people, not fighters, but haters of slavery, willing to help though not raise a hand. From this place in '55, Brown had traveled south to Kansas. After a long journey west from the mountains of New York with the intent to start the war, these gentle people were a Godsend. He rode to Kansas to begin his quest alone in his wagon with a message from God in his mind. His sons were waiting there, organizing fighters, all abolitionists ready to die. With little money, no plan and a vision, he went into Kansas to change the world.

The Quaker men came out and welcomed them, chin beards, suspenders, round brimmed hats; the women followed, bonneted and stern but modest, shy; the children, cautious, tame, respectful.

Brown stepped weakly down from the teamster wagon. He tried to stand straight to make a short welcoming speech as he had in Lawrence, to say something appropriate about the Biblical importance of the occasion, some few phrases signaling the potency of this mission in his grand scheme, but he slumped and leaned against the wagon, almost slid to the ground. His sickness was obvious to all and they helped him inside a cabin, led him to a loft, where he could be tended to. He lay down in a stupor and fell wearily to sleep.

———◆———

In his fevered mind John Brown dreamed. He saw himself with a long beard, rocking on a coach traveling to Kansas City. It seemed the other riders were looking at him, but averted their eyes each time he looked their way. He thought there was blood on his skin that would not wash away. But no other could see it. He was not riddled by guilt; there were no haunts in his nights. He did have visions of the bloody murders along the Pottawotomie. He heard the sounds of sword on dull bone, images of severed arms, heads turned askew and bodies unnaturally still, blood running, puddles in the clay, blue brains on his sleeve, the crying women. He thought of the battles he had fought, skirmishes, ambushes, night forays, rear guard actions. And he was proud of his work, his generalship, his commitment. God had given him much strength. He was firm.

He might have damned himself, damned his own children to the eternal flame for breaking a commandment deliberately, but he was calm, in the face of punishment, of total damnation. It was God's will. He knew he was not yet finished. It had just begun. He was called.

He needed money to birth the plan growing in his mind. He knew these thoughts were inspired. He had never been so sure of a thing. He was not wracked by doubt or fear. Each step of his life had been a disappointment, though he followed the way of the Lord every day. But now he was clear; he knew his calling.

The coach passed through a small town and in a fleeting vision he thought he saw his first wife, Dianthe, who had died years before in child birth. She stood by the roadside with his four dead children. He tried to call to her, but a passenger was in his way. Once he could look out of the small window they stood too far away, alone, expressionless, looking at him, as dust from the coach blurred his view. Sadness came upon him for he knew she surely died in child birth, and he knew she was a just a dream, a mirage. In his heart he had never stopped feeling the loss, though he had remarried.

Once in Kansas City, a city too filled with proslavery men for him to feel safe, he planned to sleep a night in a hotel and the next morning board a steamboat down the Missouri for St Louis. There get a steamer down the Mississippi to Louisville, then get on another steamboat above the Falls of the Ohio to Wheeling, West Virginia. From there, take the new train down to Baltimore, and a steamer on to Philadelphia or New York. Then catch a boat to Boston.

He was going to the place where the storm of his soul returned for strength. There were wealthy men in Boston, men who wrote in newspapers, spoke at large gatherings brave words of this tragedy, the beast, slavery, who would now listen to him and be proud to know him. They would write of him, use him as their symbol. They would provide the money for his plan, armies would rise up, multiply a thousand fold, like bees to a hive returning. His murderous night he hoped was the lantern dropped in the hay, the conflagration's fuel, the war's passions stoked. Armies for freedom, armed disciples, formed to wipe the scourge away, to be sent forth to trample this unholy vintage, to skim the dross of slave holders from atop the molten metal of our race, discarding them as the wastes of humanity, would march for him. His murderous night at the creek was the lode stone, pointing true north, to the future, showing the way to freedom for the oppressed.

A round faced suited man sat opposite John Brown reading a newspaper and stealing glances at this silent, intense stranger. A front page story blared out in bold letters about the battles between Law and Order Missouri proslavery forces and the Free Soil abolitionists. It gave a long complete description.

The politicians in Washington who spoke words cheering or damning Sumner's caning, depending on their domicile and party, and who now heard of Brown's nighttime disembowelments and gore in Kansas, the tears of the widows, the severed hands, the slashed necks, the bloody ultimatum—free the negroes or this is your fate—voiced words more inflammatory then yet ever spoken. They sent speeches to the press to ensure they would quote them correctly. Their voters, whether from north or south, responded in kind to the incitement of their politicians. Tensions built up with each word printed about Brown, like ice heaves on a frozen river piling upon each other in the deep of winter, uneven and jagged, pushing, force against force, the water slowly backing up, until a thaw would release them in a destructive torrent, flooding the village.

Brown's bloody child would not long be an orphan. Many would seek to adopt it, seeing different qualities, different exploitations. Politicians from the north would claim parentage because of what the child might grow to, its future prospects, a rebellious, unwavering yet principled child. Politicians from the south wanted to succor this babe for a precious while, display its mongoloid head before they publicly destroyed it in the name of all chivalry, honor and tradition.

The round faced bespectacled man sensed his fellow passenger's eyes on his paper and said, "Quite a horrible thing, those killings."

Brown nodded but did not answer.

The round faced man adjusted his spectacles and said, "I take no position myself, seeing justification on both sides. It is the very root of democracy, that a man be not beholden to his government other than to pay a small and reasonable tax and to vote, this cannot be debated. But once a vote is cast, a law written and the outcome decided we must follow. It is law. Law is law. Slavery is so against what we stand for, but it is the law. Quite a conundrum."

Brown stared ahead.

The man continued, "I hope this shall pass. I cannot bear the thought of choosing a side. The very marrow of worth of our democracy is at test."

Brown said, "There is a higher law than those written and debated by men. You will need to choose. One day soon you will need to choose between the law of man and the law of God."

The man sighed, "I suppose you are right. But I do not wish it. I do not wish to choose. I am a simple man of commerce, not a deep thinker. I just want business to grow and for my family to live simply and prosper. I do not mean to pry but what is your name sir, you look familiar to me."

The stagecoach pulled into Kansas City. Brown paused seeing some worth in letting this man know how close he had come to the genesis of the story in his newspaper.

Brown said, "Nelson Hawkins. I do not think we have met. Perhaps someday we can spend some time and wrestle with this topic. I do know where I stand. I believe John Brown to be a hero, a warrior for God and all that is righteous in this land," he said as he climbed out of the coach and caught his valise from the driver.

He walked calmly into the town, past people waiting for the coach to arrive, some coming, some going, all stealing glances at him. Their eyes met then broke away. Brown thought they might recognize him but he could not tell; he did not care.

He walked down the stark hoof-trampled street, past the town drunk who blathered aloud, "God damn your soul," then vomited and was knocked over by a passing horse.

He walked past a hotel called Wormwood, past a saloon where a wooden legged whore sat outside on a stool, past the land office and a sleeping sheriff, past people reading the headlines on Pottawotomie Creek.

Brown then bought a newspaper at the general store and walked into the telegraph office the next door down. Going inside, he sat patiently and waited his turn with the clerk in the eyeshade. He looked to the floor boards seeing the blood of his rampage in the worn wood.

A woman dressed in mourning black cried lightly, touched her nose with a rose embroidered handkerchief and recited the words of her message to the clerk, who focused as he tapped the key of the telegraph, sending the words running along the cable to reach the destination in mere seconds. The message was going to St Louis, then forwarded to Saratoga, New York, near John Brown's current home by Lake Placid. Her husband had died; he had been a taxidermist and she was shipping his effects to the family.

When she finished her transmission, John Brown heard the click and roll of her coins as they fell from the counter. They rolled across the floor interrupting his bloody vision. He picked them up and handed them to her, and when he did she paused and looked deeply into his blue eyes. He thought for a moment she might know him, her look was so penetrating. But she looked away and he was brought back to his visions of slaughters in the night, the wailing of the women and children. He saw himself kneeling over the men he had killed; he considered the pain he had brought them. He felt sorrow for their loss, but briefly, only briefly.

The plight of the slaves of his nation retook the castle of his mind and he subdued that shivering barely contained anger by saying to the widow, "May he rest in peace, madam."

"Thank you kind sir," she said as she turned to look at him, "You do not know the loss I feel. Bertram was such a good man. We traveled here so he could collect samples, pelts, specimens," she said as she cried into her hand.

Brown answered, "I think indeed I do madam. Life is a precious thing, I wish you comfort."

She responded still dabbing her eye, "If only I could find it. I am now a poor widow sir. I am alone in the world and will remain so. There is little I can look to. I travel home to Saratoga, near Albany to mourn with family. I must bring his art back to them, his work, his life's endeavors, his beautiful still creatures must be returned, they were to be in a museum in New York, you know? And I, alas, I cannot stay in this place. It is immoral and decrepit, filled with gamblers, swindlers, passing traders, whores and murderers. Have you read, sir, the newspapers, about the two governments in this Kansas Territory, one voted in legally, one populated with rebels, the supporters of those killings?"

"The government is not legal, but voted in by folks from Missouri," he retorted defending his cause.

She continued, "We are here to civilize, we instead become the savages we seek to redeem."

He said with consolation, glad to avoid the argument, "Let us not speak of politics or the death of others. I am sure your heart is heavy with your loss."

"You are so right sir, so right," she said. "I bid you, good day."

"Yes madam, Good day," he repeated.

She looked for a moment into his steely blue eyes and then left with a wipe of her nose and a sweep of her black crenulated dress.

Brown rose and said to the clerk, "Sir, I wish to send a message to Boston." The clerk wrote as he said, "To the honorable Franklin Sanborn, Boston. Arrive Boston September 10. Please meet, much to tell. Money needed, Yours, JB."

"Will that be all?" asked the clerk as he readied to tap the code.

"Yes, thank you kindly, sir," said Brown.

"That'll be two bits," said the clerk.

Brown put his coins on the counter making sure they did not roll off, looked straight at the clerk then walked out the door. He walked past the whore and checked into the Wormwood Hotel. Once in a room he knelt down and said a silent prayer, then still on his knees he opened his Bible and read:

Jeremiah 6:9
Thus says the Lord of Hosts
Glean thoroughly as a vine the remnant of Israel;
like a grape gatherer pass your hand again over its branches.
To whom shall I speak and give warning,
that they may hear?
Behold their ears are closed,
They cannot listen;
behold the word of the Lord is to them an object of scorn,
they take no pleasure in it.
Therefore I am full of the wrath of the Lord;
I am weary of holding it in.
Pour it out upon the children in the street,
and upon the gatherings of young men also;
both the husband and wife shall be taken,
the old folk and the very aged.
Their houses shall be turned over to others,
their fields and wives together;
For I will stretch out my hand
against the inhabitants of the land,
says the Lord.

For from the least to the greatest of them,
everyone is greedy for unjust gain;
and from prophet to priest every one deals falsely.
They have healed the wound of my people lightly,
Saying, Peace, peace.
When there is no peace.
Were they ashamed when they committed abomination?
No they were not at all ashamed,
they did not know how to blush.
Therefore they shall fall among those who fall;
At the time that I punish them
they shall be overthrown.

Brown then sat on a captain's chair with a broken rib and spindle, placed a soot smudged lantern on the bedside table, and spread the newspaper out on his bed to read the account of the battles, his escapes, his righteous killings. The newspaper recorded the details of finding his victims, the Doyle family, and the others. It described the contortions, said he'd desecrated the bodies. The paper said he had killed them all with his sword, with his nigger loving rage, not mentioning his sons or the others. This was, he thought, good. They used many words to describe the pitiful widows: crazed with grief, too weak to stand, in shock, able only to babble his name, John Brown, John Brown...

They wrote about the capture of his sons, Jason and John Jr., by Captain Henry Pate and his force of Missouri Law and Order men; law and order, such a lie. They had made the boys watch as their homestead was burned to the ground, dust unto dust, he thought. He worried briefly about John Jr. and his unsteady mind but it was God's will, his cross to bear.

They wrote of Frederick's death, shot through the throat. He croaked loudly for his father to save him. They wrote that cowardly John Brown had scurried away. But that was not true; he had carried his dying son a hundred yards, across a river trying to save him. But he bled to death. There was no time to grieve; he was left where he expired. His son's body was picked at by birds, they said. God knows he had tried with all his might to save him. But God wanted Frederick back. My sons, he thought, my sons. The loss pained him, one dead, two captured, he knew God had planned this, so he did not dwell on it. He looked fate in the eye grimly, blessed it saying God is always just.

His other men, some dead, others scattered, waited for their leader to rise again like the Phoenix with their next call to action. Such was Holy War: a tumult, a sorrow, lies and deception, great sacrifice, great confusion, when law was a lie and order was corruption. But all the loss was for a great purpose, God's eternal will.

They wrote that David Garrison was killed with a single shot, but that was not true.

Wounded in the belly he tried to crawl away but he was shot in both legs, then both hands for sport. His skull had then been crushed by a rock, stoned to death like Stephen in the Bible.

But they did not write of Captain Pate's most dishonorable action. Chased as fox by hound, Brown and his men, forty of them, had hidden, let Pate go past, then ambushed him from behind, pinning them, capturing Pate and some twenty of his men. A treaty was signed, Brown with Pate, bartering Pate's release in exchange for Brown's captive sons. So agreed, so done and Pate was released as John Brown had promised. But Jason and John were to this day still in jail. John Jr. had gone mad as he was prone to do, raving from anguish, nerves, from melancholia. Pate was not a man of his word. No honor coursed through the veins of this defender of slavery, just corruption and greed and lies.

Brown thought it better to sever his own arm than ever again to shake the hand of a proslavery man.

He had a vision of himself cutting off his arm at his elbow with a sharp Bowie knife, amazing the people with his pure will.

Brown had fled, the newspaper said, followed by his bedraggled tired band. The paper did not print of his defensive stand some days later along a road firing hot lead into his pursuers, one General John Reid, killing many men. They only reported the second attack and this time Brown and his thirty eight men fled, low on ammunition, seeking to preserve life for another battle. One was killed, four captured in this retreat. Brown had hidden in a corn crib, helped by a family of sympathizers, then rode four miles on a white mule to Lawrence.

Triumphant he rode in, praised, cheered for his boldness, with handshakes all around. He stood on a wooden box and convinced the people of the town to fortify, to plan for an onslaught of ruffians seeking bloody revenge. And they came, as he prophesied, with vengeful eyes they encircled the town; but with Brown in their midst the people stood their ground. They would not relent, they would not surrender. Then the Kansas Governor, afraid of such disorder, pardoned all and sought a cease fire in exchange for the disbanding of the fighters, ending the episode with a plea for calm.

Brown knew his plan was a complete success. It told the whole world: Be prepared to fight if slavery spreads past the borders of Kansas. Fear now dwelt in the hearts of the mighty and ill gotten riches had deadly new risks.

But in the words of this newspaper, John Brown was nefarious, a demon. With great disdain the writer noted that northern newspapers called Brown's massacre southern atonement, the skirmishes that followed they called military genius, his escape was deemed brilliance. He was compared to great Roman generals, Julius Caesar against the Carthaginians. They reached for ancient allusions seeking to enshrine his action with quotes from Homer, comparing his stand to the Spartans against the Persians at Thermopylae.

John Brown folded the newspaper and lay on the bed. His mind pondered the praise and bloated allusions and he dismissed them rather than allow himself to believe such self important blather. He wandered then along the deer paths by the creek near his killings, saw the faces, heard the sounds. He hid from whistling bullets in battle and saw over and over the death of his son. He remembered the dead weight of his body as he carried him. He felt the dampness of Frederick's blood soaking his clothes, running into his boots, which sloshed as he ran. He pondered on his sons behind bars, of the abuses they must have borne. These thoughts recurred, leaving sleep far away in an unknown place he would not reach that night.

At the first sound of the cock, he was up for some breakfast. Never at a loss to eat, even in the days of dying children, failed businesses, struggling partnerships, he ate well and had his coffee. A brief wash, then he settled his bill and walked out of the hotel, past the one legged whore who snored on her stool and down the street to the docks.

He bought his fare for the steamer 'The New Lucy', a gallant paddlewheel riverboat.

Brown watched as slaves carried armloads of wood up the plank, toil and sweat and despair in their eyes; the boiler huffed steam as a soot-faced stoker fed fuel to the hungry fire inside. On the platform in a black dress was the widow standing next to a large wooden crate stamped Albany. She waited impatiently for them to load it.

"Sir," she said, "I want this put on last and stored closest to the door. I will not be left to wait upon my arrival."

The porter said, "Yes but madam, there is baggage and mail to unload before you reach your final destination."

Piles of baggage and bundles of cotton sat in random clusters along the dock. Drayman moved the parcels, passing by the crate marked Albany. The widow's anger rose and she said, "I do not care a whit about the others. I have lost my husband sir. He is buried here in this God-forsaken town. Who will get off your boat first is not my concern, I am a widow sir, this box is filled with my husband's belongings, his works of a lifetime. I will not be denied the right of a widow, this crate is to be near the door."

Seeing a crowd of passengers building the porter said, "Yes, yes, all right madam, all right, you'll have it your way. There'll be more work on your account but it will go in near the door."

The crate was loaded last by four hefty black slaves and set near the door as she watched satisfied.

John Brown took his seat alone and looked out the window, at his reflection in the glass, at the calmly passing river. Water. How he loved it, the baptizer of souls, a great blessing to all.

The widow entered the cabin. She walked past him, nodding as she strolled by and sat on a bench three rows ahead. He was pleased from this vantage point. He could stare unnoticed at the whale bone combs in her hair, scrimshawed with pictures, unrecognizable patterns of fanciful scenes. He did not need to look away in embarrassment with her seated in front of him, he could study her unseen. She was richly dressed, her hair perfectly pulled in a bun, wound tight in a snail shell pattern. She was a good looking woman, a person of some pedigree. He did not find her unattractive but he would bury this thought.

The ropes were thrown aboard and the large wheel started to turn. Driven by gargantuan horizontal drive shafts and stalwart pistons the ship began to move forward. It pushed toward St. Louis, two and a half days downstream. In a short while the widow walked down the aisle and said, "Good Morning Mr. John Brown. It is my pleasure to meet you. I do believe I am in your debt, yet I do need your assistance."

John Brown stared at her in disbelief. He felt as if he stood naked to the world, caught and possibly in danger.

Journey to Manassas

The rain fell hard, mists so thick I could see only two horses ahead. Hoofs sunk in drenched turf as we rode in a single column weaving through the prairie, shoulders shrugged against the cold, slickers shining, brims dripping. Horse's heads down, they plowed forward into the fog. Rachel, Esther, Buela, and Hanna cried when we left them alone with Ben, who complained and bawled because he wanted to come. 'Joseph was going,' he argued, 'and they were almost the same age.' But Joseph was a guide, a compass for certain direction, essential to the journey despite his age. Ben was too young; he needed to stay to help his mothers. His talent was protection he was told. He was to be the man of the house in Zephaniah's absence.

The women had baked and packed food for travel, rolled the blankets, cleaned the rifles, made the bullets, sewed the tears, oiled the boots. Left at home, they went about their work; they knew their part in the mission.

We had ridden off under an overcast sky, the rain not yet coming down. Gray skies hung like funeral drapes, like black bunting. The dogs followed, roaming, trailing, sniffing, to the main wagon road then Zephaniah ordered them home. They cowered, no wag in the tail, ears back, eyes low. Sent back to protect the homestead, they followed the command of their master, same as us.

I was so in awe of what I had witnessed the night around the fire that when I woke up before dawn, in the shed with Sagebrush standing near me, I knew I could have just rode off, but I did not. Something had happened there, we all saw it. I could not deny it. This encounter and captivity had led to something, I did not yet know what but it was real and I was part of it—a mission, a common experience, a dangerous magic. And since God was the source of inspiration, I felt called for the first time.

This queue of Zephaniah and his offspring atop their horses riding on to Manassas, all well trained to follow, taught to listen and not to argue or debate his orders, was one in spirit. As we traveled I began to notice their unique qualities.

First behind Zephaniah Diana rode. She was brought along to support, cook and help, but she was strong and tough. She could shoot, load, handle a knife as well as any man. I saw her throw a bone handled knife and bury it in a tree at thirty feet piercing a wanted poster.

Zebulan rode next. He spoke often of seeing the ocean. He begged

Zephaniah to let him continue past Manassas to go to the sea. He longed for it like a boy with a crush, silently yearning, then voicing his angst to others. It kept him up nights he was so giddy over it. He could not wait to see the Missouri River, even that thrilled him. Water was a mystery, a supernatural being and the great sea was a great living fluid. Just the thought of it, the vision of its vastness, was like something out of a fairy tale. It could not be believed unless seen. His favorite stories were the verses about Noah's ark, the forty days of great rains, the floating ship, pairs of all animals saved, tossed about on the great waters. He also loved the power of Moses parting the Red Sea, escaping across its exposed sea floor and then the crashing waves drowning Pharaoh's soldiers.

"That Pharaoh," he would say, "sure never saw anything like that sea swallowing up his boys."

But he wondered why Pharaoh chased them saying, "Now why'd he change his mind? Why did God harden Pharaoh's heart? You would think Pharaoh would want them gone after all those plagues? Those poor dead children, no lamb's blood on their doors had to die. He could have let them go after the locust or the blood in the River Nile. Imagine that," he would say, "an entire river turned all to blood."

Asher, a particular lad, always sought to be served. He was more refined than the others, more concerned with his hair and his appearance. He cleaned his nails with a knife, rubbed the dust from his boots every day. He hoped to meet great people on this journey. He spoke of going to Washington, seeing a great parade from a stand near the President, perhaps joining the army and becoming a General, smoking large cigars in the parlors of the rich and famous. He was a gambler by nature willing to bet which side of a falling leaf would touch the ground first, anything to get others to think about the odds of life. He once said, "Betting is the act of guessing the mind of God, you can never know, never win all the time. If you get lucky, you've been blessed. Any bet is a good bet, but it's up to God if you're supposed to win."

Isachar was the worker. He would gladly do whatever was needed. He was tireless, strong, simple minded, reliable. If firewood or water was needed or if food needed preparation, whatever it was he knew his time was at hand. Uncomplaining he dove into the work. He was the most serene, his purpose was so clear to him.

Naptali was handsome, stunning to look at but empty as a horse collar hanging in the barn. He would engage in conversation with distinct interest but had nothing to add. His mind went blank when asked to make comment. His brain could not put thoughts to words with any confidence. He knew speaking knowledgeably was important so he would pretend interest and start a discussion on politics or religion as we rode, but then he would go blank, confused on where to go next. I noticed in my encounters with him, a distinct sense of loneliness. For one so handsome, one who would be so desired by women, he lacked all confidence. The shallow depth of his brain scared him. A look of panic crossed his face as he realized he was lost and could go no further, that he missed something crucial to success. It was as if the exposure of his vacuous mind was the signal for the four horseman of the apocalypse to descend on him.

Gad was just out for a fight. It was plain to see and simple as that. He was a scrapper and he kept a keen eye for danger that could come our way. He was not much for conversation but he had a quiet confidence that made you glad he was there. I thought Gad would be a good person to have in a tough situation.

Judah and Gad were of one kind. Their thoughts worked together toward one end, winning in a fight. Zephaniah said they had always played as children like wild cubs, fighting, sometimes to the point of blood. But it was training, a test, a sport. They talked as they rode of what they would do if an Indian showed from behind this hill or that tree.

Dan was a conniver. You never knew if he was being honest, if what he said was meant at face value or for its reverse intent. Dan made you suspicious by his countenance, made you wonder what he thought of you. When he spoke he came up close and half whispered, breathy in your face. Dan's strangest trait was talking to his horse. He would ride along speaking low in her ear. But I could not hear his words. He carried on long conversations as they rode together. But no one seemed to notice. When we rested they would sit off to the side as if conspiring.

Home was five days behind when we rode into sight of an Indian village, a collection of lodges, one large and ten or so smaller. We looked on from the cover of a rise for a time. Gad and Judah watched for weaknesses, counted warriors, women, children. Dan wanted to create a diversion and trick them, draw out the warriors then surround them and slaughter them, kill them all. Levi and Simeon wanted to sneak in the night and hamstring the horses so no one could follow as we escaped. Reuben, Naptali and Isachar sat silent, ready to do as anyone said. Zebulan, wanted to go another way and avoid a fight, keeping the goal of Brown's hanging in mind. Asher wanted to bet on which Indian would be killed first.

I remained silent seeing Zephaniah was unconcerned at their comments. He let them whisper on while he watched. He wanted to ride right in. He could have left the trail, bypassed these Indians, but he saw all of them as a lost people in need of redemption. God deigned this meeting. It was not to be avoided. So against every impulse in my being to sidestep this trouble, I followed his order, mounted up and went straight toward this dangerous and unknown future.

Roaming dogs barked protectively when they saw us coming, women pulled the children into lodges, the men ran for weapons. We kept our guns holstered as Zephaniah ordered. As we rode closer, the warriors encircled us, ready to kill us for any hint of danger. There were perhaps one hundred of them, intense, filthy, sullen, seeing us as fourteen prey on good horses. They were a desperate looking lot. They had fallen away from their ancestral ways, lost the patterns of their former lives. Anger replaced pride, drinking replaced hunting, rebellion replaced authority, squaws became whores. It was the time of the seasonal buffalo hunt, but they had not gone, they preferred stealing, trading, drinking.

A chief came out of the biggest lodge and two fat squaws followed him; others, curious, gathered around, women, children, firm-jawed glaring men. Zephaniah dismounted, his sore hip not yet able to hold his full weight. He limped over to the Chief and stared him in the eye.

The Chief asked with some incredulity, "Who enters our camp?"

"White men call me Zephaniah, but I am also called Coyote by the red man," he answered with pride and bluster in his bearing.

"Where did you get this name?" asked the Chief whose curiosity was piqued.

Zephaniah said still staring him in the eye, "An Indian named Moroni gave it to me, Tirawa-atius told him?"

The Chief looked to the others and considered the power of this statement, the spirit world encountered, the name of the Great Father spoken, the quality of his horses, the value of his guns, and he took particular notice of Zephaniah's daughter, Diana, as if she were a valuable horse, a jug of whiskey or a rich blanket.

"What is it you want?" asked the Chief.

"Nothing but to pass through peacefully and preach to you about the one true God," answered Zephaniah.

The Chief smiled, looked to his young men then to Zephaniah and said, "You are welcome, you and your people. Where are you going?"

"I am seeking a murderer. I mean to bring him to justice. But I come here in peace," said Zephaniah staring still.

"Camp here, Coyote. You are our guest. The girl, she looks strong and ready to bear young. Is she your daughter? We have much to trade for her," said the Chief.

On hearing this I wanted to move on. I did not like the feel of this place, the look of these Indians but Zephaniah was in control, he knew their ways. He said, "I thank you for your kindness, we will camp on your land but this is my wife. We will leave no one behind."

The Chief's eyebrows rose up and his head tilted slightly as he said, "You marry the young ones, you still have great powers for a grey beard."

"Yes," said Zephaniah with unblinking eyes.

"Camp near the brook. Come to my place tonight, we will talk," said the Chief pointing off to a place across the field near a grove of trees by a brook some distance away.

We tied off the horses, set ourselves up near the brook, comfortably far away from the lodges. We cooked and ate some food. The rain had stopped, leaving the ground wet, so we cut branches off a cedar tree, shook the water off, layered them over the damp grass and lay comfortably on the evergreen. Diana set her place away from us, tired of the snoring, the sleep talkers, the early risers. She'd learned in the past days she did not like to camp with men.

Zephaniah went to the big lodge and sat with the chief by his fire. They talked quietly and drank the Tennessee whiskey. We, in our weariness of riding, fell asleep while Zephaniah was away.

Sometime in the night a young Indian put his dirty hands over Diana's mouth as she slept and, muffling her screams, he dragged her off noiselessly. She tried to fight but he was too strong. She bit his hand and was struck in the face. She tried to run but was dragged down. Her clothes were ripped off and he raped her. When done, he dragged her into a hut on the outer regions of the tribes site. She was bound, bruised, gagged and kept as a toy.

Zephaniah slept that night in the lodge of the chief, out of respect for his invitation and hospitality. And while he slept he dreamed. A voice whispered in his ear, "Wash them in the blood of the lamb before they die." Then he saw a fading image of himself baptizing an Indian.

When he awoke, the chief stood over him and said, "You lied to me Coyote. She is not your wife."

Zephaniah looked at him, his eyes squinting from the morning light beaming in through the opening, trying to fathom the Chief's meaning. These Indians would not buy a man's wife but a daughter or relative was fair to barter and an even better gift. But a liar was not worthy of such fair consideration, and Zephaniah had lied. He had been brutally deceived in return.

Zephaniah sat up and said, "What have you done?" Then rising to his full height he threatened the chief saying, "If you have hurt her there will be trouble."

"She was not your wife. Her skin was not broken. She is my son's squaw now because you are the liar," the Chief said defiantly, with finality.

Zephaniah wanted to kill him right then but he thought about the safety of his family. Mad at himself for trusting, he hurried from the lodge back to the campsite. We all still slept soundly when Zephaniah returned and found Diana gone. He raged around the campsite, throwing things, waking us. Then he went off and sat in silence. Zephaniah went to his knees and as we watched he prayed about what to do. He then rose and walked over to us telling us how we had failed Diana. We looked at each other, ashamed we slept while this crime occurred. The loss of this young girl's innocence was like a valuable jewel, lost and not to be found again.

He said, "Get your rifles; we are going in to get your sister or die trying."

The Bargain

Zephaniah's words were like a flash flood, a call I had waited for my whole life. I knew this was real. I'd always wondered how I would react when the situation called on me to risk my life. Since it was a young girl, I was ready to fight, to die in her rescue. I was prepared for the worst. I loaded my rifle and both pistols and went in ready for a war.

We walked, wordless, across the sunlit field toward the village. The dogs barked as before but there was not a big commotion, everyone knew we were there and they continued going about their morning work. Zephaniah grabbed by the hair the first child and squaw he came upon, dragging them toward the Chief's lodge. They screamed and cried. The noise brought others out of their lodges and they looked on angrily, bringing out weapons, yelling at us. Anyone who came toward us we held off with our guns and with the child and the squaw at risk they stayed back, unsure of what to do. The noise brought the chief out, followed by his women. And before the second old squaw could get out of the door, Levi had a rifle to the Chief's head. A serious look crossed their faces.

Zephaniah said, "Give me my daughter or you will die right now, you will be Chief without a head."

The Chief said, "Is this any way for a Christian to act?"

There was silence as they stared each other down. Finally the chief signaled for one of them to go and get Diana. She emerged from the hut, damaged, led by deerskin ties around her wrists. She staggered out and fell at her father's feet, crying hard and noiseless.

With guns pointed at the chief and his squaws we backed out of the camp, not letting the hostages go until we were past the village's farthest boundary. By the time we made it to our camp the young men of the tribe were mad as hornets, yelling, getting in a lather to go and kill the whites. The chief looked toward us then he spoke and calmed them saying, "A squaw is nothing to lose your life over. There are many more to be found."

We sat in our camp with an eye out for trouble while Diana cried and washed in the brook. Zephaniah tried to help but could do little for her. It was a sorrowful sight, a broken child, a painful knowledge between a father and daughter. Then Diana came out of the water and sat by a tree in silence, tears running.

We stood aside until we could look no longer and Simeon said, "We should go in there and kill them all, they defiled my sister."

Zephaniah was seething, his fury tempered by his concern for his family. He was not a rash man and he too wanted revenge, but knew he would get his children killed if he followed that instinct. There were just too many.

He said, "Simeon, I want to kill them worse then you. Diana is my only daughter, but they outnumber us, if we kill half, half will still be coming. How many of you will I lose killing just half? The rest will be massacred."

Zephaniah went over to Joseph and walked with him a while. They sat beneath a tree and spoke for some time. He came back and said, "I had a dream last night. God spoke to me. I know what to do."

Diana asked from the base of the tree, "Why did God not tell you to avoid this place?"

Zephaniah answered, "God put them in our path. This is our test."

Diana answered, "Test? Look at me, look at me. Look what they've done. If God put them in our path, then God wanted this to happen. And God calls us to act to right this wrong. They deserve to die."

Just before dusk while Diana slept, the Chief signaled he wanted to talk. Zephaniah met him at the middle of the expanse between the camps. I watched as these two lone figures stood parlaying my future.

The Chief said, "I do not want a fight. We will both lose much."

"We have been grievously wronged, my sons want revenge. I could kill you right now before your men could save you," Zephaniah said containing his anger.

They stared at each other knowing they were at an impasse in a dangerous place. The Chief finally said, "My son did this, he wanted her as a young man does. This is no reason to die. Do not fight us, we are too many. My son wants your daughter as a wife."

Zephaniah without pause said, "That will not be, she can never marry him."

"Why?" asked the Chief.

"She is a Christian, you are a heathen," answered Zephaniah.

"We have gods, she will have gods?" said the Indian.

"We will ride away tonight while you are asleep." said Zephaniah as he began to turn away.

"They will follow," said the Chief. "Red Ember, my son, wants her. I will pay a good price; she will give him white children."

"She is part Apache, they will not be pure," said Zephaniah. "She is my daughter. Your son raped her. He will not have her."

Zephaniah looked all around. He looked to the sky; then he followed the pigtails of smoke, down to the lodges; around these wandered panting dogs tracing the steps of round faced children, playing games, hiding beneath the buffalo skins stretched and drying in the sun. He heard the singing of mothers as they worked pounding meal, saw babies wrapped in bundles propped up and sleeping. Finally, he fixed on the eagle feathers in the hair of the warriors, blowing in the building wind in one direction, as they looked on, waiting to see their fate, war or not. Zephaniah knew they could not kill them all. So they could not all get out alive. He thought about his mission to get John Brown. He thought about his dream in the Chief's lodge. This is not the war he had dreamed of and Joseph had deciphered. This fight had to be avoided.

He said, "I will make a bargain, but a hard bargain."

The Chief smiled, "We have many guns, horses, blankets."

Zephaniah answered, "I do not need horses, my daughter I trade only for the souls of you and your people."

The Chief screwed up his eyes and said, "How can we trade this?"

"If you want my daughter you must all become Christians, I will not leave her if you are not converted from your heathen gods."

The Chief asked as he scratched his forehead, "What must we do?"

Zephaniah answered, "You must believe in Jesus, know the one God, swear off your old gods. I will teach all of you, I will wash away your sins. Then you need to be circumcised."

"What is this? Circumcised?" asked the Indian trying to grasp the meaning.

"You must have the skin at the top of your manhood cut off," Zephaniah said clearly gesturing to the groin and making a cutting motion.

The Chief looked down concerned. "Why? No warrior will cut this. White men do this?"

"Yes we do," he answered.

"Why?"

"Because the Bible says so, God commands it," answered Zephaniah.

"White men are strange," said the Chief. "Why not wash in the water like the missionary at the Fort, or cut something else?"

"You must be baptized and you must be circumcised. It is our way. Are you scared?" asked Zephaniah. "We have all done this. Are Christians braver then Pawnee?" he added.

The chief thought, took the bait and said, "No, we will do this, all the men will do this, we will be Christians, your daughter will be one of us." And they parted.

Zephaniah's family waited, guns ready. We were all primed for a fight. So when he told us he was going to teach them to be Christians and make Diana marry a raping savage we were shocked. He said, "We will all die if we try to run, we will die if we try to fight. I have seen what Indians do to captives; I do not want this to happen to you. Diana, you will marry here." The discussion was over. All stood dumbfounded, never before confronted with such a command.

So each day the Indians gathered around and their Chief served as translator since few knew any English, and they listened to Zephaniah teach. The process was slow. Zephaniah patiently read them Bible stories, taught them about Jesus, and knelt and prayed with them. They listened and learned just as the chief had told them.

They had many questions. They wondered why the Jews did not simply kill the Pharaoh, why the Jews in the wilderness did not hunt for food and why they wandered for so long. They loved the story of Samson, his great strength, his battle killing the Philistines with the jawbone of an ass, his conquest of women, the great lover that he was. They touched their black hair hoping God would put the same power in their tresses. And they wanted to hear over and over the final twist of the plot: tricked by a woman to reveal the source of his power, she clipped his hair, sapping his strength, and making him a prisoner. Then blinded, eyes burned by a hot sword, Samson pulled down the pillars of the temple of the Philistines, destroying it and their God, Dagon, killing many.

They marveled at Jesus and had one question over and over. Why did he not use his power to save the world then and there and stop all of us from waiting and suffering? But as time went on and the Indians heard more and more I could see they grew tired. It was easy to see they were only satisfying their leader. The chief was very interested though and asked many questions. He worked at understanding this new God, the one who inspired the murders of his race.

The sons and I went to these meetings, at first in case a fight broke out, later on to pass the time. So I listened and learned as well. More things I never heard before. I was amazed at how Zephaniah had studied, could page though a Bible, chapter and verse, making his points, explaining it all. The sons, having sat through years of this teaching, found it worthwhile to take the measure of the warriors, look for weaknesses, take note of their weapons and patterns; to scout their lodges. I was not sure if Zephaniah had a plan to get us all out, or if he was just crazy with religion. He did not tell us. But he was giving all his being to this barter of his daughter for their savage souls.

Time passed slowly. Each night around the fire for entertainment Asher would take out a deck of cards and we would play. I had never been much of a card player and neither were the others, except Joseph. He did not always win but this boy had a way of knowing when to drop out, when to bet, and often he would win. He was a wise card player. Asher just loved to watch the turn of the cards and the perplexed expressions of his brothers as they considered what move to make next. Joseph never thought much about the game but watched the procession of numbered cards and royal cards and aces with a kind of idle intensity. This frustrated all of his older brothers. It was easy to see they were tired of Joseph's special status, his father's attentions, his unusual intelligence. And when Joseph won, Simeon would often throw his cards down and quit the game.

We all in our own way kept an eye on the Chief's son. It was very hard not to hate him after he had done such a wrong to Diana. Zephaniah said this was our battle, this was our test, to forgive, to move on. I wondered how this could be when our journey was one of vengeance. But there was no mystery to Zephaniah, the journey was ordained, this encounter was as well. This was but a stage of the mission. It had to completed, so we could continue. It was another ordeal; the fact that Brown was gaining time and distance on us did not matter right now. Zephaniah knew where he would be. Manassas.

The brothers spoke privately in somber disagreement with Zephaniah. Simeon wanted to sneak into the lodges, slit sleeping throats in the night one by one. Reuben wanted to set fire to the village, ride away and escape. They tried to appeal to Zephaniah's urgency to get Brown, to forestall the war, but he saw this as part of the mission God had put before him. They would do this his way as always. But they could not understand how he could give their sister over. Females did as their fathers commanded, happiness being second to obeying, so Diana did not argue, but there was a general feeling that this was a wrong. She was angry, hurt, wronged now in more ways than she could understand. Diana also came to know she was pregnant so she was even more confused about her future. Unmarried, unblessed, her future in question, a bastard on the way, she did not want to live with a tribe and be a squaw even though she was part Apache herself.

We soon noted that the chief's son was enamored of Diana. He tried to communicate with her to no avail. Her mixed white and Indian features attracted him. He looked on her with moon eyes as if his violation was the sign of his love. But Diana hated him. She looked at him with razor eyes that could slice his neck; she would have nothing to do with him. It did not matter what Zephaniah wanted or said, this marriage was going to be hard. This Indian wanted the status of a warm white body at night, a worker, white children, and perhaps if she could be one, a companion. Her white skin could make up for many faults. She would learn to be a good squaw.

Each night around the campfire I too learned something new about Zephaniah, about his family. He would tell stories to us, family stories, stories of the ancestors, the missions from God they were sent on and what happened. One night Zephaniah spoke to me alone of his marriage to his wives.

On a journey to the Mexico territory he rode through the canyon lands of Rachel's people, the Apache of Chacos. He rode around a massive crescent shaped canyon wall, its smooth edges eroded by sweeping winds. He saw her, sitting in the shade of a sandstone ledge beside a teardrop spring, the sun's low lean rays sweeping across the precipice, the shadow of its wind worn shape cast across her perfection, her lovely image waving in the heat and reflected in the waters of the azure oasis, stunning, beautiful as dawn. He knew as if struck by a stone she was to be his. She rose calmly, assuredly, said nothing, and watered his horse. She looked straight into his eyes, a long knowing look and the thought was in his mind clear as day. God wanted him to marry her.

Her poor Apache father needed his daughters to work, not marry, or at least he needed a bride's fee, goats, sheep, guns, horses. But Zephaniah had nothing so he agreed to work for her, to earn her, since her father would not agree to their union otherwise. He would work one full year, one maize harvest, to prove his worth for Rachel's hand.

He toiled like a loyal son, hours meant nothing, if there was work he did not sleep until the job was done perfectly. He was pure in his desire; all was done with honesty and in good faith. Whether in the corn field, with the sheep, collecting wood, tending the melon garden, picking in the orchard, anything, he worked harder than any other.

When the harvest was brought in, he could wait no longer. He had looked on Rachel for so many months, dreamt of her, endured the pent up longing of unrequited love. However when he raised his eyes and sought his reward her father's face showed deep concern. He lingered long on his answer, thinking, speaking slowly, carving his position in stone.

The aging Apache explained he regretfully could not keep his pledge. He had learned from a Shaman he could not let Zephaniah marry Rachel. It was a matter of Apache law. It would be taboo and a disgrace if the eldest sister were not married first. Rachel's father was sorry, he had thought hard on this while Zephaniah toiled. He said he would only let Rachel go if Zephaniah first married his eldest daughter, Esther, and only then if Zephaniah would give two more years of service for Rachel.

Zephaniah was furious but he was held captive by his love of this woman. He felt betrayed but determined to win Rachel. He was in a strange land, among a foreign people and there was no honorable way out. So he smothered his anger and toiled on, trapped by emotions of deep love, obsession, stolen time, unpaid labor, justice revoked. And he agreed to marry Esther. She was not the object of his desire but he spoke of her in favorable terms to me. He spoke of her talents, her spirit, shielding the truth of his feelings in the armor of years together, in the joys of his family.

Two long years went by. In this time of labor to buy the right to marry her sister, Rachel, Zephaniah and Esther had their first two sons, Reuben and Simeon. But when it again came time to marry Rachel he was called off to join the young warriors to fight the soldiers who invaded their land. It was at this time he crossed paths with Kit Carson, who was a murdering, drinking, traitor; living with Indians one day, even marrying one, and killing them for pay the next, according to Zephaniah. He was wounded by Carson, he said, as he rubbed his arm, but he spoke no more of him. I have heard much of those days since.

Carson and the soldiers burned their corn, chasing them to the cliffs. The Apaches ambushed, then ran off, evading the soldiers like King David from Saul. So Zephaniah was away another year, hiding high above the labyrinth of deep canyons, surviving to kill soldiers, scalping some, desecrating others, cutting off ears, genitals, gouging eyes, enough to scare off others from chasing them.

In the first months he was gone fighting, Levi was born to Esther. Upon his return, Rachel's father tried again to find another obscure tribal rule for yet another year of labor for Rachel, but Zephaniah had done enough, seen enough. He had waited long enough for love's requite. War had changed him, he was hardened. And he was no longer under the spell of her father's authority. His reverence for tribal rule was stained by too many scalps, too many bloated gray bodies mutilated in the desert sun. Her father was as any man, he could be killed, challenged.

Zephaniah just took up Rachel and married her. He then took his two sister-wives, his three young sons and moved north to Kansas territory to live on his father's land. Zephaniah was so strong willed, so determined; it was hard for me to imagine him so dominated by another man. But love will do strange things to us.

I asked him also one night by the fire when all were asleep about Joseph. He thought long before answering me. He told me that there was once a long drought but the moment Joseph was born, as soon as his head followed the gushing waters from within Rachel, as he cried out, there was a golden burst of lightening, a brightness followed by a shotgun crack of thunder and right then it rained gloriously, steadily.

It rained a soft sweet rain for days, filling the brooks, greening the fields. That year there was abundance. He was born crooked, quiet, but very intelligent, insightful. He could speak in different voices and languages. He spoke to trees in sing-song poetry only he understood and he felt pain when they were cut down, as if mourning a lost brother. Zephaniah felt Joseph understood much about God and the spirits spoken of by Jesus, of the gifts of the Holy Ghost, of grace. Joseph spoke too of lights he saw around people, good or evil pulsed in those rays, telling of their spirit.

Once, years ago, when he was just a small boy, a bad storm was forming, the purple torrents drew dangerously closer. Joseph told them to run, to get away; there was a disaster on the way. And he was right. As they climbed up and away on the prairie a funnel cloud formed. It swirled and weaved a destructive tear toward them. And in a cataclysm of noise and power it swept up everything in its path. It tore up their cabin and scattered their possessions for hundreds of yards, even miles. It carried things to far off places never to be found again. Surely it would have killed them all, but Joseph had saved them.

Another time a neighbor had died and Joseph knew of it like a needle pricked him. He told Zephaniah where to go and where to look. Joseph however waited in the darkness, hiding, afraid to see death; he was still very young. The body, an old woman who sold herbs, was found crumpled and rotting beneath the blankets of her bed, dead from consumption and living a hard life.

Joseph once said their dog was lost before they had come home. He said it had chased a fleeting deer and did not return all night. When they arrived they saw he was right. But that was not all; Joseph had felt the dog's pain and led them straight to her, found her caught in a trap. He said he heard her though she could raise no more than a whimper.

Joseph could smell a fire before it burned. He could often tell when a rider was headed their way, not always but some of the time, and if his intentions were good or ill. He visited with dead ancestors and spoke with them.

Zephaniah said Joseph was often exhausted by being around too many people, the noise he heard from their minds confused him, and so he stayed alone mostly, preferring solitude. He said Joseph always had the gift of the inner eye, as he called it. Once when Zephaniah had dreamt their cow died, Joseph's dream reader ways were made clear. Joseph heard him talk of it at breakfast then simply told him to go in the barn and look under the hay. Sure enough a few layers down mold grew, set to tangle the cow's innards and kill it.

Zephaniah prayed that night, thanking God for this blessing on Joseph. But it did not always seem a blessing, for as many times as there was water divined, as many more times there were mysteries and unknown fears. More than once Joseph had told odd tales of other worlds in his dreams that made no sense to anyone. Joseph captured amazing thoughts in his mind that could never be deciphered. It was a blessing to know the unknown but a curse not to know the unknown's meaning.

Once when we were praying before dinner Joseph started to talk very fast. Rattling on with such speed, we could not understand him. As we listened to the school of words swimming from his mouth, we picked out a catfish of meaning, cut it open and read the gizzards. He told us of the end times, the horrible battles, nation against nation. He spoke of great destruction, of two great steel towers falling down, toppled by men claiming God in their blood lust, killing for God. But he could not explain its meaning; he could not answer our questions.

I once tried to trick Joseph. I lied to him, telling him about a dream I never had. I created an elaborate story to test him. He smiled, gimp walked away and looked over his shoulder at me, showing his disapproval and disappointment. He kept his distance from me after that.

On another night I sat and talked to Simeon. He told me that when he was a boy his father had brought him on a journey into the hills, off to a lonely high place. He said Zephaniah had bound him and laid him across a large flat rock. Then he prayed over him for a long time. There was a brilliant thunderstorm and the rains came, drenching them as he lay prone across the rock. Zephaniah stood over him, his face revealed in the flickering lightening with a long knife in one hand. He prayed and called out to God for answers, his fingers digging the air, calling to the heavens, yelling aloud, 'Tell me what you want of me, Oh Lord!'

Simeon was afraid of his father; he thought he'd gone mad. But having faith and trusting the Lord, he did not try to get away. And nothing happened. The rain stopped, the night cleared and the storm in Zephaniah's mind was over. But Simeon came away understanding the demands of God on man, of a father on a son. He was not ever sure if his father would have finished what he felt called to do. But he accepted it.

I said this sounded just like another story in the Bible.

He looked at me unsurprised. "My whole life is in the Bible," he said.

Zephaniah had taught the Indians as well as could be done by any missionary. So by the end of four months the Indians were to be baptized in the creek. It was a dark, cold, All Hallows Eve, as best as I can remember. Ruddy October, cool nights had chilled the water. The warriors shivered in loin cloths and waited their turn to be washed in Jesus water. They did not understand what made the running brook different today, or what it was the white man had said to transform it. But the chief had decreed and they did as their leader wished.

They had all learned The Lord's Payer, which they said as part of the ritual,

R fotter
Hwart in heavon
Hollow be dye naaayme
dhy keeegdum comb
dhy wheel be dung
on eart as in heavon

The Chief stood watching by the fire with pride and said, "My people, you learn well. You have followed my command and listened to the words of Coyote. You said the words his God hears and now be washed in his God's name." And all were baptized, including the Chief.

When they were washed of their sins, they walked shivering to the Chief's lodge and stood warming themselves around the fire. The Chief said in Pawnee, "Now, you will be marked for our new God, you will be circumcised and have the skin cut off end of your manhood."

The warriors looked around at each other, unsure of what they had just heard. They talked in whispers as fear and disbelief painted their faces.

Then one stepped forward and said, "Great Chief, we do not understand."

The Chief answered, "The white men mark themselves this way, so God knows His people."

The young man asked, "Did God not see us pushed under water? Did he not hear us say the prayer's words?"

The Chief challenged, "Are you afraid? You do not need to be. See, I have led the way, this is why I am Chief, I do not fear."

And the chief pulled aside his loin cloth and showed that he had already been circumcised. Zephaniah had suggested the chief be the first one cut to demonstrate his bravery. He had played on the basic fear of all men not to reveal that they are in fact afraid. The Chief knew he had been bested, cornered, and while he did not like it, he did not want the white man to see that he feared anything in this world. So one day in late September Zephaniah performed the task. It was painful and not perfect. There was infection, even though whiskey had been poured to disinfect it. There was painful swelling and a fever. This had angered his wives when he would not sleep with them and he was too sick to stand. But the fever broke one night and in the morning the Chief said in his delirium he had dreamed he saw Jesus robed in shining white with the bleeding wounds on his hands and feet. He said Jesus spoke to him in a language he did not understand; and while he did not comprehend the words, he felt his power and loving warmth. He awoke weak but happy with his dream, even his wives' dismay was dispelled.

The tribe looked at the shape of their Chief's nether appendage and they still wanted to avoid this painful experience. The young man said, "We will become Christians but without this, we will not cut ourselves there."

The Chief said with his voice rising to the challenge, "This is how Christians mark the men, just as we wander with no food, this is the test. We must show this God the Pawnee men are brave."

Zephaniah then spoke, "You must be marked like the Jewish Tribes of God's Bible or you are unclean, you will not be a part of the Christian family. Christians are not afraid of pain."

So while they did not like it, their Chief had shown the way and, with their bravery challenged, they saw it was not to be avoided. And they lined up and waited their turn for this strange ritual. Zephaniah went to the corner of the Chief's lodge and they came to him, one at a time. He said a brief prayer over them as they took out their organ and held it out for the operation. Zephaniah took hold of it, poured some whiskey on it, and delicately, like cleaning a fish, cut them quickly, expertly, throwing the bloody foreskin in the fire. They winced, exhaled in pain, but did not yell. Then they wrapped their sore bleeding organ in a piece of shredded cloth and went off, in a male way, a bent over walk, and laid down, sore and confused about why a God would want this.

Seventy two males were circumcised that night. Zephaniah was exhausted. He washed his hands in a bucket and went straight to the camp. He told his sons to pack up; they would be leaving in the morning, while the Indians nursed their soreness.

He walked Diana over to the lodge to marry her, she was sullen and teary. A small group, the chief, his squaws, and a few other female relatives stood while Zephaniah performed a brief ceremony. He said, "Diana, Red Ember, I marry you to each other in the name of God the Father and Jesus the son, may you live together in peace and happiness as husband and wife." And that was it. He hugged his daughter long and hard, whispered something in her ear, then turned and went back to his camp, leaving his daughter to this unknown world of newly baptized Christian Indians.

Zephaniah then walked back seemingly not bothered by the decisions he had made, or the delay in the mission to kill Brown, or the loss of his daughter. He was content. He laid down and fell asleep.

In his sleep the Indian Moroni appeared in a dream and mocked him saying, "Coyote, you cannot protect your children, you are not a good father."

That night, as Diana slept next to her sore snoring Indian husband, she took a knife out and jammed it into the neck of Red Ember, stabbing so deeply into his Adam's apple he could not make a noise. She yanked the knife hard over toward his ear and ripped apart his jugular. She looked down on his wide eyed face, as the life sap ran out, and she spit on him.

As she ran from the wedding hut, Simeon and Levi hamstrung the horses. Reuben, Gad, Dan and Judah went from dwelling to dwelling and they cut the cord on any bow, tossed arrows into the fires, dismantled guns. That done, they slaughtered in silence, hoping to end as many lives as possible before the village awoke.

Reuben crept into a lodge stealthily, silently stalking, but in the darkness he tripped over something, rousing a sleeping Indian. The Indian leapt on him taking him to the ground. As Reuben wrestled his opponent, they rolled across hot coals, knocked over cooking pots, fighting hand to hand to the death. But Reuben was much too strong, his powerful arm turned the knife on the Indian and slowly pushed it into his stomach; Reuben held him still as his life drained painfully away. When the fight went out of the gutted Indian, Reuben rose to walk away. But there was still revenge left in the wounded warrior. He reached for a hatchet hidden beneath a blanket and buried it in Reuben's calf. Reuben howled, turned and grabbed the handle, pulled the weapon from his leg and left it sunk north to south in the face of the Indian, features askew, war cry forever muffled.

Horses screamed crippled in the night, one leg raised, as Levi hamstrung them. Women screamed too as children cried and men ran about and the fires grew. Joseph sat at the campsite and watched mesmerized as the fires spread. He said he was awakened by the scream of Diana's husband, but she later swore he had made no sound when she killed him.

Zephaniah and the rest of us awoke from the flickering brightness of the burning village and the distant sounds of distress, not knowing at first what was happening, thinking there was some natural calamity. But once Zephaniah noticed his missing sons he knew and ordered, "Get up, saddle your horses. We are leaving, now!"

We all rushed about our business knowing there was something greatly wrong, something we should have expected, the odd events of the previous months so out of place with our original plan: first on a mission to kill John Brown, then teaching Indians to pray and skinning their peckers for God.

Zephaniah ran to Beersheba, saddled her, jumped on and headed for the flaming village. He encountered Diana running across the field and they stopped and looked at each other. She stared ahead, avenged, defiant. He looked on her knowing what was in her heart.

"What have you done?" he asked in disbelief that she had actually disobeyed him.

"I killed him Pa, I killed him," she said defiantly.

"I told you I would come for you. Now you will kill us all," said Zephaniah.

By now the village was in a roiling fury putting out fires, saving the wounded and comforting the burned. In the chaos mutilated bodies went unnoticed as if they were inanimate debris frozen in the shape of horror itself. The warriors grabbed for weapons but many were damaged, useless. When some were found, shots rang out; bullets zipped the night air like devilishly fast horse flies. The warriors tried to mount horses but so many were hamstrung they ran from animal to animal like they could not decide which to choose. And the men were swollen, too sore from their religious conversion to run.

Simeon, Levi, Dan, Gad, Judah ran from the site of destruction with Reuben limping painfully behind. The secret plan with their sister complete, they looked grim faced, vindicated. Defilement avenged, Diana returned safe. Now the task was escape, saving the rest of the family. They ran, dark figures against a flaming village, toward their father on Beersheba.

Zephaniah called, "You have disobeyed me. Get to your horses. This may be our end, we must ride hard and fast."

In a few minutes we were all on quivering horseback heading off in the acrid night.

Joseph sat riding behind Zebulan, facing backward, a stove pipe hat on his head, staring almost wistfully at the orange glow in the night sky, a small smile on his face. It was early morning November time, cold and moonlit, the silver light showed our way in the ebony shade. We rode down the trail, hoping our horses were sure footed, toward the rising orb of night. It would be some time before the Christian Indians could regroup and come after us. There would be no redemption, no forgiveness for us this night. They would be after us by day break, only three hours away.

We rode hard, lathered hide foaming, for a solid 10 miles before letting the horses rest. When we stopped Zephaniah, his rage barely suppressed, his energy wound like a wagon spring, looked at the waning moon and said, "They will track us now, a war party will be on our trail."

Simeon stood up from the log where he sat and said, "We had to avenge our sister Pa, we were not going to leave her with those heathen."

Zephaniah said in a near whisper, "I wasn't either, they were peacefully disabled. They were converted, my work was done. I was going to get her."

"You married her off. How can you say that?"

"I did not sanction the marriage in my heart. That is the answer. I have the power to revoke the vow," said Zephaniah rubbing the wet shoulder of his horse.

Diana then said softly, almost wistfully, "I was going to kill him and run anyway. It didn't matter what you did. He was a pig and I stuck him."

Simeon's eyes were narrow, as they were when he was scheming. He looked around at his family and said, "Well it is done. It's done and over."

Zephaniah stood quietly, unwilling to debate the point. He then said quietly, "You have defied me. You killed the Christians I was called to save."

Reuben in his slow way said, "You are going to kill John Brown, he's a Christian."

"Brown must die to avoid an even greater slaughter," said Zephaniah.

Diana said, "He's right, it is done, I could not bear being left with those savages, Christian or not, we need to leave now. I've seen enough fighting."

Zephaniah looked at each of them, unhappy but looking for a lesson. As always he decided on prayer and commanded, "Kneel children." And we all knelt. Then he prayed aloud, "God save us from this calamity. We have sinned lord, killed, we did not follow your will shown in the dream. Forgive us and teach us to act on your will. Lead us to walk in your ways. Give us strong horses and a strong will to survive. Let my family live, Lord. Amen."

We rose then and climbed on our horses. We rode toward the harvest moon, hooves kicking up turf, manes bouncing like satin lapels, and a cold wind numbing our faces, tearing our eyes. Finally we went toward the hanging gallows of John Brown.

The Story of Ruth

The single smokestack on the paddle wheeler heading down the Missouri sent long gray entrails to the northeast. After confronting him, the widow sat down on the bench next to John Brown. He felt trapped, exposed, anxious. He was not a killer of women but he was dead set on completing his task fomenting war to free the slaves. She could not get in his way. The rotation of the paddlewheel and the tossed waters were the only sounds churning in the background. The pistons pumped on in a drone of work, chugging, and driving like the great arms of Zeus. The paddle wheel blades cut and lifted the brown fluid of the Missouri then unable to grasp and collect the formless creature, it fell away and sprinkled and clapped the waters below, escaping. Thoughts raced through Brown's mind; his calling was from God who must be obeyed at all costs, and he could not to be further delayed, not by a woman. There was no one else in the cabin so if he was going to act it must be now. Should he kill her, throw her body in the river as if she had fallen? What of the blood and the noise and the floating body? Should he wait until dark to kill her, to expedite his escape? How could he keep her quiet?

He reached for the knife, strapped to his lower leg, hidden but ready. But in back of these thoughts like a whispering ghost were questions about her actions. Why was she not afraid if she knew who he was? Would she not have been better off to say something in Kansas City and have him arrested? Why did she feel so bold as to sit right next to him?

"John Brown," she said looking straight into his eyes, "It is my pleasure to meet you."

He stared at her unable to move, frozen, assessing her intentions.

"I am in your debt, sir; you are a great, great man, a man who has advanced my own cause. I applaud your actions. Do not be alarmed, as one of your greatest admirers, I am at your service, sir. If there is anything I can do to assist you in your journey to sanctuary, in any way, please call upon me, please sir, do call upon me," she said as she put her hand gently on his leg.

He thought of her sex but felt the hickory switch on his back, as his father, Owen Brown, whipped him for his evil thoughts.

She continued, "Please be sure to let me know of any need you may have. You are a man of strong character and will; a man of principle, unafraid to act of your own volition, but even the lion of the jungle needs the help of the lioness at times. I am at your service."

He took his hand off the knife and relaxed. "What are your intentions madam, may I ask?"

"My intention is to barter, to trade. I will offer you my assistance in your mission in return for your kind assistance in mine. My name is Adelaide Grossinger."

"What is your mission, Mrs. Grossinger?"

"My mission is…Sir, I am indeed a widow but my husband has been dead over six years now. He was a taxidermist but his works are already ensconced in New York. My crate carries another cargo. I am a part of a railroad. I am a customer, nay a conductor, of a secret railroad. A railroad whose riders are in gravest danger if found out. My crate carries contraband, sir, contraband of a human nature, negro contraband."

Brown stared at her, a smile widening on his face. They looked long into each other's eyes and he laughed, for the first time in many months he laughed well and said, "I see now, widow, I see. You don't know how close you were to leaving this mortal world." And he showed her the knife as he laughed on.

She however stopped laughing at the sight of the knife, bringing a sharp end to her humor.

Brown said, "I know this railroad well. I will help you, if I can, surely. But I am partial to finding my own way until I am in friendlier territory. I cannot, however, let your mission, the noble cause of freedom for one so degraded of natural law hinder my plight."

"And what plight is that, sir?" she questioned then continued, "You have accomplished your goal, trepidation stands on the auction block, fear roves this nation, slave owning can now be a cause of death. You are the rallying cry, the spark, the leader of a cause gone from theory to flesh."

"There are things yet to accomplish. I am not yet done," John Brown said.

"You may be General of our cause, a genius for tactics but the art of escape is new to you. It is one of prudence, disguise, where assistance is an asset to be sought dearly. Your picture, bearded as it is, was drawn from a tin type of some years ago. It is beginning to make its way into the larger newspapers in our great cities. I am so glad you have shaved your face, it is kinder now, but unfortunately still one of some notoriety," the widow said trying to convince him.

She pulled out a St. Louis Recorder from a week prior, a line drawing of him in a raging pose, sword in hand, beard flowing, hair blowing in the wind, was capital of a long column of prose on his killings. Brown stared at it, unimpressed at his fame, trying to figure how this aided his overall plan, thinking of his benefactors and their reaction. This would bring him the money he needed.

She then said with a sly hint, "Perhaps in the towns I may bear the pretense of being the wife of this calm and reserved, shaven man, as no one expects you to travel in marital bliss. Your wife, in the hinterlands of New York, would surely prefer this charade than never to see you cross her foyer again."

"What is it you want of me?" he asked.

She said after first looking around to make sure no one had entered, "In the crate, cramped, dark, provisioned but alone, afraid, is a young woman escaping the ranch of a lascivious slave owner who counts her as but one of his breeding cattle. If there is a list of those you seek to kill on your next trip west, I propose him for the top of it. He is a dog."

"His name?" asked Brown.

"Solomon Sanders, he is the slime of the earth. She cannot last long in this crate, a two day journey is the limit, we have learned by one poor man's calamitous experience," the widow said with some urgency.

"She has food, water?" Brown asked with deep concern.

"Yes, but she must be spare, as relieving herself is a challenge that can reveal her," she said covering her mouth at the indelicate subject.

"What are your plans?" Brown said his interest growing.

She went on, "Once unloaded to the freight warehouse in St Louis, I need to remove her, transport her to the house of a certain wealthy man for hiding until we are sure our way is clear for the next leg of the journey to Louisville."

"What do you want of me?" asked Brown.

"Quite simply to assist me in opening the sealed crate so I can pass her on to the drivers," she said staring into his eyes for some hint of acceptance.

Brown looked down at his weathered hands and said, "It would be best for me if I quietly continued on my way. There is much I must do. This assistance you seek has some risk."

"But John," she said touching his arm, "I do not know what you plan next but suppose this next step does not come to be? Suppose you are jailed before you can reach your goal? What concrete thing will you have accomplished? You will be but a killer of a few men, will you have saved anyone? No, you will have killed but not yet saved. This is your chance to at least say you are not just killer but savior. I am connected, sir; well connected I assure you. I can help you, you can be sure of this, if you so choose to assist. It will add to your myth, your allure. Indeed, I know powerful people who can get you whatever you need."

Brown thought on this and said, "The Lord is my guide. Let me pray on it. Must I answer you now?"

She removed her hand from his forearm and said, "No, you are right, there is time, of course, you may consider it."

Brown turned his head, looked out the window at the mud laden waters of the Missouri, paying no more attention to her, back to his thoughts, now more complicated, invaded by this new situation, this new opportunity, this new danger.

They passed each other walking on the deck, but spoke no more. John

Brown looked across to Adelaide Grossinger, thinking. Helped by many in his quest in Kansas, now God asked him to assist another. He had hidden slaves, travelers on the same railroad, in a secret place beneath his barn floor in the mountains of New York. So this was not new to him. Scared, tired, hungry they rested beneath his floor before settling in the hills above the lake regions near his home. He thought of the poor woman in the crate, her fear, her need for freedom overcoming it. So his drive to continue unscathed was overcome by his pity for his black brethren. Perhaps this task would lift the heavy thoughts of the events on the banks of the Pottawatomie creek, on the death of his son. The Lord who knew all put this task in his path so he must rise to the occasion. Who knew what role this freed slave was to play in the grand plan? The slave girl Ruth, who laid inside the damp hold in a crate, frightened and desperate, sealed in darkness, had crossed his path for a reason.

Saint Louis

The New Lucy was tied off at the pier like a barrel of whiskey on a lopsided mule; strapped on one side bound only, rolling and binding and rubbing against rope mats laid down to protect it. John Brown and Adelaide Grossinger walked down the gangplank to the dock, one behind the other, and joined arms at the bottom like husband and wife. They sought the freight master and Brown insisted the crate be moved to storage as he watched. He collected a receipt and stepped off into the muddy main street. It was near dinner time, it would be light for a while yet.

They checked into Barnum's Hotel on Second and Walnut as Mr. and Mrs. Hawkins. He signed quickly, took the key, left a dollar on the register, turned to go upstairs. As he turned around, John Brown and Adelaide were met by a porter, a Negro.

"May I assiss you with ya bags sir?"

"No, I can carry these on my own."

"I be happy to turn down ya bed, pour ya water, whateva ya needs for ya comfort massir."

"I am not your master. No man is your master. Now, yes, please, thank you kindly for your help," Brown told him changing his mind.

The Negro porter picked up the bags, climbed the stair with a spring in his step, walked down the narrow hall, slid the skeleton key into the lock, turned it and entered the room. He pulled aside the curtains, put the valise on a chair, poured water into a bowl, folded and set a towel nearby.

"If ya be needin anythin juss call for me massir. Ise here to hep n serve. Juss ast for Dred."

"You don't need to serve me. You are no slave."

"I is a slave, but I'se a workin man, a slave workin man. I been fightin for my freedom in the highest court in dis here land. Name's Dred Scott."

Brown paused.

"Praise God. I have heard of you, man. You are famous in my circle. You have fought them. Good for you. The rest of your people will fight them in time as well. You have found a weak link in their legal chains. I am proud to meet you," said John Brown sincerely as they shook hands.

"Yessir, they sez Ize no citzen causin I isa nigra. I duz not even ekzist ceptin as poperty, don't think Ize ever gwoin to see my freedom, I be in and out of coat, hepped by the chillren of my Massir Peter Blow, who live rightchere in Missoura, hee I live, hee I work, but my pay goes to de sheriff, I keeps on tryin to get me and my wife Harriet free."

"Well sir, soon you and all your brethren will be as free."

"I doan know bout dat sir, there ain nuff massirs gwoin give em up. Dis coat sez they cain't be nuthin but poperty. An dey owns em for life."

"In time Dred, in time," said Brown. "Pray for it, your prayers will be answered. I can promise you that, as God is King."

"Yessir, I sorely will, yessir, I be prayin hard, sure nuff." And he left the room.

John Brown splashed water on his face, toweled dry, sat in a chair and looked out the window. He stared into the distance. Adelaide stripped naked, wiped her body with a damp cloth, toweled off, then lay on the bed to rest, covered only with a shear sheet. They did not speak. John Brown did not look at her, not once, but looked bullet eyed out into the empty streets. Most folks were in for dinner, horses tied off, the day's work over. After an hour Adelaide rose and dressed and they went down to the parlor together. Dred saw them to two seats at a long empty table, served a mutton stew, a glass of buttermilk and biscuits as they went on with their act of being married. They retired soon after speaking to no one.

When all was silent in the hotel and they saw the lanterns were dimmed and hearing no noise from the clerk who had fallen asleep in a chair in the office, they quietly closed their door behind them and walked softly down the hall. Creaking boards made them stop, hearts pounding, though there was little real worry. There was nothing wrong with a late night promenade between husband and wife though it might appear sordid to congregate with some of the folks out at this hour. They made it past the snoring clerk whose breath shuddered past an untrimmed mustache and out into the lilting summer night air.

It was warm and sultry; the evening felt like it was wrapped in a wet wool blanket. Once outside they started walking faster, looking around to see who was about. The only sound was a piano tune coming from a saloon called The Gallant Stag. They stepped over mud tracks in the street which crossed each other in conflicting paths, past a black cat whose pearl eyes glowed with eager warning to stay away and hurried to the docks.

The widow looked to a darkened alley as they walked across from the warehouse noting a waiting wagon. The driver tipped his hat.

They climbed briskly up the plank stairs to the docks, seeking relief from their painful visibility, and hurried to the shadows. Looking about to see that no one was there they moved toward the offices.

The freight office was locked, the warehouse was padlocked. With his elbow on the window to the freight office door, John Brown pushed slowly in until the steady pressure cracked the pane. He continued to push slowly until well defined pieces of glass could be seen, broken and partially separated. He wrapped a handkerchief around his hand and pulled out the slivers, one by one. Then he reached in and unlatched the door and looked around the office for the keys. He finally found them on a hook beneath the freight clerk's desk. Mr. and Mrs. Hawkins walked stealthily across the platform, unlocked the padlock to the freight room, slid the door aside and quickly found the crate.

Adelaide whispered loudly, "We are here; we are here to get you."

No answer

Again she said, "Are you safe, can you hear me? We are here to save you."

Inside there was a rustle and then a soft knocking but no voice.

"Quick, John, you must open this right away," she said urgently.

Brown looked frantically for a tool in the warehouse. Finally after much rummaging he found a crowbar in a back room hanging off a window sill, forgotten or stashed for future use, left there by a carter. He set about to pry the wooden jail open, piece by piece, to free the crated negress.

As the planks splintered and pulled away a stench of human waste arose from inside, an overwhelming smell of humiliation wafted in the air.

"Tanks God yous hee, tanks God," came a soft voice from inside.

As soon as one side of the crate was removed, out poured the female Negro, and her odor; her dress was drenched with urine. She had defecated in a corner of the crate and covered it with her blanket.

"Ruth, we are here, you are saved, we have made it," Adelaide said with her handkerchief over her nose.

No sooner had the words left her mouth. Then a call went out, "Who goes there? Who's in there?" And a lantern's light split the darkness, crossing the floor from the side window that held the crowbar. A watchman stood outside the freight office looking at the broken glass.

Brown and Adelaide dragged the fugitive slave woman across the floor to the nearest wall, flattened themselves against it and watched the door hoping he would not enter. The watchman went into the office, gun drawn, found no one, saw the safe intact and started looking around outside for the culprit of the break in. Then he saw the open door to the freight room.

"Who's in there?" he called, "Come out now? You've been found out? No sense getting in more trouble."

Silence.

The barrel of the gun probed the darkness of the door opening and became more and more visible to John Brown. The watchman stepped pensively, his fear growing, as he moved closer, closer. He cleared the door when Brown brought the crowbar down with a sickening crack, splitting his skull. The watchman's reflexive jerk pulled the trigger, setting off a loud explosion echoing inside the warehouse, a bullet ripped through the roof and he fell dead to the floor.

Adelaide screamed in horror, "Oh, my God. You didn't have to do that."

"Shut up woman and move," said Brown.

They dragged Ruth still groggy and nauseous from the floor to her feet. Each took an arm, moved quickly out to the dock and heading away from the entrance ramp. They jumped down to the ground and moved around the dark outside of the warehouse, through high weeds, tripping over discarded refuse, old parts, cracked bottles, piles of bricks. Once they reached the building's corner they could see lights coming on in the windows of residences along the street and folks parting curtains to see the cause of the gunfire. The Sheriff ran out of his office toward the docks, gun drawn.

Across the street in an alley was a wagon with a driver who waited nervously. As they struggled across the street assisting the fugitive slave the driver waved them to the alley. A trunk was strapped to the wagons rear and already opened. They put poor Ruth inside yet another coffin, sealed it, then John Brown and Adelaide stepped into the wagon's rear and sat down side by side. The driver, clad in a cloak and cap, looked back and said, "It's about time. Now just sit down, look like you are having a grand old time, you're drunk and in love."

Brown was uncomfortable with this order but complied burying his head in Adelaide's hair, smelling lilacs. The driver cracked the whip and the wagon jerked into motion out to the main street directly toward the approaching Lawman.

The Sheriff did not look at them as they rode past but then sensed something suspicious and he yelled, "Hold there. I said stop." And the wagon was brought to an abrupt halt.

The driver said innocently, "Yes sir, may I help you."

"Did you not hear that shot? Did you see anyone?" said the Sheriff as Adelaide and Brown held a long embrace.

"Yes sir, they were on horseback, they rode on toward the mill."

The Lawman looked at the occupants and did not quite feel right, his instincts were awakened by the gunfire, keen he asked, "Who is this riding in your wagon?" And he stepped up to look at the couple.

Brown pulled out his gun and shot him square in the face.

"My God," yelled the driver.

Adelaide was white as a ghost, unable to speak.

"Driver, drive out of town," yelled Brown.

The driver mechanically snapped his whip and looked aghast over his shoulder at the dead Lawman. His involvement in the murder of a Sheriff dawning on him, the driver grew rigid and his arm whipped faster, urging the horse on and out of town. As they drove past the Sheriff's office a deputy came out on the porch, alerted to trouble by the gunshot. He saw the Sheriff down in a pool of blood in the street, arms flown up and back in surprise, his face like succotash. As the wagon flew past him, he drew and he started to shoot. The Lawman emptied his gun, bullets flying like shooting stars, the boom of his big pistol sounding like a cannon.

He hit the driver in the shoulder, blowing a hole clean through and he shot

John Brown in the back. Adelaide slumped over as if asleep on a porch reading the news with a bullet in the back of her skull. The driver hunched over, bleeding profusely from his shoulder, tried to keep the horse from running wild. Brown was passed out and Adelaide was dead. They drove away as fast as the horse could run.

Several miles outside of town, the driver pulled on to a side road, drove across wide cultivated fields of tobacco, trellis' standing waiting to dry the long brown leaves. A large estate home with candles lit stood off in the distance. They rode up to safety for now.

Francis Gardener came out to meet them and seeing the condition of the driver knew that something was terribly wrong.

He called out, "What happened?"

"Trouble," gasped the driver. "Freight watchman caught them, I think they killed him. Sheriff came out. This one shot him in the face, I am sure he killed him.

Deputy fired at us, hit me, and Adelaide, the stranger's shot too."

"She's dead," said Gardener in painful surprise, "Oh Adelaide." Then Gardener asked, "Who's he?"

"Don't know," winced the driver.

Francis Gardener opened the trunk. The bullet holes already signaled her demise, but upon opening the lid of the black luggage the lifeless body of the slave woman Ruth in a blood soaked dress rolled out and fell to the ground. Just then his wife, Beatrice Gardener, came out followed by a teenage slave girl and two adult male slaves. She looked horrified on the bloody scene. But she did not flinch, she took control.

To the driver Beatrice Gardener said, "Franklin, we'll help you get down into the barn, poor man. We will care for you there, you must stay out of sight for now. Missy, you and Jessup help him from the wagon."

She pointed to Brown and said urgently, "Zacariah, you take this one to the root cellar in the barn too, go on now. Bring water, clean sheets." Then looking on the dead body of Adelaide and stroking her face she said tenderly, "Oh Adelaide, my dear. Oh my dear. Leave her in the wagon." Beatrice told another slave named Giles to drive the wagon with the bodies of Adelaide and Ruth to the far side of the field through the trees to the clearing beyond. She told him to bury them, to burn the wagon and not to leave a trace. Giles, an older slave, jumped and did as he was told.

Brown was carried in through the barn, lowered down a hatch door into a root cellar beneath it. He was dead weight. They had difficulty managing his limp body and lost their grip, dropping him hard to the dirt floor below. Something popped in his knee when he landed.

Missy stayed below with water, torn linen, witch hazel, tending the wounds of the men by the light of a candle. The trap door was shut and a bale of hay put in place, blocking it. Firelight arose through the trees as the wagon was burned and two shallow graves were dug off to the side, one for Ruth, one for Adelaide.

In town the deputy did not know the wagon, a common buckboard, or the driver, a man not seen before. He had a dead Sheriff and a dead night watchman but he would not be able to do anything until morning. He needed men and he needed to think.

River Crossing

I n a few days we reached the Missouri River north of Kansas City. We were tired, still scared of being chased by Indians. I was hoping we'd go into town, get some food and sleep in a bed. I spoke my mind but Zephaniah smiled at my weakness like he had seen it in men before and kept riding toward the river. We kept away from town but passed a wagon on its way in, plow horse pulling, cow trailing, children in the back in the hay. They looked to be selling the cow to get some cash but we did not stop to talk. Blue sky was all I could see like an indigo bowl was set over us. In the distance chicken hawks circled and drifted, rose like ashes on updrafts in the chimney flue. An eagle circled above for a while, a vantage point I would not know till dead, assuming of course I rise.

Ahead we could see the banks of the Missouri, a slow moving body, mulatto brown, easy, wide, but ten to fifteen feet deep in spots, and swifter then it looked. There were places to forge the river further up or down, there had to be, but time was now important again. The mention of extra miles of riding searching for a crossing did not please Zephaniah; he was not sure how hard the Pawnee would be on us. Looking south we could see a man waving at us.

As we rode closer we could make out a negro who operated the ferry crossing at this place. A rope was tied across the flow to the other side. It passed through a set of rusted metal rings bolted to the ferry's plank deck atop some logs, sturdy enough but small. As we spoke to him it was clear by the milky color of his rolling eyes and the uneven blinking that he was blind.

"Is this your raft?" asked Zephaniah.

"Well yez and noz. Ise opratin it, dohn own it. My massir, owns it," said the slave.

"How much to pass?" asked Zephaniah.

"How many is ya?"

"Fourteen."

"Dolla for crossin the lot o ya, one horze and a man at a time, no mo or we get tipsy.

Free ride back, doh," said the slave as he felt his way over to the raft.

"That's dear. We're not coming back soon," said Zephaniah.

"Ize didn set it, juss charges it, dohn own it," answered the slave as he sat down on the ferry.

"What is your owner's name?" asked Zephaniah.

"Massir Solomon Sanders," said the blind slave.

Dan said, "Ole King Solomon, Ise calls im," and Gad laughed at his impersonation.

Zebulan rode down to the water's edge, got off his horse, bent over, touched the river. He'd never seen a river this large, such a wide beautiful expanse of flowing life. He was not worried about crossing, he just wanted to be near the big river, see it, gaze into it.

The slave said, "Not smany horzes coming thisaway nomore. Yer first ones in a few daze."

Simeon whispered to Levi, "We could knock him out, make the crossing ourselves, no harm done."

Zephaniah dismounted gave the slave a silver dollar then turned and looked to Simeon and said, "You've caused enough trouble for now, just pass, we're moving on."

"Where yo comin from, sir," said the slave as he pushed his ferry from the shore.

"From out west," answered Zephaniah.

"You a travelin on to yo destiny, ain'tcha," said the blind ferryman.

"Just get us across, slave," said Zephaniah ending his questions.

The raft was hard work. Pulling the rope against the current with two men and a horse on board was not easy. The river looked mild but it was swifter out on the water and it was wide.

The rope rubbed and tugged as it passed through the thick pitted rings. The metal groaned of rust and many crossings, clanking on the boards when the tension was released and taken up by the brother ring. But the old blind ferrymen was not strong enough that day, his last day, not for that much weight, for that many crossings. The sons were forced to help for fear he would not get them across. His black hands grew weaker of grip and his arms slower to pull with each crossing. The Blind man sang:

Riva Jordan runs deep n wide,
Riva Jordan runs deep n wide
Jacob cross when Esau come
Lef'is wife on da udder side.

Stole his blessin, his birthright
Stole his blessin his birthright
Dress lak Esau, lambs wool on,
Fool old Issac whoode loss his sight.

Cross da Jordan, filled wif feah
Cross da Jordan, filled wif feah
Esau's comin wid his troops,
Esau's comin dohn cha hear.

He sang this on every trip. But with each crossing the words were more strangled, his breath more labored.

On the last trip across the brown silted river, one of the metal rings yanked from the deck turning the raft sharply downstream. Zebulan and his horse fell in. He was able to recover and grab the reins, while his mare dragged him to shore. He was really very pleased to go in, though he could not swim and saw floating as some game. The blind ferryman pulled hard, as hard as whatever was left in his ragged old body could, trying to right his raft and bring it home against a river's force he could feel but not see. He strained against the rivers tug. But the River, older then the slave and stronger than the man, the River which can run on for hundreds of miles while the blind negro, too old, too weak, too tired from fourteen crossings in a row, a life of crossings, of unpaid labor, could hardly move. He was no match on this his final crossing. He finally gave in to the River, gave out to the slaveholder.

Out of breath, weakened from pulling too much, he fainted, leaving the raft straining against one old metal ring.

Reuben swam out, jumped on the raft and pulled it in. Once secure on some river stones we dragged him to the shore. The blind man lay wet, dying, out cold. He coughed softly, straining, feeling pain in his chest as he stirred. Then he laughed low from inside his black slave bowels and said, "I knows you, you Zephaniah Jacobs. I knowd dat voice anawhay. You owd me once. Sole me off. Kep my wife, Roof, my daughter, my Buela, broke my heart, just broke it. Damn you slave men, I'm a man, ya know. Whay she iz now? Whay iz she?

Zephaniah looked on, showing nothing, grasping everything he said. "Your wife died some four years ago. Buela still lives with me, she's my wife's helper now. These here are her sons." Dan, Neptali stepped forward, knelt down, white skinned.

The blind ferryman reached up, grabbed them, pulled them in close, face to face.

"Yur mommas a slave, a concabine, ya should fight to free de slaves, free ya own momma. I knowd I'd die hee, knowd it, knowd it.

"Let us pray for you," said Zephaniah.

"Pray for me? Pray for me?" He laughed then he coughed from the exertion. With all his remaining might he said, "Free me. Free me. Dats whatcha shoulda dun. Butcha couldn't do dat, ya needed mah work, mah back. Ya said cause it's in the Bible it must be true, must be real. But God don't want no slaves, no men shud make slaves, da men wrote the Bible had em, but don't make it right. Now

Ise dieing, ya killed me, little by little, ya took everything. I gots nothin. I come here wid nothin, Ise leavin wid nothin. Nothin but a name. A slave name, a name my owna give me. Ise Charles to you but Massa Solomon he names me Charon. Charon, like I steered a raft to Hades. Dis here river be da river Styx. Only difference is Hell is on both sides of dis river. I bi livin in it. Gonna jump the broom to Jesus."

He spoke no more after that. He lay quietly, looked around at us until he closed his eyes. They never opened again and his breathing became more labored. In about a half an hour his chest did not rise again. He died.

Zephaniah was disturbed at this blind Negro's words. He told the boys to dig a shallow grave and bury him and cover the site with the smooth gray shale and washed up timber near the shore to keep the dogs out. He went off to an eddy by the river to pray alone. We buried him, said a prayer for God to take his poor soul, knowing the first ice flow of winter would tear apart his grave and drag his body downriver. Dan cut the rope, let the raft run free. We watched it like we were waiting for it to wave goodbye. Solomon Sanders would need another raft man, another slave to make his fortune. No one would cross here for some time.

Plantation Sanctuary

Outside St. Louis, Missouri

John Brown rose gaunt and pale for the first time from his cellar hideaway. Over the weeks he awoke from his delirium only to slip away soon after. The dim light in the root cellar and the voice of the black slave girl who tended to him came and went and did not seem real. He did not know if he was alive or dead, dreaming or awake. His wound festered, the fever grew. It would break and return, week after week. He could not eat. He became emaciated, shrunken. The look of death settled darkly around his closed eyes.

The driver, Franklin, died. He'd bled too much, went to sleep and never woke up. Brown had a foggy vision of Franklin's body being dragged through the hatch, the limp torso being carried aloft in a blinding ray of light.

The Law had tried to find out who was behind the killings. The Deputy went from home to home asking questions but no descriptions came forth, only a common wagon, an unknown driver, a woman, possibly wounded, alive or dead, no one was sure; and so his search came to naught. When Deputy Crocker arrived at the plantation, Francis Gardener asked him in for lemonade. His newly deputized men stood on the whitewashed porch, noting blood drops missed by Jessup near a column. They inquired about them but were assured it was from an injured slave. And even though Roscoe served drinks with a towel wrapped hand, suspicions were aroused. The Deputy asked to see their wagon and he was walked over to the barn to see that the wagon was just fine, clean of clues, no blood visible, even when the hay was pulled off. Gardener had always owned two wagons, one for hauling hay and tobacco, the other equipped with the trunk for hauling human cargo. They could not suspect so prominent a citizen, a slave holder whose interests lie in foiling runaways, of helping them escape to freedom. No one knew the slaves on Gardner's plantation were part of the Underground Railroad. They toiled as any common chattel but had a greater purpose. Franklin, the dead driver, was an employee of Francis Gardener, hired to handle the secret transfers of fugitive blacks. But he never ventured into town, a solitary Bible reading man, dedicated to his role, he was unknown to anyone. He was buried secretly on the far side of the fields in the slave cemetery, alongside two nameless slaves who had died in transit the previous year.

The baggage left at the hotel was a mystery too. No one knew what happened to Mr. and Mrs. Hawkins, where they came from, where they were going. But small books in a valise, with notes, names, figures, and records of financial transactions became of great interest. The deputy guessed these missing lodgers were the killers who'd fled in the wagon, but he was not sure, no one was sure. The broken, reeking crate in the freight storehouse told the Deputy slave stealing was involved, but they did not know of Ruth in the trunk or her fate.

Gardener's Underground Railroad operation was delayed for a while until things calmed down. The only remaining loose end was the sickly man who moaned names in his delirium beneath the barn floor. There was a faint hope he too would die, so they could bury him and move on from this calamity but he did not.

So after weeks, Brown, whose knee was damaged in the fall to the root cellar, limped slowly up the ladder into the light. His eyes squinted from the brightness; tightly slit they ached from the sun's prying rays while he became accustomed to the aboveground world. The slave girl, Missy, who had nursed him through was proud to see she'd saved his life. She followed him around tending to him.

In a few days he sat on a wicker chair on the veranda in the front of the plantation drinking cooled tea and talking to Francis Gardner.

"What happened to Adelaide?" he asked.

"She was killed, shot in the head, poor woman," said Gardener.

"My head's a fog," said Brown. "I remember so little."

Then, after a pause, Brown asked, "You and she were partners in the Underground Railroad?"

"I will miss her. This was her first, her only mission. She came here a week before going to Kansas City, insisting she was the right person, this was her calling. Sent here by my cousin in Boston. She was of strong fiber, a stout soul. She was determined to make a difference after the death of her husband."

"I am sorry," John Brown said looking him straight in the eye.

"All the goings on out west have motivated many to get involved. The killing in Kansas was the final straw, it empowered the timid, the destruction of the free press, the ballot stuffing, we are all angry. She was a committed abolitionist. But she had never acted beyond attendance of meetings. This was her first involvement. She felt her sex would be a diversion, a disguise. How did you come to help her?" asked Gardener.

"She asked my help on the steamboat. I could not resist," said Brown.

"But why you? Why would she reveal herself to you?" queried Gardener.

Brown could not answer.

"No response?" asked Gardener honing in.

Then Brown added, "She said we could act as husband and wife to avoid detection?"

"Yes and …?" Gardener said waiting for Brown to finish his words.

"And I agreed," said Brown matter of fact.

"But why did she approach you? What in you did she find so attracting that she would reveal the whole purpose for her disguise?" Gardener said as he leaned in and returned the look in the eye.

"She needed a man to open the crate?" said Brown plainly.

"And she happened to guess you were one who would support her cause?" asked Gardener.

"She did. She was lucky," Brown countered.

"Indeed. And you killed the watchman?" he asked looking deeper.

"Yes," admitted Brown. "To free the slave woman, Ruth."

"And the Sheriff?" Gardener probed.

"Yes, there was no other way to avoid being caught," said Brown after a pause.

"Have you killed before?" asked Gardener solemnly.

"Yes," said Brown.

"What is your name?" asked Gardener.

"My name is John Brown," he answered.

———◆———

Several days later John Brown sat in the barn looking at the rafters, at the farm implements hung from the walls like condemned men swinging dead in the breeze, dropped through the gallows floor. He had been through much; his life was always such a wearying challenge. It was time to move on at a great pace, much time had been lost. He thought about his family, two wives, one dead, twenty children, four dead as mere babies. It was all God's plan. He did not blame himself for the death of his son; he did not know where his men or his sons were. His wife Mary was alone in the mountains of New York fending for herself on a farm, left alone for years at a time for the cause. He never felt he should let others carry the load, leave the Jews in Egypt, let the course of events have their way, the Red Sea remain one, let the powerful Pharaohs carry the day. Someone must make a stand, must throw down the staff and he knew sure as blood coursed his veins he was the one. He knew this thing in a deep hard way.

He threw a riding crop to the floor and it became a snake. He watched the bright green serpent cross in the dust in rippling rhythm like cursive writing in the dirt, a slithering pattern of mysterious words.

He thought of his deep admiration for Francis Gardener, for his slave smuggling operation, taking great risk to aid the poor people caught in the net of the slave economy. He admired Gardener's Negros who were free but chose to live in bondage incognito, devoted to the cause of their own people's freedom. He felt sorry for the loss of Ruth the runaway, Adelaide and Franklin the driver. But they too were part of the plan; they had their reward, as he would get his.

It was cooling into November, time to move east before ice plated puddles froze in the road ruts and shattered under hoof, before sleet chattered his brim and bounced from his wool coat to the hardened ground. Brown was leery of the steamboats now, the exposure. His chance of being recognized while remote was always there. Had Adelaide not seen him he would be off to Boston already. But God had a reason for everything. Time was a precious thing, each day he wasted others worked without wages beneath the yoke. He decided to ride on alone by horse.

The day he left the sun's rays spread over bulging mountains of clouds like a fan of many colors. He gratefully shook the hand of Francis Gardener, as well as each of the slaves. Beatrice Gardener hugged him. He mounted his horse and did not look back. He rode east languidly giving permission to his horse to carry him onward. In his mind he heard a choir singing Onward Christian Soldiers and he hummed it as he rode, stroking the air lightly with his hand:

Onward Christian soldiers, marching as to war,
with the cross of Jesus, going on before.
Christ the royal master, leads against the foe,
Forward into battle, see his banners go,

Onward Christian Soldiers marching as to war,
With the cross of Jesus, going on before.

At the sign of triumph Satan's host doth flee,
On then Christian soldiers, on to victory!
Hell's foundations quiver, at the shout of praise;
Christians lift your voices, loud your anthems raise.

Onward Christian Soldiers marching as to war,
With the cross of Jesus, going on before.

Like a mighty army moves the Church of God,
Christians we are treading where the saints have trod;
We are not divided, all one body we,
One in hope and doctrine, one in charity.

Onward Christian Soldiers marching as to war,
With the cross of Jesus, going on before.

Crowns and thrones may perish, kingdoms rise and wane,
But the Church of Jesus constant will remain;
Gates of hell can never, 'gainst the Church prevail;
We have Christ's own promise, and can never fail.

Onward Christian Soldiers marching as to war,
With the cross of Jesus, going on before.

Onward, then, ye people, join our happy throng;
Blend with ours your voices, in the triumph song;
Glory laud and honor, unto Christ the King;
This through countless ages, we with angels sing.

Onward Christian Soldiers marching as to war,
With the cross of Jesus, going on before.

———————

John Brown awoke from his fevered sleep in the Quaker home in Nebraska. The image of the slave woman, Ruth, in the crate was imprinted on his mind's eye. His dream seemed so real. He thought about his son, John Jr. and the whipping punishment, the son striking the father over and over again, thirty times, for believing dreams could be true. He knew Ruth and her plight were real. And he felt sorry for his stern ways with his children. He had a sense he understood the source of John's madness. And he thanked God for it.

Massacre

The line of wagons, seven of them, rolled westward pulled by massive slender-horned oxen and teams of work horses, big boned, large hoofed. Some men trailed and explored off a ways on horseback. Children and their dogs walked like small insects in harassing clusters by the snaking Calistogas. From a rivulet between two mounds of greening earth fifteen men on horseback galloped out toward the settlers with intent, evil portents in their faces. They might have been thieves, messengers, a posse, the settlers couldn't tell, it was hard to see at first. The settler's guard went up right away, reaching for guns, calling in the horseman, the families, the children, pointing at the oncoming fear. They felt vulnerable. All they had, all they loved was bundled in a rolling wooden crate bouncing along like cloth covered coffins.

It was a solemn scene as the wagons pulled up and braked and as the riders approached training their guns on the families, testing to see if the settlers would shoot. But with women and children about they did not dare for fear of what might ensue. They thought they might get a chance to talk, to explain themselves, to find out if there was not some mistake. After all these were not Indians but white men. There should be no conflict except if these were the dreaded proslavery men.

After some talking and then some shouting, a driver, a father, was shot. He fell to the ground from his perch on his wagon seat, his wife screaming, his children shocked to tears. All the riders' guns were cocked and aimed on the wagons. The women shielding their babes in a chorus pled for peace and screamed, "Let them steal what they want." But this was not a robbery.

The families then climbed down from their wagons and gathered together. Guns were taken and the people were gathered like sheep surrounded by herders.

The open landscape left no place for flight that would not become a turkey shoot. After a few minutes the riders conferred and the leader shouted out. The men, women and children walked in a jumbled line, heads turning, looking about in dismay and confusion, trying to figure what was happening, where they were being driven. They walked about one hundred yards with cautious steps and concerned airs. The herders pointed and the settlers climbed down to the bottom of a ravine.

They looked up on the circle of men with pistols and rifles aimed at them like a congregation waiting for the final benediction, eyes rolled heavenward, women with hands folded to their breasts.

One man in the ravine yelled out, "You can kill us now but you'll never kill us all, we'll keep coming. Kansas will be free man's soil."

"You'll go to hell first, along with the rest of the nigger loving squatters," said the leader.

And they opened fire.

They emptied their rifles. Shotgun blasts sprayed faces and bullets punctured caving chests as the horses reared up and their nervousness brought forth equine voices of fear. Heads rolled up in agony and bodies folded as the cleave of final screams and the pained groans of the like of lowing cattle rose and fell. Bodies piled atop each other some not yet fully dead crying for mercy, blood everywhere, pooling, running out where spring rains course, life draining away.

The riders looked down on them with grim finality glad they had done their duty. They rode off in a rumble contented they had once again stemmed the tide.

Jesse's Rod

Clay County, Missouri

A teen aged boy walked with a basket through a field next to four slaves pulling out tubers and turnips, the last crop before winter set in, a source for soup. He stopped and looked up, saw Zephaniah leading us in toward his house, a large plank building with a porch on two sides, a newly painted barn, three slave quarters off to the side.

We'd ridden two days since the river with no more than short stops for rest, really more in consideration for the horses than the riders. It had been tough, my backside was sore; my thighs were worn from standing in the stirrups to save my rump. We rode determined, for we knew waiting could bring our deaths. There was no complaining though we were hungry. While we watered the horses I noticed a fox quietly watching us from a tree, a grin on its pointy snout, it lay across a branch blending in perfectly. I thought it was an illusion. I was so tired, I simply stared at it. Joseph had caught two fish and cooked them fast on sticks but that had not held us long. We needed to find a place to provision and decide the next course of action.

The boy in the field dropped his basket and started running in, calling out, unsure if we were trouble or visitors. His mother and father came out on the porch to see. She was a hearty woman, heavy set, round faced. The man was lanky and awkward. An older boy stood in the door. There was a retarded boy sitting cockeyed on a rocking porch swing, looking on mutely.

Zephaniah rode up and said, "My name is Zephaniah Jacobs, this my family. We've been riding hard for some days now. We could use some help. Shelter in your barn, some provision? I can pay."

The boy ran up, flushed and wary. His mother said, "Get in the house, Jesse." But he did not listen.

Then she asked, "What have you been riding from, may I ask?"

"We had a fight with some Pawnee a few days back. They were in the wrong. I think we have left them far behind," answered Zephaniah in his normal straight forward tone.

She said, "Damned Indians, you're not the first we heard of who run in with them. How do I know I can trust you? You ain't no abolitionists are you?"

"No, I give you my word. I am a family man, a slave holder, like you. If we meant you harm we would not be standing here talking. We follow the Lord," said Zephaniah declaring the last word loudly.

"Some declare that then kills the unwary. But I guess you do." And she looked at each of us, one at a time. "Two dollars a day for the lot of you," said the woman.

"Thank you kindly, that'll be fine," answered Zephaniah.

"My name is Zee Samuel, Zerelda Samuel. This is my husband Dr. Reuben Samuel. This is my son Jesse and this here's Alexander Franklin, call him Frank."

Six other children of various ages wandered out to the porch behind their momma.

Zee said, "This here's Susan, Sara, John, Fannie, this here's Archie, he's slow witted but good hearted."

Zephaniah climbed down from his horse and said, "Pleased to make your acquaintance. This is my daughter Diana, this is Joseph."

Joseph got off his horse and walked right up and sat next to Archie. They looked into each other's eyes and smiled.

Zephaniah continued, "This is Reuben, Simeon, Levi, Isachar, Judah. Zebulan's there on the white mare. Gad, Asher, Dan, Judah, and Isachar, and over there is Neptali. This is my cousin Hiram." We all tilted hats.

Zerelda said, "You're all a sight. There's room and oats for the horses in the barn. You're all going to sleep in the loft, it's dry up there. There a tack room in the back for the girl, stoves in there, it's getting cold."

"We're obliged," said Zephaniah.

Demonstrating who was in charge, Zerelda said, "Rutherford, Luke, Sam, Charley, help them with their horses." The slaves walked over. Then she said to the young boy, "Jesse fetch some water, bring it on in to them."

"How about Frank?" he sassed back.

His mother said sternly, "You watch your lip, Jesse. You're not too old to be put over my knee. Frank, go snap a chickens neck, two chickens, we'll need some stew for this crowd."

We tied off the horses and set out buckets of oats for them. We were dragged out and tired, so we rested in the hayed loft until dinner. We ate a hearty chicken stew, bitter with turnips and onion, out of tin cups, crowded around the hearth. The talk first was of family. Her name was Zerelda. Her man was a doctor; he tended to Reuben's injured leg. It did not look good, but seemed to clean up alright. He put a herb poultice on it. He was her third husband. The boys, Jesse and Frank, were from a previous marriage. Their natural father, Reverend James, a Baptist minister, left and died looking for gold in California. Her third husband, the doctor, owned the neighboring farm. They joined families a few years back. The rest of the young ones were from that union. Zephaniah did not elaborate on his wives; he said only that his wife was back on their stead in Kansas. Talk then turned to Brown.

Zee's face grew dark at the mention of his name and she railed on about his murders. Zephaniah joined in, but he did not tell her where we were going. The families both listened, eyes going back and forth as each parent spoke. Zephaniah's clan was so tired they could barely keep their eyelids up, fighting submersion in the warm dew of sleepiness dripping over them.

Joseph sat on the swing with Archie. They were playing softly, counting finger games, hiding their eyes games, guessing which hand games, in slight whispery voices and tittering soft laughter. Zee stopped talking and listened to them and said with amazement, "Now ain't that something, that boy's never played a minute with anyone, let alone laugh."

Zephaniah said, "Joseph is a very special boy, he has a sense we don't have."

"Archie is too," said Zerelda warm to the kinship. "I wish I knew what was going through his mind. He doesn't talk much," she sighed.

Joseph said, "He's happy, and he knows he's loved. He loves all of you, especially Jesse. Jesse stood up for him at school. Some kids were calling him names, Jesse punched them."

"Jesse, is that true?" asked Zerelda.

"Yes ma," said Jesse.

"Now ain't that something, how did he know that?" she said looking in Joseph's blue eyes. "Jesse, there'll be no more fighting. It's no wonder Miss Little is coming calling next week," she said frustrated with her untamed child. "This one's a wild horse, will not take a cross word, don't know where that spirit came from."

Zephaniah said, "Life is a fight, it's better to challenge it, it wins out in the end anyway."

"This life's a mystery," Zee said lighting a pipe. "The good Lord's testing us, wants to see if we're true, if we're worthy of the final gift. He gives us signs, sure as the sun rising. Just never sure which signs to follow, which ones are His, which ones are tricks of the devil? But we know He's there. We know no matter what befalls us. We know it in our bones, most of us, the blessed ones." And she pondered the night for some time as we dozed and Zephaniah considered her words.

Where you heading?" she asked.

"East. Virginia," Zephaniah answered finishing his stew.

"That's far off. What made you up and leave, taking your children but keeping your wife home."

Zephaniah put down his cup and said, "I am called by God Almighty to capture and kill John Brown."

There was a silence.

Zerelda sensed the conviction of his words, "Well then you must go," she said. "You think he'll be there, waiting for you?"

"He'll be there, I know it," said Zephaniah.

"Are you not afraid to leave your wife alone, with all the goings on in these parts?" asked Zerelda.

"They are strong. They will fend for themselves. The planting was done before we left. It was the only way," he answered.

"They?" She pondered out loud, but asked no more.

Zephaniah did not answer right away, but simply looked at her.

Zee continued, "Why did you not leave your boys to help?"

"I left one son, Benjamin. I need these boys to fight Brown. I raised this family for this calling. And God called." Zephaniah answered calmly.

Archie went and brought out a fiddle. He was a natural fiddler, played sweet melodies, jigs, ballads. We were all amazed but too tired to truly enjoy it, but we sang a bit though, The Water is Wide, Green Sleeves. He was odd looking, small eyed, large round head, rosy cheeks. When the night's entertainment ended, we went back to the barn, found a comfortable place, quickly fell asleep, bellies full, tired from two days riding, running away from trouble.

The next day we cleaned guns, checked the horse's shoes, mended tears in our clothes, cooked corn cakes, got ready. Zee gave us a smoked ham, it was a beauty. I had finished cleaning my gun and oiling the stock. I was tired and laid down outside for a nap in the sun near the barn wall like a contented cat.

Across the field was a tree break and beyond that a brook ran, Kidron Brook they called it. Joseph fished there with Archie while Jesse shot river stones from a slingshot a ways down the bank, hitting a partridge squarely and killing it. At some point two lads approached with trouble in their step, in everything about them. These two boys were somewhere around fifteen, bigger and stronger, proud of their size and power. They thought it would be fun to steal Archie's fishing pole, and they tugged it from his hands making him cry. As they teased him, Joseph watched, dark countenanced, knowing trouble was coming. Jesse looked down the brook, saw the bullying and came straight on.

The bullies broke the fishing rod and Archie rose blurting out an expression of anger in no discernable words. Jesse walked right up and kicked one of them square in the balls. Then he punched the other's nose so hard the breaking bone could be heard across the field. Jesse then picked up a rock and was about to hit the boy. He might have killed him but Joseph held his arm back, keeping him from striking.

Off near the edge of the woods a war party of ten Pawnee crawled quietly in the leaves, horses tied off many yards back. Sore, with blood stains in their crotches, they looked on from cover at the fight between the white boys. In a second an arrow zipped in and penetrated the body of the boy bent over in male anguish. Jesse heard the thud and saw the shocked expression on his enemy's face. He dropped the rock, grabbed Archie and Joseph and ran for cover. Arrows kicked up dust where they struck the ground, missing them, ricocheting askew.

The boy with the broken nose did not know what was happening. He just sat there, holding his face, blood running onto his shirt. Then an arrow sank into his back separating his heart. He yelled loud, fell over, and died.

I heard this yell, looked on, sensed by the tenor something was wrong. Jesse knew he had a wide field to cross and that the boys would be exposed so he stayed down. I could see the boys hiding behind the rock pile. I saw something fly by, saw Jesse look up then duck back down, and I knew there was trouble. I called out loud as I could, "Indians!"

Zephaniah was in the loft of the barn. He got up, put on his holster, grabbed a rifle, climbed down the ladder, ran with his limp to the crack in the door of the barn. I'd backed up, put the barn to my shoulder as Zephaniah alerted everyone with a gunshot. Sure enough, coming low, rifles in hand and crouched in a run, five Indians approached the boys, knowing they were unarmed.

A shot rang out from Zephaniah, then another and one Indian fell, another was hit in the leg, it looked to go clean through. The other three fell to their stomachs and started firing. Shortly the pop and echo of guns reverberated from the woods, the barn, the house, as everyone joined the fight.

Jesse, Joseph and Archie were pinned down but young Jesse, fearless and with a spirit for action, took his sling shot and started shooting rocks. He hit one Indian in the ear, which made him mad and thoughtless. In his anger he dodged and ran toward the boys. Jesse kissed one stone, just stood right up and when the Indian was no more than five feet away launched it straight and true, and shot him directly in middle of the forehead, dropping him in a heap, the dust blowing off with his spirit.

Zee and Frank, rifles in hand, shooting and scanning from the window, yelled to Jesse to stay down. They both shot simultaneously and tore one Indian asunder as he ran toward the boys, such perfect shots from such a long distance.

Zephaniah knew Pawnee were well schooled in stalking prey so he told Simeon, Dan, and Levi to go around behind the barn and cover the rear. In minutes there was gunfire and three Indians were caught mid stride. They were blown down like saplings in a gale, sprawled across the ground, spirits fleeing.

Two Indians remained in the trees and they did not like the odds. They ran to the horses, mounted and rode back west. No more shots were heard.

Zephaniah told his sons to ride after them so they could not return to the village and alert the remaining tribe of our whereabouts. He said, "Do not let them get away. Kill them." And off they rode.

Later they told us they had stalked them all day and found them where they'd stopped to rest. The boys tied their horses off at a safe distance and waited. Once settled down, with the Indian's fear smothered in fatigue, the boys overtook them, encircling them. They shot them down before they could grab a weapon.

And so we were safe, the Pawnee would chase us no more and no one in the tribe would know where we were. Too late in the fall for flies, these newly baptized and circumcised Indians stiffened as the sun rose and hungry turkey buzzards flew rotating courses in the air, circling ever tighter over the meal of the day.

Zerelda was glad to have killed some Indians. She held them as savages, thieves, killers, drunks, devils. In her life she had witnessed Indian murders, the Kelly's, the Stuarts, whose entire families were mutilated and their farms burned. So she was firm jawed and stared straight into their dead faces. She noted the bloodstains on their groins. She poked with her gun at the bluish bodies lying lifeless and rank among the flat pumpkins, rotting and deflated as if unleavened on writhing brown vines in her field.

The bodies were dragged to a place in the woods and buried in unmarked graves.

Zephaniah did not explain why he prayed over them. He did not tell her the story of the rape, the bargain, the circumcisions.

The two dead boys, the bullies, were taken into the barn, while one of the slaves rode to get their father and mother. It was a sorrowful sight when they arrived.

The next morning at breakfast Joseph looked at young Jesse and said, "You will be a famous man, a wanted man. There is no home for an outlaw."

Zerelda laughed and looked at the others. They did not know what to make of this crooked boy and his odd statements. But I now know Joseph's words carried truth. Years later these two boys would be famous outlaws, Frank and Jesse James. They started out with Quantrill's raiders, burned Lawrence, worked the borders during the war. But even later they kept the fight up, though the war was over and everyone yearned for peace. They stopped fighting Yankees and started robbing banks. Perhaps it was an act of bravado for their lost cause, maybe boredom. I am not sure. Jesse was angry deep inside after Federal troops beat his step father and burned their house. It is sad now to think on them; Jesse shot dead by a coward who sought fame, Frank giving lectures on the 'Wild West' after serving his time in prison.

Zephaniah thanked Zerelda and Dr. Samuels and said, "Time to move on. We've brought you enough trouble."

So we mounted up, rode off at the morning's first light, leaving them in Clay County, Missouri with newly turned earth over dead Indians, neighbors mourning their lost boys, gun barrels in need of cleaning and a life of heartache and trouble ahead.

It was cold and snowing a bit, windy. Snow swirled but did not stick; it filled the pockets of dead leaves blown together in secret alcoves among the trees and brush. It blew in our faces wetting our skin as we rode east once again.

Pawnee Prayer

On a hill looking over the razed village, lodges yawned, caved and empty. Mourning squaws toiled in malaise and fatherless children trudged aimless in play. The leaning funerary beds extended crooked fingers topped with waving bristled feathers. Rotting corpses, all leather and knobs, stared over the landscape. The rigid lines, like spears through the raw wilderness, killed. Tendrils of smoke rose laconic over still smoldering ash. Weariness and tears were in the eyes of all. Wailing rose from the lonely women, children and dogs waited for the men to return but they did not.

The Chief stood with his one living squaw, mourning his losses, chanting to the winds, carrying his grief across the universe.

He hated the white beard, Coyote.

"Great Father," he prayed, "give us the power to strike down the white invader. Give us the power to stand up to their armies, to kill their laws, to slay their God."

The wind rose gusting an answer blowing his long gray hair in wafting strands; it chilled his carved wrinkled face.

"Take these dead warriors, give them good hunting. Let our men yet living chase the white dogs, capture and kill the family of Coyote. We are your children, Great Father. Protect us, show us the way to victory."

Dead Woman

We rode away from the Samuel's place, moving again in the right direction, eastward. Weather stayed clear though cold, fingers stinging, noses red. I was not happy about sleeping in the open. It was not too bad once asleep, but getting there was hard, toes cold, body wrapped as tight as you could, snuggled up against some other shivering back. In the morning the stiff joints and frost on your head was not pleasant.

In one place we crossed a barren open plain and thousands of rabbits lay scattered about, frozen and dead. I did not understand what could have killed so many. We passed beyond that place, trying to pick our way through the carcasses but stepping on many. It was eerie seeing so many animals dead for no purpose. They had rotted and been exposed for some time, so we could not eat them. I do not think I could eat them over a life time there were so many. For as far as I could see, dead rabbits.

Joseph liked to ride backwards on Zebulan's horse, trailing his saddled horse behind him, looking into its large brown eyes. Along the way I tried talking with him, but he would not answer, he just looked at me, too wise or too removed to speak, I am not sure. Perhaps he still remembered my lie about the dream. He would make statements but not in response to anything I said. It was as if he was carrying on another conversation with someone altogether unseen but greatly more interesting. Once he told me that my mother was fine. He just looked at me, said it.

At different times I rode alongside each brother and talked with them. Zebulan continued to talk about the ocean.

"The Atlantic," he would say, "the Atlantic Ocean. I always thought I would see the Pacific Ocean first, but now I go toward the Atlantic. I wonder how big it really is. I wonder how many fish are in it. I hope to go in a boat, catch me some. Maybe I'll just keep on going right across to Paris, France. I hear the waves are high as a house. There are great leviathans, like swallowed Jonah. They talk of sea monsters, mermaids, half woman, half fish. I've read of ships sinking with no survivors, lost at sea forever. How does it feel to float alone in such vastness? How deep is it? How many colors of blue and green can it be?"

Zephaniah sang hymns to himself as he rode along, I could only catch a few phrases,

"Rock of Ages, cleft for me,
Let me hide myself in thee,
Let the water and the blood,
From thy riven side which flowed,
Be of sin the double cure,
Cleanse me from its guilt and power."

Sometimes we would talk and I asked him many questions. I was worried about the women with only one small boy to defend them, and asked, "Why did you not leave more sons home, to help, to protect them?"

He did not answer at first and rode ahead. Later he slowed and came back to me and said, "I created this family, built this army for a purpose. I was never sure what I would be called to do. But these times have come and now I know. This Brown always has a contingent of men; he is supported by men of money. I have none of this, but I do have my own army, my boys. The women will fend just fine. They are smart, learned in farming, Ben will help them. Buela, Hanna are both there."

"How will Ben help them if there is trouble?" I asked.

"You do not know Benjamin. He is a ravenous wolf, resourceful is he. I spoke with him before we left and he cried and felt left behind. But I told him this is his test, he is the man of my land while we are gone," he answered content in his decision.

Isachar rode off at a distance, always looking for food, hunting for small game from his perch on his horse. All knew there would be supper that night with him on the hunt. We ate rabbit in some places, prairie dog in others, deer, ground hog. A shot would echo past, triple bang—far, near, past. He was a natural stalker, patient, focused, never giving off to other desires, never distracted, like he could get no pleasure without a captured prize.

Asher the gambler would speculate on what his brother had killed. He would seek bets on what it would be as he groomed his hair and talked about the meal to come. In the evening after our meal he would break out his dice. He loved to gamble for just about anything, a piece of food, a coin, a bullet, or for nothing but the bet itself. He loved to watch his opponent's mind turn over the possibilities, choose a position, then make a bet and watch the dice roll. This was his greatest joy; it was not in the winning but in exploration, the leap into the unknown odds of life.

One day as we came up over the arc of the horizon, we saw off to the east a group of wagons, burned and smoldering. As we rode closer we saw in a ravine not far from the wagons, the bodies of settlers, all slaughtered, in grotesque positions, piled randomly as they fell, putrid in the wind. A terrified woman emerged, frantic, filthy, mad, talking nonsense. Three bloated bodies she'd dragged from the fetid draw lay in an uneven row. A swollen man lay beside the crumpled, sorrowful body of a girl, her daughter. Another man, face covered with a dress, was beside the child. She held a gray baby, who was dead, starved, face wrinkled like an old man. She'd been there a week, keeping the birds off the bodies.

She ran out, pleading, raving, she said, "They need your help, can you help them? Are you a doctor? See my baby has a fever. Help them, please help them."

Zephaniah said, "Diana, walk her over there, calm her. Reuben, Isachar, Dan, Zebulan, bury them. Hiram, Gad, Asher scout the area, make sure the Indians are not around any longer."

The boys buried her family. But there were too many dead settlers so they covered them with blankets or clothes or the tattered canvas from the wagons. Once they were buried, Zephaniah came over and sat by the woman who was eating ravenously.

"What happened?" he asked.

She said between bites, "They rode in, just shot everyone?"

"Who?" asked Diana.

"Don't know. Men on horses," she said dripping food.

"White men? Why did they do this?" asked Zephaniah.

"I don't know," she said still eating from the metal plate.

"What did they say?" said Zephaniah.

She stopped eating and tried to remember, "They said… they said…. they would not let us settle if we were against slavery."

"Are you?" asked Zephaniah

"I don't care," she said.

"Where did you travel from?" he asked unsure if her answer was true.

She stared at him. Zephaniah and Diana were the first people she had spoken to in a week; she was still getting used to hearing voices from the living.

She said in a monotone, "We are from Sunbury, Pennsylvania. My husband had a good job with the railroad, a carter, but he wasn't happy. He wanted land. His brother came with us. He was always a drunk, but stopped the bottle, so he could come here; he said he was moving on to a new life. So we went by wagon, one month, out to Pittsburgh, down to Wheeling on a flatboat. Ran aground there, waited for the water to come up."

"Then on down to Louisville. But we ran out of money, we could not afford to go on by paddle wheeler with five people plus our belongings. So my man he worked a bit on the docks, we lived in our flatboat tied up. Moses was born there, on the flatboat. We called him Moses because it was like he floated up in the reeds, just like on the Nile when they found baby Moses in old Egypt. We bought two wagons, nearly stole them they were so low-priced from a family who'd failed, turned back east after losing two little ones to the pox. We hitched up with this party of settlers, financed by a man from Boston, an abolitionist I guess, but we didn't care, we were just happy to have a party to travel with, we took no position."

"Indians followed us two days, a small group maybe five. I dreamt each night they'd ride in and take away my children. Torture them. I waited in my dream for them to come at us, so I could fight. But they did nothing, they tired of following us and wandered off. I did not think white men would do worse than them. Oh God, I did not think men would do this to one another. So here we are, this is what happens, this is our lives. My girl, my Margaret, where is she? How's Moses? Is he better? He was having trouble taking my breast."

Zephaniah said flatly, "He's dead. They're all dead."

"Liar," she yelled and she threw her food, leapt forward, fell on her knees, weak, crying. Zephaniah grabbed her arms, held her off until she lay on the ground and cried it out and she lay there, moaning lowly. Diana covered her with a blanket, and she stayed like that all night.

But when we awoke, she was dead. Just cold, dead. Not sure why. Her heart did not beat, she did not respond to us. After a considered silence, Zephaniah told us we were to bury her next to her family.

The ground was getting hard, Zebulan's hands were blistered, his feet sore from pushing down the spade, trying to chip away the soil. So only a partial hole was dug, flat stones were piled near the side to cover her body.

We stood around her looking at her still countenance. Death was again the victor; only a few hours before she had life and she was talking to us. Now she was gone. Perhaps her heart gave out, broken from the grief of her loss, the tragedy of the whole scene.

Zephaniah prayed, "God, we ask you to take this woman, whose name we do not know. Jesus told us in your house there are many rooms. We ask you to give her one of those rooms for her and her husband and her brother and her girl Margaret and her baby Moses and the rest of these souls if they be Christian."

We had not yet buried, baby Moses. His face, drawn, lips going black; this grimy bundle, was lying near a charred wagon. Diana went over, picked up the cold lifeless child and lay it on its dead mother's legs, head on her belly where he had come from a few months earlier.

Zephaniah continued, "Take their souls, if it be your will, take them in your paradise. This life of ours is your will, Lord, we accept its trials, its tribulations, we come home to you when you call us. We ask only for your blessing, the chance to show we love you. If you have a miracle in mind for us, tell us lord, show us. We will follow."

With that Reuben picked up some flat stones and started piling them around the edge of her form, building a crypt, a pyramid of stones over her, to keep out the dogs and the birds. Joseph started as each stone was put in place like they brought on a twitch. He stuck to Zephaniahs side with his face in his ribs looking into his coat.

"Father, she is alive," he whispered.

Reuben dropped the first stone on the woman's chest. Suddenly her eyes sprung open like she'd been stuck by a needle and she stared up, straight ahead. We were scared enough, first staring at death and now at a dead person staring back. She gasped out, made a soft airy noise, inhaled softly but deeply a chest full of air, coughed, spit as if a plug had been stuck in her chest, as if she'd drowned and her lungs were filled with water. Reuben in startled response removed the stone from her chest and she sat up, color coming to her face, looking about confused.

Zephaniah fell to his knees and looked at her, then held her. Joseph jumped, clapping his hands. The dead woman, too stunned to know what was happening, looked as if roused from a century's sleep, unaware of where she was, who she was. But she was indeed now alive as Easter morning.

She looked around but did not seem to recognize us. She fought to voice her amazement but no words could come from her. She could not speak, her voice was gone, lost. Neither could she stand, her strength sapped by her near grave. We helped her up, carried her over the stones to our side, the life side, wrapped her in blankets, rubbed her to bring back life warm blood.

The baby did not move again. Its face crinkled with ageless death. Reuben tried dropping a stone on it, hoping for the same magic, but it did not rouse it. So we completed the burial, though the fear that we might be piling stones on a live thing sat heavily on us. Dead woman as we would call her not knowing her name, looked on dumbly, unmoved by her child's funeral, a near person, a near corpse.

The family then went on packing up. They put Dead Woman on Joseph's horse. We all mounted up and rode on. Joseph sat backward on Zebulan's horse as usual, but now he stared at the empty eyes of the dead woman riding behind him, curious and smiling. She stared and did not speak to him or anyone ever again.

The others rode on as if nothing new had happened. She was indeed dead but now alive, yet Zephaniah and his clan did not show any amazement, so used to these things I'd guessed. They looked ahead and moved on as if this mute woman was a sister born anew to their family. I had seen some strange things up to this point. But nothing caused me to wonder as this did. I rode on feeling not usual, knowing I had seen what I had seen, knowing there was a woman who was dead who was now sitting on a horse riding east with us looking into the light that I thought she'd left forever.

Shields

Shields Green was a house slave in Charleston, South Carolina. He worked in a thirty five room mansion on East Battery Street which overlooked Charleston Bay and Fort Sumter. His master's family was one of the original families of Charleston and he reveled in an atmosphere of the French court in the period of the revolution. Shields was commanded to dress each day like a courtesan, with knee high socks, ruffled shirts and short pantaloons which were much to the taste of his owner. Shields also wore a powdered wig in the style of his master's colonial forebears, something he detested. The house was enormous and gaudy. It had fourteen foot ceilings bordered by ornate plaster molding. The rooms were adorned with elaborate crystal chandeliers which cast glittering sparks and shadows on the walls when lit. There was a grand sweeping staircase that rose like a conch shell beneath a seventy-five foot dome painted with fat angels and messianic looking men. There were twenty six fireplaces which Shields was required to keep clean and stock with wood. His master insisted that no ash or, if not in use, dust ever be present on the tiles or in the flue. Behind the house was a Roman garden with faux broken pillars and milky marble benches. The exterior brick walls of the yard were covered in ivy and were to be kept meticulously manicured. In the middle of the sculpted space was a fish pond filled with carp from China which required cleaning and emptying weekly for fear the prized fish would perish. The pleasant winding walks were for Shields a curse since his master was obsessed about weeds or any out of place shoot of grass. If a pebble from the path was in the garden or if a leaf or tendril found its way onto the stone path there was hell to pay in extra work. Shields walked that path countless times making sure neither leaf nor weed nor deceased insect disturbed the order and tranquility of his master's special place.

In the music room, where many a night was passed entertaining, there was a glass skylight lending an ethereal atmosphere whenever a cello and piano might serenade guests as they sipped juleps and waxed artistically. Shields would stand in the shadows in the back of the room at attention, tray in hand, waiting to serve a drink or retrieve a glass. He would bow and smile and seek to attend to every need of his white masters. And then after a day of serving and doing the myriad of duties around the house, he climbed down a ladder and slept in a bunk in the dank basement near where the potatoes were stored.

As the lives of slaves went, Shields days spent inside this comfortable home would not seem as tragic as some. Shields, in truth, felt some guilt over that fact, but he had to endure trials of his own that he too could not escape. His master was not physically cruel. There were never beatings. So in these surroundings you might expect a slave to flourish. But while Shields was not dealt blows to his body, he was dragged into a personal hell in another way.

If there ever was a problem, if laziness or lack of attention to detail, forced his master to act; if the spoons did not shine or the shoes were not lined up perfectly, there was the inevitable wagon ride into the country. Still dressed like a servant from the days of Marie Antoinette, Shields and the other household slaves would be taken by his master to the plantation of a friend who would upon request put on a display. This spectacle was often something as simple and brutal as the whipping of a runaway. Once he saw the finger of one poor man who had stolen some food cut away like a fish head. At another time he watched the public humiliation of a young girl who had offended her master, perhaps by failing to please or for crying during a sexual encounter. She was tied to a tree and covered in dung. It was rubbed into her hair and over her face. It was smeared on her arms and body. She was left there one full day amidst the stench and the flies. And whenever the waste dried more was applied. She cried and moaned in disgust and dismay and Shields could only watch while the masters sat on the veranda swatting gnats and sipping cool tea. His master's message was clear: selling Shields off to his friend was always a possibility.

And in this life of total humility, where honor or courage was completely absent and character was built by letting none accrue except servility and attention to endless and futile detail, Shields was then forced to deal with his master's wife.

She had a perverse streak in her which she indulged whenever the man of the house was away. She and a few of her lady friends thought it quite a treat to have the house slaves spend the day in their under clothes. And later at night, after she had been titillated all day by the sight of the partially clothed bucks prancing about her house, she would call Shields to her boudoir for a most degrading encounter. Shields' shame was so great he could never speak of what he was forced to do. But he knew his master would surely kill him if he ever found out about these sexual escapades; he also knew his master would never believe him if he tried to reveal his wife's blackmailing bedroom abuses, so he kept silent and dealt with the snickers and whispers of the other slaves. Whenever business called away the master, Shields knew he would have to carry on his tasks with an even more degrading status, that of the naked nigger; and he knew his night would be filled with indignity.

Shields endured this humiliation for ten years and then one night when a hurricane blew in, he slipped away. He found his way into the hold of a ship when all was battened down and waited out the storm. He landed in Philadelphia and started a new life. He felt lucky and, while not an articulate person, he could always make people understand how much he appreciated his freedom. But, while his back was not scarred, his shame remained palpable. He had lived as well as any slave might expect while he witnessed the terrible suffering of others. His guilt arose from not being able to do anything to help them. And his soul suffered because he could never tell anyone what he was forced to do on those sweaty nights while the master was away. These realities in his life weighed on him and he sought only to be helpful to others, win their respect and, if ever possible, their admiration. Shields always prayed to God to send to him a special calling, a task on which he could embark so he could stand tall and have others say, 'that Shields Green is a great man.'

The Doctor

In the next few days of riding we were mostly alone. I saw a homestead a ways off, smoke rising, but few signs of life. We did not approach it. The land had flattened out, far sightings were not hard. The weather was clear.

We grew accustomed to the chill, slept together in a pack each night, a blanket wrapped around us, a large oil cloth over groups of three. Reuben slept loudest, snoring one deep rumbled breath after another. Zephaniah was peaceful, sound. Simeon seemed to fight in his sleep, restless, turning hard, exhaling long. The dead woman kept to herself; she did not sleep I do not think, or if she did she slept alone sitting up. All day she spoke not a word but in a time became aware of us. She responded when we spoke to her like a dog on command and started to help with chores in camp. But she was not the same, not normal, whatever that is.

In three days as we camped in an area known by some as Haun's Mill we could see a wagon rolling up across the expanse. As it got closer I saw it was different than any I had seen, larger than most, pulled by four pure white horses, legs splattered knee high with mud. Its back section was a small wooden house with a peaked roof. There were faded paintings on the sides, pictures of planets, stars. A fancy lettered sign announced, 'Dr. Leroy Sunderland, Scientist Extraordinaire, Mesmerist, Phrenologist, Sage, Fortune's Told.'

The man driving wore a stove pipe hat, a city suit. I assumed he was the good doctor Leroy, the proprietor of this wagon. He rode up slowly, we could watch him coming for some time across the gold prairie. I looked to Joseph. He had a way of knowing when there was trouble but he was looking in the fire with a puzzled expression. He did not look up even as the others rose to see who was coming. It took a long time for this horse drawn creaking contraption to come up. The driver raised his hands to show he had no weapon.

He called, "Good day, my good men. It is late in the day, may I pull up, join you in this nights repose? I and my good steward would enjoy your company tonight."

"Who be you?" Zephaniah asked.

Removing his stovepipe hat he said, "My name sir is Dr. Leroy Sunderland. I am a practitioner of medicine for the mind, the body, the soul. My partner, curious as he may be, is Manasseh."

From inside the wagon there climbed out a tiny little man. He stood on the seat and at full height he did not reach the seated doctor's head. He had large hands on short arms, a big head over a tiny torso, short legs. He was the first dwarf I had ever seen. He looked around with a regal countenance as if looking on a group of peasants, arms folded, little legs wide; he looked out upon the world knowingly.

Joseph moved to stand behind Zephaniah. He wrapped his arm around his waist and looked askew at this strange creature, uncomfortable at the visage.

"He's bad, Pa," he whispered.

The doctor gestured toward his short cohort as he rose and said, "Please meet Manasseh, a dwarf, one of the little men spoken of in tales of yore. He is a scholar, a chef, a magician, a world traveler, a warrior, a student of mankind. You will find him very interesting but I must warn you he does not think of himself as a little man. The last man who insulted him he killed. I am a doctor, schooled in Vienna, Austria. Graduate of the Arch Duke's Academy established by his Majesty's personal physician, Heir Franz Joseph Gall. I have traveled to the far reaches of the world in search of my art, studied with the healers of the Himalayan mountains, mystics, ancients, elevators of mind over matter. So if you have a malady of the body or of the mind I can cure it. Everywhere I go there are souls who need me. Some seek me out to cure their affliction; others do not know what ails them and want my diagnosis.

He gestured to the dead woman and said, "I see this woman here, her light is low, she needs my assistance, by the very expression on her face I can tell this. May I step down?"

"You can," said Zephaniah.

Manasseh the dwarf swung athletically from the wagon to the ground, grabbed a rope and lowered a ladder for the doctor, who climbed down, step by step, cautious to keep his footing. They made quite a pair standing side by side. Manasseh had a large head and stood on his stubby legs thigh high to the doctor. He dressed in boots and a coat made of Buffalo hide. He wore a derby and his bushy hair fluffed out the sides of his little hat like overgrown weeds. The doctor in coat and tails, with his collar long since lost of starch and a stained stove pipe hat, was long armed, long nosed, with rings on every finger and skinny as a pea pod. He took a deep bow and Manasseh the dwarf removed his derby and bowed the same. We all nodded, sensing danger, but not sure where it would come from.

The doctor said, "Let me diagnose this woman." And he walked over to the dead woman, bowed to her saying, "May I?" She did not respond.

The doctor looked around to blank expressions. He then put his hands on her head like an upside down bowl and felt around for bumps saying, "Witness, my friends, the science called Phrenology. You see her head is the map to her health. The regions of her head reflect her personality, her future, her past. Her cranial bone is of a very interesting shape. I can tell that she has drives from her brain organ which cause her much harm. She needs further diagnosis."

He felt all over her head, as we looked on. Then he spoke in a strange language to Manasseh all the while looking off in the distance considering his explorations of her head.

"What brings you to these regions?" he asked as he probed her scalp.

Zephaniah said, "Declare yourself first, are you an abolitionist?"

The doctor said, "I take no position sir, it is not the realm I dwell within. The world makes us serfs, as I see it all men are slaves, black or white."

"Are you a Christian or a worshipper of pagan Gods?" asked Zephaniah.

He answered, "No sir, the God of Abraham is my God but men's misinterpretation and misapplication of his word has taken them astray. I, dear sir, am a new type of Christian. I have raised my consciousness, I have met with angels; I have learned a new way."

Zephaniah looked on not sure he wanted to hear more. The boys had relaxed their hands on their gun belts.

The doctor then looked to Diana and said, "This one, she is pregnant, has she seen a doctor yet?"

And he stepped up to Diana and was about to put his hands on her belly when Zephaniah stood in front of him and said, "We do not need a doctor."

"As you wish," he said smiling, taking his hands away, avoiding confrontation. Then he said to the rest of us, "You may wonder how I know these things. I have witnessed the great Aurora Borealis in the hinterlands of the north. The lights of the universe flaring in glorious color are in all of us. We are made of the same stuff as the stars, you see, the same minerals in this rock fly through the heavens, they are within our bones, our souls. I see this light about all of you. It looks to me like a halo of colored mists. A strong healthy body will show bright light of many colors. A weak light and there is a malady, someone needs help. It is one who has need of Dr. Leroy Sunderland."

Zephaniah asked, still unsure of this man's intentions, "Are you a settler or moving through?"

"No, I am a visionary, I cannot settle down. It seems when I do, when I try to explain myself things change. When I foretell, when I cure someone, when I tell of the mysteries I have encountered some believe me, some want to follow me but some want to ride me out on a rail. If you have not yet been tarred and feathered you have not lived. You have not stood up for your beliefs, if you have not been so attired. It is the raiment of honor of a great mind, for a prophet is not welcome in his own country. And so we move on seeking the place where I can gather fellow mystics. Perhaps you are they. Tonight, I can show you things; tell you things, things of wonder. Things you need to know."

Manasseh spoke to the doctor in the language none of us knew.

"Manasseh suggests he prepare a meal for all of us, he is an expert chef.

This food is a meal for the Gods. Then we will perform for you our assortment of mystic arts."

The doctor went back to exploring dead woman's head while the dwarf went behind the wagon, pulled down a small step ladder and climbed in. He started to pull out pots, pans and other utensils and carry them to the fire. He rearranged the fire stones and erected a steel spit. He then went into the wagon and brought out a piece of hind quarter which he skewered on the spit and started turning. He said something in the unknown language to Reuben and motioned for him to tend the meat. He then went back in the wagon but did not soon come out again. We heard a bump, a clank, a jostle every so often but we did not see him for a while.

We sat watching this succulent piece of meat dripping its juices, flaring the coals. The doctor thoughtfully let go of the dead woman's head, walked off to the brook and washed his hands and face. He knelt, prayed and then returned.

Dr. Sunderland said," I can take her with me, I can cure her."

But no one answered.

When the meat was cooked, Manasseh came out from the wagon with two bowls, one in each arm, and a pile of tin plates balanced on his head. He set them down with the ease of a juggler spilling not a drop and took a brush and brushed the meat with the sauce. He then said something to the doctor who said, "Manasseh says it is time for us to eat, we should get plates."

Zephaniah said, "First we will pray. We never have a meal without thanks to God."

The doctor asked, "To what do you pray?"

"To the One God, provider of all life," answered Zephaniah.

The doctor demurred, "You may go ahead, we will stand aside. We do not follow this practice. Food is here for us to take, it is not a gift. God has created all but turned all in the world loose to fend for themselves. It is meaningless to thank him."

"You do not give thanks to God?" asked Zephaniah.

The doctor thought for a second then explained, "I was told some time ago by ancient beings who visited me in a wood that Christians are misguided. You pray for yourself. God is all powerful; he does not need your prayers. God does not hear your small voice."

Zephaniah looked at him then to us and said, "That's not what Jesus said. Kneel."

So the rest of us knelt as he said, "God, we thank you for this food we are about to receive. We thank you for all the blessings of this life. Show us the way Lord, we ask only that we may fulfill your will. Teach all who stand here now that you are the one God, that you hear us, that you guide all that happens in the world."

All said, "Amen"

Dr. Sunderland and Manasseh did not respond at all. When we rose to our feet the dwarf went to the fireside. We each took a plate. He carved the meat, poured from a ladle some sauce on each plate. We all ate very well; it was amazingly delicious. I'd never tasted such a tender meat or such a tasty sauce.

Zebulan asked, "What is this?"

The doctor only smiled and said, "It is a secret recipe from the depths of Africa."

He looked around pleased we were enjoying it so.

When the meal was over, as we sat around picking at our teeth, burping, the Doctor rose and announced, "Now Gentleman, if you will be so kind, please gather round my wagon."

Manasseh went to the wagon pulled on a rope that fed into a pulley and the side dropped down to a small stage, legs on hinges supported its front edge. Behind it was a painted backdrop with a picture of a desert and a pyramid, a bird God hovered over the pyramid and a river ran to the foreground as if flowing onto the stage. There were very different looking trees along the river and people were kneeling down in supplication worshipping the bird God. Manasseh ran to the fire with an unlit torch. He lit it and returned to the wagon to light the torches placed all around the stage. As he did this the doctor withdrew to the interior behind the illuminated proscenium.

We waited for the exhibition like children at a circus freak show. We had been alone on the trail so many nights; we found this much more interesting than silence, a crackling fire, a snoring Reuben. Zephaniah was remote, guarded but not dismissive, he may have even been curious. Joseph was silent, fearful.

Manasseh walked out. He was dressed like a tiny medicine man, a Buffalo's head atop his and paint on his face and small leggings on his little lower limbs. He said in perfect English, "Witness now the Genius of Dr. Leroy Sunderland. Those who are present when these magical arts are revealed can only but attest to his great powers in the future. Hear his words. To yield not to them is to put your own lives at risk." The dwarf stepped slowly backward off the stage.

From the other side of the stage the doctor walked out. Except for a small loin cloth and his stove pipe hat he was buck naked.

"Listen, oh children. I appear naked to the elements. I can give you nothing but what I know, what is in my mind. What you are about to see is no trick, no sleight of hand, simply a lost art. Manasseh, bring me the stones."

The buffalo headed dwarf came out with his arms held straight forward. Five round blue stones were in his fingers displayed around for all to see. They were sky blue, polished shiny, hazy, seemed to be perfectly round. The doctor took off his hat, took the stones from Manasseh and they bowed to each other. The dwarf removed himself from the stage, walking backwards with high exaggerated steps, his head down and probing back and forth like a tiny buffalo retreating but wary.

The doctor showed the stones to the audience again, all around slowly, a look of mystery in his eye. We looked on, Simeon squinting, Dan biting his lip,

Zebulan in awe, Reuben wide eyed, Diana passive even bored, Levi with hand on gun, Joseph glaring, Zephaniah unmoved. The Doctor put the stones in the bottom of his stove pipe hat, raised the hat to his face and looked straight down the pipe toward the stones. He stood there for some time. The wind kicked up, flaring the torches, casting odd shadows of the man and his hat on the wagon and the woods.

The doctor spoke, "I have counseled the angels whose names I cannot say aloud or I will die. I have seen the visions. I have eaten the gifted mushroom and flown with the eagle that carries all Truth on its wings, the All Seeing Raptor. Tonight, we will eat the magic plant together. You will see the truth only I have seen. I will teach you about God, the real God. The book you read is a lie, written by liars, its truth, its meanings, long hidden away, make you like cattle, like sheep. Your family will be scattered to the wind, your home will burn like incense in an urn, the smell of death rising to sanctify the temple of the heavens. You will be the sacrifice; you will be the burnt offering. Time has moved on slowly to this moment. Now it moves on faster, faster toward your end."

Diana bored and not feeling well moved off into the darkness to pee. She squatted in the woods. From the shadows she could see into the rear door of the wagon. The little man was very busy inside, sorting, gathering, setting things up. He looked to be whittling or carving. She stepped closer, silently, moving close enough to see into the little house. Behind the dwarf was set a platter with round buttons, another strange food for them she thought. There were several rifles, a pile of assorted clothing, jewelry. Hanging on the wall were leg and arm manacles. By the light of the torches she could see him take up a bone and begin shredding the meat off it with a knife. As she looked closer she saw a human foot at the end of that bone.

"My God," she thought, "what had they eaten?"

The doctor went on saying, "Coyote, Moroni beckons to you. He says you are on the wrong trail, says you cannot catch Brown, you will not find him." And he removed his hat from his face and continued, "If you want to know what will happen, how to change your future, partake of this food. You will then understand my words and become one with the raptor."

He clapped his hands and out came Manasseh with the tray of small circular bits of unknown food. The family looked to see what Zephaniah would do. Zebulan had already stepped up to take his piece when Diana said, "Father, come here."

Zephaniah walked over. She whispered to him, "There's a human leg in the wagon. I think that's what we ate."

Zephaniah did not hesitate, he turned, pulled out his pistol and shot the dwarf through the chest, raising his little body a few feet off the ground, the tray spinning end over end in the air, the impact of the bullets forcing his body backward, slamming him against the back drop. He slid down leaving a slash of red across the pyramid.

The doctor was so stunned he wet himself right there on the floor of the ungodly stage. Zephaniah did not shoot, he just looked at him for a short while. We had our weapons drawn and trained on the urine dripping doctor and stood waiting to see what was happening. Zephaniah went to wagon and came out on the stage holding a human bone, a leg shorn of muscle with a fully fleshed foot on the end.

"What was your plan doctor? Did you plan to kill us? Eat us? Is this what you fed us tonight?" said Zephaniah glaring at him.

The doctor was speechless; looked around caught like a rat in a kettle.

Zephaniah stepped back and nodded our way. Dan, Simeon, Reuben, Levi, all opened fire at once. They emptied their guns, shot the Doctor full of crimson holes, small in the front, gaping in back. His insides flew backward as if caught in a twister. He too fell against the backdrop, bleeding over the depiction of the worshippers of the raptor God.

Zephaniah walked over, took a torch from the stage and set the wagon on fire. We stood back and watched, murder still in the air. The wagon blazed high catching fast, exploding as ammunition burned. I looked on amazed and reviled at what had happened.

'Did we have to kill them?" I asked.

Zephaniah said to me, "Tonight we have eaten of human flesh. They have made us as savages. When there is an abomination before God we must kill it, wrench it, stamp it out then and there. There is no denying, no waiting, no bargaining with evil. We know it when we see it. It is our duty before God to stop it or we become like them. Be a man, Hiram."

The wagon fire flared and spewed streams of vapors coiled with fumes of wood and corpse. It spread about the still night air a devilish haze, an odor of death. What we had seen and what we had eaten made me sick. Diana fell ill, as did Zebulan. I vomited near the brook, splashed water on my face, unable to wash the sweet odor of burning flesh from my skin. I had seen more death in these last months then in my whole life. I remember thinking for the first time; I was not made to be a warrior.

Holy Night

J ohn Brown sat alone in the last pew of a small clapboard church. The Christmas
Eve service flowed sweetly on but it could not overcome the conversation in his
head. Was he mad? He did not think so but he was convinced, firm in mind,
compressed hard as ancient stone. Children sang of joy to the world, preachers
spoke of peace on earth, but he had visions of a slave war in his head. A tear ran
down his cheek. He loved the slaves so, he could think of nothing else. He was
kneading his raw hands thinking of the day of slave freedom not the birth of
Christ. He did not hear the words retelling of the story of the wonderful baby, the
message of love. It conflicted with what he was told by God to do. There could be
no love, no peace until men were no longer enslaved. He stared at the preacher,
saw the words in the air by his mouth, hovering over the congregation but knew
they were intended for a future time, a future he would help bring about.

Brown gazed around, tired marrow deep, eyes blurred and bleary, mind
driven. His body was saddle worn. He'd ridden for days on end, thinking,
planning, organizing, dreaming strategies for killing whites and freeing blacks.
He was as weary from thought as from riding. He'd avoided people and would no
longer transport on steamers. But he could not bear Christmas Eve alone though
years before he swore to never enter a church again when they would not seat
blacks and expelled him for trying.

The preacher read:

*"In those days a decree went out from Caesar Augustus that all the world should
be enrolled.*
This was the first enrollment, when Quirinius was Governor of Syria.
And all went to be enrolled, each to his own city.
And Joseph also went up from Galilee, from the city of Nazareth, to Judea,
to the city of David, which is called Bethlehem,
because he was of the house and lineage of David."

"Did you hear that… of the house of David? Now if we look to the
beginning of Matthew what is the first thing he teaches us? It starts with the
lineage from Abraham to King David, fourteen generations, from David to the
deportation to Babylon of Israel fourteen generations, from the deportation of

the Jews to Jesus, Fourteen generations. Why do we talk of this? Because it is God's promise, Isaiah 11 tells us, foretells to us: There shall come forth a shoot from the stump of Jesse, and a branch shall grow out of his roots. And who is Jesse? He is the father of King David:

> *and the spirit of the Lord shall rest upon him,*
> *the spirit of wisdom and understanding,*
> *the spirit of counsel and might,*
> *the spirit of knowledge and fear of the Lord,*
> *He shall not judge by what the eyes see,*
> *or decide by what his ears hear:*
> *but with righteousness he shall judge the poor,*
> *and decide with equity for the meek of the earth:*
> *and he shall smite the earth with the rod of his mouth,*
> *with the breath of his lips he shall slay the wicked."*

"So he is not the sword bearing Messiah, the warrior of the Jews come to smite, to conquer the world with force. The Messiah will smite with his words, with his wisdom not a sword."

> *"The wolf shall dwell with the lamb,*
> *and the leopard shall lie down with the kid,*
> *and the calf and the lion and the fatling together.*
> *The cow and the bear shall feed;*
> *their young shall lie down together;*
> *and the lion shall eat straw like the ox.*
> *The suckling child shall play over the hole of the asp,*
> *and the weaned child shall put his hand on the adders den.*
> *They shall not hurt or destroy in all my holy mountain;*
> *for the earth shall be full of the knowledge of the Lord, as the waters cover the sea."*

"And so the baby in the manger was told of by the prophets of old. They said he would come out of Egypt. Then they said he would be born in Bethlehem. Then they said he would be a Nazarene. How could this be? We know now these three disparate prophesies happened. He was born in Bethlehem due to Joseph's journey for the census. He escaped to Egypt to avoid the slaughter of the innocents by jealous King Herod. He returned to dwell in Nazareth. Three different prophecies seemingly at odds, came true."

"Angels told the shepherds and a star brought the magi with gifts. These kingly visitors were not Jews but Gentiles. God was to be for all men, his words were meant for Jew and Gentile alike. The Angels said to the shepherds, the common men,

"Be not afraid for behold I bring you good news of a great joy,
which will come to all the people for to you is born this day a savior,
who is Christ the Lord.
And this will be a sign for you,
you will find a babe wrapped in swaddling clothes and lying in a manger.
And suddenly there was with the angels a multitude of the heavenly host praising
God and saying Glory to God in the highest and on earth peace among men."

A choir stood and began singing 'Silent Night' in quiet peaceful tones. John Brown seemed to pray or slumber but each time he closed his eyes his visions returned. He forced his thoughts to transfer from his killings to his cause. Brown sat thinking of his family, dead, killed, distant, alone, about his mission for God, about the plight of the slaves.

Some sat on this Christmas Eve in cold quarters, burning scant wood for warmth, singing this same song with African harmonies in longing tones. They rubbed together cold hands calloused from unpaid labor, stood on unshorn feet, ripped and thickly padded from long days toting. They winced from hobbling, whipping, branding, yoking, amputations.

After the final verse the congregation rose, shoe cadence in unison, one people, one motion. Candles were brought to each pew; the flame passed person to person, a lighting of lights until all were lit. Now the small pump organ started again humbly, slowly. And all sang. Small children wondered at the candles, transformed from mere illumination to Holy Light this night. Brown saw the children's eyes as the pleading eyes of slave children, looking up, innocent, runny nosed, amazed at the confluence of light, music, words, hoping for a savior, hoping for a future beyond bondage, beyond anguish and separation.

Women gazed longingly at the light. Brown saw them black faced, chained, motherless, childless, with bone deep anguish at the lives ahead of them, praying to God to hear them, to bring them home, aching the ache of life, from suffering, pain, loss, yet still with some joy at the awe, at the mystery of birth, the mystery of life in a womb.

Brown opened his Bible in his mind and read from Isaiah:

Let the earth listen and all that fills it;
the world and all that comes from it.
For the Lord is enraged against all nations,
and furious against all their host,
he has doomed them, has given them over for slaughter.
Their slain shall be cast out, and the stench of their corpses shall rise;
the mountains shall flow with blood.

He left the church in silence, speaking to no one.

Riding along a winter stream on Christmas day, he looked at the rivulets of frigid water tunneling through the iced cover, breaking through in random creases. How cold must it be for all water to freeze? What a cold desert it would be across the world.

He'd lived through winters burning a cord of wood a day to keep warm, crazy with desire to feed and house his sickly children. The cold blue water—always he had thoughts of water—the miracle of water. He loved to gaze at it. He stopped his horse, looked deep into the coursing stream, bubbling and pulsing past iced channels.

Water. He thought of John at the river Jordan, baptizing, giving freedom from sin, of the dove's flight as Jesus stood in the river Jordan. He had thoughts of Jesus walking on the water, of Jesus learning of his mission, learning of the death which awaited in Jerusalem as he rode his mule toward Calvary hill. He knew how Jesus must have felt. He wanted to be like him in every way, even in death, a sacrifice for the evil of slavery. Brown would not live long; he knew it surely, a few more years perhaps, maybe less. He could be captured, hung by the neck, shot by an angry slaver, scourged, humiliated. But like Christ, someone had to be unafraid of death, someone had to have faith.

The water moved on over stones, under drifts and snow prows. He remembered the flatboats, and how they passed day after day over the water, filled with settlers, carrying them on to new lives, promises of land, promises of prosperity, of ownership, a family homestead. Were they drawn by the call to populate Kansas to stop the spread of slavery or the call to seed it in the territory? Did they care? Were they simply ignorant and selfish, or driven as he by a vision of the world they would not know in this life but foresaw for others? People wandered the earth, seeking something always better, the endless journey, some with a goal, some simply surviving. It was the way.

On the journey they latch on to something, take a risk, choose a path. And if they are lucky their path leads them to success and success becomes their new God. Water always brings them to it, water. Common settlers were the stewards of ruination on the waters of the Missouri, whose waters mixed with slave blood and ran to the sea, yet the sea was not full. John Brown rode now to call up the winds to make this ocean rage white capped, wrecking the ships that carried slaves to lives in bondage, sinking the new false god to the depths of the sea.

The people he sought to kill had done just this. They found success, a way to feed their family, a way to create a future. But they grasped enslavement as their means, their new god. They could not give it up. They could not be expected to ruin their lives, to become destitute by choice, by reason of their own judgment. That would be unnatural.

The government was torn between factions who worshipped the new God and those who loathed it. Free men had moved to Kansas and saw elections stolen by Missouri's southern sympathizers, who crossed the border fearful a free Kansas would infect their state, killing off their farms, their livelihood, their futures. Since his slaughters there were new actions in Kansas against this God of Greed: a separate free soil government was voted in by his anti-slavery brethren. Now there were two feuding governments fighting for the loyalty of the people in Kansas.

He knew he acted for God.

Man had strayed before and he would again. But with each diversion from the true path a prophet arose to speak wisdom to the people. Isaiah, Jeremiah, Elijah, their words warned the people. Perhaps his would be heeded. A new name would enter the pantheon of those who foretold what would befall a sinning nation. The name was John Brown.

Christmas Gifts

It was Christmas Eve day. We rode outside of Columbia, Missouri. I was reflective of all that had happened so far. It had been quite a journey for me, not at all what I had expected, but we do not know what is around the next bend in the road in this life and yet we must travel on. So I acted like a reader with a good book, turning the page.

The Dead Woman still rode with us, staring ahead, straddling our world and still a part of the nether region she'd had a glimpse of, shocked still by her journey to the dark side, I'd guessed.

Reuben's leg had become much worse. The wound festered and a thin lace of spidery veins ran up his calf to his thigh, it had turned a purple color and the pain was growing. But Zephaniah did not want to stop; he thought the leg would heal if we prayed for divine intervention. It had been so in the past with other illnesses, other injuries. So he prayed for Reuben every night. He said the battle with the Indians was preordained and if it was His will surely God would heal the wound.

As we approached the outskirts of Columbia, a place Zephaniah wanted to avoid for a reason he would not say, we saw people walking and some riding buckboards toward us. When we were about a half mile apart they turned and headed in another direction, northerly.

As we came upon the spot where they had turned we saw a sign on a tree announcing a Christmas Eve service and an arrow pointed up the road we would not have taken. Since the others had gone that way and Zephaniah said Reuben's leg needed some extra prayer, we turned left, headed north up the curving road toward a set of uneven rolling hills. Over one stunted hill and sitting askew in the middle of a flat moraine, a small white church stood with a meager but proud steeple that claimed a place for God beneath the chalky sky. A house behind the church, the parsonage I assumed, echoed the sanctuary. Horses were tied off and wagons arranged along the roadside. No one was about as the service was just beginning. Churchy voices of men and women, bass and soprano and those switching between the two and perhaps some others as well crowded inside singing about Jesus' birth. They sang 'Joy to the World.'

We rode up, tied off the horses and walked in. It was considerably warmer inside among the people. A stove squatted hot and black in one corner and the room was filled with hat wearing women and neck tied men. It felt good to be with folks again though I was never comfortable in church for some reason. All eyes turned toward us as we walked in and looked to take a seat. People scuffled and rearranged so we could sit in one polished wooden pew together. We were stinking, dirty, welcomed, made comfortable. We nodded humbly in thanks, Reuben leaning on Zebulan and Levi, limping and looking pale as marble.

The preacher looked at us in double take and stopped singing like the devil stole his vocal chords. He stared at us, mouth agape. Dead woman showed no reaction as someone handed her a Bible and a song sheet and smiled urging her to open it.

As they sang the last verses of 'Joy to the World', the preacher walked to the cross ceremonially and raised his arms in thanks. Zephaniah's face went blank and eyes went wide and he stopped singing at the sight before him. The preacher then looked straight from the cross to Zephaniah. Their eyes locked for some time and neither joined the multitude in song.

When the hymn ended with 'heaven and nature' singing, the minister lowered his arms, turned and looked at the congregation and said, "My fellow Christians. We are here this Christmas Eve day at the cusp of this night of miracles and we have in our midst a miracle of our own. A miracle of miracles. In this pew visiting our church is my brother, Zephaniah. I have not seen him in 30 years. Praise God. We are reunited."

Zephaniah stood rigid as a statue showing no recognition and making not a sound. We all looked to him unsure of what to think, what to do. The congregation tittered with startled commentary which only halted as each turned to look at their minister's long lost brother. Zephaniah remained still as the minister stepped down and walked to the end of pew then opened his arms and waited for him to step up and embrace.

Zephaniah said, "Esau" in a puzzled tone, nearly a question, and he walked slowly past his sons to the center aisle and looked his brother in the eye. Then he grabbed him tightly, put his face into his collar and hugged him. The church folk looked on touched by the emotion, moved by their minister's apparent joy at this Christmastime revelation. They erupted in applause.

The Pastor asked for calm and tried his best to continue the service but he was clearly distracted. So he asked the organist named Mariah to strike up a hymn. He picked up a hymnal and leafed to page thirty four, 'O Little Town of Bethlehem', and asked all to sing. The organist, at first shaken and appalled by the abrupt alteration of her service, took up the request with Christian understanding, found the page and started playing with her normal vigor. While everyone sang Zephaniah tried to join in but could not keep his eyes off his brother and eventually closed the hymnal and just stared. He could not seem to believe he was in the presence of his brother. It was such a stroke of luck. He would not have found him had John Brown not committed his crimes, if he had not dreamed, if

Joseph had not interpreted. Surely this was a message from God.

Much of their lifetimes had passed by but between the glances of these brothers long lost was a distance much greater than the span of the church.

There was a physical resemblance; they looked to be family, though the pastor was clean shaven and balding, also smaller and rounder. His face was pocked but their close set eyes and hook noses were clearly of the same lineage.

When the hymn was over, Zephaniah said, "Brother Esau, I must ask a favor. If you would be so kind as to say a prayer over my son, Reuben, we would be grateful. He has a wounded leg, it steals his strength. We need God's healing ways, we need your prayers."

Esau walked up, laid his hands on Reuben's head and said, "Gracious Lord, we pray for my nephew Reuben. Please Lord, heal him, let him serve you longer. Amen."

With that said Reuben fainted, dropped to the pew. We all rushed to help. Zebulan grabbed him preventing him from sliding to the floor. Someone brought water from a crystal pitcher near the preacher's seat which we splashed on his face, but this did not revive him. Pastor Esau told us to bring him to his house in the back of the church and put him in a bed upstairs. So we carried Reuben out. It took seven of us; one holding each limb, two at his sides, one opening doors. The rest followed concerned and trying to help but getting in the way. We removed him from the church, carried him across the yard, up the porch stairs, through the front door then up the stairs and into a bedroom.

We waited in the parsonage and shortly a woman ran to the house and said, "Zephaniah, I am your sister-in-law Elizabeth, praise God, we are so glad you are here. It has been so many years since you've seen your brother. He thought you were dead. What brings you here?"

Zephaniah said, "Providence, Elizabeth, God brought us here. I did not think I would ever see my brother again in this life."

"He's a changed man, Zephaniah. There is nothing of the past in him, do not think on it. We carry on the work of the Lord here, we do not think of those days. He forgave you long ago," Elizabeth said in a healing tone.

Zephaniah said slowly, "Forgave me?" He looked at his sons and repeated, "He forgave me?" But he would not speak on it further.

Elizabeth avoided the topic and said, "You are all a sight. Of course you will stay with us, have Christmas dinner, there is so much to talk about. How is your son's leg? Has he awakened?"

"No, I am afraid not," said Zephaniah.

"Has he seen a doctor?" she asked with concern in her voice.

"No, I have prayed for him," said Zephaniah straight and true.

"Well if you're praying, pray for a Doctor, he needs one," said Elizabeth.

"God's will is God's will," said Zephaniah.

"God gave us the brains to train Doctors, that's his will," returned Elizabeth with a look of disdain. Then she continued saying, "Now which one of these boys will ride into town?"

Zephaniah paused absorbing the insult and then said, "Levi, do as she says."

She looked at Levi, walked over, grabbed his shoulders, looked in his face and said, "Levi, ride southeast on the same road you came in on. On the outskirts of town is a white house with a porch, there is an evergreen tree in the front, it's the first house you'll see. Tell Doc Hyssop we need him."

"But its Christmas Eve," said Levi.

"He'll come. Esau's his preacher. He'll come. Now go and get him," she ordered. And Levi left. He rode off in a hurry, his horse rearing and unwilling to leave the good grazing.

Elizabeth went upstairs after sending a slave out for some water. Reuben was running a high fever. He was still unconscious and did not look good; his color was almost yellow, same as the sheets.

The service ended and the church emptied of congregants, and as the wagons and horses departed down the winter hardened ribbon of road, Pastor Esau came in. Zephaniah and he looked at each other for some time. They exchanged some uncomfortable pleasantries. Then, with the tension building from a need to speak about difficult things, we were asked to leave the room. The glass doors to the parlor latched closed and we went into the kitchen.

Zephaniah and his brother Esau spoke for some time. I never did hear what had happened between them. I know it involved land and was some kind of family dispute from long ago. Whatever it was, it was over and they left the room after shaking hands, the past was sealed.

That night the doctor came riding in with Levi. He sat for some time with Reuben. After his examination he spoke in hushed tones with Zephaniah, Aunt Elizabeth and Pastor Esau. I heard the words 'infection, fever, delirium, amputation.' There was a long silence after he said that last hated word. It could mean sure death.

Then the doctor left and they sat around the table staring at the floor. They did not speak for some time until Esau said, "What brings you here, brother?"

"I travel east seeking John Brown. I am to find him and kill him. He seeks to bring an end to God's rule over our nation. He will bring war, I must stop it."

There was a silence.

"I see," said Esau. He thought on it for another time and then said, "Brother, stay with us a while."

"Yes," said Zephaniah, "We will wait a few days for Reuben to recover, then we will leave."

"He will need longer than that. He may lose his leg. If he lives through that it will be months before he'll walk," protested Esau.

"If he will live then he will live, it is God's will, but Brown must die, that too is God's will," answered Zephaniah.

Esau apparently knew not to cross his brother once his mind was set for he did not debate the point. That night we had a delicious dinner of venison, corn mush and bread. There was enough for all, though sixteen people crossing the threshold were a surprise.

Reuben started to rave in his sleep as we ate. I looked in on him and his skin shined; it bubbled with beads of sweat as he mumbled confused phrases. I was concerned for him; I thought he might pass on before my eyes. His leg had been cleaned and bandaged by the doctor but infection had long set in. The Samuel's poultice had not helped. It was in the Lord's hands now if he would keep his leg, if he should live.

That night we sat in the parlor while the Pastor and Aunt Elizabeth exchanged small gifts. When it seemed the gift giving was over Pastor Esau said, "Elizabeth, thank you, this muffler is especially nice. Now why don't you go over there and open the door to the pantry."

Elizabeth, in humorous anticipation, feigned uncontrollable desire to open the door. Each time she reached for the door knob she acted overcome with emotion, squealed and then backed away dramatically. We all laughed at her antics, which she played with much fun three times, then the fourth time as we all waited for her to open the pantry door she did it again, reigniting our laughter. Finally, she opened the door and there sat with crossed legs a small Negro girl.

Esau said, "Elizabeth, this is Eliza. She is your Christmas gift. She will help you around the house, assist in your every need.

This was a valued gift, probably worth $400 with many years of work and future child bearing. She was a fine creature, a fine gift for many reasons. Esau motioned to the slave girl to walk forward. The dark child had been sitting quietly in the closet for some time, perhaps all through dinner, so she was slow to react. She was clearly afraid, squinting at the lamp light as she walked out coaxed by Esau.

Elizabeth said coyly, "Well now, Pastor Jacobs, did we have a good collection this year?"

He answered, "Well not exactly, Eliza was a donation from the Geary's, it is a tithe of sorts. She will assist in the church as part of her duties. But it was made clear this was a personal gift, a way to make the church run smoother and a way to soften the hardship on your life."

The little chocolate brown girl stood alone with fearful cow eyes, a black among whites, a child among adults, with no parents, no home. She was taken to the slave quarters out back to live with a new family of niggers she did not know. I thought she was an odd donation to a church and a unique Christmas gift. But I also thought she was a lucky slave girl having found her way into a churched household.

That night as we slept Joseph had a dream. It did not upset him but he knew he must tell his father of his visions. So Zephaniah spoke to him behind the closed doors of the parlor in the morning, in seclusion, to hear what news he may bring.

As we sat at breakfast that Christmas day, Zephaniah came into the room and said, "Joseph says Brown was in St. Louis. He murdered a freight watchman and a Sheriff. He had a room in a hotel and his personal effects, a log book of expenses, of weapons bought and accounted for, money owed, names of supporters, was left behind. We leave today."

"But what about Reuben?" asked Dan.

"Will you care for him, brother?" said Zephaniah.

"Well of course," said Esau, "but he may die, he may lose a leg, he is your son; you should stay until he is well."

Zephaniah said, "The Lord has called me. Care for him?"

There was a silence as Esau considered this sudden request. "I will, of course," answered Esau.

As we gathered our things, Diana noticed that some time the night before, on Christmas Eve, the Dead Woman had walked away. She just wandered off, probably with the same expression of incredulous emptiness as always. She went off on her own, dumbly, mutely, quietly, her face mirroring her lost soul. We never knew what happened to her. We did not know where she had gone. I thought we might pass her on the road. But we never came upon her and I cannot say I ever saw her again, though there were times I thought it was her and others swore they saw her as well, in a crowd, on a street, but we must have been mistaken. The only place she surely still lives is in my dreams and I wonder if they might be real. But so much of the past is like a fevered nightmare and then we die and both are gone together, and we are then just a memory which someone will soon forget. But I exist or existed. I know since I leave footprints in the snow and my bed sheets are wrestled in the morning and my pillow indented. So what of that?

In the years that followed I wondered whether she might have been a part of my waking imagination; someone I saw like a vivid walking mirage, lifelike but a phantom, or a spirit wandering the earth whose path crossed ours for reasons I could not explain. Perhaps Reuben still in a fever dreamed of us. Perhaps Joseph created all of us in one of his visions and we wandered the realms of his mind. I think on these things and do not know the answer.

Zephaniah packed quickly, hugged his brother and sister in law; after thirty years they had just one day together and they never saw each other again. He whispered something in Reuben's ear though he was out cold and we left and rode hard for St. Louis to pick up John Brown's trail and leaving Reuben behind to his fate.

Legal Tender

John Brown sat on a stage in Cincinnati, Ohio. He looked on the audience before him; his tired eyes wandered the sea of floating faces. Probing, curious they watched him trying to fathom the depths of the man. All waited patiently for their featured speaker, the General of their cause. They met in a room that served as a church, a court, a town hall, housed a quilting circle and acted as a local meeting place for Bible study. These were dedicated Presbyterians, serious about stopping slavery. They had supplied money for rifles, paid to have them smuggled past Missouri slavers who could hang you with no trial, just shoot you on sight if you carried either human contraband or weapons. These good people paid the way of those brave enough to challenge the laws of avarice and greed.

Brown was nervous. He had only spoken to small groups, ten or twenty at a time, in meager homes, paltry parlors and poorly stocked general stores but his name had grown and his company was much sought after by some, near worshipped by others. Nearly seventy supporters crowded the hall to see this fighter, this actor of divine will. A Franklin stove near the stage drew dewy sweat from John Brown's forehead which rolled down his cheeks to his now bearded chin. He used his jacket cuff to daub it back staining his sleeve darker, his handkerchief was accidently left crumpled and dirty in his satchel. The suit he wore was threadbare and rumpled, much of the cord gone from the corduroy, knees and elbows smooth as parchment. He traveled with few personal items, owned little in the way of dress clothes, certainly nothing fine enough for such an occasion. In fact, even could he afford such things, he thought such adornment vain; he did not seek to own anything appropriate for any occasion. Not while men still rotted in the holds of ships or suffered the lash and shackle. He could not dress in a prideful way or celebrate life in any way while others suffered injustice.

The crowd knew he had gambled everything for this cause and he was honored for his stoic celebrity. His rustic look was exactly what the people expected, even what they wanted. He fit the image they had seen and read about; they were not disappointed.

The opening speaker, a rotund local official whose squeaky voice vibrated his pronouncements in a way course to the ear, was seeking re-election in the fall. He drove his points home hammering his fist on the podium exclaiming this and proclaiming that. The audience tolerated his staccato delivery and declaratory fingers poking the air while they waited patiently to hear from the lips of John Brown a tale of punishment for iniquity, a story of redemption for a sinning nation. When he was finally done, he stepped back from the podium and smoothed his hair and adjusted his coat and looked with deep sincerity at his audience, severe and savoring his last moments of control.

"And now," said the speaker, "without further delay, I give you our honored guest, a man who needs no introduction as words cannot convey the weight nor breadth of his character. Please welcome, ladies and gentleman, a true hero, a man of incalculable worth, a freedom fighter for the enslaved millions, the honorable John Brown."

John Brown rose and moved toward the podium to tell his tale but he was stopped by a loud blast of applause he had not expected. He stood as if a stone wall as ladies, men, and children rose to their feet, their hands frenetically clapping amid rolling rounds of cheers from some, hurrahs from others. He stared around warily amazed and awestruck, waiting a full five minutes as wave after wave of applause and calls of "Bravo" and gusts of "Here, Here", came at him.

When finally the applause calmed someone yelled, "God Bless you, John Brown!"

He looked out and some said he seemed to grow a foot taller, but still he spoke not a word. The audience looked on this solemn man, his eyes glistening with emotion, a man who had given up so much for their cause, his son Frederick dead on the field of battle, his wife and children, his means, his soul. A long silence followed. Uncomfortable rustlings, coughs and cleared throats were all that was heard as the stove blared out a siren of heat. Brown was at a loss, frozen in place by a new revelation. He was hunted, wanted dead or alive in some parts. His family was scattered, his business in ruins. He had sinned, broken a commandment, he had killed, had encouraged others to kill, had helped his sons kill. He had witnessed the death of one of his sons. Now he was here to raise money so he could yet kill more.

His mind wandered back to the cattle drive with his father when he was just a young lad, when he first saw a slave boy whipped to a pulp for laziness, left to sleep in the cold with no blanket and dressed in but shreds of clothes. He had hated slavery from that day forward; even as a boy he knew it to be a plague. He had declared his opposition to it on that trail ride, but waited his whole life to finally pronounce it to the world with his bloody actions.

He was betting with this visit that the money he needed would flow to support him and further his plans for an end to slavery. Tonight was a kind of hunt, a beating of bushes with a speech about life in the territories, his battles, the conditions of slaves. Now he had reached a point of some fame he did not expect. He was used to scraping by, convincing others for his means. But now it was clear to him for the very first time that his message was out, a force was gathering, his plan was unfolding before him. It was within his reach, a certain blessing by God.

His jaw tensed and he took a deep breath as his resolution congealed. He looked at the staring eyes, the empathetic faces of the men and women who waited for some inspiration, some validation of their deepest beliefs and said, "I thank you. I thank God Almighty. He has blessed me. He has called me to act in his cause, to strike as with the power of the total sum of your arms, to strangle the life out of slavery as with the total sum of your hands. I will continue. I move on but only with the total sum of your aid. I am willing to fight on; only money keeps me from returning to the battle."

He paused and looked out at the good people before proceeding to explain the life of a slave, the shackles they wore, the separation of parents, women from husbands, children from mothers, families torn, hearts broken apart. He spoke of the injustice and the cruelty, the fornication and tortures, the punishment and endless unpaid toil.

He spoke of the theft of Kansan's democracy by the Missouri slave supporters, how they had stolen elections, murdered innocence, aborted the constitution in their rabid quest for the spread of slavery. Lastly he spoke of the commitment of those who followed him into the fight. He spoke of his battles, the death of his son and the lost soldiers, as well as the seething opposition he faced from those ill tempered devils seeking to save their enriching bastard called bondage. He was simple, sincere, authentic, true.

When he had finished his speech, when the tempest in his soul had spread out across the gathering like a blessed plague lashing them with the turbulence he called up like Prospero, plates were passed from person to person, row to row, plates which overflowed with legal tender, espousing 'In God We Trust.' It was a large collection, a good response, solid support. He could now get to Boston where greater sums could be found. He could now afford to make a down payment on the guns, supplies, ammunition, and the pikes, implements designed by him, long poles with Bowie knives attached at the end, perfect for the slave untutored in the arts of war but ready to be led, to be used in the rebellion he would start. God had blessed him once again. This convinced him further he was on the right path.

In his room that night he read from Isaiah:

Behold I am laying in Zion a foundation, a stone, a tested stone,
a precious cornerstone, of a sure foundation:
he who believes, will not be in haste.
And I will make justice the line,
and righteousness the plummet;
and hail will sweep away the refuge of lies,
and waters will overwhelm the shelter.

Then your covenant with death will be annulled,
and your agreement with Sheol will not stand;
when the overwhelming scourge passes through you will be beaten down by it.
As often as it passes through it will take you;
for morning by morning it will pass through,
by day and by night;
and it will be sheer terror to understand the message.
For the bed is too short to stretch oneself on it,
and the covering too narrow to wrap oneself in it.
For the Lord will rise up as on Mount Perazim,
He will be wroth as in the valley of Gibeon;
to do his deed – strange is his deed!
And to work his work – alien is his work!
Now therefore do not scoff,
lest your bonds be made strong;
for I have heard a decree of destruction
from the Lord of Hosts upon the whole land.

Look to Beersheba

The road to St. Louis went by in a two day blur of foaming flanks and featureless land and heavy lidded sleeplessness and horses worn, their flashing eyes grown dull and bloodshot, their gaping nostrils struggling for sweet cold air. We rode on. Zephaniah would hear nothing of slowing down. He pushed and drove us harder and harder. We stopped to water the horses briefly at a brook of no consequence and as we sat looking at our feet considering our fatigue, Beersheba just fell over dead.

Zephaniah limped over, fell to his knees beside his lathered lifeless horse. He was visibly distraught, aware surely that he had killed this regal creature with his drive. I thought perhaps his until-now concealed emotion finally flowed out over his horse, leaving his home and his wives and abandoning his son Reuben had taken some toll, surely this was the proof. But it was a horse, and a fine one for sure, that finally reached into him and pulled out a softness for something in this worldly existence and broke his focus on God and God only.

His sons whispered among themselves: they knew this would happen. They knew it. They never wanted to leave Reuben, but they had listened. They did not want to leave home, but they had followed as they always had without question. They looked at their prone father mourning his horse and knew he had said not a word about the plight of their mothers or their brother. He had never showed such emotion for them, for Diana. There was a rumor of new found doubt in their eyes and hints of questions in their whisper's tone. Diana was silent and kept to herself, cold, alone among men, pregnant; her woman's intuition told her Beersheba's death was the talisman of things to come.

Zephaniah prayed over the horse asking for God to take her beautiful soul. Then he took his saddle off Beersheba, strapped it onto back of Joseph's saddle and told us to mount up, which we did. He climbed on to Levi's horse and helped Levi up behind him. I saw the look of doubt pass among the boys and Diana. But they would obey; it was the only way they knew. It was at this time I think I saw the fabric of this family begin to pull apart.

We rode on, hard as ever with no words said about the motionless body of Beersheba, as if she had never existed, whose fine spirit now wandered green pastures beside still waters. We rode on, across the expanse leading to the city and into St. Louis.

When we finally entered the city limits we followed Zephaniah up Walnut Street and tied up in front of the Barnum Hotel. Zephaniah dismounted and limped straight into the lobby, looking about as if Brown might still be there, but he was disappointed.

The Negro porter approached him and said, "Can Ise assis you with yo bag, sah?"

"I have no bags boy. Just show me to your clerk."

"Heze gone right now, sah," said the porter.

Zephaniah frustrated at this answer asked, "Were you here when the murders happened?"

"Murders? Lotsa murders here, too many guns."

"Is this the hotel where the bags of John Brown were left?"

"I doan know dat sah," said the porter with doubt in his wide eyes.

"Do you know if a man left his bags?"

"Oh yez sah, yez," said the porter glad to be able to answer in the affirmative.

Zephaniah stared at him, calmly reached across and grabbed his spotted red lapels, pulling him in close he said in a slow sinister voice, "Don't lie to me, boy."

"It happen, tings get loss."

"Tell me what happened?" said Zephaniah emphasizing each word.

The porter visibly nervous answered, "Man and lady check in, lef in da night, lef his bags, Sheriff come here, took da bags."

"Were there books left in the bags," asked Zephaniah his interest peaked.

"I don't know. Ise just a poor black porter, no buddy tells me nuthin."

"Where is the Sheriff's office?" asked Zephaniah letting him go.

"Rightchere on dis street, up some, thataway," he said pointing to the place.

Zephaniah limped out of the hotel and said nothing. He turned left and walked up the street, his boots striking the boards like a ticking clock. We walked along too, keeping to our horses, cooling them, looking at their streaked eyes to get a sense of how they felt, concerned for them. He strode into the Sheriff's office and waited in front of his broad oaken desk.

The Sheriff looked up from his papers and considered the man. Without a word the Sheriff rose and walked out to stand opposite Zephaniah, sizing him up. We could see them talking through the paned glass window. They talked for some time, Zephaniah probing, thinking some, then questioning some more.

The sheriff, tentative with this stranger, looked at him with puzzled suspicion. Down the street near the docks a steam whistle from a paddle wheeler squealed a shrill demand as Zephaniah came out of the office.

Once again he said nothing to us. He limped back down the street tick-tocking the boards straight to the livery and we settled the horses. Then we walked back to the hotel. We checked in and each signed the register for the first time in their lives. We had three rooms for the men with the eldest getting the beds and one for Diana. The cost, five dollars, was expensive by all calculations. But dinner, a clean room and a soft bed was well worth it to me. I would have paid anything after the ordeal of riding so far.

At dinner we learned from a newspaper the good news of more border crossings between Kansas and Missouri by Law and Order men. They were pro slavery heroes to us, scaring more Godless scum to repent from seeking to change God's will. We heard of small battles with abolitionist sympathizers in Lawrence. We heard about killings by abolitionists copying Brown. Homesteads had been burned. There were murders, rapes.

When dinner was over Zephaniah stood and said, "The Sheriff said Brown was not here. He would confirm nothing. There is no bag, no book, no notes, says he. But I know Brown was here. Joseph is right. I know it. Let us pray."

We all bowed our heads and he said, "Lord we thank you for your blessings, for the will to continue on this journey. We ask you Lord to give us strength to carry on, to complete your mission. Let us find John Brown and stop this war and save thousands from a bloody death, preserving our nation; preserving the ways you taught us in your Holy book. Show us the way Lord. Show us the way. Amen."

That night as we slept Joseph had a dream that it can only be said terrorized him. His bed was soaked with sweat. His flushed skin pinked deeper as jumbled fearful words poured out. Finally he sat up and yelled aloud a cry no boy should make. He was terrified and shaking like he was freezing. We heard him yell and stumbled from our cavernous slumber, soundly exhausted from our long ride, and we ran to him like we were knee deep in mud. Zephaniah ran in and looked on Joseph with an eye of caution. He knew right away he had dreamed something terrible. So he told us all to leave and he closed the door and stayed with Joseph for some time.

We could hear Joseph's muffled cries and the hum of Zephaniah's soothing words garbled through the simple pine door. We could not make him out, except once Zephaniah said, "My God." but that was all we could get. Our weary senses were doused with acid speculation and raw they burned with each hum and whisper beyond the door. We looked at each other, afraid to say what might have happened.

Eventually Zephaniah came to the door. Drawn and sallow skinned, he let us in. He looked on us and sat down with forlorn resignation on the bed near the wan, spent body of Joseph. We waited while our thoughts and fear of disaster permeated the air.

He hung his head and said to the floor boards, "Calamity has befallen our home. Evil has walked on our sacred ground."

Then there was silence, a long pause, and he looked up at us with pleading eyes saying, "I cannot say what has happened. I simply cannot."

"What is it?" asked Simeon, his ire rising.

"Tell us," said Diana.

"I cannot," said Zephaniah, confused, emotional, eyes downcast once again.

"Tell us, we have followed you on this mission, now tell us, we deserve to know," said Dan.

There was another long silence until Zephaniah rose and walked to the window. Then gathering courage he turned to us and said slowly, looking from face to face, "Joseph had a terrible vision. Men came to our farm, abolitionists; they stole away Buela and Hanna. They are gone, forever. They burned our farm. Ben. Ben is dead, he died in the fire. Esther has gone to God too."

We stood with unblinking eye, every muscle tensed; this moment was permanently etched on us like an ancient rune, pain's carved letters blotting out whatever signs of joy we had ever known.

He continued, "Rachel, she is alive but Joseph cannot say what happened to her."

My sinking heart rose at this news of Rachel. I looked at Joseph and thought of his terrible night visions but leapt at this last hope. The specters of pain and the suffering of loved ones, these rude violations, which littered Joseph's young thoughts, transformed him, aged him, sucked out whatever spirit of boyhood remained in him. I looked at his small form in the sweat soaked nightshirt which stuck to his crooked back and at his hair pushed back off his forehead and his hands trembling still and his screwed up brow and crimped mouth drawn shut by the taught strings of his mind—signaling his belief in his dream, in his words— and I dared to hope Rachel might be alive. His unquestioned dream brought both hell and redemption to me in its message.

Simeon, Levi, Judah, Isachar, Zebulan, Diana, all looked lost. Their lights had been extinguished by the news of Esther, Ben, Buela, Hanna, by their worry for Rachel. Just today their mothers and brother wandered their imaginations alive, preparing food, working, laughing. But now they were cold, dead, even buried. The family wanted to flee, ride west, right away, home, to their core, their warmth, their life spring.

"I must think," said Zephaniah his eyes betraying his anguish. "Go to your rooms. Try to sleep. I will make a decision in the morning."

Hollow, remote, spent, they all went to their sleeping places to await their father's decision.

It was a slow night of restlessness, thoughts racing between tosses and turns, imaginations free to run, worries building walls holding off rest. It was a mostly sleepless night, even to sleep seemed to be awake, the tension and fear was so palpable. Tears flowed even as we slept. All visited a place none had been to, carried there by a horse called Grief.

I opened the Bible to the place I went for comfort and read Psalm 23 about walking in the valley of the shadow of death, fearing no evil. How could that be so if you were being murdered?

The next morning before the sun, when the day was just a dark blue rim on the horizon, we met over breakfast. No one had a word to say. All talk seemed useless, ridiculous, frivolous. Joseph was so trusted in his foretelling that all had believed immediately. There was no doubt. Decisions were based on his dreams; we traveled because of his visions; we mourned due to his nightmare.

Zephaniah looking pale and weak from sleeplessness spoke, "We will continue after Brown. Finish eating. Mount up."

There was quiet all around, no comments, no answers, no words. Unspoken thoughts collided in the air; the tension was sensed by all. There was a clamor of silence muted by Simeon who stood and walked to Zephaniah. He stared him straight in the eye showing he would not be dominated and said, "No Father."

This had never happened before. The words "No Father" had never been said. 'No Father' was never an answer to anything. They all looked on in total awe. An awareness dawned of a dangerous new relationship, an uncomfortable feeling bristling with rebellion filled the air. Their entire lives Zephaniah's words were law, as if written in tablets by God. But now something had changed. Tragedy had intervened. God had always ruled their hearts, if not because they feared the deity then because they feared Zephaniah. But in the night, in Joseph's terrible vision, the question was raised: follow God, follow their instincts or follow their father?

Simeon said, "Father, God is telling us to return home, this is the meaning of Joseph's dream."

"No son, this is the devil putting fear in your hearts, trying to keep you from finishing this quest. What has happened has happened. You cannot change that. We have been called to this mission to hang John Brown, we must go on," argued Zephaniah.

"Father, why is Joseph's dream only understood by you? Doesn't God speak to all of us?" asked Diana.

"He does, you know He does, I have always said so," said Zephaniah.

Simeon looked around and moved to the center speaking to his brothers and sister saying, "Our mother and Ben are dead. Buela and Hanna are stolen. Rachel might still be in danger. Our home is in ruins. That speaks to me. I am not sure if it is God or not but I am going back. Anyone who wants to follow me, follow." And Simeon walked out.

The others looked at each other. Until one by one they walked out. Only Joseph stayed, still stunned silent by the violent dream he'd had about his mother, the things he'd witnessed as if he were there. Then Joseph stood, walked over, pulled his father down to his height by the arm and kissed him on the cheek. He then walked out the door quitting the mission, forgetting his vision of Brown, leaving his father, following his brothers, heading home to mourn his dead.

I quietly sat waiting. I wanted to return and save beautiful Rachel. But I also wanted to get Brown. I had not come this far to quit. By all rights Zephaniah should have been on a horse riding home harder even than he rode to death poor Beersheba. But he stood firm, his course was set by God. Nothing could break his will or deter this quest. Hardships sent by the devil would not keep this warrior from buckling on his sword. He did not show anything; he absorbed these blows like a grizzled prize fighter. I knew there was a deep hurt, struck black and blue with fists of fatherly failure. His family would not follow him, it had fragmented and the devil was laughing. So though part of my heart wanted to go back, I did not have the heart not to go forward.

I had gone along as Zephaniah stubbornly followed the meaning of his dream. He was single minded, almost in a way not human, intensely driven. I was drawn by such a force, such a will, I don't know why but I could not leave him.

The family mounted up and did not look back once. They rode west whence we had come. We watched them go until they turned the corner to the river. And then Zephaniah and I rode east, continuing the journey in silence, burdened by heavy thoughts of the suffering at the homestead, of Esther and Ben dead.

As we rode he said, "They raped Esther and then they stabbed her. Ben slept through it all. He died in the fire and knew nothing of their pain. Rachel, too, was raped I think, Joseph could not say it aloud, but I think she lives. I will hang John Brown as God has willed. Then I will find the tormentors of my wives. And I will kill them."

Two days later, as the family rode homeward, Zebulan could not control his desire for the sea. He knew water was somehow in his destiny, he knew it as he knew his name. He was pulled to it as a moth to a candle and now that he had seen the splendor of the Missouri it was irresistible. The great river spoke to him and its undulating voice told him the sea was his home. He simply had to go to it, to see it, to touch it, even though he knew he should go to his terrestrial home. He left his brothers, getting on a river boat outside of Jackson. He said he would travel down the Mississippi to the Gulf, wander the shores of Florida, up the east coast or perhaps catch a ship to the islands. He did not know anything for sure only that he was passionately drawn to the sea. This he knew.

Forgiveness

R achel cooked over the open fire singing bits of a Christmas Carol as she prepared their meal.

"What Child is this who laid to rest, on Mary's lap is sleeping?
Whom angels greet with anthems sweet, while shepherds watch are keeping?
This, this is Christ the king, whom shepherds guard and angels sing.
Haste, haste to bring him laud, the babe, the son of Mary."

She stirred and sang and smiled peacefully. Esther, she and Ben had fared well these months. They had worked extra hard with the men gone. There was a good harvest of corn, they gathered as much as they could, set some aside for feed and ground up the rest for meal at Snyder's Mill. They had put up preserves of berries picked in August, slaughtered a bull then smoked the hind quarters, boiled the head, made head cheese, burned the heart in the fire to God, boiled the bones for the marrow and the gelatin, stretched the hide to repair shoes and make a coat. They had wasted nothing.

She now stirred a stew of beef, potatoes, corn and cream. Esther sat sewing. Feeling her way along a seam she winced as she stabbed her finger, her poor eyes of little use in this task. Ben slept in the loft, tired from digging a new well, off to the side of the house as it seemed drought was coming on. Buela and Hanna were in their cabin.

There was a knock on the door and Esther looked up. Rachel, staring into the embers, deep in prayer, deep in thought, turned her head at the sound. It was strange for anyone to come to their door. Rachel could not recall the last time she had heard a knock on the door and a caller had crossed their threshold to visit. Her first thought was how nice it was for a caller to come so near Christmas, but that thought dropped and knotted in her stomach as a voice she could not trust called out, "You in there, we're passing through, we need some directions, step outside, we want to talk."

Esther squinted and looked around alarmed. Eyes fluttering, she dropped her sewing, stepped up and felt the hearth's corner for the rifle. Finding the warm metal barrel she took it up, familiarly checked the charge, loaded a ball. Rachel rose, touched Esther's arm to calm her, to tell her she would manage this. So Esther stood behind the door, gun in hand.

Rachel stepped to the window, pulled aside the linen curtain and peered out. In the dark she could make out three men, rifles in hand, but she not see any definition nor recognize them, only their outline and the shadow of faces beneath their brims. They were bearded, grim and threw off an evil energy. The fourth knocked again at the door and the voice came calling, "Step out, help us good neighbor, we mean you no harm."

Rachel whispered to Esther to keep the gun down. She turned the door latch and stepped out on to the porch, confident and friendly and said, "Good evening. How may I help you?"

"Where's your men folk?" the leader said, a lean pointy nosed man with a wart on his cheek.

"They are to be back any time," she lied, "they rode to the woods yonder after some quail crossed our field."

"How long ago?" he asked acting curious.

"Perhaps an hour, I heard some shots I expect they caught one and will return shortly," she said in a friendly voice.

"You're a liar, we been watching you from the trees. Ain't been a man here all day," he sneered.

Rachel stood calmly. They had not mentioned Ben; perhaps they had not seen him.

She took a deep breath and said, "My sister and I are alone, you are right, sir. I am sorry I lied. We will be happy to help you, what is it you need to know?"

The men looked around at each other and smiled a bit with their eyes. "Need to know? Well pretty woman, what we need is for the fat one to come outside. Now! Or I am going to blow the brains from that little squaw head," he said as he pulled out his pistol and moved quickly toward her.

Rachel's mind raced, she wanted to protect Ben and move this encounter to a peaceful ending. Calmly, sweetly she said, "Esther dear, come outside. These gentlemen want to meet you."

Esther stepped to the door, propping the rifle inside the door jamb within easy reach. She then stepped into view in the doorway, her arm just inches from the gun.

"She's even fatter close up," said one of them.

"You're a slave holder. That's a crime against God. We're here to take away your slaves, to free them as God intended, set them on their way north. You're days of living off the sweat of others have come to an end," announced the leader.

Rachel, unable to keep from her voice the fear welling in her throat, said in a pleading tone, "The women are our friends, we love them, they love us, we have been together for so long."

"Step down to the ground, off the porch, both of you," ordered the leader.

Rachel looked to Esther knowing she did not want to leave the gun. Rachel worried that if shooting were to commence there was no telling who would be left standing. Ben could be killed, all of them could be. Rachel took Esther's hand, pulled her gently as she stalled, digging in, not wanting to leave the security of the gun behind. They both stepped hand in hand from the porch to the ground.

"Get over to the barn," the man commanded.

The women walked ahead of the four men who chuckled and prodded at them. "She's a beauty this one, this one she's a hog, look at how she does jiggle," said a toothless man whose lips puckered when he closed his mouth, whose brown gums were the only color in his smile. He then reached in front and grabbed Esther's breast and said with a cackle, "It's a soft feather bed, this one is."

Esther jumped away, pushing his hand. She started to wheeze, a heavy nervous breathing that could not keep up with her racing heart. Rachel was moved to panic as the situation seemed to get out of control.

They entered the barn and the leader said pointing to a horse stall, "Stand over there."

They walked across, turned and faced the men.

"Now strip," he ordered.

"You do not need to do this. We are good women; do not do us this dishonor," Rachel said as her fear broke to the surface.

"This is not going to be dishonor, this is going to be subjugation. You're going to see what it's like to be a slave, to be sold, to be used like an animal. Now strip," he commanded again.

Rachel said trying to save her sister, "I am the more beautiful, let my sister go, she is fat and blind, nothing men such as yourselves would want. Take me."

The leader walked across and slapped Rachel hard across the face, grabbed Esther's dress, roughly tore it open in the front, chaffing her neck, exposing her sagging breasts.

"Now strip or I will shoot you dead on the spot," he said as he put the pistol to Rachel's head.

The men chuckled in excitement at Esther's nakedness. Esther started to cry but Rachel stood firm, tilted her head, closed her eyes and began to undress. With each nervous unbuttoning of her dress the men's attention grew, they stepped closer. Esther, sorrowful at her fate, worked at getting the remnants of cloth off of her. She stood naked first, arms crossed on her chest, breasts contained, womanhood hidden beneath folds of fat. Her patched button boots the only thing left on her.

Rachel's dress dropped to the ground and she stepped out of it. Then she resignedly pulled off her undergarments and stood also with nothing on but her shoes. The men laughed at Esther but stared in wonder at Rachel.

The leader put his pistol in his holster, saw Rachel's birthmark extending from her face to her breast and then he grabbed the purple stained breast and squeezed it hard, not a caress but a clamp that was meant to hurt, pulling her towards him. Rachel winced.

He said, "Well look here, a purple teat and a red teat, now there's a sight. Does that hurt you squaw? What's this teat worth? Is the red one more then the purple one. You're an expert at buying colored flesh, what's purple flesh worth?"

Rachel was silent.

"What do think it's worth boys?" he called to his men.

"Well hers are worth two bits each," said the younger one, who looked scared but aroused.

"Maybe three for the purple one," said the toothless man.

The other spoke with a German accent and said, "This hog here ought to charge by the pound, she'd be expensive. But for this fatty, I won't pay but a penny a teat."

"What's your name?" the leader whispered to Rachel.

"Rachel," she whispered back hoping her tone might save her.

He said wistfully, "Rachel, like Jacobs wife in the Bible, she was a whore too. Jacob traded her for his safety, didn't he?" Then he prodded her breast with his pistol and continued, "I estimate you're worth more than your sister. Now that's five bits for your teats to her two penny teats. So I think I'm going to save you for last."

He nodded to the other men who sprang like fleas to a cur toward Esther. They swarmed around her, grabbing her, slapping her fat, kissing her neck. She groaned and said, "No," over and over. They pulled her lumpy body to the dirt; the young one held her arms over her head, the German pulled her legs apart while the toothless one started prodding between her legs with his dirty hands.

Rachel did not want to see but the leader turned her head and smacked her face hard. He then tongued her, neck to cheek across her purple birthmark.

The toothless one dropped his trousers and climbed on top of Esther, who was breathing so heavy from fear she might have passed out. He entered her, started pumping away, leaning on her arms pinned above her. The young one was grabbing her breasts while the toothless one was arching, grunting, thrusting. The German at her legs looked on with a sick expression, a smiling sneer, trancelike.

Rachel's spirit melted at the sight of her poor sister. The toothless one had his pleasure then changed places with the German who pushed aside the young one.

The leader put his hand between Rachel's legs. She resisted, holding her legs together, so he roughly drove his gun between them. She gasped as he said fiercely, "Open up, you purple teated bitch."

Rachel stood legs apart and he removed the pistol. Then he put his hand in its place, ramming his fingers inside her. This kept him busy while the others finished with Esther.

Then with violence and lust in his voice the leader said, "Lay down."

And as Rachel sat down on the hay he undid his pants. She begged him not to. He kneeled down and tried to force her legs part but she resisted, so he slapped her twice with the fore and back of his hand and she laid down and submitted.

She looked at the ceiling while he entered her and worked away. She looked around the barn, focusing on farm implements, a harness, piles of hay, the mute animals, then she saw Esther, saw the knife in the hand of the toothless one, saw it plunged into her chest, saw the life run out of her onto the ground.

The leader finished and got off Rachel and noticed the bloody mess that was Esther, blood trickling among the fat layers. "Now what did you do that for? This was for some fun, not to kill them. Now get, get. You two head out back, get the slaves. Joshua you burn it all, everything. And you," he said to Rachel, "if you ever own another slave or if you ever tell anyone about this, I'll be back for you. I swear by God, it'll be your day of reckoning." And they left the barn and walked across the field.

Rachel lay there numb. She heard some arguing from Buela and heard Hanna scream. Orders of some kind were shouted. She knew her women did not want to leave, that they were at home. They'd had children and this was where they lived.

The German stood over the cemetery pouring forth his stream of hot piss on the stones marking the graves. He yelled, "I piss on your ancestors," as the house started to burn and crackling flames poured out the broken window.

A feeling of dread came over Rachel and she rose and ran naked from the barn past the torch wielding man, who threw his flaming club into the stall with the horses. The barn caught fire as if doused with animal fat. Rachel ran to the house but it had quickly become engulfed in flames. Above the whinny of the horses and the moaning of the cow she yelled frantically, "Ben, Oh God, save my Ben."

She tried to pull the front door open but flames shot out like a stove starved for air. Her hair afire she ran about helter-skelter striking her palms to her head to put out the flames. She ran to the horse trough and plunged her head in. Then she came up and fell to her knees. Her arms raised she cried to the universe, cried to God, asking why she was being punished so.

The men put Buela and Hanna on a horse together, then mounted themselves. They laughed at the sight of a naked woman running around in the firelight in her shoes. Buela and Hanna looked on, tears streaking down their black faces. Then the men rode off into the night taking Buela and Hanna away forever.

Rachel lay in a trance for a time until the waning light from her burning home subsided, when the chill spoke to her louder than her grief. She walked past the remnants of the barn to the slave quarters, found some clothes of Hanna's which she put on, tied a rag around her painfully burned head, over her remaining uneven and disheveled hair. And she fell onto a bed and stared at the black ceiling.

In a few hours she rose. It was near midnight she thought, unsure why time even mattered to her. She laughed to herself at the absurdity of caring and knew her life had changed forever. But then a thought, a mission reached out to her, pulling her magnetically to stagger from the slave house.

In the smoldering pile of the house and the barn the remains of her Esther and Ben lie blackened and charred; only her heart felt blacker. She tiptoed around the hot embers to find them and she looked at her loss for a while, her flesh, her bone mingled before her eyes with dirt and ash, reduced to debris. She went to the cemetery and found a flat stone and scraped a single hole to inter them together, to bed their remains for all eternity near their ancestors. Then she gathered their seared bones and the muck that was their fluids in a bucket, taking several trips to carry each of them to the cemetery. Bucket by bucket she carried them over and poured them into the shallow hole. She buried them, pressing the damp earth as neatly as she could, putting some order to the sacred soil like a crying child devoted to her creation in the dirt.

Then she prayed, crying but thanking God for the gift of these two people who had been so important in her life. She kneeled dressed in her slave clothes, praising God, crying aloud, singing with a whimper in her voice:

Praise God from whom all blessing flow
Praise him all creatures here below
Praise him above ye heavenly host
Praise Father Son and Holy Ghost.

She walked forlornly back to the slave cabin and fell in an exhausted heap on Hanna's bed.

Secret Six

John Brown waited in a red velvet chair, plush and comfortably soft but too straight in the back and too low to the floor. His knees sticking up, his hands folded, he practiced words he had said many times in preparation for this meeting. He felt like a child again waiting to see his terse grandfather, to explain himself, to say his piece about his sin, to confess to an angry God. But this was to be no confession; this was to be a revelation.

When he arrived from his long journey from Kansas, he was aware his tattered clothes, dirty hands and odor would offend these city folks. He was sure they would send him away thinking him a vagrant. So he stayed in a tawdry room over an oyster house near the docks, bought a bath but had no money for new clothes. He washed his old suit in a basin, two times, let it dry, wrinkled but clean.

At the correct time he walked up the cobbled street past Fanuiel Hall, past the red brick State House to a stately townhouse atop Beacon Hill. From the rise of the hill Brown could see in all directions. The air was cool coming off the harbor. Ships sailed boldly, gleefully, some sat at anchor, a few at the wharves unloaded goods with paid white labor, another sat a burned hulk in the harbor, still smoking, set ablaze by an unknown arsonist who was aware the ship carried other cargo at times, black skinned cargo, chained together, vomiting, dying in their own waste. He smiled at this sight.

To the west a few skiffs crossed the Charles to Cambridge. Up river, Harvard's steeple stabbed the sky, landmark for a mountain of thought, for the new religion, Unitarianism. The cemetery down the hill held the body of the patriot Paul Revere, the rider with a message of war to come, a message now to be delivered by Brown to these astute and wealthy Americans for those not yet enjoying freedom.

A sour faced butler leaned over formally and said, "Mr. Higginson will see you now."

Brown was shown through elaborately carved double doors with bas relief of American patriotism; Washington set in mahogany, a scene of Valley Forge with frozen, wounded, ragged soldiers, sufferers, martyrs for freedom for all mankind.

Into a room of exceptional taste, of such garish expense he felt awe at the incredibly frivolous luxuriousness of it, walked John Brown, to seven men who rose from various chairs around an antique table of the Art Nouveau style of France.

They crossed the carpet to shake his hand. Brown was a little nervous but not afraid, just somewhat unsure of himself in such society, a common rustic, dressed as such, more at home on the range or in a battle or preaching against slavery than in and among the niceties of the upper crust.

The first who spoke, a man with long hair, a mustache and sorrowful eyes said sincerely, "Mr. Brown, it is so good to finally meet you; I am Thomas Wentworth Higginson at your service."

"Of course, you know Mr. Sanborn," he said with a gesture to the man. It was Sanborn who Brown had gone to first. He had arrived at Sanborn's office in Boston many months later then his telegram indicated, delayed with his illness. It was Sanborn who arranged this gathering.

The next to speak wore a strange beard on only his throat. His face was homely and his expression far off as he finally focused on Brown saying, "Mr. Brown, I consider this a distinct privilege. I am Henry David Thoreau. Thank you for all you have done for our cause. You will go down in history, sir. I hope you do not have to become a martyr to become a saint. For you surely are a saint to millions in bondage. Many want to crucify you, but they are the Pontius Pilots, washing their hands of this scourge of slavery."

"Mr. Brown," said a small man with a very long curling beard, "I am George Luther Stearns. I am an admirer. I support you sir."

The next said, "Gerrit Smith." He was an aged and wealthy merchant, bald headed, with a voluminous gray beard which parted in the middle as he gave a brisk bow. "Very pleased to see you. I trust your wife fares well on the farm in North Elba,"

"Yes sir, your kindness in giving us that land is greatly appreciated. I am in your debt," said Brown with respect.

"Nonsense, we are in your debt sir," the older man replied with a chiding tone.

Brown said honestly, "You have done much Mr. Smith. The land you gave, thousands of acres to the runaways, was very kind."

"Thank you Brown. If only they could have fared better. I forgot to consider their lack of skills; farming is difficult in such a climate. It is a hard place. I am sorry to say it is largely a failure," confessed the spry old man.

"But the Underground Railroad ends in your town sir, that says much," said Brown with some intensity.

"It does, it does indeed, and it will continue to do so until all four million are free. Hence we must stand our ground in Kansas. You have drawn the line sir. Bravo!" said Smith.

Thomas Wentworth Higginson introduced him next saying, "John Brown, please meet the Reverend Theodore Parker."

"You have done our cause a great service. I hope to get more details, I am writing a piece on you," said the bald Reverend Parker who glared at Brown with dark sparkling eyes beneath a large forehead and deeply furrowed brow.

"Of course, Reverend," answered Brown. "I read something you wrote some time ago. It bolstered me much in my convictions," said Brown though he could not remember the name of the piece.

"I am so glad to hear that Mr. Brown. It did so for many. It also caused me much grief, not to mention my church position. 'To a Southern Slaveholder' it was titled, made a tempest for a while," said the Parker with a small laugh, rubbing his shiny dome.

"There is a large Negro congregation waiting for you, sir," Brown said warmly.

"Thank you Mr. Brown. I am afraid however my ideas about God, the Bible and its inaccuracies, the contradictions, the outright mistakes have closed all the pulpits in this city to me and cost me many a friendship as well," said Parker unaware of Brown's beliefs.

There was an uncomfortable silence in the room.

Brown looked at Parker for some time and then he said, "You believe in God, that is enough for me." He decided this was not a time to discuss religious interpretation.

Higginson then showed him to Dr. Samuel Gridley Howe saying, "Mr. Brown, meet Dr. Samuel Howe."

Howe, a newspaper editor, reached across with inked fingers and said, "I am receiving many letters in support of you, sir. Rest assured the editorial page of the Daily Commonwealth rings with your praise as it exposes the nakedness of slavery. I would like for you to sit for a picture. Let the people see you as you are, rather than that terrible ink drawing circulating."

Brown responded practically, "I would rather not have my likeness known to so many just yet. Fame will hinder me, I am afraid."

"I see, perhaps you are right, shall we sit then?" Howe said.

Brown waited while these titans took their seats, not wanting to assume a place among these great men. He stood holding his hat, lacking confidence amid such wealth and education; the wrinkled worn man, dulled by weather, by cares, by large ideas and no means, waited. He was not long idle for once the subject of slavery arose it was as if the world stopped for him, his cares evaporated.

"Please sit Mr. Brown," said Higginson.

"I think I would rather stand," Brown said quietly.

"As you wish," said Higginson.

George Luther Stearns asked, "Are the accounts correct we read of the fight in Kansas?"

Brown spoke calmly avoiding a direct answer, "I have read but a few, they are largely correct in the North. Those in the slave states are another thing altogether, they are full of lies."

Stearns followed with his true question, "Did you, Brown, kill the settlers or did members of your force?"

Brown stood still, not wanting to lie, not wanting to condemn himself or anyone. He wanted to trust these men; their lives were dedicated to the same cause. Stearns had sent much money and guns to abolitionist settlers. Higginson was head of the New England Emigrant Aid Company; he had spent a night in jail after trying to free a fugitive slave named Anthony Burns. Howe's newspaper was a beacon of abolitionist opinion. His wife Julia Ward Howe, a poet and strong anti slavery voice, would soon pen a song about Brown. Gerrit Smith, a wealthy philanthropist, unafraid of any consequences, perhaps brave due to financial power and political connections, was stalwart in his support of abolition. Reverend Parker had donated much money, preached the word of freedom for blacks all over New England. Franklin Sanborn as Secretary of the Massachusetts State Kansas Committee, formed to support the anti-slavery settlers in Kansas, had been a fighter for the cause for some time.

Henry David Thoreau was a philosopher of the day, a leading Transcendentalist, a compatriot of Ralph Waldo Emerson, whom Brown wanted to meet. These thinkers wrote words pondered by a generation, illuminating the status of man as both a spiritual being and an animal of some curiosity.

Brown said instead, "Let me tell you of the place."

And then he told them of the realities of the situation in Kansas. He brought to life what they had been pondering from afar. As he spoke they listened raptly as all of the stories in the press, all of the evils they were against, were brought to life by this tired, worn, corduroy suited fighter, fresh from the frontiers of freedom, an authentic Puritan warrior, an epic character, powerful, vengeful, and yet serene in his demeanor.

"And so sirs," Brown finished. "You can see it does not matter who has killed for until this battle is over, for it to be over, all must either kill or support the killing. So we all carry the sword. Congress will not act, hampered by the need to compromise. Laws cannot respond, those who vote pollute the outcome. Gentleman, I need to go back to Kansas. I will act for the paralyzed politicians. I will free more slaves, add fuel to this righteous fire, this fire that must burn. I must bring pure desolation before the hearts of the slave lovers will change."

And then he said plainly, "I need more money."

No one answered. There was silence in the room until Thoreau stood.

"I support you, John Brown. I will write about you, speak for you, for our cause.

I am not a man of money but one of thoughts, of words. I once wrote of civil disobedience.

"I have heard of it," said Brown, and they all laughed breaking the tense spell in the room that was as thick as the cigar smoke circling their heads, wafting near the ceiling like a celestial halo.

Thoreau continued, "Yes, yes, this slavery scourge means we are not yet civil. We must disobey until it is slain. We must act. I will make sure your cause is known."

They shook hands warmly as Thoreau said, "I must take your leave sir, but I must request an audience at a later date before you depart."

Brown agreed wordlessly. And Henry David Thoreau left the room.

Gerrit Smith stood up and said, "You will have my support."

And around the room was heard, "And mine."

" And mine."

" And mine."

" I am with you."

" As am I."

Brown's elation showed only with a deep glow in his blue eyes. His mind was swirling with great ideas now closer to reality, with the severed fetters of the oppressed. This group of six, this secret six, were joined together to finance him, John Brown, the abolitionist warrior, leader of God's army, he knew they were now blood brothers in his cause. The circle widened with these men of worth and influence. They were his assurance that he was going back to Kansas to kill again. Then with success as his collateral, he would reveal to them his ultimate plan and obtain his due.

Cold Morning

I n the morning Rachel awoke with crushing remembrance weighing mercilessly on her. A powerful grief ripped at her insides as if she entombed a hungry beast in her belly. A bright milky white sun showed it to be mid morning and the incongruence of a bird's song outside the cabin only highlighted her pain. She felt totally alone and miserable, a moral filth had seeped down to the very depths of her soul. Her first thought was to open Hanna's Bible. She opened to the Song of Solomon, Chapter 7 and read:

> *How graceful are your feet in sandals,*
> *Oh queenly maiden,*

But tears came to her eyes blurring her vision and she could read no more. She was numb. She could feel nothing; the night before seemed a dream. As she rose she kept her head down not wanting to look about, rejecting the sight as a way to avoid the reality. But she was drawn like a spirit to the cemetery. She just had to look on the new grave she'd made the night before. She knelt gently by it and could smell the burnt sweetness of body's inches below the surface.

Esther was dead. Ben was dead. She was alone. Rachel felt like a shell, empty inside, brittle brained from painful thoughts, worries about family or future brought a dull ache to her head, the nausea of complete despair grew in her stomach, loss over loss, pain over pain. She had to stop when visions of her sister, of her son, flooded her mind. Then the tears poured forth, unstoppable, anguished gushes from thoughts too real, too strong to contain in the small cavity of her head, needing to push out, contorting her face, collapsing her knees, convulsing her body. She had never experienced such overwhelming grief which took control of her muscles, her instincts, her mind.

That first day and several to follow were a blur. She could not eat, had not much of anything to consume anyway, but she did not care. She was without sensation. She could not feel anything until a thought formed that led her down a lonely path of thoughts, which led to a river of pain, dammed up, needing release. And her soul could not hold back the waters of grief. They flooded over her body for a time until it passed, drained away, taking with it some of her spirit.

She finished each grief episode with thanks to God though. She knew God tested us in ways we could not comprehend. She had never been tested so before, though she knew others who had. She knew the men who took Buela and Hanna, who killed Esther and Ben, who raped her, had also tortured and killed others, or that others like them had. She knew she was not alone in grief; grief was always a part of life. A time to laugh, a time to cry…

John Brown brought this suffering. He was God's instrument to test her faith. So she prayed for the forgiveness of the men who did this, knowing they were creatures captive to the devil. She prayed for John Brown even as her husband pursued him. She prayed for the hope for a brighter future; she prayed for her family, wherever they might be, prayed for God to accept her thanks for her life. She prayed to Jesus to teach her not to hate, she prayed for Ben, prayed for Esther. She prayed that there might be a pleasant, peaceful, joyful place for them in heaven, with all of their ancestors, with eternal joy, worshipping God forever.

She lay down in the slave hut, now her only home, and stared up at the roof boards, cobwebbed and water stained. Thoughts of better times, of Ben as a baby, of Esther and her father, of her entire family, started her down a path of happy images of her life. But the path swerved and painful thoughts were lurking around a turn. She wandered again among the evil images of the night before, their power still too overwhelming to simply erase with games of the mind. The pain, the death, her attackers were real and present to her. She wanted to forgive but could not forget. She knew that forgiveness, the forgetting of anger, took time. But the act of forgiveness did not take away all wrongs, did not condone what was done. There would be something in the lives of evil men that would bring what they had done home to roost. There would be some pain, some loss, some compensation required. But it was God's will to bring it, not hers.

All she could hope for was to forget, to reject hate, the last portion of evil left behind, the most powerful, destroying more than fire, corrupting more than perversity. Hate was what would ultimately decide who won and who lost. Hate was the creator of the future soul, to live in hate was not to live; to be consumed by it was to no longer exist as before. She knew this and fought against the desire to strike out, to kill in return. An eye for an eye? Jesus spoke of it and defined it. It was not to pluck out the eye of the offender, only the law, only God could do that. It was to forgive, to live with one eye, overcoming the desire to match pain for pain, loss for loss.

So she walked out to the pond, stripped off Hanna's clothes and walked in. The waters were cold enough to form a stained glass rim of ice around the edges. She waded in, singing to God as she washed. Saying over and over, "Forgive them Lord, forgive them Lord, those who did this to me."

The Lawyer

Zephaniah and I rode east, crossing the Mississippi above St. Louis, a larger ferry operated there. We crossed with ease then walked our horses onto the land of Illinois. But we took the wrong road and headed too far north. There was some spring in the air though winter was still on. Red buds showed on the trees in a mirage of color, painted by my hope for spring, seen only from a distance, disappearing close up. A hint of green brushed the earth, seen only as you gazed across the new downy grasses in certain light.

Our party had shrunk so with the boys gone home, but Zephaniah did not despair. He had strong faith and knew who he was, what he was called to do. He was resolute. He did not tarry on Simeon's rebellion or on his pledge for revenge for the suffering of his family, of Rachel, though I did.

I thought on her constantly, not knowing her condition, injured, living, sick, dead. I wanted to turn back to follow the trail west to where my heart was, not to follow blindly east into unknown territory. I began to doubt, not knowing where Brown was or if he would be in Manassas, if the dreams were true. I was quiet but dark spirited, thinking of Esther and Ben, their horrible deaths. I hoped for the first time Joseph was wrong, that we would find out he'd dreamt someone else's pain, another's destruction. But if that were true this journey was a false hope to begin with.

We rode across Illinois for two days, slower now, still in an easterly direction. We slept one night in an abandoned house. The urgency that had taken hold of us had died with Beersheba. Zephaniah knew he could not afford to keep killing off the horses, running them to their deaths, hearts busted.

At one point a long lanky lawyer, whose legs nearly touched the ground from atop his tired mare, rode in our direction and nearly passed us. He wore a stove pipe hat, a soiled suit jacket, a cloak. A satchel of books sat behind him, moving side to side with each step of the horse's hind legs. He was an odd looking man, all the more reason to remember him. His ugliness left a strong impression due to a certain kindness emanating from his awkward features. His ears were large, his face bore warts, his nose big, pointed, his clothes ill fitting. He nodded as we rode toward him.

Tipping his hat he said, "Gentleman," in a high reedy voice unbecoming of his frame, unexpected from a man of such size. A small sign hung from his valise of books. It read: John C. Fremont for President.

I was too tired to see it but Zephaniah took notice of the sign, reading it aloud. Ever concerned about the position others took in the battle to save God's way of life, he could not pass this man in silence and he said, "Who is John C. Fremont and why should he be President?"

The man paused on his horse, raised a long finger to his face, wiped his nose and rubbed his whiskered chin and said, "John C. Fremont is a good man, a great man. Explorer, Indian fighter, he opened up much of the west for our expansion. I will be speaking on him tonight in Beardstown. Why don't you try to attend?"

"I do not have time for political meetings. We must continue on our way," said Zephaniah.

"Well, I am most sorry. I would hope to gain your vote for Mr. Fremont," lamented the lawyer.

Zephaniah asked, "Is he the same Fremont who rode with Kit Carson back in '42 into Apache country?"

"He is, sir," answered the lawyer.

"I married an Apache. I was there. I tried to kill him and Carson. So I will not be voting for your candidate," said Zephaniah with a look of disgust on his face.

"It is a free country. Good day gentleman," the lawyer said trying to avoid a conflict.

Zephaniah called out as he rode off, "Fremont is a murderer, a liar, a torturer of women and children. If you knew what he'd done you would not ride in his support."

The lawyer stopped, turned around and said, "I ride as a circuit judge, but I attend meetings for my party. I will take your comments into consideration. Those were difficult wars, as all wars are a plague to mankind. I do not endorse him for Indian fighting, but for President, he is a leader of men. I see many men in my work; greatness is hard to come by."

"Who be you?" asked Zephaniah.

"My name is A. Lincoln, I am a lawyer," he answered tipping his hat.

"My name is Zephaniah Jacobs; I am a fighter for God's ways. I seek John Brown. I mean to kill him," said Zephaniah without a pause.

Lincoln took this in and said, "John Brown? I am against him as well. He has raised the pitch of the argument between north and south. The law will catch up to him."

"No, he has been pardoned, as I heard it. It is up to me to find him," said Zephaniah.

"Good luck then in your quest," said Lincoln as he turned to go again.

Zephaniah followed on his horse and asked, "Is Fremont an abolitionist?"

There was a silence as Lincoln was aware of the passions this topic could raise. It was debated across the land with bitter dispute. He stopped his horse and said, "He is, sir, he is a leader in the movement."

"Well, I am against him then, Mr. Lincoln, even more so, I would sooner kill him than vote for him," said Zephaniah.

"Those words can cause you considerable trouble. Candidacy for the highest office in the land makes assassination threats rise to no small thing. Speak freely but carefully Mr. Jacobs," warned Lincoln.

"I speak my mind," retorted Zephaniah.

"You may need a good lawyer if this phraseology should bring you trouble, please remember my name. I will defend your rights but not your intent. We'll find a defense in your painful life that a jury will agree with, I assure you. Of course, for a small retainer," Lincoln added with a smile.

"Are you an abolitionist?" said Zephaniah not responding to the levity.

"I am not sir, but neither do I want slavery to spread. Slavery is protected by the Constitution but its expansion is not guaranteed in the document. We can effect that," said Lincoln.

Zephaniah said, "It is God's way, sir, it is tradition. God made the black man to be our creatures."

Lincoln answered ready for a debate, "I do not disagree, they are not as we are. They cannot live on their own. I favor sending them back to Africa rather than giving them freedom here. What would happen in our cities were they to be released from serfdom? But I do not endorse slavery's wholesale elimination either. I take a middle road."

"If it please the court Squire Lincoln," Zephaniah said, chiding him in a lawyerly tone, "there is no middle road for Slavery. You are either for it or against it. The middle road is for fools. Know that I am against your middle way, Mr. Lincoln; I am against John Fremont and all who want to steal my rights. Lawyers can make anything seem to be true but truth is bare in the eyes of righteous men, A. Lincoln."

Lincoln looked to the sky and said, "You are free to raise hogs, Mr. Jacobs, but painting a pig doesn't make it less of a pig. Slavery is a swine. I want to keep it in its pen, let it wallow in its familiar mud, but wander no further or it may become feral."

Riding closer to Lincoln Zephaniah said, "You watch your tongue, A. Lincoln. You insult me, you insult my religion."

Lincoln asked, "What religion is that sir?"

He answered, "I am a Christian. I follow the God of Abraham and his son the Lord Jesus Christ."

Raising one hand Lincoln asked, "So you love your neighbor?"

"I do," said Zephaniah.

"Does a man's color determine the neighbor?" asked Lincoln.

"I did not make them black, I did not start slavery, God did," replied

Zephaniah.

"So you do not love them as neighbors?" Lincoln probed.

"I would not wantonly harm them; they are slaves, not neighbors. I treat my slaves decently, like members of my family," Zephaniah said in defense.

"Will you let them leave?" continued Lincoln.

"No, they are slaves. They would not thrive. Do you not understand the difference?" Zephaniah said, his voice hinting at his growing impatience.

"I do sir, I am afraid I do. So God, Jesus, speaks only to love white men?" Lincoln said.

"That's right," came the answer.

"Not red men or yellow men or black men?" asked Lincoln, rubbing his chin.

"No they are inferior," said Zephaniah with some force. "They are part of the world we have been given to care for, we are stewards of their welfare, like the animals on our farms."

"And yet you married and Apache, curious. Do you know where Jesus was from?" said Lincoln.

"Yes, Bethlehem, along the Mediterranean sea." answered Zephaniah.

"Near Jerusalem, the lands around Egypt, Arabia. Do you know what those people look like?" asked Lincoln.

"I know them, they look like us," he answered.

"In those lands skin is dark, even black, they are Semitic. Jesus was a Jew from the land of Jews," said Lincoln.

"Are you saying Jesus was a nigger?" said Zephaniah putting his hand on his gun.

Lincoln countered quickly, "No sir, but Jews from that part of the world are darker skinned, as are their gentile neighbors. Jesus was surrounded by them; he preached to them, he spoke to Jews and non Jews alike."

Zephaniah had enough and said, "Now Mr. Lincoln, I been listening to you but you've been saying a lot of nothing. That doesn't change the fact that niggers are property. Your words can never, never change that. You're a good lawyer, twisting a phrase as you do but you can never change the fact that I have a bill of sale. I own them. The government cannot take away that fact. I have the right to my property."

Seeing the end was near to this conversation Lincoln said chuckling, "You are a wise man, Zephaniah, perhaps you should be a lawyer."

Not seeing the humor Zephaniah said, "I am God's instrument. I will do as He tells me. If lawyering is my next calling then I will see you in the courtroom."

"I hope that I too will be God's instrument in a great cause someday, perhaps I will. The only way we can survive as a country, as a union, is not in the elimination of slavery and not in the expansion of it, but in co-habitation.

Otherwise we will tear apart. The question is, can we compromise?" said Lincoln
ready to move on.

"There will be no compromise, not after John Brown," said Zephaniah.

"I hope you are wrong, I sincerely do. Good day sir. I hope your journey goes
well," said A. Lincoln as he rode on while Zephaniah and I watched.

———————◆———————

I would see him again, his coffin borne by a caisson, led by a rider-less horse,
boots reversed in the stirrups. He would lie in state on a black draped catafalque
in the Capitol rotunda. I would watch his crepe covered train heading home to
Springfield. I will always remember the words he spoke, the irony of his position,
the myth he would become. The years ahead brought much discord. He would
become President with the Parties split along radiating fissures of this issue of
slavery. He sought first to save the Union without freeing slaves, despite the
beating of the abolitionist drums in the north. He truly felt Negroes inferior.
But he would not let me and mine be free to own them, to live as we wished in
Kansas. We hated him for that, another fence sitter politician.

He only freed the niggers when he had no other way to win the war. We
had them beat at every turn, until he did that.

Walden Pond

John Brown shook hands with Henry David Thoreau at the trail head leading into a grove of second growth trees near Walden Pond. Thoreau's small house where he had lived studying nature, writing about life and society in his essay Walden, had stood not far off, but it was gone now, dismantled for the value of the wood. This place was only a mile from Thoreau's aunt's home in Concord, where he now lived. It was remote, tranquil, bearing an atmosphere of his generous thought. Young sprouts of trees poked through the green ground cover racing to the sun, shading decayed logs, scattered and burned from a fire mistakenly set by Thoreau the previous year. Summer heat reigned over this verdant haven, a moist haze sweat through the light fabric of the afternoon. They walked side by side, two different men in many respects yet in one great way kindred spirits. They loathed slavery.

Thoreau's ugly beard, one thin band of hair on his neck well beneath his chin, a curious facial hair unique to Thoreau, grew in stringy strands down to his collar. He was a member of the Transcendentalists, believers in an intuitive spiritual state which did not rely on established religion or human intellect or experiences in this world to get closer to God. It was a sense to be developed, an intuition for the eternal. Thoreau's friend Ralph Waldo Emerson spoke of the Divine Soul and the movement was a spiritual revolution, romantic and irrational.

Brown said as he stepped on some stones crossing a brook, "I was moved by your essay Resistance to Civil Government. I had never heard it put so, it seems so natural, so right."

"Did it motivate your actions in Kansas?" asked Thoreau.

"It did," said Brown.

"Why did you not choose more peaceful means?" Thoreau asked as he stopped near the edge of the pond.

Brown threw a stick in the water saying, "It takes an axe to cut down a tree. It takes a shovel to uproot a stump. You cannot save the tree and remove it. Slavery will not die without many mortal wounds. This I believe."

"I fear you are right," said Thoreau. "I would help you if I could. But I have never been a wealthy man; I am a simple worker in our pencil factory. I write as it befits me but few read, fewer buy."

"Not all great works are read in their day," said Brown as he sat on a rock.

Thoreau said, "It is true, we shall see. But I regret I have little else I can give you. Just some words, well written, well placed, is all I can offer. Look, did you see the fish jump?" Thoreau said pointing to a spreading ring on the water.

Brown said, "Yes, it was a beautiful fish. A bass I think."

"Yes a striped bass," said Thoreau. "It was big. Beautiful to see, even more beautiful to eat."

Brown then said, "Your words are a powerful weapon. Your influence is great, you know many warriors of words. Emerson is your friend, he supports me. Others read you, they support me too. Your night in the jail was the inspiration that endears you to them still."

Thoreau said leading Brown deeper into the wood, "That was the spark, indeed. I did not pay a poll tax. I did not support the war so I would not pay it. I did not feel we should steal California from Mexico. Freemont, Carson murdered and lied to get that treaty. Such is the way of this world. Now to be clear, this government's tolerance of slavery is a crime. I do not want my taxes upholding this sin against all mankind. But you know why I was released from the Concord jail? My Aunt paid my tax, so I came out the very next day. Not so dramatic a term of confinement."

"Sometimes it is not the duration of the act but the power. It may not even be the act but the communication of it," said Brown.

"Yes, you are right. But you, sir, will not have the luxury of a mere night in prison."

"I know this," said Brown.

Thoreau continued, "You may die in battle, you may be captured, you may hang."

"You are right, I accept this. I accept my judgment. I do believe my financial supporters could hang too," said Brown.

"Do you?" Thoreau said stopping near a large oak.

"Yes I do," answered Brown.

Thoreau said with some concern, "Certainly not for providing you money? We do not control what you do with it."

"No not just that, but for what is to come," said Brown pulling a cattail from the mud near a standing pool.

"What will come?" asked Thoreau curious enough to stop and turn to him.

Brown said in a solemn voice, "I know that I can trust you. But I will only say I am making a plan. It will turn the tide in our direction."

"I am not sure I want to be a part of the inner circle," confided Thoreau.

Brown added, "You already are. You taught people it was their duty to disobey when a wrong is afforded by government with our taxes. But also I follow the words of Jesus who said we must free the oppressed and the poor. Now God has shown me what must be done. I will do it."

"What will you do?" asked Thoreau.

"In due time, Henry," said Brown biding his words. "I must gather men and arms. I must drive a wedge between the slaves and the slave owners. I will provide them the means to rise. Empower them. Lead them into the battle for their freedom."

Thoreau considered this and said, "I see. A lofty goal. Are you sure that docile race will fight, they are simple minded. They seek only to please. They do not seem to have a suspicious bone in their body. They are simple brutes, not trainable."

"They will fight if given the chance. Cinque on the Amistad, Nat Turner, both slaves. They did it; they proved slaves will fight. With the right leader, the right weapons, the right tactics, in the right terrain, we can fight on, live on, win. We can strike and retreat like Wellington on Napoleon. They will come to me if I raise the cry to revolt. Like bees to the hive," said Brown with confidence.

"How do you know this is what God wants?" queried Henry David Thoreau.

"God wants slavery eliminated from the earth," said Brown plainly.

"Did he speak to you?" asked Thoreau.

"He did," said Brown.

"What did he sound like?" Thoreau asked wondering if he was mad.

"Like the sound of many waters," said John Brown.

"Indeed," said Thoreau. "That is something they can't explain at Harvard Divinity. Unitarians. Let them explain a vision. Rationalists. They think Christ a great man, a teacher, though not the son of God. But they revere his peaceful words. As I see it there is no middle ground. The words are meaningless if he was just a preacher. They would have to say he was both deranged and a great teacher, for he himself said he was from God. It is divinity that communicates truth, not a mere man. So if you think his words are the truth, he must be divine."

John Brown did not answer but looked at him, considering Thoreau's words.

Thoreau continued taking the measure of the man before him and said, "'John Brown, your certitude is not a hard thing for me to see. Had it not been for Kansas, I might doubt you, but I know what you did. You are the very symbol of what we only write. I know there is money being gathered to support you. Perhaps you are right. This may be the time," he concluded.

"It is. I assure you it is, sure as God created the world," said Brown.

They walked on for a time in silence until they stopped beneath a large pine tree. Thoreau said, "I am not sure all men of God will agree. I have met some preachers, here, in Maine, out on Cape Cod. They are pacifists, abolitionists, but pacifists."

"Then they do not want to end slavery or they do not understand it," countered Brown. "Jesus is my Lord. I walk in his ways. I will sacrifice my life for my brothers. I will set free the oppressed. I will protect the innocent. Pacifists stand idly by while millions suffer. What good is a philosophy of inaction in the face of evil? I will not love a neighbor who holds a slave, who sells a child, who impregnates, who whips, who hobbles, who brands, who lynches. I must stop it."

"When will you leave?" asked Thoreau.

Brown's pace quickened and he said, "I do not have money enough now. But as soon as I do, I go back first to Kansas. They will need another dose, another shock to drive home the point. I will go back, free more slaves, but this time I will deliver them to safety."

"What about your grander scheme?" Thoreau went on, his curiosity getting the better of him.

"There is the thing about money," Brown said heading back to the trail entrance.

Thoreau followed. Noticing a furry caterpillar walking along a log and he stopped to watch it as John Brown continued on.

The Book Seller

A s we reached the falls of the Ohio we crossed into Louisville, Kentucky. There we heard of the Dred Scott decision. The decision came down on March 16, 1857, but we'd just heard about it from a stable boy in Louisville. Black men were property; the Supreme Court of the land decided it so. It was official, it was the law. This decision borne out by both the Federal Courts and Justice Taney's Supreme Court, with no further appeals possible, was a landmark. Justice Taney had the final say. The news bolstered us as we rode.

We read the newspaper aloud, repeated a few key phrases over and over: 'Slaves were legal property protected by the Constitution. They had no legal standing to sue for their freedom.' This would shut the likes of A. Lincoln up for good. But would it stop John Brown? We did not think so, in fact it would drive him on we thought. So we continued to ride east, determined as ever to see him hang.

Western Kentucky was a flat green land with some blue hills in the distance. We rode and rode, seldom speaking, deep in thought. I thought across the boundaries of time to the memories I carried, some heavy, some light, the good, the bad, the times I wished I could relive, do again. I thought of my granny, how I'd failed her. She had asked me to help her but I would not. I was just a boy wanting to play. She fell carrying wood for the stove and broke her hip. She died weeks later. She told me not to cry as I sat by her bed but the guilt is with me to this day.

I thought on the one love I'd ever had who I left out of spite, not wanting to be controlled by a woman. She had married another, a fact that still caught in my craw. I rode along thinking of these things and others that brought me pain, like a monk who whipped himself in a lonely cell, my self-flagellation covered by a mourning coat of self pity with all the mistakes of my life jammed in its pockets.

As we approached Lexington, Kentucky, we passed a bookseller in a wagon. Zephaniah had a love of books, he'd read more books than I ever saw, so this interruption from our ride's monotony was the very tonic for him. We stopped and asked to see his wares.

The man stepped down from his wagon, gracious and happy for customers, and opened several small wooden crates. Setting aside the lids, he displayed a myriad of books on many subjects. His collection was extensive. He had eight different translations of the Bible. From Greek to Latin, Latin to English, English to German, German to Dutch, a version of each directly from original Greek, bypassing the Latin. He had a Catholic Bible with more books then I knew of. He had collections of books that were not included in the Bible. He had Bibles with documents for the recording of family trees, of marriage records, birth records. He had Thoreau's most recent writings, 'Walden Pond' and 'On Civil Disobedience.' He had Walt Whitman's 'Leaves of Grass.' He had Tolstoy, Dosteyevski, 'Moby Dick' by Herman Melville, Nathaniel Hawthorne's 'The Scarlet Letter,' 'Communist Manifesto' by Karl Marx, 'The Mayor of Casterbridge' by Hardy, Dante Alighieri's 'The Divine Comedy,' Victor Hugo's, 'Les Miserable,' 'The Age of Reason' by Thomas Paine. He had the most recent Blood and Thunder about Kit Carson, dramatizing his Indian battles, his explorations of the west with Fremont.

But when nothing was to our fancy he asked, "Perhaps you would like to see some of my more exotic works?"

"We may," Zephaniah said, his interest growing.

The bookseller struggled through his boxes to find a few particular tomes in his collection and then he said, "Books like these are what some may call controversial. This one was written by one of our local celebrity authors. She wrote it from her home in Ohio but she's from Kentucky, yes she is. Now your tastes may not be partial to this but literature is free to explore the human mind, what some may think but cannot speak."

And he took out a copy of 'Uncle Tom's Cabin, Life Among the Lowly.' It was a simple black and white cover, a picture of a family of darkies on its face, in front of a cabin. Zephaniah had heard of this book, as had I. It had made quite a stir in Kansas and all over the world. The north loved it, bought thousands of copies; the south despised it but read it to see what lies northerners were writing and what northern radicals were reading. It raised our ire, spreading its lies in a heart rending story.

Zephaniah held the book, turned it over in his hand and said, "I consider this all a lie.

The bookseller asked, "Have you not read it?"

"No I have not," said Zephaniah.

"Then how can you hold such an opinion?" asked the vendor.

"I have heard about it, sir, it is unholy refuse," said Zephaniah handing it back to him.

"Refuse? I am a book seller; to me this is the golden goose. Good controversy sells books. I have sold many copies of this refuse," the bookseller said eagerly.

Zephaniah pronounced, "It is the Golden Calf, erring human thoughts worshipped though corrupted, blinding us to God's will. I bet you do not sell as many as you say in this land. Folks here seem to be a God fearing people."

"Nay, nay, not two hours ago in Frankfort, I sold a copy to a man, he was thrilled to see it in my collection. He said he'd waited so long to read it. A man named Brown, he was," said the bookseller making his point.

"Brown?" asked Zephaniah.

"Yes, he was sitting outside the hotel. He came to my wagon and bought it right away. He said he felt deeply about the Negroes plight, said he'd been away a long time, had not read it yet but admired it," the merchant added.

"You're sure his name was Brown," Zephaniah said coming in closer.

"Yes, he told me his name. I remember because I wrote it in ink inside the cover of the book for him," said the bookseller confused at the questions.

Zephaniah threw the copy of 'Uncle Tom's Cabin' back into the crate and said not another word, mounted up and we rode hard for Frankfort.

When we got into town there were only four buildings, one a livery, one a general store, one a hotel, and aside and attached to it a saloon called the Whiskey Inn. It was a small, dilapidated, unpainted structure. There were a few people sitting outside, imbibers of spirits no doubt by their condition. An old bloodhound slouched near a rain barrel, its eyes as drooping and bloodshot as the nearby humans.

We tied off the horses, went directly in and approached the bartender.

"Is there someone here named Brown?" Zephaniah asked the man as he stood polishing a glass, his handle bar mustache waxed to a fine point.

"Yes sir," answered the bartender who put down the glass upon hearing the low menacing tone to the query.

"Where is he?" asked Zephaniah with his hand on his gun.

The bartender's color drained as he pointed to a medium sized older man with a straw hat and his back to us watching a card game. Zephaniah walked up and stood right behind the man. He pulled out his gun and puts its cold barrel right to the back of Brown's head.

Curling smoke rose from cigars in the bulging mouths of the players. The air was so still the smoke floated straight up and spread out on the ceiling in a gossamer gauze drapery above the table. The room tingled with deadly surprise. Intent on their game the players were ready to toss away cards for the draw when their eyes rose to focus on Zephaniah and the gun on Brown. The sight leaked cold fear to their poker faces and they ceased chomping on the cigars in perfect unison.

"John Brown." asked Zephaniah.

There was no response.

"John Brown." he repeated.

Slowly the man put his hands up. "No sir...Thomas Brown," the man stammered.

"Thomas Brown?" Zephaniah said with a hint of confusion.

"Yes, that's right, now be careful with that gun. Who is asking my name?" Brown said, still looking forward, afraid to move.

Zephaniah did not respond. The gun was holstered.

Thomas Brown stood up and turned around. He was old, sixty years or better, and gray. He seemed to be hungry or at least yearning to consume some more of life. A weary meanness was beneath his eyes, like he'd been beat too many times.

"I don't appreciate you putting a gun to my head," he said irritated but still afraid, he was not a strong man but he was proud.

"Now Tom," the bartender said, "You just got out of jail don't be causing any trouble or you'll be right back in."

Brown smiled, showing two missing front teeth, and rubbed his stubbly chin.

"No, I ain't going back. They me beat in there plenty, whipped me good, flayed my skin with a bull whip, so it hung off me like a shawl, so I'll let him be. What do you want of me?"

"Do you have a copy of 'Uncle Tom's Cabin?'"

"The book? Yes I do, what's it to you?" said Brown now fully confused.

"Nothing, I'm sorry. I am looking for one John Brown," said Zephaniah.

"John Brown?" the old man said in amazement. "You mean, the John Brown from Kansas?"

"Yes and you are lucky you are not he," said Zephaniah turning for the door.

"What do you want of him?" asked Brown.

"I want to…I want to talk with him," said Zephaniah stopping in his tracks.

"With a gun?" Brown said gaining some courage then yelling, "If I do see him, I want to congratulate him. I would gladly spend three more years in jail for his cause."

"What were you in jail for?" Zephaniah asked turning around, his mind preoccupied, not really interested in the answer.

"Jail? It was no jail, it was hell, a pit. This state's prisons make evil blush. Me, I was in for kidnapping slaves, kidnapping them? Ain't that funny? But it's not so, I wasn't kidnapping them, I was setting them free I was."

Zephaniah stared at him, hating him, and said quietly," God will punish you for that."

"God will punish you for making men slaves," Brown returned as loud as he could say it.

With that, we turned and left, embarrassed at our mistake. The drunks on the porch and the blood hound did not rouse either at out leaving. We took no notice and rode off. John Brown was still our quest; we started riding east again.

Faith

In Eastern Kentucky we began to encounter the foothills of the Appalachians. This was the land of Boone. There were ancient damp forests covering deep diving ridges, layered stone, generation upon generation of shale. We crossed a river as it snaked through a gap, on each side the towering striations twisted, heaved sideways, as if a large shovel had cast them off, stacked them up. I felt a great cathedral rose around us; a worshipful feeling emanated from its crevices and pipe organ stone chutes. But the size of it, its grandeur, its massive scale spoke of forces far greater than I could imagine. These vistas, far more than the stars and the seas, made me think of God, made me strain my neck in awe. They were a part of my world I could touch and see and climb upon, places God had once moved with his mighty hand. Somewhere way back in time forces of God created all of it.

I think that moment was the first time in my life I truly believed in God. I dismounted and stood seemingly in the center of the universe, turning around, neck craned, eyes rising, brows arched. I could not live long enough to understand how the rocks could be so. I somehow had the idea that this had once been the floor of a massive sea before the great flood that put all the world in upheaval, before all things lifted, changed, creation recreated, dry land turned to sea, sea to dry land. Before then there was another sea, whose dried, caked bottom we looked upon. The hand of God had passed there, commanded the disheveled stone to rise, decreed the river to change course, I said reverently to myself.

But what of the loss of His creatures? Did all who were called enter the ark, all species? Who called them? How did they know to walk to the ark? Could one unintended creature have been left behind to drown? Was it supposed to die or was it an error? Were they the lineage of some Unicorn or other mythical creature we now miss and dream of, extinct and subtracted from the grand plan?

And the people, those who mocked Noah, who perished for not listening to their prophet, their doubting words swallowed with the rising sea, were they meant to die as well or was it their choice? The evil man perished and the innocent man was not given reprieve. They all drowned alike for not listening. All surviving life was determined by one man, inspired by God, listening to God. He and his family survived to reseed mankind.

So I asked a question I have asked all my life. How do we know who is the leader, who hears the word of God? Who is the true prophet and who is the false prophet? Does anyone truly hear God speak to them? Can we know anything of the mind of God? Can we guess his mighty plan? How does he tell us? Can we read his thoughts or know his ways? Is it in a book, in a dream, or in a mystery of nature? Is there is no way to see, no way to hear? How do we know if we are called to act for God?

This is what attracted me so to Zephaniah, his faith. If only I could have such faith. The skeptics are left wanderers, riders on the range, waiting for each encounter to come their way, some proof to bring them on board the ark. Hope on hope. They want to see Him, hear Him, put their hands in His side, see His punctured palms. Some folks say life is haphazard. But haphazard means no God. Haphazard means emptiness, coldness, randomness. I could not believe that.

So I believed finally and it was the rocks of Kentucky that spoke to me, that passed the eternal message of God to my mind, a gift I cannot ever repay. I say each tiny moment, all of time, is strung together, all are planned, all are intended to bring us somewhere. The entire world, all experience, is a tapestry with one thread through it, God's great work. The mysteries of God are revealed to us in the twists and turns of our lives. This is what I came to believe.

There was a reason why I was riding across Kentucky, farther east then ever in my life alongside this man Zephaniah Jacobs, because I knew this experience must have been preordained. I was not sure if I was in the presence of a Prophet, if Joseph was a true foreteller, I did not know for certain. But I had followed. And I felt I must go on, the quest had to continue.

As we rode clouds were building in the south, moving our way. Sure to be a mighty storm we put on slickers as we looked at the purple roiling mountains blowing toward us. But we kept going, feeling closer to our prey with each step. We pulled our coats closed to cover our guns, to keep our saddles dry but the wind was blowing, the rain slapping sideways to our faces, thunder and lightning erupting with the force of a volcano.

As we came into an open area, a knoll along an overflowed brook, past a cryptic ancient cedar, a jagged bolt was thrown from the heavens splitting and splintering the tree, a brilliant blue light striking Zephaniah. Its explosive radiating power killed his horse, sent mine to her hind legs in fear, throwing me. Sagebrush then ran, panic overtaking, off into the enveloping stormy darkness. I fell to the ground into puddles of new rain mixed with wispy dust. I crawled about yelling for Zephaniah. Hair plastered to my head and rivulets of rain as thick as rope coursing down the anguished draws of my face, I called and called into the night.

He had been thrown against a broken limb of the tree. The smoldering trunk smelled like a cedar chest, its saw mill odor lingered in the air released by the power of the fiery message from heaven. I thought he was dead; he did not move and seemed not to be breathing. The rain splattered on his salt white face, a bleeding streak was burned across his scalp, over and through his eye, down his cheek. He was branded forever by the lightening, lifeless, aged ten years in one instant.

———◆———

Zephaniah had seen the flash, felt himself in the air flying then he landed softly into someone's arms. He could feel arms beneath him, catching him, holding him safely. Light encircled his body, surrounded him. He was not afraid but felt warm, calm, with no need to fear or flee, awe struck silent, but safe, very safe. He tried to look up but had to shield his face, the light was so white, so perfect. He was totally wrapped in light, filled with it. All he could do was close his eyes and give in to the power around him. And he heard distant music and smelled flowers and herbs, fragrances he wanted to breathe deeper and deeper. This further relaxed him, letting him give in to the light even more, forgoing all his will power as he had never done before.

He rose to his knees, then to his feet. He put his hand over his eyes, shielding them, trying to look through his fingers. He looked down and saw sandaled feet. As he pulled his hand away, he was able to look on what he said was a Shining Man.

———◆———

I could not pick him up. I dragged him through the mud across the road, beneath the green bows of a sister cedar, a sprout from the root of the stricken tree. I sat there all that night near the old tree, cold, wet, holding him across my lap for warmth. His breathing, shallow and irregular, seemed to come and go, in and out in a call and response with the gusting winds.

As the storm's anger slipped away further north, my horse wandered back, sheepish, guilty, shy, glad to find us. Sagebrush stood over us, looking down like a doting parent, quiet, staring. At first light I tried to lift Zephaniah across my horse, but he was so limp I could not. He slipped from the saddle and before I could grab him he collapsed like a gamecock dropped by buckshot. So we sat all day. I built a fire, tried to give him water and waited for him to revive.

Finally after many hours, I looked at Zephaniah on the damp ground and a slight shade of pink had come back to his face, his breathing came on stronger but his eyes were yet closed. Then he sat up suddenly but said not a thing, did not respond to my questions. He rose to his feet with some effort and let me guide him to the horse. I was then able to get him back on Sagebrush.

Zephaniah, eyes closed, oozing wounds on his head and across his face, was helpless but aware, blind, mute, and possibly deaf. I led the horse and talked to him as I walked, not sure if he could hear me. But I explained myself anyway, as much for my loneliness, as my worry for him. I told Zephaniah many things, what

I heard, saw, felt, the sorrows of my life, my new found belief, my fear for him.

In a short while he just climbed down from my horse and walked alongside me, head down, unsteady gait, limping still from his injured hip. He said later that wherever we went in the following weeks a Shining Man walked alongside him, softly strolling, quietly listening to the sounds of nature, to my words, to Zephaniah's thoughts.

Brother's Keeper

The sons of Zephaniah Jacobs rode into Kansas. They had pushed the horses hard to get to their home, hoping for reunion with Rachel but expecting a sad time, thinking on the death of their mother Esther, the loss of their mothers Hanna and Buela, dwelling on the pain of their brother Ben, asking themselves what had befallen Reuben, and with thoughts of their brother Naptali, where he might be, what adventures on the waters he might be having. And Zephaniah, what of him? And, of course, they wondered about the fate of John Brown.

Joseph was especially quiet, withdrawn to one of his secret places. His happiness gone, he looked off in distances, missing his confidants from other worlds, apparitions his brothers could not know in their ordinary minds. His brothers did not speak to Joseph except to command him so he did not look to them for comfort or inspiration. Unused to taking orders from his brothers, who had become cruel with their new responsibility, their rebellion, he did not want to eat, did not want to fish when they stopped.

He sat sullen and more remote, missing his father and his mothers. Joseph had been damaged by all he had seen, his mind was not sound, a witness to great pain at so young an age, to cruelty and the suffering of those he loved. He could watch unspeakable horrors in the real world, the slaughter of the Pawnee, the death of the blind old slave by the river, the killings in the Samuel's field, the fetid remains of the massacred settlers, the shooting of the Doctor and the dwarf but he could not cope with the most severe visions he conjured in his mind. His emotions could not be shielded in his sleep.

Simeon had assumed leadership. Second in age to Reuben, he found himself pleased his elder brother had been left behind, proud to finally be in charge. He felt he deserved to lead due to his superior strategic skills. The others had talked briefly of going back for Reuben, but Simeon convinced them he might already be dead and beyond saving. It was the farm, the catastrophe, their mothers, they needed to think of. Simeon was sure to illustrate his anger, his drive to address this family emergency, and how he was like Zephaniah in so many ways; but beneath it all was cunning, a concise manipulation of their emotions. He was always working toward the domination of the will of his brothers, who were so clearly less able than he.

In the past when Reuben as oldest had tried to assert himself it was clear he was a slow thinker. He could not manage logistics or strategize. These things came naturally to Simeon; he had a perfectly suspicious nature for the job ahead. But Simeon led in more ways than to order the breaking of camp or the choice of which paths to follow, which direction the wind blew and the sun tracked.

He led them in the paths of their anger. He sent the disease called revenge to fill their hearts. He led them to talk first of the capture of the criminals who invaded and ravaged their home, then of the ways to torture them, the pleasure of the kill, the length of it, the way of it. During the slow journey of many days they reviewed the ways of death in great detail. They spoke of it around the fire at night. It darkly filled them so they dreamt of death, thought of it as they rode and ruminated in private silence. Most conversations between them turned inevitably to their grief and then transformed into red hot hate.

They rode one behind the other until they saw a curved line in the prairie horizon, the sunset casting familiar shadows on a place they felt they had been before, like a recurring dream shaped like a dead newborn. They knew they were close to home. Hope attached to remembrance of previous lives and still indwelling touched a part of each of them in unison. Their horses sensed this and increased their pace. But the violent dreams they'd had, conjured by Simeon these past weeks, stained their speeding hearts.

Rachel was cutting wood as they came into view of her. The boys and Diana were happy to see her alive, yet the sight before them made their hearts sink. Their home was destroyed. It no longer smoldered but jagged blackened wood stood bleak and rough, detached and alone, howling like wolves in the night. Remnants of the hate visited there was still present. Rachel, not yet seeing them, was lost inside a thought as she worked. But soon she sensed them, caught a whiff of her family's approach, knew in her heart they were home. She did not turn though, but dropped the axe, stood there shoulders even, waiting. She knew this time would come. When she would say things she did not want to.

She turned and saw them. They rode faster to reach her, the long delayed reunion within grasp. They jumped down from their horses, converged on her and held her.

All the past months of separation, of loss, melted into tears, watering at last the drought of suffering so long endured. Consolation floated in the air like the sweet smell of lilacs in spring, encircling them to bring with each draft a fresh moist aroma.

They wished they could walk into their home, dwell in places they had grown up in, where memories were swept in every corner, but they could not. Like so many nights when insects lived but once their old lives were gone in a twinkling. So they went instead to the slave hut. They crowded in to find places to sit in so small a room, so inadequate for all of them. They needed to immerse themselves in their tragic story, to sit, to talk, to hear what had happened, to let it pour out.

Rachel said, "Where is your father, where is Reuben?"

"Reuben was hurt and left to recover with our Uncle Esau. Father continued on, he still seeks John Brown," said Simeon

"Uncle Esau? You did not stay together?" she asked puzzled.

"No, when we heard about you I told him we were leaving," Simeon said proudly to display his leadership.

"Heard about me?" she interrupted.

"Yes, Joseph saw it all," said Gad.

"He dreamed?" said Rachel shocked at the thought.

Simeon said, "Yes, as soon as we heard what happened I told Father we were coming back. I left and the rest of them followed me. I led them here. We will find the men who did this. We will kill the men who killed our mother and Ben."

"Killed?" said Rachel feigning she misunderstood.

"Yes, tell us who they were," said Dan.

"They were not killed," she said.

"What do you mean?" asked Diana.

Joseph sat quietly as his brothers each in turn looked at him and their suspicions converged. They had gone through privations, lost a brother, another wandered off, thought their mothers were dead and kidnapped, their father traveled a misguided path, as they followed Joseph's dreams. And now his dream had brought them home with welled souls bursting with hate and the dream was false? They waited to hear Rachel's explanation.

She gazed at the floor, unable to say the words and look them in the eye. Then she said haltingly just as she had rehearsed, "Esther and I had gone to get water and there was a fire, the house was in flames. I think some fat was set too near the hearth. It started and burned so fast. Ben slept in the loft. He died. We were left with nothing. Nothing. The loss of my Ben and the privations were too great for me. I blamed Esther for Ben's death. She had left the fat by the fire. I was angry, in mourning, not myself. I mistreated Esther. I could not bear her, any of them. It was my fault. I could not accept my loss. I became intolerant. I blamed everyone. I could not lift myself from the pit I had fallen into."

"We argued often and I said things I should not have. They grew to hate me. And they left. They left and I am not sure where they went. Esther, back to our father in the canyons to the south, perhaps. Perhaps. Hanna and Buela, roused by all this talk of abolition, just walked off one night. I do not know where. Please forgive me. Please."

Dan went to her and held her as he was nearest. "So our mother is alive?" he asked.

"Yes," said Rachel.

Dan looked up from Rachel to Asher to Gad. They considered each to himself whether they should search for Hanna and Buela. But if they had run off on their own, abandoned them, what then? If they were to try to find them where should they start? All were still angry at the loss of their mothers, their home, their brother. Their desire for revenge still hot, they wanted still to chase, to capture, to torture, to kill. Their long nurtured rage could not be dulled. They were confused, pulled apart as if drawn and quartered.

Simeon, Levi, Judah, Isachar, and Diane looked at each other. Diane now fully pregnant, her domed belly grown large and uncomfortable—she was but a few days or weeks away from bursting—was noticed by Rachel who, being so mesmerized by tragedy, did not yet mentioned a word on her motherly condition.

Simeon's mind raced. This was all too much for him. He raged out of the hut, his spleen molten, tempered only by thoughts of searching for Esther, their mother now lost. Should he spill his anger on Rachel, pitiful as she was now, for her reaction to Ben's death, the cause of all this? How could this be? How could the past months be so wrong? Reuben, Esther, Hanna, Buela, Ben, gone? Then his darting eyes set on Joseph.

The new object of Simeon's rage sat with his usual blank expression and his ruffled blonde hair. Simeon backed away from the door into the dark, looking on as Joseph rose and sat next to his mother and, hugging Rachel, laid his head on her shoulder. Always jealous of the special attentions Joseph received, Simeon came to a conclusion; his young brother had caused all of the suffering. Simeon had always questioned Joseph's visions, hated that his imperfect dreams were bought whole cloth as truth. Joseph was the reason for all this pain. That heavy thought sunk like a millstone in a lake of hate. Simeon walked off into the dark to strategize on what to do next.

———◆———

As days passed they worked and tried to rebuild what could not be replaced. In a week's time much had been accomplished though. The good timber was long gone; the straight wood was used up years ago for the cabins. So, they set about rebuilding with stone and sod a structure they could live in.

Rachel was burdened by her lie, her denial of Joseph's dream. But she did not think long of the effect her lie might have on him. She knew Joseph saw things others could not, surely he would understand her motive. She was still deeply affected by death, mourning veiled her face and worry for Reuben and Zephaniah hid behind most thoughts. She felt somewhat stronger, a little more productive, enveloped as she was once again by family and her role as mother. She hoped against hope her lie's true worth was in altering the vengeful course her sons would so cruelly have followed.

Simeon talked separately to his siblings, planting a seed of hate for their brother Joseph. Their hearts were fertile ground for his bile. He circled them with a well reasoned conspiracy; brought them to a conclusion they'd each harbored but could not speak. He converted evil thoughts to hateful words and a full understanding of what must be done. He plied also their greed.

He said, "Father may not return. His quest is a false one, this will break him, kill him. He may be dead already. He may never return. Who knows what wrong path he follows, mistaking a dream for the truth. We cannot make the same error again. If Father is dead, this land is ours. This place is my inheritance and you all know that to be true. As the oldest, I will get the blessing. It is mine but I will share it with you, with each of you. We will all be rich together. So pledge to me. If I promise to share my inheritance equally, you must promise me one thing."

"What is that?" asked Isachar, enticed but wary.

"Do you promise?" asked Simeon leading them to the abyss.

"What is it you want of us?" asked Dan eagerly stepping first into the void.

Simeon gathered himself and said reasonably, "I want what each of us knows to be right for our family. As your leader that is all I am concerned with. Joseph is a blight to us. He is a weakness that has nearly destroyed us twice. He must be shunned, culled for us to avoid further devastation. His false dreams could be our destruction. Also, just think if Father should return, which is not likely, you know he will still trust his dreams and visions. You all know this to be true. There is only one choice. So say it."

"What?" asked Asher.

"You know what must be done, say it," said Simeon looking into their souls. "Say it."

"What must we say?" asked Dan.

"You know, you all know," said Simeon pressing them.

"We must kill him," said Levi.

And the words hung in the air like the smell of rancid meat.

Abandoned Hope

The next day while Isachar and Dan worked, Simeon, Levi, Judah and Joseph rode away together, off for one night on a hunt. The need for meat disguised Simeon's scheme: to shoot Joseph and his horse, to leave the bodies on the prairie to be consumed by animals. This plan was built in his mind like a gallows, plank by plank, over the past days. He would tell Rachel Joseph had ridden off in the night dreaming some nonsense, chasing some ghost. He knew Rachel was so distraught and fragile she would believe anything.

Miles out they stopped near an abandoned homestead to set up camp as Simeon had planned. Simeon left Joseph sitting by a crumpled stone well looking into its blackness and he stepped aside to explain his final plan with his brothers. He said, "All of you can ride out. I will shoot him, take his body away, then kill the horse, and leave them on the plain in the open."

Judah said, "Why get rid of the horse? That would be a waste?"

Levi added, "Why kill him at all? That would be a sin. Better if he dies on his own, this removes the sin from us. Throw him in the well, leave him there. We'll say he wandered off leaving his horse and was killed by wolves. He'll die on his own, we won't have his blood on our hands and we won't lose a horse."

"Yes," said Judah. "Let's kill a deer, rub his clothes in the blood. We can tell Mother he wandered off and that the clothes were all that remained."

Simeon looked at Judah and Levi. He liked their plan but was angry he had not thought of it. He sighed heavily and to prove again his worth as their leader he walked over and pushed Joseph into the well.

As Joseph tumbled he reached for stones trying to save himself, but they were loose and Simeon kicked and stomped on his hands. Frantically, Joseph tried to hang on, grabbing and gripping at anything. He held onto Simeon's leg scratching bloody rows into his flesh with his nails. But he could not hold on, a force was pulling him downward as his brother peeled off his hands. The rocks he grasped fell before him and splashed first in the murk below. Then Joseph fell into the shallow water and mud at the bottom of the well. He landed knocking the wind out of himself and his head struck the stones. He remembered feeling pain and gasping for air, then all went black.

◆

At the same moment back at the Jacob Homestead, Diana's water broke. Rachel knew it was time. She led Diana in her wet dress into the slave hut, set her down on a bed, brought in a bucket of water, some rags and told the Dan and Isachar to boil more water. She then looked between Diana's legs and saw that she was still a time away from crowning. So Rachel went and ate some corn mush and smoked hog, knowing she had a long night ahead of her.

As the long day and night wore on, Diana's anguish grew, rising and falling with the pangs of birth. Rachel held her trembling hand, rubbed a cool damp rag on her forehead and sang to calm her. She sang the songs of Diana's youth; lullaby's first sung for her own babies, and now sung for her nascent grandchild.

God's Care,
All through the night,
Will keep us safe,
Til morning light,
And awaken us
And awaken us
To sunshine bright

This baby was stubborn. Hours went by, night turned to day, the pain growing with each degree of the suns slant. Diana pushed and pushed but the child would not come forth. Seeing it was a breach, Rachel reached inside and tried to turn the baby, to rotate the child inside Diana's womb and pull it out, but only a leg could be grabbed. Poor Diana knew she was dying then. She looked on her mother's frantic face working so desperately below her. Numb now to pain, she looked across the land that was always her home place, into the blinding sun in the clear cobalt sky, at the soaring eagle riding the invisible currents.

She knew she would be leaving here soon and asked Rachel to pray. But Rachel had lost enough, she could stand no more and she cried with determination, "I will pray but not for you in heaven, I will pray for you on earth. You will live, you cannot die. Have this child, my grandchild, I want this child, a child of rape, I don't care. Just live, just live."

But Diana bled too much and the life went out of her like a fading wind, she died holding Rachel's arm.

Rachel was as stone. She picked up a knife and in one slice cut open Diana's stomach. Hiding her grief in determination, she yanked the lifeless child from the still warm womb. With the purple marbled umbilical cord coiling from Diana's gaping stomach, Rachel raised the child to the heavens and she prayed, "God, let this child live. Let it live. Let it live, God."

And she brought it down and smacked it on the tiny buttocks, the sound of skin on skin echoed but no cry came forth.

She smacked it again, and once again there was no cry.

Then, one last time, she looked to the heavens and smacked the child. Around the farm the ringing cry of a baby was heard.

Rachel held the newborn to her breast and cried. She exhaled greatly falling from exhaustion and grief beside poor dead Diana. And still holding the small child close she cried for her loss and for her motherless granddaughter.

———◆———

As Simeon, Levi, and Judah rode home without Joseph, trailing his horse, they were serious but triumphant at their success. Dan and Isachar saw them riding up. Afraid of what their brothers had done, they ran to them. They all met, excited but pensive, out of earshot of the hut.

Simeon, Levi and Judah dismounted, and Simeon said proudly, "It is done."

The forbidden thrill of the scheme was shattered with these words; the finality of their act fell like an executioners axe. They looked from eye to eye in silence.

From the slave hut the vibrating cry of an innocent baby pierced the morning air. The rise and fall of the newly born child's tiny howl played like a squeeze box. A sound that should have been a beacon of joy for a new life in a troubled family, fell flat and juxtaposed to the anger they had just acted so cruelly upon.

Simeon's scheme now had to progress to its final evil stage.

Crossing into Virginia

I stopped at a cabin and a wrinkled parchment skinned woman came out with a rifle, her yellow husband was coughing in his bed beyond the door. His phlegm clogged throat emitted strained wheezing sounds as he rattled and hacked unsuccessfully and could find no relief. She told us to get out. I showed her Zephaniah's condition, told her about the lightening. But she did not care; she had her own problems with her husband dying. She told me to move on, said Zephaniah was jinxed or punished and she'd had enough bad luck. I did as she said, the gun was a great convincer; the pitted barrel speaking much truth to me.

I found an abandoned barn to lie up in, a few miles beyond her place. We stayed there nearly two weeks. Zephaniah was like a walking dead man. He'd lost everything that was his except the ability to move but even that was more labored; he looked to be a crooked old man, joints stiff, strength gone.

One day when walking to pass the time, I came upon an abandoned peach orchard, its fruit in perfectly ripe condition. Orange pinkish yellow globes of luscious fruit hung from the branches, calling me with a primitive love song to reach up and enjoy. I picked them until my arms were full and carried the soft fuzzy balls back to our shelter. They were as juicy as I had ever had, succulent, delicious, dripping with sweet nectar I could not get enough of. I could only think of God as I ate them.

I was amazed that a tree could bear such a gift just for me and that they were sustenance for my body and soul, something I needed. How did trees give us what we needed to live, simply there for the picking? I knew it was no coincidence. Zephaniah loved each slice, savoring each bite, the juice running down his hands. But we both ate too much. We paid a price for consuming such a large amount of the ripe fruit. But they were absolutely delicious and well worth some discomfort.

When I saw Zephaniah was getting no better and that he could not travel on horseback, I took some of his money and bought a wagon from the yellow woman whose husband had died. And laying him in it, we set off on the road, heading east again.

I remember when we crossed into Virginia I could see a great ridge ahead of us. It stretched as far as I could see from left to right like a large blue wave

that never broke, the Blue Ridge it was called. Manassas was to the north and
we needed to cross this ridge to get there, to the place foretold to us. We were
close to Brown, I knew it.

Before this large long mountain there was an even plain, a pleasing valley
with a river running down the middle of it, swerving, ambling, soothing, light
brown, rippled, fed by many brooks hopping off the Blue Ridge. It was called
Mechum Creek.

We trod a narrow path that would lead us eventually to the meandering
river. As we rode a great storm blew in. A big rain came on fast and torrential
cascades of water poured to earth as if from Jove's great bucket, the lowlands
filling, the flood plains backing up. The river swelled as great waters ran off screed
slopes and gushed through gaps, over ledges, feeding the river's rapid runaway
energy. The building waters met resistance at the many turns and floating debris
caught in the meanders, causing the river to expand. It cut us off, leaving us on
a knot of soil between the confluences of two overflowing washes, separating
above us, thrashing around our island, crashing together below us. It roared with
a primitive sound of an irate Zeus on Mount Olympus, a sound of wet fear.

Zephaniah lay dumbly in the back of the wagon as the waters rose to the
wheels, then to the wagon bed. Sagebrush grew panicky and decided in her fear
to run straight into the current and she pulled the wagon in. I grabbed a tree and
held on and I watched helplessly as Sagebrush's leg was caught in the crux of a
floating tree, it sounded like a cracking whip when it snapped. She was pulled
under, no footing, no grasp, helplessly dragged by the strong downstream force.
The wagon and she separated; she struggled so as the water pulled her away,
faltering on her broken limb. I lost sight of her, sure she'd become trapped, fearing
greatly Zephaniah and she might drown. Zephaniah drifted away on the free
floating wagon, as I climbed the tree amidst the torrent and clung to a limb for
my life.

In the rising waters, the wagon caught on trees and was snagged by branches.
The wheels weighed down with accumulated debris caught in the spokes. The
rushing stream pushed the wagon forward. It bounced off random obstacles,
spinning in turn, knocking off boulders. Hitting, spinning, jarring, bouncing,
then reversing momentum, and almost turning over, it moved along like a toy
boat. Eventually it became wedged; other flotsam jammed it in tightly, forming
a dam. Zephaniah weak, blind, dumb and deaf lay there and he knew his time
had come.

Afraid, soaked by the rain and chilled by the cool wind fueling the storm, I
held on for my life, blinded for moments by shattering lightening then left alone
to the haunted whim of the darkness after the flash.

The rain stopped before dawn. I was able to climb down and pick my way
on rocks to drier ground. But Sagebrush and Zephaniah were nowhere in sight.
I scoured the muddy water's course looking for him, calling his name. Though I

knew he could not hear me, I yelled anyway. When I could see from a height the path of the river I realized he could be far downstream, drowned probably given his condition. And I was brought low, lower than ever after so much. I was alone now, in a strange place with no horse, no leader. Tested beyond my capacity, I wondered why God had let this happen just as I had believed in Him.

Then I came upon the body of Sagebrush. She was mud covered and flies swarmed about her, eagerly hurrying to consume her, a banquet of decay. Her leg was twisted in an unnatural bend, like she was running backward. I pulled away the knitted waste from the flood trying to uncover her body, to try to look on her unsoiled as if she were alive, but found it useless. I knew I could not move or bury her so I had to just leave her there. I was able to get my saddle and gun and a few of my possessions, which I found along the way, though they were all filthy and wet. I hated the thought of her dying so and I was sick with grief as I left her there. She was such a good horse. She had carried me so far. I loved her for her quiet labor, her trusting spirit. But she was gone. Her dark hazel eyes were dull and dry, they did not flash her salutations, they did not express her love. It was a sad, sad moment. I felt awful and tears for her, for me, soon flowed. I was very lonely as I walked back to a town eight miles away, wet, tired and unsure of my future. I still had the money in my coat pocket but no horse, no leader, no friends. I felt I was truly with no safe harbor. I needed to get a horse and go find Zephaniah.

I looked in a faded red livery stable for a new horse. The owner, a Scott, had a dapple gray for sale. It was older and cheap in price. But she had no personality, was boney shouldered with a sagged back and tired out. He said her name was 'Precious.' I did not like that name for a horse, maybe a lapdog, but not a horse. Then I looked into another stall and there stood Beersheba, I swear it was she.

I could not believe it. It did not make sense. I'd seen her dead by the river in Missouri. It could have been a different horse but the match was too perfect. The markings were identical, the size was the same, the eyes were the same. The stable owner said an old Indian dressed in overalls had walked into town, traded this horse and then left. So I was completely perplexed. But Beersheba or not, I had no choice but to try to buy her. I bargained hard but he held to a dear price. I could not leave this horse there after the loss of Zephaniah, supposing this horse might be Beersheba, so I paid too much for her. I depleted my funds and had just a few dollars left. But she was Zephaniah's horse, I was almost sure.

I rode her by the river heading south. We picked our way through the waste left behind from the flood. For a full day I tried to find Zephaniah but he was nowhere. So I turned north and, knowing he was driven by a cause, I figured he and I would converge at the same place, Manassas.

I rode along the west side of the ridge for several days and covered much ground. I passed through several towns seeking him out. When I arrived the sluggish inhabitants seemed only to sit in the dense heat and mull their existence, waiting for something to occur or someone to come and enliven them. I was not it. They looked at me and said they did not remember the blind man I described. With each town my doubts grew but I could not believe him dead. I had to keep trying to find him.

I came across the ridge finally, crossing near Harrisonburg, a spring vista ahead of me as I descended. The view was bursting forth in young life, a rich vernal green. I felt I'd crossed into the promised land but no line of freed Jews followed me out of bondage.

Then, after many more miles, I finally saw a sign for Manassas. The name had loomed large like a mythical city; its name spoken in hushed tones, brought forth in a dream inspired by God. When I saw the sign the name Manassas was printed with one more 'S' than I expected, this made me pause and wonder, could it matter, one 'S', was it still the same. Its proximity was close, one more day's ride away, and I wanted to rush to it, but I was too tired to hurry. After much toil, much suffering, losses, death, I was almost to the place where I would find John Brown. There I would kill him and finish the mission, but I did not have it in me to push harder. So I rested beneath a hickory until the morning.

The next day I rode into Manassas, a small pastoral farming village with a common general store, a pillared bank, a fly ridden livery, a church, a school, a hotel with a fancy saloon. Manassas was a center for commerce, for business exchanges, where produce met coin and value was derived. But I'd expected more of Manassas. I assumed it would have a mystical atmosphere. I thought it would be larger, brighter, more of a royal kingdom then a town.

I rode past slaves hauling grain from a wagon to the feed store. I saw a group of slaves chained together, manacled at their ankles, standing in a cluster to be auctioned in the town square. One had a back so rippled with the scars of whipping, of countless lashings, he looked to wear tobacco leaves on his back. Another was as muscled a slave as I had ever seen but he lacked one eye. A woman stood naked before the crowd, her embarrassment long cast into a permanent expression of her plight so as to make it barely noticeable. She was buxom, quite a value for breeding. The block was surrounded by the buyers of humans and the auctioneer called to them barking the qualities of these slaves. He pointed to their fine features with a riding crop, prodding their rumps, baring their teeth, lifting a handful of breast in his effort to earn his commission. The slaves brown eyes were cast downward and their hopes were sucked out by the endless undertow of life.

I looked into the crowd and thought for a second I saw the dead woman who'd wandered away from us. But I could not find her face again and thought I'd imagined her.

I continued to look about for Zephaniah. Everywhere I inquired about him people looked at me blank faced, considering me some troubled stranger. My distraught look was feared. They thought I might have a scheme or ruse in play, mistaking my distress for a caginess to be wary of.

When I asked the question, "Is John Brown here?" they looked at me with hardened eyes then told me to leave. They did not like John Brown, would not countenance his presence and did not want to hear even the utterance of his name. They wondered if I was trying to inflame them by raising such a mean topic. They did me no violence but neither would they tolerate me.

After a time of searching I realized neither Zephaniah nor Brown had been there yet. But I still believed, my faith was drawn from some deep well of hope, from a strong conviction to the quest. So I decided to settle in and wait.

Due to my poverty, I needed to find a way to exist. So I rode out to a pretty place along the Shenandoah River and asked a tobacco chewing farmer if he needed a farmhand who was skilled with horses and slaves, an overseer. I lied about my slave experience but he took it and hired me for a dollar a week. This was low pay but I was happy for the roof and the money.

Work was something I had not done in some time. It was a pleasure to have my mind absorbed in labor rather than riding in monotony thinking of the miles yet to go. I was glad to settle and while I felt so lost in this land called Virginia, I was at least safe for a time. I was glad to have a dry tack room to sleep in, having slept outside for so long; but I did not like that slaves slept not far from me in the same building beyond my wall. They were my charges for work. So I made sure they knew I could apply sound discipline to control them. Being like simple children they yearned for the order a good overseer could bring.

I spent much time reading the Bible and other books I thought Zephaniah would approve of. His influence on me was great. I missed him, and in a kind of homage I tried to live as he would approve. I started going to church regularly for the first time in my life of my own accord. I listened to the preacher. I prayed for the future, for guidance, and I began to live by a new rule that made my life much simpler. I learned from the preacher a new phrase, 'Let God do it.' There was nothing truly in my control, so I decided to 'Let God do it.' I kept one eye on the heavens, one eye out for Zephaniah and John Brown.

I worked and lived this way for many months, then one day as I rode the horse I thought to be Beersheba, as I watched the slaves gather pumpkins in the field I heard about John Brown's raid on Harpers Ferry.

Wide River

As the raging waters sucked the detached wagon downstream, Zephaniah did not feel the need to save himself. He did not care for his life; he was immobile and with no feelings. He felt as when he'd been struck by lightning, airborne, afloat, protected, embraced. He was calm, unconcerned. After he saw the Shining Man walking along the banks in the storm, nodding in approval to his thoughts, he was peaceful, ready to let events take him over, to let God have his way. He had spent so many years fighting to structure his life to follow God, to be something God would approve of, that this new approach was a pleasant, easy way.

When the wagon finally lodged on a boulder, water overtaking it, bubbling up through the grooves in the wagon bed, forcing it to lean precariously and finally rising over Zephaniah's chest, he started to slide, to give himself to a watery grave. And as he slid off a hand reached in, grabbed his wrist and pulled him to safety as the wagon rolled over and broke free.

In the darkness Zephaniah was led by an unknown hand from the swelling river to safety. Blind, dumb, unaware of the identity of his savior he was led over rough ground on a winding trail. He climbed over rocks, through rain filled brooks and through a pine forest, the needles refreshing the damp air with their clean smell. He then started to smell smoke from a cooking fire and meat roasting, its charred aromas spicing the atmosphere.

He was led into a shelter, helped to sit down and wrapped in a blanket. Food was brought, some kind of fowl, roasted, moist, plain but good. With no sense left to him but touch and smell, he could do nothing but trust. Zephaniah ate his meal and then slept deeply.

While he slept he dreamed. He was climbing a mountain leading to the sky. There were choirs singing and a multitude of beautiful sounds. First, as he reached the highest place he saw many blessed creatures, cherubim and seraphim, he saw all manner of beasts, he saw angelic creatures, beautiful faces, beautiful eyes. They floated and hovered around, always looking up toward a great light. He wandered closer to the light and there were ever more robed people who sang or hummed or sighed in awe and peace. Then off in the distance with a pathway of ruby and diamond stones, there was a large door. He walked up and turned around to look back on the glorious place he had just passed through. The faces of all were looking to him. He then turned and took hold of the large door knocker and rapped at the door. The sound echoed greatly within and he was surprised that this noise caused all singing and joyous sounds to halt. Then the door opened slowly and standing inside dressed in a robe was Archie, the mongoloid child on the farm of Jesse James. And he knew not what to say.

Living Water

A lone old Indian walked across the parched plain leading his aged horse, pallid and faded in color. They stepped in slow unison with stoic determination, returning to the home place of the tribe for this season. The bright light bleached his old eyesight with its whiteness. His craggy face was crisscrossed with lines dug by life, a warren of deep gullies from years in the sun. Thirsty and dry, clutched as by searing hot tongs, water as scarce as the future before him in this driest of seasons, this eon of months absent of rain, he walked on.

Rude drought took hold as it had across the centuries, its fingers wrapped around the throat of the land. The heat rose like fever on a pox ridden child. The grass a brownish yellow was brittle, withered and sallow, the land, dried to dust, choked itself.

All life seemed suspended when as in a mirage he saw the old homestead, the fallen walls of his enemy. After all the years of depredations by white invaders this sight of final failure brought a glimmer of joy. But a rise of his eye was all he would give them; a still yet sweet revenge was satisfied. His slight gloat at the plight of these misguided settlers killed off by disease or righteous slaughter was soon over taken by the most urgent of hopes for a drink from the dark depths of their broken down well.

He walked up to the stones, collapsed in on themselves, dropped the reins of his horse and knelt slowly down on his aged creaking knees to gander below. The smell of moistness drifted past his dry skin and was drawn in as a tired runner gasps for dear breath. The horse too smelled it, flaring its nostrils, the cool air rising from the circle of darkness. His old dimming eyes burned from the daylight looked to the well to see to its bottom. And as his eyes adjusted he was surprised to look on a white boy, white hair, white skin, in the water, eyes opened and staring straight back at him.

The boy looked to have expired with death's gaze on his face. The old Indian, startled at first, thought he'd seen a vision or a ghost but then he looked back more closely and knew it was real. He was there for sure, a white, white boy. He wondered what had happened. Why was he at the bottom of a well in this place?

He took a ragged rope from a sack on his horse and dropped it down until it landed on the boy's chest with some force. He lifted and dropped it a few more times trying to see if he was dead or alive.

Joseph roused from the contact, his eyes, opened but unfocused, looked up to the ring of light. He saw something move, something new. There was a wagging dot intruding into the saucer of light above him. He thought he was looking at the moon in the night and a beetle crawled slowly across its face. Then the ropes rough whiskers rubbed against his cheek and he dreamed his father whispered in his ear, telling him to wake and rise from bed in their cabin. Then his vision cleared and he could see a man.

Like he was pricked by a needle his mind lurched awake, a hope for survival jumped past his stupor. He reached up and touched the rope, then grabbed it tightly. The Indian called in a language he did not know but was clear in its urgency; he coaxed him to hold on, to tie the rope around him. The child, hungry and languished, frail and small, weakened but able, put the rope round his waist and then held on tightly, seeing life coming back into focus, a chance to survive, a way to go on.

And the old Indian pulled him up, a great effort for such an aged man, to the surface, to the world as we see it, saving Joseph from the hell of a death from starvation, bringing him back to life in this mortal sphere.

John Brown Returns

J ohn Brown rode vengeful into Kansas with the wind at his back and his sword
pointing northward. He came on like a mighty savior of the oppressed black
people, confident, bearing on his shoulders the wrath of God. He always
had the will, the desire, the energy, the zeal, but never, never the resources or the
commitment of the powerful. He was truly now representative of a movement,
not just nebulous ideas and fierce passions.

His reunion with his men was as the returning general victorious. They
awaited him, they needed him. He was the militia's general, the leader of their
cause. He looked with stern pride as he rode up to his sons. He released the reins,
climbed down from his horse and embraced each of them tightly, infusing in
each hug his upright force. There were warm handshakes all around, as he read
the faces of each of his men.

These weary warriors had no time for farming, no time for families. They
lived as vagabonds but stood as straight as soldiers in any army in the world. There
was no pay, no rich reward for them, no master plan for power, just a moral cause,
a cause they would die for and a leader named John Brown.

They sat down to conference in a spare country cabin, meeting to discuss
what had transpired in the past months for their General, old Osawotomie Brown.
They talked of the support of the Secret Six, not by name, not by profession;
Brown had pledged his silence on this. They talked of recent political news, of
divided and distant family, talked of those who'd died in the months that had
passed. And then Brown, once reacquainted with his men, laid out the plan they
had waited to hear.

The next week they would mount up and raid the farms of slaveholders to
liberate their Negroes. In a symbolic act they would take the owners as white
hostages then put the slaves in full control of the masters. Lastly, this time he
would finish the work, assuring himself a better outcome than that of poor Ruth
in the trunk in his dream. They would all ride to Canada, one thousand miles
to the north, and deliver the liberated slaves to a new life, beyond the reach of
Justice Taney and the United States Supreme Court, with their bogus Dred Scott
decision. Then he would travel across New York to Boston, to his benefactors with
his worth again bolstered and he would get the money for his war.

The following Sunday they rode out to free a slave named Jim Daniels.

Brown heard he was to be sold off to Texas that same week, separating wife and children from husband and father, from whatever home life they knew together. But this would not be, Brown would not stand and let this happen.

Harvey Hickson's farm was the first place they stopped. A bucolic setting with sheep and cattle grazing, tails wagging and swatting, ears twitching, a tidy house and a well kept barn with several cats sleeping in the grass near the corner.

Brown and his men rode up, rifles raised and guns cocked, and called in to the house to show themselves on the porch. Hickson looked through the wavy glass panes of the windows he'd bought in Kansas City three months before and recognized John Brown. Knowing his reputation, he decided there was no sense in fighting, death would be sure and he would lose everything. So there was no bloodshed, he easily surrendered and Jim Daniels walked free for the first time in his life.

Brown stole Hickson's horses, some mules and a wagon. These spoils of war he declared for the slaves. Then he took Hickson as hostage and forced him to walk, bound about the wrists, behind his wagon chided by Jim Daniels who could not believe his good luck. Jim Daniels walked alongside with his wife and his daughter, pleased to see his cruel owner tied up, saying the good Lord Jesus had come to his rescue and his good fortunes were the work of almighty God. But when Brown handed Jim Daniels a gun he was truly amazed; he had never been trusted with such a fine instrument of power.

Then the next place they went to was John B. Larue's. This place was less picturesque. There were no animals in sight; crows seemed to be the only crop. Unkempt farmland surrounded a large dilapidated house with broken shutters hanging from several windows, a porch rail was missing and the roof sunk between the joists like a starving man's rib cage. The place was in a general state of disrepair. Brown and his multi-racial posse rode up with wagons, horses, a glowering white hostage and newly freed slaves with broad smiles on their faces like they were on a great holiday, feeling some pride and wondering at the wide open door to their future.

Larue opened his door and stepped out on the porch. When he saw the men and slaves with rifles and pistols raised, he sensed danger and stole back inside. Slamming the door closed, he pushed a roll top desk across as a blockade and the lid came down on Larue's fingers with a heavy zip and a crack. He danced about shaking his aching hand, a white line of shocked flesh across his fingers, and he looked back out the window confused and mad.

Brown called out, "We've come after your Negroes and their property. Will you surrender or fight?"

Larue called back cradling his hand, "I'll fight."

Brown said, "Alright, we'll smoke you out. We'll burn your place to the ground."

And he signaled to Daniels to grab the kerosene.

But Larue, with fingers now bleeding, looked about at all his possessions and then lost his courage. He thought the better of fighting this many men and so he surrendered giving up five slaves, one of whom said, "Poor Massa, he got him a big probem now, cows gots to be milked and his woikin niggers done took off."

So Brown and his booty walked off to freedom. They walked to the north, where all human life was precious. First to Nebraska, where they could rest and re-supply, to the settlement of Quakers who would clothe and assist the slaves, and then on to Canada.

Along the winding road heading north, somewhere beyond Kansas City, Brown sat on his wagon with his frayed straw hat on his head and the eight newly freed blacks, four of them riding in the back of the wagon, one driving the stolen wagon with weapons and plunder, three walking barefoot behind and nine white men on horseback in the rear. They trod slowly to a free country, Canada.

Brown, unafraid of who he might encounter, rode past a group of armed men guarding the road, a crude posse raised to capture him—John Brown the slave stealing criminal. But once they recognized that it was in fact John Brown who passed with his beard and righteous countenance, they were so awed at his presence, so afraid of his reputation for murder and mayhem; they simply stood aside and just let him pass like the gates of heaven were opened to him.

The next day Brown's collection of abolitionists and the newly freed slaves approached a group of people, three rangy men and two Negro women, resting by the roadside. These weary travelers sat crossed legged in respite, eating apples. By the look of their impatient movements and the way they peered down the road from time to time, they seemed to be waiting for someone.

At the sight of the wagons and the small band heading toward them the men put down their fruit, they pointed and spoke together; it seemed they knew who was rumbling toward them. They did not appear surprised. They clearly recognized John Brown as he climbed stiff legged down from the wagon. They talked together for some time.

When the deal was struck, there was a round of handshakes passed between them.

Then the two Negro women rose to their feet and joined the walking free blacks behind the wagon on their way north to freedom. Buela and Hanna looked to the smiling Jim Daniels and wondered why in the world he was so happy.

Children of God

Rachel walked out exhausted from the slave hut and looked on her sons as she held the tiny baby to her breast. Her granddaughter, Helen she called her, so beautiful she could launch a thousand ships, was crusted with blood and the waters of birth. Rachel walked over to her sons and showed off the baby to each uncle, a smile breaking through her grief.

"Look at this, oh my. Is it a boy or a girl?" said Simeon.

"A girl," Rachel answered holding back the rest of the truth.

"How is Diana?" asked Simeon.

There was a long pause as Rachel struggled for the words.

"She's gone?" said Rachel in a flat forlorn voice.

"Gone?" said Dan surprised and confused at how this could be.

"Yes gone, she died giving birth," said Rachel looking at each of them.

They stood dumbstruck until Simeon said, "Damn Indians."

The others could not think of anything to say. This knowledge of Diana's death weighed on them like a boulder. It balanced awkwardly atop the anvil of guilt they carried for Joseph's murder.

Then Rachel noticed one was missing and asked, "Where's Joseph?" And there was a silence as no one could say it.

"He's gone too, mother," said Simeon finally as he went to his horse and untied a sack from his saddle.

"Gone too? What do you mean?" asked Rachel fearing the worst and going after him.

Levi looked from Rachel's eyes to the ground, avoiding her, and told the story, "He wandered off in the night as he dreamed, I guess. He was gone in the morning. He walked away, he did not ride, so we searched everywhere and then we found...."

"You found what?" said Rachel, a weary frustration entering her voice.

Levi continued, "We found him, dead. He was killed by wolves in the night."

Simeon brought over his blood dried clothes as proof and handed them to Rachel. She fell down to her knees with the baby and she lay Helen down in a bundle on the clothes. She then crawled away on her hands and knees to a place several feet off, as far as she could go with this new pain. And she gathered some dried grass and dust, raised it over her head and let it fall over herself in mourning. She continued this quietly. She did not cry for her losses, as her son's, the killers of Joseph, looked on.

Rachel said to the sky, in a whisper no one could hear, "How much can I bear? How much can I bear? Oh God, how you test me? Why God? Why God? Why do you test me so? Forgive me Dear God. Forgive me. You know that I love you," she said to the wind.

She prayed then in silence. She prayed for her lost son Joseph, she dwelled on his terrible death, ripped apart by wild animals; the thought was too terrible for her to consider. She prayed for all of her sons, her husband, her sister, for Buela and Hanna. She sought forgiveness for her lies spoken to protect her sons from their vengefulness. But as she prayed a picture crossed her mind.

She thought of her sons, their cold looks, their blank faces, expressions worn like the same bolt of sackcloth. Their eyes went narrow and they would not meet hers. The avoidance was familiar to her. She knew what it was to lie. Their words of what had happened were too perfect, too measured; their countenances too tentative. The story about Joseph seemed too contrived.

It was her lie which denied Joseph's dream, spoken for all the right reasons but hers nonetheless. She had set this tragic stone rolling and she could see the terrible swath it cut across her family. She knew. She then remembered the baby in the midst of her grief and she rose and walked over and took the child from Dan's lying arms. She put the baby to her breast, though she had no milk. She wanted to suckle her to help her stay lively. Then she looked with recrimination at her sons.

Rachel said calmly, "You've killed him, I know it. A great evil has taken over your souls." And she started to walk in the direction they'd come from. And her sons watched her leave.

The sons were greatly bewildered at what they'd done. It seemed so clear and sure when they were scheming but now it seemed confused and perverse. They wanted to run after her, grab her, say anything to change the future they saw, even add new lies to those that had caused this, but Simeon stopped them.

"Let her go," he said, "She'll be back."

But Judah ran after his mother anyway. Trying to retrieve the irretrievable, he stopped her at the top of the hill where days earlier they'd crossed with Joseph as they returned to their home.

Judah said, "Mother, he is not dead. Wolves did not devour him. We did not kill him."

"Then where is he?" said Rachel.

"We left him in a well by a homestead, miles away, over yonder, over there," said Judah pointing and looking down in shame.

Rachel looked to where he was pointing then she looked back at him as if she did not know who he was and said, "Bury your sister."

She turned then and left him standing knee deep in guilt, mouth open, totally immersed in the regret of his evil error. He watched her walk away, knowing there was little he could do, so great a damage had already been done.

Rachel walked all that day in the blistering heat, like a force of nature she pushed ahead to find Joseph, to save him or bury him. She held the sleeping baby close to her, out of the sunlight, concerned for her well being but unable to leave her behind with her murdering sons. She stopped at a farm and begged for some milk, holding out the child so they could see she did not lie. The woman, thin and worn, took pity on her and gave her a water sack filled with milk in which was fashioned a nipple and the child suckled. She also gave Rachel a linen blanket, torn and stained, and Rachel wrapped Helen tightly in the old way of her people. The child slept warm and quiet, lulled by the rocking of Rachel's steps to the east.

She walked all that day, mile after mile, and when she saw the homestead with the well her hopes rose and her steps sped to a run. On reaching the farm, she crawled up beside the well's broken stone wall and looked into the darkness, praying to see him.

She called his name and it echoed in the dark well, "Joseph."

But there was only quiet emptiness, a void that is a mother's worst fear when she knows her child and evil have met. "Joseph," she called again.

But again there was nothing, a nothing that leaves goose bumps on even the hottest of days. As her eyes grew accustomed she could see to the water and she realized resignedly with a groan spilling forth from her lips that Joseph, her son, was not there. And while she knew this could be the wrong farm and she might never find him, she sensed there was a secret known by this murky chasm. Sitting down, tired and depressed, her losses mounting, this series of disasters the reality of her new life, she prayed to God and asked Him to consider and convey her next steps.

Just then she looked to the dust and she noticed fresh hoof prints. At once her Apache senses, still strong enough despite the passage of time, shouted like a trumpet and she felt him to be alive. She knew he was saved. So she looked to the north, rose with Helen and followed the trail of a horse which carried her only living son away, to where she did not know.

White Slave

Joseph rode on the old horse weakly. There was no joy at his rescue, no attempt to communicate thanks to the old Indian. He bounced along limply with each plodding step of the old pale horse. He spoke not at all to his Indian rescuer. The old man was unsure if this silence was from shock or if the white boy was indeed mute. He walked alongside Joseph slowly for days with just glances between them. The Indian watched for some sign of a life force, some drive other than a need to breath and eat. Joseph's gaze was directed to some far off place. His mind seemed lost in a thick morning fog, the kind that comes off the rivers in September filling the valleys with whispering opaque spells conjuring fall's approach. He seemed at times drunk but there was no whiskey, and at other times he seemed like he had lost too much blood and might faint but there were no open wounds that would leak his life away, there were no arrows or bullet holes that penetrated him.

On and on they rode until finally they made the Indian's village. These were buffalo hunters. Joseph thought they might be the same Pawnee as before. They looked like the tribe Zephaniah had circumcised, but he was not sure. He kept his eyes down and did not challenge any gaze, he hoped no one would recognize him.

As soon as Joseph arrived it began to rain. It was a cool summer rain that quenched the land. It filled the river beds. The runoff replenished the pools and the low places. Skins were filled and rainwater overflowed the bowls left out in the hot sun. The whole tribe came out to the blessing of water brought by the white headed boy.

In a time the rain passed on, the sun came out and a spectacular rainbow arched across the sky, its several colors clearly defined, it glistened and lived for many minutes, bringing a feeling of wonder to all.

But this event did not change the fact that this was a captive white boy whose lot in life was now to be their worker, their slave. Joseph's Indian rescuer made a valuable donation from his journey and passed the white slave boy on to the women. They put him to work almost immediately gathering wood and dried buffalo dung, for the cooking fire, for the meal, which he needed so badly.

He was now a white slave among red men, treated like a dog, struck for being too slow. He slept in a leaky lean-to near the horses and worked beside a slave boy captured from another tribe. This was a common practice among the Indians. Any conquered foe was useful, their children, their women, after they killed the men. The captive was a pitiable boy with desperate looks ever in his eyes. He cried and spoke in his sleep but never said a word or looked up during the day. His eyes darted about as if suspicious and hungry, which he was since they only were fed scraps, the left over mash, the bones before the dogs.

Joseph paid no attention to him and kept to his work, aloof as always, watching and waiting for a chance to escape.

The Plan

ohn Brown looked around the room at his Boston benefactors. The Secret Six, as they would come to be called: Gerrit Smith, Franklin Sanborn, Theodore Parker, Samuel Howe, Thomas Wentworth Higginson, George Luther Stearns, and thought about how far he had come. He had recently returned from his journey to free more slaves in Kansas. And he had led them all the way to New York on the shores of Lake Ontario, where they set off by steamer for Chatham, Canada, a haven for runaway slaves. It was a large community with a famous Negro school. There Hanna and Buela, Jim Daniels and his wife, along with the others, would attend their first classes. They would live among free Negroes and learn to stand on their own. It had been a long arduous journey but all had made it safely, in total awe and reverence of their savior, their leader to freedom, John Brown.

On his last trip to Canada, before he'd gone to Kansas the second time, John Brown had met Harriet Tubman in St. Catherine's Ontario, a free Negro woman, a leading operator of the Underground Railroad, an inspiration, a talisman for the anti-slavery movement. They spoke together for one full day and he still carried a kerchief she'd given him to remember her by.

He then went on to Chatham and called an abolition convention. He hoped to enlist support for his cause, perhaps some fighters as well. They met in a small white church, thirty four blacks and twelve whites were present. He introduced himself to the hushed room, who knew they were in the presence of someone great, someone who was a leader, a visionary. Though plain spoken and corduroy clad he appeared as any admiral or great chieftain. He spoke of his journeys, his battles, his vision for the future of America. He wanted a world of total equality for all mankind, black, white, red, female. He was a striking figure. Rather than the stiff Calvinist firebrand they expected, he spoke of a world of peace, goodwill, equality. He was not a fierce murderer but a man of vision and sensitivity to the oppressed. But then he also spoke of his mission and he told them of his plans for a raid in Virginia. He told them that a new government, a provisional government, was needed until these changes could be fully realized.

So, Brown then held a vote to form this provisional government. His vision was for blacks and whites to serve together, elected officials sharing power, as

President, Vice President and all the critical positions of a governing body. They
would serve until the United States Government could be reorganized. Brown
became the Commander in Chief. They voted in a Secretary of State, a Secretary
of Treasury, and Secretary of War, and several Congressmen from among the
black and white common men in the room. Brown sought also a revision to the
Constitution of the United States, a document interpreted as supporting the
enslavement of others by Taney's Supreme Court. He wanted to be very clear
on the language, so no lawyer could twist the words (as if the words 'All men are
created equal' were not enough). They sat for days and debated the content of
this new charter.

Brown also thought of his visit with Charles Sumner in Boston the previous
day, who was as yet recovering from his clubbing by Brooks in the senate chamber.
He walked with dropsy step and he had terrible headaches still, his face was
numb and his mouth drooling, his voice forever slurred. But Sumner served on
in the government. He returned to his Senate office despite his disability, an act
of defiance by both he and his constituents.

Brown asked if he might see the coat and shirt he wore the day of the attack.
And Sumner took the clothes dried stiff with his blood from a cedar closet.
Brown held them reverently as if absorbing some deeper truth or examining an
ancient relic of the church.

As these thoughts dissipated Brown stood again in the opulent home of
Thomas Higginson in Boston and looked around at his august audience. These
men of influence, the Secret Six, looked at Brown and waited patiently while he
gathered his thoughts.

He said," I will read to you what we have done in Chatham. The Provisional
Constitution and Ordinances for the People of the United States." He then
cleared his throat and continued:

*"Whereas, slavery throughout its entire existence in the United States, is none other than
the most barbarous, unprovoked, and unjustifiable war of one portion of its citizens upon
another, the only conditions of which are perpetual imprisonment and hopeless servitude
or absolute extermination; in utter disregard and violation of those external self evident
truths set forth in our Declaration of Independence: therefore, We, the citizens of the
United States, and the oppressed people, Who, by a recent decision of the Supreme Court
are declared to have no rights which the White Man is bound to respect: together with
all of the people degraded by the laws thereof, Do, for the time being ordain and establish
ourselves the following Provisional Constitution and Ordinances, the better to protect
our Persons, Property, Lives and Liberties; and to Govern our actions.*

Article I
Qualifications for Membership.
All persons of mature age, whether proscribed, oppressed and enslaved citizens, or of

the Proscribed and oppressed races of the United States, who shall agree to sustain and enforce the Provisional Constitution and Ordinances of this organization, together with all men or children of such persons, shall be held to be fully entitled to protection under the same."

And as he read his voice went hoarse and he said apologetically, "Forgive me gentleman, I will ask your patience. My voice leaves me, I have not been well."

Higginson stepped up to fill the void and said, "Bravo to you Brown, you are truly a man of your convictions. Freeing those slaves, leading them all to Canada, then a Herculean ride right back here. One thousand miles, you are amazing."

Brown retorted in a trance and raspy voice, "No God is amazing. He gives me the strength to continue. He leads me beside raging waters that feed me."

Higginson went on somewhat mystified at his tone, at this revision of Psalm 23, "This most recent action, as well as your other previous adventures in Kansas, convince me of your mettle."

"I will change the world," said Brown still with little emphasis. "I will shake its very foundations, if you'll only get me resources."

"We want to talk about that, Brown. We want to find a more peaceful way," said Parker.

John Brown said, "There is no peaceful way. Every day we think of peace is another day men will be in bondage. In America, bondage in America. There will be a great war in this nation. The south will never agree to relinquish slavery, not without a fight. The loss of free labor will break them. They know this. It is like taking the bottle from a drunk. They will not give this up easily."

George Luther Stearns waded into the conversation, asking as he rose, "And how do you propose we advance the cause further. We've funded your adventures in Kansas. The Underground Railroad has been running for years, we can't free them all. We would smother our cities in idle Negroes. The crime rates would climb, the poverty would be debilitating to our economy. And some propose we ship them back where they came from. Well how can we ship four million Negroes? How long and how costly would that task be?"

"Mr. Stearns you are very right," said Brown. "There is much to be done. God wants them free. I will free them soon, soon. No amount of preparation will ever be enough. We must start now. Recreate the legal structure, have a new set of founding principles for all men. I have started this in Canada; I have formed my provisional government, with anti-slavery leadership and freed runaways who have the most at stake, who want to lead us to a new millennium. We have written a new Constitution abolishing slavery. See here, this is the new phrase, 'Liberty to all, Black and White.' It is this document that sets the course, that gives my actions meaning. We do not want a fight, we want reform. But to get reform we must free them where they live. For this there will be a great fight."

Parker's bald pate shined with nervous sweat as he asked, "You suggest a revision of our Constitution. How do we ratify it? This is a democracy, we cannot overthrow the government, force its signing down the barrel of a gun. Stop sir, I can hear no more of this. This is insane."

Brown said with no hint of defeat, "No more insane then the battles I won in Kansas."

Howe said shaking his head, "What you propose will be tear at the heart of our civilization. You will bring chaos, we will split apart."

Brown said, "You must rethink it, sir. We will create order and justice. It is civilization that seeks to spread slavery to Kansas. That is a chaos God will not endure. We must kill the snake at its head, or we will feel God's wrath."

"You propose an invasion of the south, Government overthrow?" asked Higginson. "By what? By a force of mercenaries? We don't have the resources to pay an army."

"No sir, I need but a fraction of that, but a few shekels," said Brown.

"Well who will do your fighting?" asked Parker.

"The slaves," said Brown flatly.

"The slaves?" said Sanborn who was listening quietly. "You'll raise an army of ignorant untrained blacks to fight southern State Militia?"

Brown said confidently, "They are men who want with all their hearts to be free. They will fight. They will fight. It has happened before, in Haiti, in New Orleans in 1811. Nat Turner in Virginia in 1830."

Sanborn answered, "May I remind you what happened. In New York in 1712 a slave uprising was put down, some eighteen slaves were summarily executed, burned at the stake, hanged by the neck, broken on the wheel. In New Orleans, sixty six slaves were put to death. Then another sixteen had their heads cut off and put on pikes along the plantation road."

"They failed because they fought with no leaders and no support. I will be their General," said Brown.

Stearns chimed in as he sat down, "Yes and you remember the mayhem Nat Turner raised, slaughtering white men, woman and children in their beds. Some fifty were mutilated with swords and clubs."

"Yes sir, I do know the story," said Brown. "But remember also they escaped to remote areas, avoided capture for months. We can free them from bondage, from farm to farm, plantation to plantation, bring them off to the hills where we can regroup, give them weapons, train them and keep moving south into the belly, the heart of the enemy."

Sanborn said with caution in his voice, "You will surely be chased down and slaughtered."

Brown smiled and said, "This may be true but what a glorious way to die, fighting for God's will. You were not as worried for me when I went to Kansas."

Then walking around the men he said, "It is time now to abolish slavery.

This is what you all profess to want. There is no other way. God will not let this sin stand much longer, we either act or the conflagration to follow will be much worse for all of us. There have been 300 years to talk. The time for action is now. I have 500 pikes in storage in Northampton, Massachusetts. I need money to buy guns. The rest leave to me."

Stearns said rising again, "I must leave now. As far as I know my monies go to support the Massachusetts Kansas Committee. I wish to know no more." And he gathered his hat and cane and walked out.

Brown looked around the room then said, "At least it was not a withdrawal of support. Are the rest of you with me?"

He looked from face to face.

They were cautious, uncertain, as they calculated the risk to each in their turn. Treason, insurrection, murder, incitement of a slave uprising would be the charges. They could hang for abetting, but they did not renege, though some time was needed for all of them to fully assent. In blunt and certain terms it was now time for action. The stars were aligned. But there were no signs in the heavens nor was there any portent other than Brown. Brown was the force; he was the meteor and the blazing tail. Brown was unstoppable; no force on earth could control him.

They all agreed. It was time for a war.

Colonel Naughton

A column of soldiers on the way to Fort Leavenworth waited as their Colonel and two soldiers ran up a hill, bent over for cover. On reaching the top the Colonel's leather gloved hands held his field glasses steady and he looked on the active Indian village below. He noted the horses stolen weeks earlier, then he saw a small boy working near a fire, tethered by the neck with a rawhide strap, tied to a pole so he could not run away, a white boy, a blonde boy, a captive for sure. Now here was a mission worthy of his command, to save a white captive from heathen savages.

So he crawled back down to his troops, mounted his horse and said, "There's a white boy held by the Pawnee, Sergeant. We go in for the rescue, now. Pass the word for total silence. We'll ride up there single file, just below the horizon at the top of this rise, then spread out in a long line. I'll give the order. Then we'll charge. Tell them to aim at the knees, we'll be riding and shooting, and we don't want to shoot over their heads. And make sure they're careful to watch out for the white boy. I'll go to him first, gather him up and get him out safely. Go, and give the order to take no quarter. No quarter, do you hear? But be sure to tell them to save the horses, we need them," he said without taking a breath.

And they mounted and rode to the top of the rise, spread out in a line and he gave the order to charge. Into the village they rode with all the speed their horses could deliver, blowing their trumpet, unsheathing their swords. They rode in to slaughter, to kill them all, to smote them with God's wrath. Women, children, men, old and young, were cut down, the faultless blades, swinging, cutting, were soon blemished with the blood of fleeing Indians. Rifles were emptied, shot after shot.

With his pistol drawn the Colonel rode in, killed a squaw, a child and an old man in ruthless succession and then he swept in slicing in half Joseph's tether, and lifting the boy to a place behind him on his horse like a skinny white parcel for the Pony Express.

Joseph watched expressionless as the cruel slaughter went on. He saw a spear rammed through the chest of the old Indian who'd saved him from the well. He saw children pierced by spears and thrown into the fire, he saw women clubbed by swinging rifles and brains spewing forth. The soldiers were mechanical, merciless, enraged. They shot, sliced, and killed with remorseless precision; devastation and the smell of fear permeated the air, broken bodies lay lifeless in blood stained buckskin. Their hollow unblinking eyes stared at death's horse as it rode away, mouths agape they screamed in silence for him to return their lives.

After a time as the mayhem continued, Joseph could look no more and he moved his eyes to a lone tree against the horizon while the screams and shots and death cries faded in the background. He envisioned a great wind and looked back to see bodies littering the ground like fallen leaves blown from the tree.

And then the victorious army formed up and rode off in a glorious soldierly gallop, flags and banners whipping gallantly in the air. Joseph held on tightly as he rode behind the Colonel across the solemn prairie for the safety of the fort. All lamentations were left behind by this swift running chestnut mare and new adventures were sure to lie ahead for Joseph, wherever he was going.

The Colonel's thoughts were ablaze, enflamed by the thrilling action, emboldened by his murder, proud to have saved this young boy from the hell of enslavement and conspiring how he might capitalize on this rescue.

This Colonel Naughton sought a post back in Washington. So this brutal slaughter of the kidnapping Indians and the rescue of this boy was great fodder for his official report. With little action since the border wars settled down, something dramatic was needed. The Colonel had missed the last war and peacetime advancements were so slow. He'd had enough of this duty, so far away from it all. He'd long ago tired of negotiating disputes between settlers and Indians, chasing drunk savages, horse thieves and worse. He hoped to make a name for himself in the hinterlands, in the mystical west they all wrote about. Perhaps this white boy was the answer to his prayers.

The promotions he schemed for back in Washington were posts of power, calling for action and decisiveness. Saving a white boy while recapturing stolen horses from savages was a sure way to make a glorious image for himself.

As soon as they were back at Fort Leavenworth, the Colonel started to write his report. He told his Lieutenant to bring the quiet blonde boy to his quarters to gather information on his captivity—stories of evil mistreatment, of blood thirsty savages. He wanted authentic quotes that would illustrate the situation. But the boy sat looking ahead, he would not talk. Even better, thought Naughton, he can't speak, he will never speak. They cut out his tongue. He's a mute in deep melancholia from the shock of living among heathens, pagans, beasts. His mental defect was exacerbated, no instigated, by his mistreatment. What a story to enter in his report!

He wrote all evening with a cool professional tone and added phrases with creative flair, certain florid descriptions assisted the story line. Then he posted his report with the next rider out.

The following months were filled with rigid military routines, the common life of soldiers at a fort where drilling, riding, training were foremost along with discipline, order, honor, bravery. Joseph served as a valet for the ambitious Colonel

Naughton, a stickler for detail, a very precise man. He was a meticulous dresser, who worked Joseph hard with the excruciating detail of his uniform and shining boots. He wanted everything perfect. He sported a perfectly groomed beard and had large brown eyes which gazed beneath his frequently combed shanks of golden curls, quite the dashing bearing for such a young man.

The Colonel was kind though, not of evil bearing. He had a good heart; he did no harm to Joseph. He treated him sternly but kindly, took him under his wing, like a son some would say. He talked to Joseph regularly, could see he had clear enough understanding, though he never spoke, ever. He thought perhaps if this boy would just speak he might flourish and become a fine soldier someday.

He taught Joseph to stand at attention or rest at ease in his presence. He taught him to pay attention to details, to polish his boots with gusto and spit shined reflections, to shine his sword, to march, to shoot, to parry. He found him quite skilled and a quick learner, yet he was quite concerned that Joseph still would not speak.

The lower ranked soldiers grew to like Joseph too. They taught him other things. These lessons were not intended for his professional resume. They taught him to spit and spoke to him new phrases for his own edification, strings of curses long enough to lasso a calf. Then one day they let him in on their card game. And the very first time they let him play poker he beat them.

He was drawn into the game by an Irishman named O'Rourke from Dublin, who'd signed up for a meal and paycheck fresh off the boat. He said he would send his mother his pay if it weren't for the game and the liquor, which were his weaknesses. Fresh over from Ireland, this drinking man looked across the table as Joseph pulled three queens over sixes, a full house to the Irishman's straight. From that point they all knew Joseph was a very skilled player, a brilliant tactician. He understood odds and the cards he'd been dealt.

In three months time, just as hoped, the Colonel was summoned to Washington, to a post with a prominent General, one closely connected to the President. And so Colonel Naughton and Joseph set off riding with a military escort to the east, to the capital on the Potomac, to live among the high and mighty of the land.

The Raid

Harpers Ferry was at the crux of two rivers, the Potomac and the Shenandoah. The ancient shale cliffs glowering down from Maryland and Virginia to the flowing channels below were formed ages ago, carved out by the forging waters of a great flood, a massive wash. This was a junction, a confluence of civilization, a town at a major railroad junction; the Baltimore & Ohio came through, crossing on trestles, stopping in the small village. The town was a jumble of buildings both brick and frame, rising up a few small streets and atop a sizable knoll. There were hotels and eateries, a smith and a general store; a tavern and a railroad station were perhaps the busiest. All the businesses were deeply anchored in the town with a steady flow on Federal income and regular work; Harpers Ferry thrived.

The arms foundry was created by George Washington as one of his first official acts; it was in such an ideal spot for reliable power and so close to the capitol of the new nation. It now made most of the weapons for the south. Thousands of rifles were stored behind gates on the main street in the armory. This was Brown's target.

One day in early summer, John Kagi rode up with a bill of sale in hand to an old barn, once a tannery and now a warehouse, in Chambersburg, Pennsylvania. In it were stored dusty boxes filled with Sharps rifles, Maynard revolvers and Brown's self designed pikes—medieval poles with Bowie knives attached to the ends; weapons for the newly freed slaves to stab and gut their white opponents. They had been there for months, unlabeled but assumed to be mining equipment. Kagi, a veteran of Brown's fighters from Kansas, was one of the first in the group of rabid, violent abolitionists who'd learned of the plan for Virginia. He signed in blood right away, never questioned it, though others had.

The warehouseman keyed a padlock on a chain running through holes in the uneven barn doors. He heaved open one at a time, coaxing movement from the rusted hinges which croaked like they might bind and snap. Morning light had tunneled through the ill fitting boards and lounged in uneven stripes across the stacked boxes like draping flags. Spores ascended and danced on wafts of charging hot air, rising in a million tarantellas. Kagi caught the moldy smell in the mildewed air and let it go by as he looked on this cache. The streaks of sunshine christening his wares were signs of a bright future. He had already found the gold.

The warehouseman sensed something about this quiet man, who did not resemble a miner. He did not look like someone heading into a deep pit to dig for hours on end to unearth some nugget of worth. He was no common laborer or prospector; there was something else. He saw the look of glory in his eyes. This stranger had been voted in Canada to be the next Secretary of War in Brown's new government. These crates were the key to his place in history

The crates were loaded in the wagon by a two free Negroes, hired hands for the job, and Kagi drove on toward Harpers Ferry.

Captain John E. Cook had been living outside Harpers Ferry for nearly a year. He was another of Brown's original Kansas fighters. He had been scouting the area, gathering information on the workings of the town, the presence of local gendarmes. There was no practicing local officer except for an overweight constable who spent most days sleeping in a chair inside his tiny office. He noted the train schedules: twice a day like clockwork. He also counted as best he could the location of the local slave population. He wrote down everything, noting that few soldiers were in town except for those who visited the tavern on leave or rode the trains which arrived empty and left filled with weapons.

Cook sat in a local eatery and watched the men go to work in the armory. He went there for coffee and biscuits a few days a week and watched and counted, then left as if off to work himself. He noted the sleepy workaday attitude of most and the lax security for such a wealth of arms. He thought to himself this was easy 'pickins'.

Nights spent in the tavern were detection missions as well. He befriended locals and, after buying a whiskey or three, listened in fabricated awe to their spirit loosened boasts, spoken in confidence, about the weapons they were building, how many were produced each month, where they were stored in the armory. The rifle factory just up the man-made canal was a mere hundred yards from the armory. Its drills and saws ran on power from the steady running water while skilled workers bore and machined weapons of the highest quality. They were taken down the road, a crate at a time, and loaded into the armory.

Inside the armory the oiled and gleaming guns stood on display in long racks on the walls, locked in place by a metal rod. Cook glanced in one of the barred windows once, while he stood beneath the eaves in a spring downpour, and looked at the finely made tools that would soon build a new world of equality for all.

John Brown arrived at Harpers Ferry on July 3rd, fittingly the day before the grand ceremony for the nation's independence. It was a warm sunny day, a good day to see the final stages of his plan fall in place. He had a look of destiny in his eyes. His sons, Oliver and Owen, and another man named Jeremiah Anderson (also a fighter from the Kansas wars), could sense a change in him as they traveled together. Brown was focused yet peaceful, the anxiousness he always exhibited had calmed. He knew his time was at hand. He was never one to flinch from a fight. He'd been in battles before and he always knew they were but a foretaste of this blood feast to come. But rather then rise in anger for this next and greatest of clashes, he was serene. This was the consummate purpose of his entire life, the reason he was on this earth. His sons were sturdy weapons he had forged; his soldiers were the crimson flower of his righteous crop, raised for one great ordained reason. He traveled to Harpers Ferry to put these weapons to use and to bring in a bountiful harvest.

His son, John Jr., too mentally unstable to go, had stayed behind blathering to anyone who would listen about the apocalypse to unfold. The men he spoke to knew he was touched, but knew as well who his father was. John Brown had risen to fame like a rocket over a besieged fort; he could surprise and amaze with his actions. Perhaps, they thought, his raving son knew something they did not. So they listened with one ear cocked and a wary eyed glance to the future.

The whole family had listened to this grand plan for Virginia for years and they too sensed finality. Mary Day Brown was as firm and resolute as her husband in the abolition business. She was his strength; she provided a source of power for him to go on when he privately wavered at the cup before him. Once when he visited her at their farm in Elba, in the mountains of New York, between his travels freeing slaves and delivering them to Canada, he told her. He was going on to his death. He knew this was to be his final act in this realm. Mary knew it too. She kissed him on that cool morning before he rode off; hugged him long enough for dew to gather and drip from the bent and withering grass. She sent him on willingly. She knew who he was and what he was. She knew this when they married. It was her role in life to prepare him for this battle. She knew it and she knew she would see him no more alive, but that black men, women and children would walk free because of what they had done together.

As soon as John Brown arrived, he set about to find a place to live, a place where he could store his weapons, a place that could house his soldiers. He found a farmhouse to rent outside Harpers Ferry on the Maryland side, a farm owned by a family named Kennedy, in a spot hidden away where few people would happen upon them. Under the name Isaac Smith, he agreed to the rent the house, $35 for nine months. He looked upon the ramshackle house after the owner rolled away and saw in it a fulfillment of his basic needs: adequate space, room to drill and practice, a broad view to see people coming upon them, and this too brought him ease. But it also seemed, as the blood orange clouds darkened into dusk, that there was a nod of assent from his maker. This was the place that was to be since the earth was created. It seemed so right. He knew in his marrow he was on the path God had determined for him. He was aged and tired from miles and battles but he felt like a spring buck. He was filled. It is as though he and God were walking hand in hand, everything was working as expected.

"Soon, soon," he thought.

His son, Watson Brown, and William and Dauphin Thompson, grown children of Brown's daughter, followed not long thereafter; they rode in to see Father Brown hard at work with pen and ink rewriting the Declaration. He greeted them but would not stop work on his opus. He had been writing for days, absorbed in this great document, he thought it soon to be lauded as a master work in American history, but only after the raid succeeded and armies of free slaves marched onward freeing others. The new arrivals understood. It was why they followed him. So they set their horses off to feed and started to clean the rifles and settle in. This was the time for rest and preparation for the unleashing of the hell they were to be part of. It was understood that each moment mattered and they all had a role in it and a job to perform. John Brown, the leader they were following, perhaps to their deaths, had always operated with this sense of divine purpose and they mirrored it.

Later free Negroes joined them at the Kennedy farm; Dangerfield Newby, hoping to free his wife who was still a slave along with his seven children in Virginia; Lewis Leary, a runaway slave, John Copeland, a free black from Ohio, and Osborne Anderson, a recruit from the Constitutional Convention in Chatham, Canada. These men saw themselves in the vanguard of their enslaved race. They had heard of Brown or listened to him speak. They had deep hatred and resentment for the wrongs they'd endured. It was their time to act. There would be no other chance for them. They all knew that they would go down in the history of their race as men of fate who saw the future as told by Brown. This was much more to them then civil disobedience, this was uncivil revolution and they were ready to wreak havoc on the enslavers and their proxies.

Other whites soon joined them as well: William Leeman, Charles Tidd, Aaron Stevens, Albert Hazlett, Stewart Taylor, and the brothers, Barclay and Edwin Coppoc. These men were also veterans from the battles in Kansas; they had drilled in Ohio and waited for their chance. They rode in ready to free more slaves come what may. This was their calling, they were not afraid of death. They could be cruel; they were killers and did not wince at it. Each had a rough look about them, something you might not trust in a card game. It was because they did not harbor any qualm for raising their rifles and drawing a bead on any man who stood in the way of their beliefs. In their injustice hating eyes pro-slavery people were dogs to be put down. They saw in their actions a deeper purpose; it was not for folly or gain they would shoot a man through the bowels. It was for a just cause. Their slaughter of men was of a higher sort then common murder.

Brown's daughter, Ann, came too with her sister-in-law Martha, Owen's wife, to cook, clean, sew and stand guard. Martha was a strong woman, toughened by years alone while Owen followed his father. Ann, though slight, was fierce

in her determination to support her siblings and father, even to death. They
revered old Brown. He was their father, their leader and their spiritual guide. They
knew the risks but they also knew success required a woman's skills. As much as
weapons and bullets, women were assets in the battles of life and war. The men,
focused on higher things, would not eat properly or keep the place up. Though
the weaker sex, they felt they would provide strength of a kind men could not
master: order, cleanliness, organization. They were not fighters but they were part
of the conspiracy. They faced the same fate: they could be rounded up and hung
with the rest of them. This they knew and they went forth anyway.

So this variety of God's children formed Brown's army. They all served the
cause as one race and gender, the sons, brothers, the Negroes, the women, all.
This was a small part of the vision John Brown saw for the world. All were equal
in his eyes, all could serve and fight and all could die.

The days and weeks of waiting were long. Summer heat roasted the roof shakes,
baking determination deeper and deeper into all beneath the eaves. While
waiting the men read, drilled, trained with guns and pikes, played cards, read
newspapers, cleaned rifles, and thought about what lay ahead. Brown's revision
of the *Declaration of Independence* was called: *A Declaration of Liberty by the
Representatives of the Slave Population of the United States of America:*

> *When in the course of human events,*
> *it becomes necessary for an oppressed people to rise,*
> *and assert their natural rights, as human beings,*
> *as native and mutual citizens of a free republic,*
> *and break the odious yoke of oppression,*
> *which is so unjustly laid upon them by their fellow countrymen,*
> *and to assume among the powers of the earth the same equal privileges*
> *to which the Laws Of Nature, and nature's God, entitle them.*
> *A moderate respect for the opinions of Mankind,*
> *requires that they should declare the causes which incite them*
> *to this just and worthy action.*
> *The history of American Slavery is a history of injustice*
> *and cruelties inflicted upon the slave in every conceivable way.*
> *It is the embodiment of all that is Evil,*
> *and ruinous to the nation, and Subversive of all good.*
> *We will obtain these rights or die in the struggle to obtain them.*
> *We make war upon oppression,*
> *nature is mourning for its murdered and afflicted children.*
> *Hung be the heavens in scarlet.*

And with all the work now done, the travels, the fighting, the recruiting, the fund raising, the meetings with luminaries, revolutionaries, runaways, mercenaries, abolitionists, authors, preachers, editors, merchants, Brown had yet one more man he wanted to convince.

In August he met with Frederick Douglass, the leading free Negro intellectual of the nation, in a stone quarry near the Pennsylvania border. They had met years before when Brown was just a committed simpleton, a convincing but directionless advocate for the cause. They sat in his meager home and he told Douglass of his vision for a slave war. Douglass sensed his seriousness, and later would know him of deadly intent after Kansas. Brown said he would first draw a line at the Kansas border and then start the war of all race wars in Virginia. He had envisioned this all long before, and told Douglass about it by a single candle on a scarred table top, pointing to a crude map of the eastern United States. He pointed out Harpers Ferry and the ragged line of Appalachian Mountains running into the center of Georgia. Douglass never thought he would get this far with his plan. But Brown had.

Douglass was impressed by his dedication to the black race and his personal sacrifices. He felt strongly Brown was of the utmost seriousness and was ready to give his life. But while their vision of equality and their dedication to the cause was so closely related, and Brown had shown his mettle on the national stage, Douglass could not find it in himself to sanction this bold and violent action. He felt Harpers Ferry was a steel trap for sure.

Douglass knew in his soul slavery's demise would come only by fighting and that a fire to free his people had to be set. But he could not bring himself to join this venture; it seemed so contrived, so wild, so optimistic of result. Brown so hoped he would agree to assist, particularly with the freed slaves. Years later he'd admit Brown was right and he was wrong, that this night encounter in the quarry was not with a man possessed or on the brink of madness but with a stern eyed soldier with a duty to perform who foresaw the future Douglass sought.

Brown searched the darkness for movement in the abandoned stone quarry. He made out a carriage approaching and in it Frederick Douglass, his straight-standing nappy hair, gray and white against the night. Douglass' black face was featureless in the dark. He walked towards Brown with a smaller black man, Shields Green, who followed a few steps behind like a trusty valet, trailing a little, not feeling the peer of Douglass.

Shields Green had escaped from the hell he knew as a slave in Charleston, South Carolina. He served Douglass as a dutiful employee not a man bound by chains. It was his choice. It was all he knew to do after his years dressed like a Frenchman in his master's large house. He still bore the guilt of the sexual perversions heaped on him like so many stones by his master's wife. He had slipped away in the midst of a hurricane. Found his way to a ship's hold and eventually to Philadelphia where he breathed free air for the first time. In time he was in the presence of Mr. Douglass at a lecture and he knew what he was to do. So he offered himself up and served him and his cause ever since. This was his calling he knew; to work for this great man of his own race and promote the ideas he espoused.

Brown and Douglass came together, shook hands and embraced. Then they spoke in the darkness.

"We will go in October. All the pikes and guns will be in place by then."

"It is a bold plan."

"It is."

"I know you do this for my people."

"Yes, for all people in truth."

"Yes, I know."

"But mainly for God, he commands this."

"I cannot find it in myself to sanction this violence. It cannot succeed."

"Perhaps, but we will go on with it."

"Will you not reconsider?"

"No, it has been too long waiting."

"You will die."

"I may be shot or hanged. But others will learn from what I did. Then they will rise up."

"Some may, but I fear it. There has been no plan set forth. I do not know if my people are ready...if they will join and fight."

"They are ready."

"How can you be sure?"

"They are ready."

"It is impossible to know, at last. I do not want to lose so great a fighter for our cause on such a gamble."

"I have not many years left. It is time, finally."

Douglass paused and thought on this a time then said, "I wish you well, John. God's speed. Let us go, Shields. We will change no minds tonight?"

But Shields Green said, "I'm think I'm astayin' with Mas'er Brown.

Dumbfounded Douglass said, "Shields?"

"This be my time, sir, I thank ya for all ya done. I be followin the ole man now."

Douglass stood for a few moments, aware of the change he saw in this man who'd been content to be his valet and was now volunteering to fight and probably die.

"I see, I see," said Douglass. "Then God's speed to you. You are a fine man. I am proud to say I know you. I am proud to know both of you. May you both succeed, I pray."

They separated and never met again this side of the veil. Shields Green heard in Brown's words something that formed a crossroad in his life. Only the decision to ride out the storm in the hold of a ship and escape to freedom was greater. Brown's way was his destiny. His years of humiliation and servitude in Charleston and his escape to the north finally made sense to him. He had found a way to gain the admiration of others. So he rode off to join the raid on Harpers Ferry and Frederick Douglass returned alone.

The men, twenty-one strong, met at the Kennedy farmhouse. A new man named Francis Merriam had joined after donating six hundred dollars worth of primers for Sharps rifles, as well as more ammunition. He was a bit of a dandy but devoted and serious, though not quite stable. He had lost a fortune gambling and did not see why he should not gamble on this outcome as well, at least, he thought, there will be some meaningful outcome.

Brown gathered the men and women and read aloud from the Bible:

"Remember those in bonds as if bound with them
whoever stops his ear at the cry of the poor,
he also shall cry himself, but shall not be heard.
He that has a bountiful eye shall be blessed,
for he gives his bread to the poor.
A good name is better to be chosen than great riches,
and loving favor rather than silver and gold.
Whoever mocks the poor reproaches his maker, and he that is glad at calamities
shall not go unpunished.
He that has pity on the poor lends to the Lord, and that which he has given will
he pay him again."

Brown then read the Provisional Constitution aloud and they all said, "Ay" to its ratification.

At six p.m. Brown closed his watch and said, "Cook, Tidd, off with you now, cut the telegraph wires, there will be no messages tonight. We leave at eight o'clock, you have two hours. When you are done join up with those raiding the farms and freeing slaves."

They all shook hands; the plan was finally in motion.

When Cook and Tidd had ridden off on horseback the rest settled into their thoughts and waited these last anxious one hundred and twenty minutes, which crept like ivy.

As the time was nearing to leave, Brown felt he needed to review the plan one more time.

"Owen, Merriam, Barclay Coppoc. You are to stay here. Once we are well gone, head to the schoolhouse."

They nodded. They knew it; they had known for some time but were pleased to hear it again.

"Once the others have freed slaves they will meet you at the schoolhouse for weapons. Arm them and show them what to do. We will all be out to meet you and take them to the hills. We follow the plan. We will regroup and begin to head south along the ridge tops. There are farms at the base of the Blue Ridge in the Shenandoah where we will free more and gain reinforcements."

Brown turned then and pointed.

"Watson and Taylor guard the Potomac Bridge, no one crosses it."

They nodded. They knew it too. They had talked of this plan for weeks now. Taylor spit and some dribbled on his chin. He wiped it without blinking.

"Kagi, Stevens, take the watchman from the Potomac Bridge to the engine house as prisoner. After we have the armory, you will head with the rest of us to the rifle factory and hold it."

Kagi smiled, he was ready. He shuffled his feet and straightened his shirt. He wondered what he would wear when they formed the new government.

"Shields Green, you head out to the Washington farm with Osborn Anderson and Leary."

They looked at each other, heads shaking in assent.

"Get George Washington's sword, the one given to him by Frederic the Great. I want to free the slaves holding that sword. Do you understand?

Nods again.

"Free Washington's slaves and bring them to me with Lewis Washington, George Washington's great grand nephew, in their charge."

Smiles crossed the faces of the waiting warriors at this thought: the bloodline of the first President in the control of his slaves, the sword of the Father of the Country severing their bonds.

"Oliver and Will Thompson, you're holding the Shenandoah Bridge. No one crosses it; if they try, make it their last steps."

Oliver could envision what he would do when the first man tried to take his charge. It thrilled him.

"Jerry Anderson, Dauphine Thompson, you watch the streets. If anyone gets in the way take them hostage, bring them to the armory."

Another pair of nods.

"Hazlett, Edwin Coppoc, Leeman, Copeland, Newby the armory is yours. Shoot to kill or take em prisoner, but take it. I will be with you."

All looked to each other, chins drawn up to pursed lips, squinting eyes met and widened, held in a captive gaze already long distant from any care of this world, convinced and converted to an army for God.

"Now gather your arms, we proceed to the Ferry."

They rose and gathered their arms, donned their hats, shifted their trousers to a comfortable place.

"Do not take the life of anyone if you can avoid it; but if it is necessary to save your own, then make sure work of it."

Ann and Martha had already left a few days before, saying long farewells.

It was a hard departure, feeling final and permanent. Brown stopped and looked at his daughters shawl, left behind for his comfort. He touched it and moved on. He walked outside and climbed into the wagon loaded with weapons. The men walked behind.

Owen Brown, F. J. Merriam, and Barclay Coppoc watched them leave. They had a long wait so they settled in, nervous and primed, for their portion of the plan at the schoolhouse.

A light rain was falling as they marched off. All that could be heard was gravel crunching under boots, a creak from the wagon, a splash in a puddle. Someone tripped on a root and cursed.

"There'll be no curses among our men."

The wagon's wheels bounced and rolled over exposed boulders which surfaced like whalebacks in a frozen sea, never sounding. A breeze blew, cooling but not yet cold; leaves were changing; they rattled in the oaks and fell from the poplars and the willows, showering them as with the confetti of cheering crowds. Along the road by the coursing river they could look on the dark waters and hear the steady wash and splatter on the corrugated banks. Each was lost in a private thought, the nerves of things to come twanging against the bone of what already was.

Kagi and Stevens led the way on the six mile trek from the farmstead to the town. They walked in silence with only a few comments along the way. Brown told them to be quiet each time anyone spoke, so they all withdrew and tried to think as hard as they could on their lives and their loved ones, thoughts rushing past like tin types thrown in the air. With each second that passed they knew they were closer to something great in this life or the next.

The whipping sound of the telegraph wires sounded funny to Cook and Tidd. With each cut and snap they laughed at the springing noise of the recoiling wires. It was a grand trick they were playing on the telegraph clerk who would be tapping away with useless calls for help.

After cutting the telegraph wires, Cook and Tidd went off to rove the countryside freeing slaves; the first step in the plan to start the war was completed.

There was a wagon path that ran alongside the railroad trestle on the Potomac Bridge and the small army of men approached it with glory in their eyes. The watchman came out with a lantern in hand. He was laughing.

"What have we a grand parade? It is too late for fun."

"This is no parade. You are our prisoner. Come with me."

He looked stunned as he was taken by Kagi toward the armory.

Watson Brown and Stewart Taylor then stood guard at the Potomac River Bridge. They each took a seat near the guard house, looking toward the darkness on the Maryland side and the lights in town on the other, waiting for whatever may come. They were ready to kill anyone who could disrupt their plan.

Oliver Brown and William Thompson stood guard at the Shenandoah Bridge. They too were resolute. Oliver had a mean streak and it was itching him. He was ready to die, preferred to kill, and knew it was just a matter of a short time for either.

At John Brown's order the rest went to take the armory on Potomac Street. They kicked in the door and entered with guns at the ready. The sleeping guards were taken by surprise. The last to enter was Brown who followed through the door, looking confirmed as a man and resolute as a revolutionary.

Brown said to the guard, "I came here from Kansas to free all the Negroes. I now have possession of the United States Armory and if citizens interfere with me I will burn the town and the blood will run in the streets."

The sleepy eyed men were aware by now this was no dream common among them, but it was bizarre all the same. John Brown in their midst, armed Negroes stealing weapons, freeing slaves, it was too fantastic to consider and yet there he was, bearded and tawny, with fired eyes and a loaded gun.

With the armory taken, John Kagi brought the Potomac Bridge watchmen to join the other hostages milling in the armory yard, then Brown went with Kagi and Stevens to take over the rifle works. There was no resistance there either, just hands raised and submissiveness. So Brown returned to the armory while Kagi and Stevens and others stayed behind at the factory.

Meanwhile Cook and Tidd joined the black fighters Leary, Green and Anderson and were off to free slaves. It was a one mile walk to the first farm. They were pleased to be once again in the slave freeing business.

Cook entered the first slave cabin and found a group of blacks sitting around a hearth. He stepped in through the door, rifle in hand.

"I have come to free you."

They were shocked and looked at each other.

"Follow me."

They did not know what to do. He was white, had a rifle and gave them orders, but they were orders they had never heard before.

"Come now, we are led by John Brown. He is here to free you and arm you."

They knew of Brown but they were confused and afraid. They followed after the shock wore off but more as prisoners than fighters. They were afraid they would be captured as runaways and whipped or hung. They were not sure who this stranger was, and although there were other blacks carrying rifles, this did not make sense or seem wise.

Along the way, after stopping at another farm and gathering a group of male slaves, a few of them ran away in fear. Cook and Tidd looked at each other considering this new development. This was no way to start a race war.

Leary, Green and Osborne Anderson, went up to the back door of the Washington mansion to break in and capture Lewis Washington. Once they had broken in, they stormed the bedchambers scaring nearly to death the Colonel and his wife. They then gathered the family in the parlor and took down the famous sword mentioned by Brown from the mantle. They looked at it with relish as the silver patina wavered along the sweeping blade, its fading grip still a soft and supple leather felt rich to the touch, its ringing edge honed sharp and clean. They held the saber, now a flashing messenger of freedom, and saw in its reflective shine their smiling faces, blurred and stretched to unnatural shapes. When they marched the prisoners outside with the sword over their heads, they smiled as slaves milled about wondering what was happening, unaccustomed to seeing their master in such a state. Brown was now the father of a new country, where black, white, yellow and red, men and women alike, were free.

Washington was put in a carriage sobbing in anguish; he was not the warrior his grandfather was. He feared for his life the entire ride into town. His fear increased when he saw armed guards on the trestle as they crossed the Potomac Bridge and even more so as he went through the town past more armed men and on up to the armory.

When Washington was brought in to the armory building he did not know who the old fighter was who sat calmly at a desk.

Shields Green said, "This is John Brown of Kansas."

And Washington's face went white; he knew his reputation.

Francis Merriam, Barclay Coppoc, and Owen Brown saw the first group of free slaves walking down the road, led by Lewis Leary and Osborn Anderson, toward the schoolhouse. They greeted them and took them to see the weapons inside. The slaves were dumbfounded.

Merriam and Owen demonstrated how to use the pikes. But some of the slaves betrayed confused looks and wide eyed disbelief. When handed the weapons they held them limply. A few saw this incredible event as the chance of their lives, the moment they had been waiting for, and they stabbed at the air ready to fight. The confused slaves, however, over time slipped quietly away. Their first free choice was to run away and return to bondage, so accustomed were they to that sheltered world.

A replacement for the captured watchman on the Potomac Bridge, lantern in hand, walked out for his night's work. Oliver Brown, who had moved over from the Shenandoah Bridge, jumped from the darkness, gun in hand, and yelled for him to stop. But the startled man did not understand and his good nature could not conceive of this as anything but a ruse. He moved forward a few more steps smiling and guessing at this sport as Oliver came up alongside. He then saw the guns and pikes and fear overtook him; he turned and punched Oliver Brown. As he ran away they shot at him and he was grazed by a bullet on his ear. The watchman ran hell bent to a tavern in town with blood trickling down his ear and neck. He told his wild eyed story to the droopy eyed men drinking and playing checkers but they only thought him a drunk who'd fallen and banged his head. They did not believe him.

So out went the saloon keeper to see what was happening. Out on the bridge he walked concerned but sure nothing was afoot, only to be taken prisoner and marched into town to the armory, where he was startled to see other townspeople held captive and mulling about unsure about what was going on.

The wounded watchman, after no one in the tavern would listen - still scared outright at almost being killed - ran in a westerly direction along the railroad tracks to an oncoming train, the Baltimore & Ohio east bound from Wheeling. The engineer saw in his lamplight a fool running alongside, bleeding at the head and yelling for him to stop the train. Sensing danger he hit the brakes, jostling the sleeping passengers in the cars.

A conductor stepped down at the same time as the engineer and both came up to the puffing man, who was bleeding and sweating and seemed crazed.

"There's men with guns on the bridge. They shot me! Look! They shot me."

"What's going on there?" asked the engineer.

"Don't know... but don't go on, they'll kill you."

Oliver Brown let loose a shot in their direction and the three men scurried to the safety of the train.

Oliver licked his lips, inhaled and blew out in frustration. He narrowly missed but scared them to the same effect. They were stopped.

A baggage handler, a young black man, stepped off the train to see why the train had stopped and what the commotion was about. Oliver Brown and Stewart Taylor drew a bead on him and both fired but missed. In fear the startled porter turned and ran away from the train, acting reflexively to escape danger. Oliver, angered at two missed marks in a row, shot him in the back and he fell mortally wounded on the tracks. So Oliver and Taylor dragged him to the bridge so they could watch him. He was conscious and in great pain with a large gaping exit wound in his stomach. He died some anguished hours later from the terrible wound.

The first person to die in the raid to free all slaves and the first skirmish of the Civil War was a free black man.

Osborn Anderson and Lewis Leery returned to the armory from their round of farm raids and told John Brown about the slaves they freed. Some, he said, would fight and were ready to die; this was their chance for freedom and they knew it. But many had run away afraid.

This caused Brown pause. The whole plan was based on raising an army of slaves; he needed them for the invasion of the south. He hesitated. He looked about at the men who followed him, on the faces of those blacks who were inspired by him, gun in hand and ready to fight. They were the men he needed. They understood. They were inspired. But what had happened? Why were the freed slaves not rallying?

He looked down, deep in thought, noticing the soil and stains on his worn shoes, dust from many places mingled together with blood and sweat; he looked around the armory at the weapons, brand new and at the ready for war. He so wanted to go on. He thought about his options. He sighed, shook his head. He'd made up his mind.

"Newby go on up to Oliver and tell him to let the train go on without further trouble."

"They'll tell everyone, the army will be riding toward us in one hour's time, at the next stop the wires will be hummin."

"Tell him. Just tell him"

And Newby left with a new look on his face.

Oliver Brown was concerned when Newby brought him the word from his father. He knew the world would soon know of their raid on Harpers Ferry. Word was already spreading around the valleys and farms. The Jefferson Guards would be brought in from Charles Town and news would soon get out to Washington, alerting the army. This troubled him, but ever the soldier he waved the train on. But this new development brought new concerns for the plan, so they gave up the bridges and Oliver Brown, Watson Brown, and Stewart Taylor retreated to the town to meet with their leader. There was no point in holding the bridges any longer. Perhaps they would regroup and escape.

Will Thompson wanted to wait on the bridge and was later captured trying to hold off the attackers. He was brought to a local hotel called the Wager House as prisoner.

The engineer wasted no time. He opened the door to the furnace and started shoveling coal. At the same time he opened up the valve and the train started with an exhausted huff and began to roll as if mired in a slough. The engineer had once dreamed of this; he remembered the same sense of impending fear growing to panic from the dogged sluggishness of his massive locomotive. He looked down at Oliver Brown with trepidation as he walked along the trestle and wished the near frozen train could move faster. The train then pulled laboriously past the crumbled body of the dead baggage man, his dark face pressed against the boards on the trestle, mouth opened, eyes shut. The engineer felt sorry for him, he had been a good and loyal person. He shoveled in the coal and fired up the engine and in short time the train disappeared in a mist of its own conjuring, spirited away with urgency carrying a most troubling message for Washington.

A portly grocer closed the door on his trackside house and was on his way to work. He walked along as he did each day, after looking in on his children and kissing his wife, with a lunch pail in hand and a fresh cup of coffee in his large belly. He waved to the train as it went past, unaware of the disruptions underway. He did not understand the troubled expression on the engineer's face or the look of dismay on the faces of passengers staring through the windows. They went by in rapid succession, one fearful face after another, as the train gained speed. The last face, the conductor in the window of the caboose, was one of perplexed pity. This whole event struck the grocer as odd. There was something different in the air this morning.

From the town Dangerfield Newby, frustrated by the message he had just delivered to Oliver Brown to let the train escape, drew the round grocer in his sight. He watched him trundle and bounce along and when he was attuned to his walking rhythm, he shot him; hit him in the groin, wounding him mortally. The grocer fell like a clown in the circus, hit where it hurts; he yelled an almost comical noise that sounded like a child's nonsense; it could have been funny if not for the blood. He died there on the ground as the train imploded to a speck in the descending distance.

Brown, now fully aware all was not going according to his vision and with the train carrying word to the rest of the world, took the most valuable eleven hostages and pulled back to the engine house to make his stand, leaving Albert Hazlett and Osborn Anderson to hold the armory.

Brown, his hostages, Watson and Oliver Brown, Edwin Coppoc, Aaron Stevens and a few other men entered the small brick structure at a run. Brown skidded to a halt and surveyed the small space in a second and gave the orders.

"We need firing holes in the walls, load weapons and set them aside to keep continuous fire. Any spare time spend cleaning and loading. Wait for my orders before we shoot."

The gunfire had gradually brought out the people poking into the early morning light like prairie dogs curious to see what was happening on the mound.

Dangerfield Newby ran to join Brown in the engine house but as he crossed the street a bullet zipped the air entering his throat and exiting his upper back; he fell to the ground choking on blood. He died quickly leaving a great deal of himself on the ground to mark the spot. A townsman who had seen him shoot the grocer took him down. He was the first of Brown's men killed that day. He would never again see his wife and children, still held in bondage in Virginia. Another free black man, like the baggage handler, was killed in the battle to free all blacks.

A group of citizens, angered to a fever pitch, feeling their lives and families threatened, and enraged that a Negro was their attacker ran to his body and mutilated it, cutting off ears, poking eyes from their sockets, crushing his head; they wounded and punctured him over and over, leaving him an indiscernible pulp. They left him to rot. His body was there for the roaming dogs. They nudged and poked and tore until he was a bloody mess that could have been any creature let alone a man. He would lie there for many hours drawing flies, rotting and being consumed.

Then the ragtag group of irate, unorganized and ill equipped townspeople gathered and seemed to be getting ready for an action. Seeing this Brown called again for his men organize the guns, load them and leave them standing against the wall. His men took aim with limited sight through the small portholes in the brick walls at his enemies, those who fought to save slavery.

"Don't waste your powder and shot. Take aim and make every shot count. The troops will look for us to retreat on their first appearance, let em come on, wait for my order, we'll drop them as they wonder whether we will fight or run," he told his men.

The mob came on firing and yelling as they charged the engine house. Brown's men opened up with a volley tearing through them, dropping some in pain and anguish. The sight of their neighbors falling and dying scared them and the mob soon fell back.

Across the river the Jefferson Guard arrived from Charles Town. They tried to hold their ranks on the march like professional soldiers, but they were so anxious for the fight that some ran ahead at the sound of shots, much to the dismay of their volunteer Colonel. Word had spread and ire was up. There was to be a fight to the death and they sensed it.

The locals cheered as they arrived and the Jefferson Guard felt proud and heroic though nothing had as of yet been accomplished. After much back slapping by those now gathered along the Maryland side on the river's edge, and after the Guard had broken ranks to speak to old friends and relatives, the Colonel called for them to form up.

The Jefferson Guard began to move across the Potomac trestle followed by the locals who were much bolstered by their new reinforcements. In a few minutes they charged the rifle works, forcing Kagi, Copeland and Leary to flee. The escaping men tried to forge across the Shenandoah River but were shot in the water. Kagi fell dead from his wound, face down and still. The bullet had exploded his heart. He floated away like a rag doll on the water, bouncing and turning in the current. The Secretary of War for the future government of John Brown was dead.

Leary was shot in the back and captured on the river bank. He was dragged ashore and beaten and taken off to a nearby farm as prisoner to await his fate.

Copeland, wounded, lay on a rock some way out in the water with his rifle. A man waded out to shoot him. They faced off with each other, frantically taking aim at close range, but neither gun fired, both were too wet. Cold and confused, the bleeding and frightened Copeland surrendered.

The forces united to protect their homes, families, and slavery massed again. They raged now as a crazed mob and with each yell and catcall by a roused citizen they surged forth in unison like geysers of anger and hate. John Brown sat sheltered for a time against the brick wall of the engine house, as exhausted as ever in his life, the glow in his eyes not fully faded, however. There was as yet work to do for God. His sacrifice was at hand. He looked around the tiny building used to house the fire wagons which had become his haven and he wondered on the beauty of the bricks, the hewn beams across the ceiling, their strength, their purpose, spanning perhaps thirty feet. The brick walls leaned in like his burial tomb, but for now his fort, and hence his friend. He was still alive and trapped in his earthly existence waiting for his freedom. But as long as blood flowed in his veins and was not spilled out on the ground like stale coffee he would strive to fulfill his mission. The Fort, as all would later call it, afforded him yet one more chance to beckon his message. He smiled and knew he was in the vault of his passion, his three day sepulcher with the stone rolled across the entrance. Three heavy oaken doors were barricaded shut, protecting him from the hundreds outside who surrounded them. They awaited the next rally and charge.

In this lull in the fighting, George Washington's great nephew sat leaning against a wall, sweating with fear, surely no hero, guarded by a freed black slave. The other hostages, guarded by the brave armed blacks, had looks of tension scarring their eyes; resignation dripped from their faces at the nearness of death's call. John Brown looked at them calmly and then turned to his uneven porthole in the brick wall, looking across the river to the precise movement of soldiers on the other side.

Time went by and Brown considered his plight. Surrounded by soldiers and angry citizens, with bullets flying, men dying, the word out and the United States Army on the way, Brown decided to send his son, Watson, and one of his soldiers, Aaron Stevens, under a white flag to parlay. He did this to try to save his men; he did not care if he died. They brought with them an armory clerk as hostage. But there was no discipline in the crowd. With no sense of orderly warfare or a command to control the guns, few would recognize a flag of truce. Watson, walking out flag in hand, was shot in the bowels and Stevens fell mortally wounded, shot in his head. Watson, holding his gut, crawled bleeding from a severe belly wound back into the engine house while the armory clerk escaped, running like a waddling duck off to the waiting crowd out of sight of the raider's guns. There was to be no negotiation, it was to be outright surrender or nothing.

In the rush of events, one of Brown's men, Will Leeman, ran off trying to escape into the river. He was shot. He floated downstream struggling to keep his head above water; stopping finally in the shallows, he crawled up on a rock. A townsman waded out with his gun over his head, keeping it dry. He shot Leeman in the face, leaving no expression of glory for his cause or features anyone could recognize. He was left to rot on the rock for many days.

One of Brown's men, Edwin Coppoc, saw from his porthole in the brick wall a finely dressed man walking along the road across the river from him. He put him in his rifle sight, aiming at the sparkling pocket watch chained to his dapper vest. He sent a lead missile stopping time, shooting him dead. He was the Mayor of Harpers Ferry, a much beloved man.

This death enraged the townspeople who looked on from the cover of their houses and from behind buildings. A mob formed which stormed the town. They overtook the Wager House, the hotel where William Thompson was held after being captured trying to hold them off at the Shenandoah Bridge. A woman, the housekeeper, pleaded for the men to take him into custody only, but they would have none of it. They dragged him out to the trestle, tied him up and used him for target practice.

He yelled, "You may kill me but thousands will avenge me. There will be liberty to the slaves."

He fell from the trestle full of holes and lay in the river, punctured over and over again from shot after shot.

John Brown cracked open one of the large oak doors of the engine house for a better look at the terrible events on the trestle. But as Oliver Brown stepped into view to take a look, a bullet screamed past John Brown piercing Oliver's shirt which quickly ran red. He fell to his knees; he too was shot in the bowels. He lay in excruciating pain and he begged his father to kill him. John Brown, mind racing with choices and decisions, held his son's head in his arms, looking across to Watson lying on the dusty floor and down again at the red mash of Oliver's stomach. He said calmly with much love, "If you must die, then die like a man." He then rose and checked the pulse of Watson, who was weak and fading. It was God's will.

Another military company arrived and ordered a charge on the engine house. The sound of gunfire rattled and boomed as if a war were on but again Brown's small group held them off. Townspeople and Jefferson Guard littered the ground and the rest retreated in the same uncoordinated manner in which they had charged. Those once enraged now ran away spent and those on the ground bled away their rage, encountering a chill that would never give up.

Across the river at the schoolhouse, Cook, Tidd, F.J. Merriam, Barclay Coppoc and Owen Brown heard gunfire. Some Negro women walking along the road told them there was all Hades breaking lose in town. So they climbed a hill to see what they could. On seeing the massing soldiers and the enflamed townspeople they had reason for concern, but the murder of Leeman in the river and Will Thompson on the trestle froze them. They could see no way to help and they stole away into the wilderness to escape north to safety.

So here was Brown with only four men who were not wounded, others were killed and scattered, with his sons dying before him, and yet with no help in sight, but he would not relent. The town's people sent some men under a flag of truce. But Brown wanted freedom and safe retreat to Maryland in exchange for the hostages. The answer was the same; it was to be unconditional surrender or death.

Brown looked across the river. The Federal army had arrived with Colonel Robert E. Lee at its head.

Lee sat on his white charger and surveyed the site and he deigned to send in his Lieutenant J.E.B. Stuart to approach the engine house at dawn to speak with the insurrectionists and seek a formal surrender. This was to be their last chance or a charge would be coming, but this time from a professional army.

Sometime in the night Albert Hazlett and Osborn Anderson stole away from the armory and ran into the night to safety.

The night was a long one. Oliver died, painfully and slowly, as did Watson, and his father prepared for battle, for his final hour. John Brown comforted his prisoners and said he would not harm them, they should not fear, killing them was not his goal. He wore on his side the sword of Frederick the Great, and he felt great pride for the Negroes who fought with him that day. He watched his men, making sure the rifles were loaded and stacked by the firing holes, and waited.

At the break of day, J.E.B. Stuart walked to the large oak door of the engine house. It creaked open and Brown's old face looked out. It was only then Stuart knew they were fighting John Brown.

"So you are he?"

"I am"

"You have caused quite a problem, Brown. I come with a message from Robert Lee, commander of the Federal Troops of the United States of America. Simply this, surrender or die."

Brown repeated his terms, "No, no, I want free passage to Maryland for all of us, or a bloody fight must ensue. There will be no surrender. The fate of the hostages is yours to decide. I cannot protect them in a charge."

"What do you want Brown? Why are you here?"

Brown nodded toward the blacks but said nothing.

With that Stuart nodded and stepped aside. He signaled and his men rushed the door, which Brown hastily barricaded. They tried to batter it in with sledgehammers, but to no avail. Brown's men shot out of the holes in the red brick walls but they could not hit them at such an angle and so close a range.

The soldiers then grabbed a metal ladder and using it as a battering ram; they charged and crashed it into the door until a splintered hole large enough for a man to enter was broken through.

A lieutenant rushed in the opening. He saw a kneeling man loading his rifle as Washington called out, "That's Brown!" and the soldier lunged at him with his sword. But the sword he mistakenly wore that day was a dress weapon, much lighter and not meant for fighting; it stabbed shallow in Brown's side and hit a bone, then it bent. The lieutenant then withdrew it and swung it at Brown, cutting his head with two crossing strokes.

Other soldiers rushed in but were shot by rifle fire from Brown's remaining men, shot in the face, shot in the shoulder, shot in the side. John Wilkes Booth, a private in the regiment entered and pierced Dauphine Thompson and Jerry Anderson with his sword, capturing them with soldierly form.

The fight was over, the hostages walked away into the daylight, hungry and weary but glad to be alive. Brown lay wounded and his sons and others were dead. Shields Green and John Copeland and others were captured as well. Some escaped.

The raid to start the war to free all slaves had failed.

Job

Zephaniah awoke from his dream about heaven and Archie the mongoloid behind the large doors, in a simple cabin. Smells of mildew and sweat mixed with smoke from a slumbering fire, spiced the air. He was amazed to realize that his hearing had returned and the sounds of chirping birds resonated as clear and sharp as bright coronets. His sight was still gone however and he groped about as he sat up. He'd lost all track of time; he did not know where he was. But he felt new, alive, awakened into a wonderful world of sounds he'd long missed. He felt unburdened, his newfound hearing cheered him and oddly the loss of sight did not cause him to despair. He felt free and blessed.

He looked to the foot of his pallet and there sat the Shining Man, calmly looking over him, glimmering through his darkness. He did not know if this was a dream or a visitation or perhaps a message from God, it surely seemed so. The feeling he received from this Shining Man was so good.

He thought of his family, of the rainstorm, of Hiram who had led him on Sagebrush and disappeared in the storm. But they all seemed so far away, a faint memory. Had he lived? He realized he was not sure. This could be heaven. Perhaps all were blind in heaven.

The next sound he heard was a chorus of Negroes singing a slow beautiful rhythmic song, like Hanna and Buela sang, worshipful and beaming:

"Swing low, sweet Chariot
Comin for to carry me home
Swing low sweet Chariot
Comin for to carry me home

I looked over Jordan
What did I see
Comin for to carry me home
A band of angels comin after me
Comin for to carry me home"

It was Sunday he felt, the Sabbath, it must be. It was the day to praise God. But if this were heaven, each day was a day to praise; all time was time to praise.

The song rose in pitch and promise, there was a clapping of hands, a joyful noise as it grew.

When it stopped he hoped for more. He tried to rise to his feet but he had lain for so long his legs were weak and he fell to the ground. So he lay listening for more. In a few minutes footsteps were heard. Someone entered the door and stopped.

An aged Negro man saw Zephaniah on the floor. He called for help to get him up. Soon more footsteps entered and strong arms raised him back to his pallet.

The man said, "Now you be layin still. You gots no strength, been here well nigh a week. Talkin nonzenze in yo sleep. John Brown, John Brown. Shinin Man, da Shinin Man."

"Who are you?" asked Zephaniah and he suddenly realized he could speak too. These were the first words he'd spoken in months, since the lightening. Something amazing had happened, he was thrilled to have his voice back

"The Negro said, "Ise called Job. I think causin Ise cursed like em."

"I can speak. My voice, I have my voice. Where am I?" asked Zephaniah.

"Yer on me farm, in Virginny. Well, my massa's farm. Ceptin he dead. Died in da tavern. Keeled right ova. Now Ise part a hiz estate till dey settle his debts. Cain't be sole till dey decide who ownz me, who ownz da farm," he answered.

"You saved me?" asked Zephaniah.

"I did, sure nuff, pulled cha from yer wagon, floatin down da riva."

"Was there another man with me?" Zephaniah asked.

"Not dat I seen? Wha happen to ya," asked old Job.

"I don't remember. I think I was struck by lightning and I lost everything. I am still blind. But I can talk now, and hear you. I was not able to until today," Zephaniah said.

"Praise de lod. youse tokkin and youse hearin. Ya talkin in ya sleep, talkin ta a Shinin man. Well, well, your heads healin but yer hairs gone gray," Job said looking closely at his wound. "I doan know bout dis eye. Lordy, lordy, you been marke by God, but yer blessed, ya lived"

"The Shining Man? He's over there," said Zephaniah pointing to the foot of his bed.

"Sho ee is, now you juz calm yo sef down, stay quiet awhile now," Job said as he crossed the room and picked up a plate. He returned and fed Zephaniah some cold Johnny cakes that tasted stale but good. He'd not eaten in some time.

The next morning Zephaniah was still weak and Job said he needed to work to regain his strength. So he helped Zephaniah walk about inside the cabin. And his steps grew stronger, day by day. They walked like this until gradually Zephaniah could walk for some distance.

Job then started to walk him to the banks of a river. He led him to sit on a quiet spot in the shade of some ancient trees. Zephaniah would sit and listen to the sounds of God's world for hours. Blind, his ears had grown more sensitive and he was able to pick out the fine sounds in the cacophony around him.

He heard, as if a newborn, the river coursing sweetly over stones in cool fluid rhythms, the birds as they skittered and hopped lightly among the brush, the whippoorwill's haunting call in the meadow, the soft coos of love birds, the rap of woodpeckers, the splash of fish leaping then returning to their water world. These sounds harmonized with the swaying of breeze filled branches and the ruffled leaves, God's bellows blowing over them, then inhaling and pulling them, waving them back toward Him. He felt anew the cool tingles of the thickly matted grass on the river's bank and the satin breath of the southern summer gusts. These sounds and feelings soothed him as never before. He felt like a new creature.

At times he and Job, enslaver and slave, conversed on life, a slave's life. Zephaniah saw the pain of the sin he'd fought for as he heard of Job's mother and father, long gone. His mother died at his birth. His father was sold off when he broke his arm. Job told him off his whippings in his youth and his year in the yoke. He told of his friend Jaze who was traveling to Durham to be put on the block but escaped the night he was to be sold and ran away to the hills, never to be heard of again.

Job would also read from the Bible to Zephaniah. He had learned to read secretly and felt great joy at reading aloud. It was for him an act of great meaning, he thought the further his voice carried the closer he was to some kind of freedom. So he would read loudly and clearly adding extra emphasis where he thought it important. And those words from Job's mouth seemed to ring new chimes in Zephaniah's mind;

Therefore I tell you, do not be anxious about your life,
what you shall eat, or what you shall drink,
nor about your body, what you shall put on.
Is not life more than food, and the body more than clothing?
Look at the birds of the air: they neither sow nor reap nor gather into barns,
and yet your heavenly Father feeds them.
Are you not more valuable then they?
And which of you by being anxious can add one cubit to his life span?
And why are you anxious about your clothing?
Consider the lilies of the field, how they grow;
yet I tell you even Solomon in all his glory was not arrayed like one of these.
But if God so clothes the grass of the field,
which today is alive and tomorrow is thrown into the oven,
will he not much more clothe you, O men of little faith?
Therefore do not be anxious saying,
'What shall we eat?'
'What shall we drink?'

Or 'what shall we wear?'
For the Gentiles seek all these things;
and your heavenly Father knows that you need them all.
But first seek his kingdom and his righteousness
and all these things shall be yours as well.
Therefore do not be anxious about tomorrow,
For tomorrow will be anxious for itself.
Let the day's own trouble be sufficient for itself.

And one of his favorites on any afternoon:

For everything there is a season
and a time for every matter under the sun.
A time to be born, and a time to die;
A time to plant, and a time to reap;
A time to kill, and a time to heal;
A time to weep and a time to laugh;
A time to mourn and a time dance;
A time to cast away stones,
and a time to gather stones together;
A time to seek, and a time to lose;
A time to keep, and a time to cast away;
A time to rend, and a time to sew;
A time to keep silence, and a time to speak,
A time to love, and a time to hate;
A time for war and a time for peace.

In this way Zephaniah lived for many months. He remained blind but he heard the world anew at the mercy of a slave. He lived among slaves on a land in legal limbo, where neither land nor slave had a rightful owner, like a man who does not know God.

Zephaniah did not know which side of the slave issue he belonged, at whose side would he stand? He knew the Bible was the word of God and slavery was in the Bible, but Job and the silent presence of the Shining Man reinterpreted all. He seemed to hear and learn new things since the lightning struck and the Shining Man was at his shoulder and when words he'd read so often came anew from the thick lips of Job. He did not understand this journey to Manassas he was sent on. His fury to kill John Brown had led him to become a helpless soul in the hands of those he'd enslaved. Trusting in God he knew there was a purpose and he would try to learn the lessons he was being taught.

The Shining Man

E ach day the Shining Man followed Zephaniah to the river. He was the only light beamed into the darkness brought on by the lightening. Finally, one day as Zephaniah sat and listened to the world the Shining Man spoke saying, "Zephaniah, listen to me."

Zephaniah rose to his feet. He could see the man clearly and now to his delight he could also see the trees and the river and the birds and the blue sky. His eyes overflowed with tears at the beauty of this vision. Then Zephaniah fell to his knees, no other response seemed quite right in the Shining Man's presence, he knew he was blessed, he knew he was at home and at peace in front of this bright creature.

And the Shining Man touched his hand and helped him to stand. He then led Zephaniah along the river and he sang softly these words:

"When the sun comes back and the first quail calls,
Follow the drinking gourd.
For the old man is a-waiting to carry you to freedom,
If you follow the drinking gourd."

Zephaniah listened to this song. He knew from Job the song was a secret message about escaping to freedom by following the Big Dipper as guide to the north.

The Shining Man said to Zephaniah, "We must walk together for a while. Will you walk with me?"

"I will, I will," answered Zephaniah.

They walked a while enjoying his new sight until the man said, "It is so good to be here with you. Feel that air, our Father made that air, just feel it. His spirit is in you, like the air, you feel it; you know it is there, you know it is good. Like the sun, just remarkable. Joseph Priestly knows about dephlogisticated air. Oxygen? Do you know what I say?"

Zephaniah answered, "Yes. I breathe it, it keeps me alive."

"Well, where does it come from?" asked the Shining Man.

"God made it, but I don't know how," responded Zephaniah.

The Shining Man smiled and said, "Of course not, no one does. Priestly discovered it. It was always there from the beginning. But you do not really know where it comes from. Some may know basic elements, the chemicals some will call it, but no one really knows what it is. They name it and think they know it. They think because they discover a process, one of countless equations, they have figured out God. But they never will. Then strangely they do not believe, when the mind that God gave them makes it possible for them to have the revelation of doubt or disbelief. As if God should make their mind free of all doubt. But that is not free will. Amazing self assurance, incredible self delusion. I often wonder how such arrogance could develop in such a simple creature. Every hundred years or so there is a new theory. You set the whole world on end announcing your brilliance. It is interesting to watch, hubris. The wind runs its circuits and comes back to the place whence it started. But we do not know where it goes and where it comes from. But there will be a new theory soon.

The Shining Man stopped, walked down by a brook, knelt and touched the water.

"I love this. Water. So completely perfect. You are made from it, born in it, live with it, need it. It is the source. It is made up of the sun and stars, the same as you. How did it get here? Who made the sun, the stars, the oxygen, the water? They are from God. Just as you are. It is so simple and right there it is, in front of your face, but they still want to see miracles, as if this isn't enough. Look at this," he said as he picked up a beautiful quartz stone from the steam bed.

He rolled it around in his fingers and said, "Do you see this? Isn't it beautiful?"

"Yes it is," said Zephaniah entranced by this presence.

"This whole creation is a wonder is it not?" he asked.

"It is," answered Zephaniah.

"But it is so wasted," he added throwing the stone back in the water.

"Wasted?" asked Zephaniah, his concern showing on his face.

"You do not know what you have," the Shining Man said as he rose and continued walking.

"I think I know...." stammered Zephaniah.

The man walked on ahead and said, "God created everything. Everything. He has given everything to you. Your life, the whole world. But you do not see him in it, you do not hear him. You walked out of the garden and set off on your own, hoarding wealth you do not own, and you, not God, made slaves to create less work for yourselves. Why do you always corrupt the temple? Now you will have to live through the flood you created. From time to time, our Father lets a great cleansing occur. He will not stop what will happen, it is already in motion. But God did not create it. Man did. It seems man cannot learn without spilled blood, without crisis. What a world. And after the suffering you forget so quickly all that transpired, and then in time you repeat it."

Zephaniah asked, "Why did God not create the world perfect to begin with?"

The bright man just smiled and answered, "Then you would be no more than an animal. There would be no choices. How can you perceive good and evil, if you cannot conceive of good and evil. There is no middle ground; a perfect world means no world. An imperfect world means knowing the difference. Then you choose what to follow.

"It is a hard thing," said Zephaniah.

"No it is simple," the Shining Man said as he stopped and faced Zephaniah. "It is only hard if you are selfish. Just remember, all things are made by God. They are God's. The things you steal. The things you sell. The things you own. If you start there it all makes sense.

He then continued to walk and added, "The next time you come across a book seller

ask him for a book called 'Origin of the Species.' It will be published soon, Charles Darwin wrote it. Another attempt at guessing the mind of God. But just remember, nothing, nothing is random. Nothing. Do you understand?"

"Yes," answered Zephaniah wondering at these words.

The Shining Man laughed a little bit as he looked on Zephaniah and said, "We will walk a while yet, man to man, all right?"

Zephaniah nodded that he would.

After a brief silence Zephaniah asked, "When will Jesus come back for all to see?"

The Shining Man smiled at this and answered coyly, "Not before man no longer enslaves men. They are Christians, you know, the slaves. If there was ever a message for the poor, for the oppressed people, Jesus spoke to them. Remember, you do not own anything here, certainly not a man made by God."

"But slaves would not know Jesus if they were not here," said Zephaniah rationalizing.

The Shining Man countered, "A horse knows how to run fast even before the whip.

Jesus would have reached them in time even without your yoke."

"But the Bible, there are slaves in the Bible," said Zephaniah.

The Shining Man stopped again and looked in his eyes and said, "All men are sinners, our ancestors were no exception. Slavery is an abomination in God's eyes. What about God teaches you to enslave?"

Zephaniah considered this and asked, "Then John Brown acts for God's plan? But John Brown is a murderer. Has he killed for God?"

The Shining Man countered strongly, "He is as misguided as those he seeks to punish. If our Father wanted to make each of you gods or angels he would have. But he made you men. It is your imperfections you struggle against, not God's. Killing begets more killing."

Zephaniah asked with a puzzled expression, "But you say all things are from God. He is in charge of the plan but the future is up to us. How can that be? It makes no sense."

The man answered, "The future is God's future, not your future. You are in charge of how fast you grow toward His future. But you control nothing."

"But how can I know what God really wants," asked Zephaniah.

The man said, "What makes you think you can ever know the mind of God? I cannot. Just as we are dwarves of the universe, we are grains of sand on the shore of God's mind. I cannot explain it in words."

Zephaniah asked, "So the Bible is wrong, it explains it in words?"

And the Shining Man answered, "The writers of the Bible tried their best to express spiritual truth. So Man wrote inspired by God, but their vocabulary, their creativity, their understanding is only that of a man's. That is why you are confused. That is why you pick out contradictions, as if sorting fruit. That is why it is hard for some to believe. They want answers but get more questions. But it is man's nature to question. That is why they call it faith."

"I have tried to follow God's way as it is written. I have patterned my life after it, what else can I do?" said Zephaniah.

The Shining Man answered, "Do not turn the Bible into a false god. You have to listen to the Bible, not just read it, do not worship words. Open up your soul to them, but do not accept the common definitions. Divine the Divine. Language is imperfect to explain God."

"Then what is the Bible if not the guide for my life?" asked Zephaniah.

The Shining Man replied, "It is a good book."

"That is all?" asked Zephaniah.

He answered, "Men wrote it. That is all? That is amazing. It is one of the most amazing things in all existence. Try writing something inspired by God. It was written as best as they could led by their understanding of God as taught by prophets, by his Son. But all of it was done by men, all imperfect men. The Bible was translated, altered by Scribes, subject to human error, copied and compiled by hand for centuries. Books are left out of your Bible, some are yet to be found, some lost forever, dust, gone. It is a compilation, written and compiled by fallible men, but still inspired by God."

"The Bible is not perfect?" asked Zephaniah

The Shining Man answered, "All things done by God are perfect, but nothing done by man is perfect, even something inspired by God. The Bible is perfect but only when you can see it. Jesus spoke of the soul of the law, not just the written word of the law. The soul of the message survives in the Bible, it lives somewhere in all of us. It is divine inspiration that lets a mere word reveal anything of God, written on Man's innermost soul, not parchment. Man's mind could not conceive of God until there was a word. The stories are true, yes, passed down, yes, altered, yes, but their heart is intact. Miraculously! A true story can never be forgotten once told. That's why in the Beginning was the word and the word was God. Do not try to understand God, you never, ever will, trust me."

"Tell me what I must do," asked Zephaniah.

And the answer came swiftly, "He does not condone the slaughters to come or those that have been. But he cannot stop them. Souls rage and once again there must be battle. Jesus weeps. He has told you before in so many ways, it is about Love. There is no map for life, just Love. If there is no love in it, it is wrong, that's one basic principal you can live by. Father, Abba, Love. You're going to have to use your instinct for Love. That's why Jesus preached Love, Love of God, Love for you, by you, revealing for all mankind the true nature of God, revealing a God given instinct. It is all man is capable of that is divine, to Love."

Then as suddenly as he arrived he was gone.

———◆———

Job found Zephaniah stumbling and wandering, talking to himself by the river. Job was amazed that Zephaniah could see, said he was blessed for sure. Zephaniah could see Job's kind face for the first time, the mirror of the good spirit inside that he had felt for so long. He laughed, touching his face, cupping it, his sight had returned and he was amazed. He was confused but happy, very happy, unsure of what he was to do and what was the meaning of all the Shining Man had said.

They sat until dusk on a bench outside the cabin looking at the sight of the fall leaves before them. Zephaniah, still in his amazement, said to Job, "Why don't you leave here, just run away?"

"Headin north to da promise lan? I doan know. Been livin here moss my life, dese hills, dese feelds dey part of me. Guessin I be in Viginnny ress a my life," said Job. And Zephaniah went inside the house to get the Bible. He wanted to read it, to find some verse that could convince Job that he should be free or not, depending on the words.

Just then the howling of a blood hound resounded along the valley floor. A group of four white men with torches and a dog walked on to the farm and called out, "We come for Job."

Job, fearful, stood, "Yes sirs, whut can I do fa ya."

"You been into town last night?" one of them asked.

"No I be hee da whole time," answered Job.

"Liar," said another.

And they swarmed him, tied his hands, put a rope around his neck and led him away, as quick as it can be said. Zephaniah had stayed inside looking on, frozen, unsure of what to do. He was torn, he knew Job to be a good man, but he also knew he was property and had no rights. These white men no doubt had good reason for being here, though he knew Job spoke the truth. But with the women crying in fear for Job, Zephaniah could not stand by. He grabbed a pistol, ran to the door and followed the torch lit beings, long shadowed and evil, into the dusk.

He ran along the edge of the field near the still leafy oaks. When he got close enough he could hear that Job was crying. He had gone to his knees, begging them saying, "Please Ise innocin, innocin. I neva did dis evil thing. I neva did."

But they did not listen and threw the rope over the thickest limb of a massive old pine tree, needles ripe, black sap spots like tears drops in the wavering torchlight. And Zephaniah just watched as Job with a rope around his neck was pulled up, swinging, jerking, lurching.

The white men said, "Nigger Boy gonna rape a white woaman, and the nigger Boy git his juss disserts."

And they left him swinging.

Zephaniah was shocked at seeing Job's lifeless swaying form. This lynching had happened so fast, so efficiently, so devoid of feeling. It was as if a spider had been crushed underfoot or a fly swatted. He owed this Negro his life. This man who'd saved him and helped him to recover was now still, dead though innocent, innocent though black. He felt he understood him as a man, as a human being even though he was just a Negro. He had witnessed his kindness and seen the world in a new way, but he could not bring himself to stop this unjust act. Had Zephaniah not been blinded he would never have seen this. Zephaniah thanked God for this revelation and then immediately he felt remorse. He could have shot them and saved Job but he had hidden like a coward. He was torn. It was all wrong, all of it, but he had cowered in the shadows of the trees, confused at what he should do.

The men left Job limp and lifeless and walked back down the red dirt road laughing and spitting, proud of themselves as they strode back to town. The sight of poor Job hanging from the tree like a shrugging man deep in thought, arms limp at his side, made Zephaniah groan aloud. He ran over urgently but too late, untied the rope and lowered Job's body. Then he carried his dead weight back to the cabin and laid him on a pallet. He watched as the women tore at their hair and cried the age old moans of loss. He saw them wipe off his body and dress him in his only clean shirt. He saw them put the coins on his eyes and sit around by candlelight crying and praying over his dead body.

Zephaniah could watch no more. A time to live and a time to die, he thought he understood the words now. He took the pistol, mounted a sorry horse and rode off in the direction of the men. After riding hard for about three miles in the gathering dusk he came upon the four killers of Job. They had been tipping a liquor jug as they walked and they were feeling happy after a good bit of work. They were not concerned about this old white man riding their way and barely paid him heed as he rode past them. Then Zephaniah turned the horse and confronted them.

Zephaniah said, "You killed an innocent man. Job was with me all night last night."

They looked at each other and laughed, "Zat so, well he ain't an innocent nigga no mo. He a dead nigga." And they laughed again.

With that said Zephaniah pulled out his pistol and shot each of them squarely between the eyes, all four. They wore flaccid expressions from drunken brains as they fell backward, a new red eye in each forehead staring, a single river of blood running down their noses. The bloodhound ran off yelping, scared by the gunfire and the smell of his master's blood. Zephaniah dragged their bodies off the road, covered them with logs and fallen leaves, and he rode back to the cabin.

The women were still singing and praying over Job's cold body. Zephaniah looked on in reverence through the night at the rope tracks on his neck, at his black face turning blue.

The next day, Zephaniah mounted a horse and headed into Blacksburg. When he arrived in town he heard the news. John Brown had raided Harpers Ferry and been captured. He would go on trial in Charles Town, Virginia, two hundred and fifty miles to the north.

Zephaniah decided immediately he must go there. So with no money in his pockets and his old mission revived, he rode out, north to Charles Town to see this John Brown.

———◆———

He traveled for ten days; day on day, mile on mile, until finally he saw a sign for Manassas. He thought of going there, but was drawn to go to Brown's trial in Charles Town. He sat on his horse at the crossroads. He still believed somehow Manassas was the place Brown would be, as Joseph had said. But he knew he was in Charles Town in a jail cell.

As it happened a newspaper blown by the wind tumbled past and became caught on a briar bush. Zephaniah dismounted, picked it up as if it was a message from an oracle and read it. He read the story of Brown's raid, his plan to free the slaves, start a revolt. He read his letter to the public and realized this man was more than an abolitionist killer. He was a revolutionary, a messenger of God. He realized Brown was starting the war Joseph had foretold, a war to free the likes of Job, and now because of the lighting and Job and his vision of the Shining Man, Zephaniah knew why.

He believed God led him to this place but wondered why, if Brown was in Charles Town, why had he been called to Manassas. Joseph's interpretation of his dream had brought him to these crossroads and his righteous rage over Brown's murders had driven him onward over all this time. But in the process God had turned his heart around and, instead of wanting to kill Brown, he now wanted to save him. He thought he understood this man. He wanted to save him from hanging, to join Brown's cause. God works in strange ways, he knew. But whether Brown would be hanged or whatever his fate, he was called to Manassas for something. So while his quest for Brown drew him to Charles Town, his compass oriented to God's will pulled the reins to the right and he headed toward Manassas. Perhaps the answer was there. Manassas.

The Trial

ohn Brown stood before his gallows looking into the noon daylight, the
unseasonably warm breeze blew his beard to the north, and his eyes, clear
blue, reflected the sky; he was thinking about his life. He had a slight smile
on his lips. He remembered his final hours at Harpers Ferry. He remembered the
engine house—'The Fort' they called it—the deaths of his sons, the hunger, the
white flags and negotiations, the men who had died. It all seemed like a dream.
John Brown stood beneath the noose, new rope twisted to a taut executioner,
and considered his trial.

Brown knew as he lay on his pallet, wounded and feverish, through the trial
proceedings that he was witnessing his dream come true. The transformation
that was occurring was remarkable. It was truly divine intervention because he
could not have planned it this well. He was reaching the nation in a way he had
not expected.

The trial was an event of epic proportions, held in Charles Town, Virginia.
It was an even greater catalyst for freedom than the raid could have been. He
never could have guessed this. It had immense future consequences not seen
since the tumult of the nation's birth. The final decision of this court, caught
as they were in a web of southern dignity and honor, unable to fathom what
these proceedings would reap, sounded the death knell for slavery and the death
hundreds of thousands in years to come.

Brown looked on the southern barristers so sure on their rules of order,
bound by codes of jurisprudence, true to legal ethics, slaves to procedure and saw
the trial added one more great weight to an already guilt ridden nation. The Law
that ruled the day served but one master; it prosecuted one crime, insurrection, to
preserve another crime, slavery. This chaffed. It could neither soothe nor repair;
there was no justice in such contradiction. There was not a rung to grasp that
was not slippery with moral ambiguity; that was not dripping with the precious
ointments poured over Aaron's head.

The tempest he fomented in Harpers Ferry swirled around this court and
spread across the land. He saw the court's earthbound powers held no sway in this
case of universal dimensions. It could not know its decision was the beginning of
the end of the South, but Brown knew it, after a time.

Virginia saw only that awful murders had been committed; warlike acts against the sacred ground of their homeland, a threat to southern honor challenging southern manhood, an affront to the integrity of the endowed rights of states.

The southern press blared headlines of outrage, words stirred from deep within its gut, striking out as a cornered animal would. This rabid rage, fueled by fear of slave uprisings, grew torrid. Imagination took control. What if Brown had succeeded? Consider the bloodshed, the murders, the rape of the gentle sex of the plantation by evil black mongrels.

In the north all the pent up angst about the heated topic of slavery was released from their souls with this act. When Brown's acts were interpreted by their leaders, by the press and the philosophers, many northerners came to understood that this law needed breaking; that verbal jousting and rhetoric were simply not enough to end the morally repulsive, ungodly institution of slavery. It filled the air with a hellish stench. They had held their noses for too many years since the Declaration of Independence. Now, at long last, Virginia and the entire south must pay for her slavery sins.

But Brown's incursion on Harpers Ferry was not a raid to simply free, it was intended to raise an army to wreak havoc, to create bedlam. Brown raised a trumpet call for runaways to rally. He set a mystical fire to ignite oppressed souls into one common purpose, toward freedom. Brown saw himself beckoning souls who would run when beacons shone, who would flee when church bells chimed; souls bearing Brown's Bowie Pikes honed to one edge, one scythe to level the wheat, to run to the hills, encamped in the mountains, banded together, to grow to a force, a fighting black movement, to transform America: an audacious vision sure to fail, almost desperate in its errors.

Brown looked back on it with a wry smile. To think they could take the bridges where a major railway crossed, take the Federal arsenal eighty miles from Washington whose wares were the munitions store of the South; to think that he might organize an army of slaves, with no prior effort to communicate a plan and no prior training, to retreat with him to some redoubt in the hills not chosen yet (not chosen yet!), how could he succeed? How? But as he had always said even his errors were part of God's plan. He could not know the mind of God; he was but an actor for the unfolding of his purpose.

When Brown's failed scheme first hit the northern pages, the philosophers of the day, the ardent abolitionists and powerful Christians, the Transcendentalists, who considered themselves the watchdogs of man's spiritual future, saw this meteor and they invoked the meaning of Brown. Emerson and Thoreau wrote with rich religious allusions. Brown was to be martyred, crucified, nailed to a cross by soldiers of Caesar. He was the Christ for the black man, who would rise again to lead another battle to free the slaves. Brown, the herald of the apocalypse, would ghostlike haunt the south for years to come, rising nightly as the spectral prophet of doom of their illicit cause.

Thoreau gave a rousing speech in Concord to a crowd, who listened to his words with keen attention as he untangled the issues at war in their minds. He led the charge to fight for Brown's legacy, the meaning of his sacrifice.

He said, *"I am here to plead his cause with you. I plead not for his life, but for his character,—his immortal life; and so it becomes your cause wholly, and is not his in the least."*

"Some eighteen hundred years ago Christ was crucified; this morning, perchance, Captain Brown was hung. These are the two ends of a chain which is not without its links. He is not Old Brown any longer; he is an angel of light. I see now that it was necessary that the bravest and humanest man in all the country should be hung. Perhaps he saw it himself. I almost fear that I may yet hear of his deliverance, doubting if a prolonged life, if any life, can do as much good as his death. Misguided! Garrulous! Insane! Vindictive!"

"So ye write in your easy-chairs, and thus he wounded responds from the floor of the Armory, clear as a cloudless sky, true as the voice of nature is: 'No man sent me here; it was my own prompting and that of my Maker. I acknowledge no master in human form.' And in what a sweet and noble strain he proceeds, addressing his captors, who stand over him: 'I think, my friends, you are guilty of a great wrong against God and humanity, and it would be perfectly right for anyone to interfere with you so far as to free those you willfully and wickedly hold in bondage.'

"And, referring to his movement: 'It is, in my opinion, the greatest service a man can render to God. I pity the poor in bondage that have none to help them; that is why I am here; not to gratify any personal animosity, revenge, or vindictive spirit. It is my sympathy with the oppressed and the wronged, that are as good as you, and as precious in the sight of God. You don't know your testament when you see it. I want you to understand that I respect the rights of the poorest and weakest of colored people, oppressed by the slave power, just as much as I do those of the most wealthy and powerful. I wish to say, furthermore, that you had better, all you people at the South, prepare yourselves for a settlement of that question, that must come up for settlement sooner than you are prepared for it. The sooner you are prepared the better. You may dispose of me very easily. I am nearly disposed of now; but this question is still to be settled, — this Negro question, I mean; the end of that is not yet.'

"I foresee the time when the painter will paint that scene, no longer going to Rome for a subject; the poet will sing it; the historian record it; and, with the Landing of the Pilgrims and the Declaration of Independence, it will be the ornament of some future national gallery, when at least the present form of Slavery shall be no more here. We shall then be at liberty to weep for Captain Brown. Then, and not till then, we will take our revenge."

So there was a kind of Olympic confluence of the violent and spiritual, of terror and the divine, of vigilante actions and religious sentiment. Most remarkable of all remarkable things was that these two most opposite camps merged in 1859 into one force.

John Brown was a descendant of Thomas Brown, a scot of the Mayflower Brown's, a Puritan, a Calvinist, an Old Testament fire brand, single minded, unwavering; a simple man, but a clear ringing bell across the cold valley in the darkness. His backers, his translators, his interpreters, were educated mystics, spiritual Christian preachers, philosophers, newspaper editors, the rich, the privileged. But a like power coursed through their veins and they marched lock step together, unified in passion for the freedom of the black man. They became as one, willing to write, to speak, to risk all, to take up the cause. One side financed and defined for the public the scope and the heart of the battle; the other led by Brown stood ready to fight, to bleed, to die, to let his children die, to watch every item of worldly gain disappear.

Standing at his gallows, a crow cawed in a leafless tree, drawing John Brown's eye. He looked at the noose swinging in the breeze and thought, "Eighteen soldiers and two more of his sons, Oliver and Watson, all dead, sacrificed for the cause; that is how many lives it took. Thirty six hours that would change the world. I have not failed. The negro will be free."

Brown's papers, discovered at the Kennedy farm, had exposed his backers in Boston. Gerrit Smith suffered a mental breakdown, was committed to an asylum soon after this news, so distraught was he over the deaths he'd caused with his support. Howe, Sanborn and Stearns ran for Canada, afraid they would be hanged for treason, saying they were unaware a Federal Arsenal was Brown's final goal.

Higginson stood firmly. He would not run. He was not afraid, as were the others. He, along with Pate and Thoreau and Emerson, stood on moral ground.

As the effect he'd had became known to him, Brown thought he saw in his death great meaning; as a martyr millions would rally for him, the battle would be joined. The newspapers and visitors to his jail cell made it clear. He had not failed but in fact had succeeded in setting afire the issue of slavery.

Thus I wondered as I looked on the courtroom, Brown on a pallet suffering still from his wounds as the proceedings droned on to their inevitable decree toward the gallows, if Brown did not plan or allow himself to be caught, if he did not hope for a Judas in his midst, so he might be hanged. I came here from Manassas to see for myself. It was such a mystery to me, I could not stay away.

Why did he let the train leave Harper's Ferry with the news of his insurrection? Why did he not escape when the slaves did not gather as planned? What happened? So I wondered, without resource enough for the cataclysm he sought, with his plan failing before his eyes, did he realize enlisting the

Transcendentalists and the press to bear his message as even more potent. But
how could he have simply sacrificed his sons? Why did he not surrender earlier
if he knew this. Was he a fool or a master, a charlatan or saint, a prophet? Was
he a false prophet? Was he mad?

I know now after many years, after living through the war and seeing the
unfolding of events, the final outcome. Brown called for a holy war and he started
one. It was Brown's call to battle, first to a band of militant abolitionist dreamers,
then to a whole population that changed America. He prophesied sweeping
freedom for slaves after much bloodshed, it eventually happened. He dedicated
his life to it. He sacrificed his family to it, abandoned all worldly wealth to it. He
traveled thousands of miles to bring it to fruition.

It was Brown's raid on Harper's Ferry which stiffened the necks of southern
leaders, who instilled new fear into plantation owners, who raised the hackles
of poor dirt farmers, love of their land over love of the Union. No overture
of peace could forestall the inferno to follow. Manassas, Bull Run, Vicksburg,
Fredericksburg, Gettysburg.

This common man who planned a battle continental in scope with little
real logistical support, a disaster in all he tried in this world, was the focus of all
attention by all political parties, by all presidential hopefuls including Lincoln.

It was Brown who fused southern opinion against Lincoln's party. The
papers said he and all northern Republicans were radical Christian crusaders,
thieves of property rights. Lincoln was depicted as an ugly ape chained to wealthy
industrialist charlatans who coveted southern wealth; whose primary tactic was
slave insurrection, but most never uttered such words. Lincoln's platform in '60
simply sought to halt the expansion of slavery into Kansas, but it did not seek
total abolition. He wanted to leave it where it was, but that was not heard in the
din.

The nomination of the rail splitting lawyer was made possible by Brown. He
caused the party schism that made Lincoln the third candidate, and eventually the
uncanny and miraculous winner of the Presidential election. His election sounded
the death knell, tore the ties of Union asunder, and threw down the gauntlet no
southern gentleman of honor could leave unanswered.

And so it was Brown who led the way to the firing on Fort Sumter by
South Carolina and the rapid unraveling of the Union through succession and
the formation of our Confederacy, what is commonly noted as the beginning of
the War Between the States. But I know where it really started; the war began
in Harpers Ferry.

It was Brown's song penned by Julia Ward Howe that made northern armies
march. Brown's image "a' mouldrin in the grave" led them into wilting fire and
exploding canisters, the belching of cannons all around, to bleed their blood into
sacred ground, hallowed ground.

Mine eyes have seen the glory of the coming of the Lord
He is trampling out the vintage where the grapes of wrath are stored,
He has loosed the fateful lightening of his terrible swift sword,
His truth is marching on,

Glory, Glory hallelujah,
Glory, Glory hallelujah,
Glory, Glory hallelujah,
His truth is marching on.

And in a few years to save the Union, Lincoln took Brown's tactics for the raid on Harpers Ferry to every southern state. He authorized the unleashing of scorched earth tactics that roved like a mighty plague. Lincoln embodied Brown's vision of slave insurrection on a national scale and formed them into platoons and set them free to fight. Out of desperation to break the South, he raised Brown's mantle of emancipation and became the abolitionist he never was with the Emancipation Proclamation.

Brown's cell was decrepit. It was an aged stone structure which had held runaway slaves and drunks. Men had died there. Men had killed themselves there. But as in so many other things, the world to Brown was an illusion and he was unconcerned with appearances. He had transcended these things many years ago. He sat in jail reading, calmly, his Bible:

"Now there was a man of the Pharisees, named Nicodemus,
a ruler of the Jews, this man came to Jesus by night and said to him,
"Rabbi, we know that you are a teacher come from God, for no one can do these
signs that you do, unless God is with him."
Jesus answered him, "Truly, truly, I say to you, unless one is born anew, he cannot
see the kingdom of God."
Nicodemus said to him, "How can a man be born when he is old? Can he enter a
second time into his mother's womb and be born?"
Jesus answered, "Truly, truly, I say to you, unless one is born of water and the
spirit, he cannot enter the kingdom of God. That which is born of the flesh is
flesh, and that which is born of the spirit is spirit. Do not marvel that I said
to you 'you must be born anew.' The wind blows where it wills, and you hear
the sound of it, but you do not know whence it comes or whither it goes; so it
is with everyone who is born of the Spirit."
Nicodemus said to him, "How can this be?"
Jesus answered him, Are you a teacher of Israel, and yet you do not understand
this? Truly, truly, I say to you, we speak what we know, and bear witness to
what we have seen; but you do not receive our testimony. If I have told you

earthly things and you do not believe, how can you believe if I tell you heavenly
things? No one has ascended into heaven, but he who descended from heaven,
the son of man. And as Moses lifted up the serpent in the wilderness, so must
the son of man be lifted up, that whoever believes in him may have eternal life.
For God so loved the world, that he gave his only begotten son, that whoever
believes in him should not perish, but have eternal life. For God sent the Son
into the world, not to condemn the world, but that the world might be saved
through him. He who believes in him is not condemned; he that does not believe
is condemned already because he has not believed in the name of the only Son
of God. And this is the judgment, that the light has come into the world, and
men loved the darkness rather than the light, because their deeds were evil. For
everyone who does evil hates the light, and does not come into the light, lest his
deeds should be exposed. But he who does what is true comes to the light, that
it may be clearly seen that his deeds have been wrought by God."

He looked across the way to his men who occupied a cell along a far wall.
John Cook and Edwin Coppoc sat on separate cots staring alternately from floor
to ceiling; they were not readers or writers. They had grown ever quieter as the
mysteries of the trial unfolded. They could not see any way out of the labyrinth
of language and motions, so they shut down and rested easy. They knew it could
come to this and they appeared calm. Though at night, restless sleep and forceful
dreams betrayed a haunting internal fear. They tossed and dreamed, speaking in
their sleep in urgent ways.

Shields Green and John Copeland, the two captured blacks, were in another
adjacent cell. Shields could not read. He spent his time in silence, waiting for the
meals to be delivered. He knew no reprieve would come his way, perhaps to the
white men, but not him. He was pleased with the small degree of fame he had
gained. He felt like his life had a purpose and he was not afraid to die.

Copeland read his Bible and prayed much. He seemed content, enjoyed
his food, and even sang a hymn from time to time. He knew he had done the
right thing. There was no way this slavery beast was good or fair and it needed
culling.

Brown spent much time writing letters to his wife and his friends, to his
abolitionist mentors. Some were sent to the press and printed in newspapers
across the land, spreading his words, reinforcing his cause, challenging the fence
sitters to join his holy mission. He used the time he had left to evangelize and to
warn of the debacle to come if they did not change their ways.

At last, when all was the proceedings were done, while the wounds on head and
side still oozed and he lay on a pallet before the judge, when the court's blood
lust was totally spent recounting the rude tale, when the last witness had testified,
and when the last motion was made, when it was time, John Brown stood, looked

about calmly and spoke his piece, saying:

"I have, may it please the court, a few words to say. In the first place, I deny everything but what I have all along admitted: of a design on my part to free slaves. I intended certainly to have made a clean thing of that matter, as I did last winter, when I went into Missouri and there took slaves without the snapping of a gun on either side, moving them through the country, and finally leaving them in Canada. I designed to have done the same thing again on a larger scale, that was all I intended. I never did intend murder or treason or the destruction of property or to excite or incite slaves to rebellion or to make insurrection.

I have another objection, and that is that it is unjust that I should suffer such a penalty. Had I interfered in the manner which I admit, and which I admit has been fairly proved—for I admire the truthfulness and candor of the greater portion of the witnesses who have testified in this case – had I so interfered in behalf of the rich, the powerful, the intelligent, the so called great, or in the behalf of any of their friends, either father, mother, brother, sister, wife, or children, or any of that class, and suffered and sacrificed what I have in this interference, it would have been all right. Every man in this court would have deemed it an act worthy of reward rather than punishment.

This court acknowledges, too, as I suppose, the validity of the law of God. I see a book kissed, which I suppose to be the Bible, or at least the New Testament, which teaches me that all things whatsoever I would that men should do to me, I should do even so to them. It teaches me, further, to remember them that are in bonds as bound with them. I endeavored to act up to the instruction.

I say I am yet too young to understand that God is any respecter of persons. I believe that to have interfered as I have done, as I have always freely admitted I have done, in behalf of his despised poor, I did not wrong but right. Now, if it is deemed necessary that I should forfeit my life for the furtherance of the ends of justice and mingle my blood further with the blood of my children and with the blood of millions in this slave country whose rights are disregarded by wicked, cruel, and unjust enactments, I say let it be done.

Let me say one word further. I feel entirely satisfied with the treatment I have received on my trial. Considering all the circumstances, it has been more generous than I expected. But I feel no consciousness of guilt. I have stated from the first what was my intention, and what was not. I never had any design against the liberty of any person, nor any disposition to commit treason or incite slaves to rebel or make any general insurrection. I never encouraged any man to do so, but always discouraged any idea of that kind.

Let me say, also, in regard to the statements made by some of those who were connected with me. I hear it has been stated by some of them that I have induced them to join me. But the contrary is true. I do not say this to injure them, but as regretting their weakness. Not one but joined me of his own accord, and the greater part at his own expense. A number of them I never saw, and never had a word of conversation with, till the day they came to me, and that was for the purpose I have stated. Now I have done."

And then the sentence: death, death for all of them.

One day in early December John Brown received a letter from Mahala Doyle, wife of John Doyle of Kansas, Mother of William and Drury Doyle. She wrote a letter to Brown cursing him for killing her husband and sons that night along the Pottawotomie creek, ruining her life:

I do feel gratified to hear you were stopped in your fiendish career at Harpers Ferry with the loss of your two sons, you can now appreciate my distress in Kansas, when you entered my house at midnight and arrested my husband and two boys, and took them out of the yard and in cold blood shot them dead in my hearing. You can't say you done it to free slaves, we had none and never expected to own one, but has only made me a poor disconsolate widow with helpless children. O how it pained my heart to hear the dying groans of my husband and children.

But Brown never answered her. He knew she could never understand. He did not take those deaths lightly but he saw them as part of God's great plan. He did not act out of spite but for his cause. It was ages ago anyway. He knew that posterity would approve of his acts to prevent slavery from being established in Kansas. The lives of a few for the lives of many; it was, after all, war.

John Brown wrote letters to his wife as well. He told her of his love for her and said she should not worry for him; he was holding up well and was cheerful. He put on a brave face for her, a pose he wanted to carry through to the end. And so he did not want her to visit. He wanted to go to his death serenely and calm, but he thought seeing his lovely wife would destroy his composure. He knew also that money, ever the plague to his existence, was scarce. So he told her to pray for him but remain at home in Elba.

But Mary would have none of it. Always strong willed, she decided she would see her husband before he died. So a letter to Thomas Wentworth Higginson convinced him to finance her trip.

Mary Day Brown arrived one day before his hanging. She had hurried there by train to Boston, ship to Philadelphia, train to Baltimore and then Charles Town. Thomas Wentworth Higginson accompanied her the whole way.

Brown's guard who had grown to like Brown said the rule was one hour visitation but he would see what he could do to let it go longer. He left them alone, standing outside the building.

It was a heartbreaking final time. They knew it was their last hours together and they hugged each other for a long, lingering time.

Tears streaming John said, "Mary, my Mary, why did you come here. You should not have"

"I needed to see you John, this last time."

"But the journey, it is too hard on you. And you should not see this."

"I needed to see you John. I love you so."

"I love you too my dear. You are Gods greatest gift to me."

"Our sons are dead and now you. What is to become of me?"

"They will care for you, there are many now, you will have enough."

'I do not want them. I want you."

"I want to be with you also"

"All of these years with you gone, I hoped some day you might tire and need to be with me. But it was not to be."

"We both knew it. It was my fate from the beginning."

"Still I dreamed of it."

"I know…Owen is safe?"

"Yes, he is in hiding, it was a tortuous journey back through the hills, hiding out, starving, but he is back. The others will guard him with their lives. He will be fine."

"And the girls?"

"They are fine as well but they worry for you."

"Tell the children I died for God's cause."

And they embraced again.

Just then the guard outside smoking his pipe let out a holler of amazement and John and Mary rose to look out the cell window. Across the sky was a beautiful meteor shower. Endless streams of racing stars, like a thousand strokes painted by a golden brush, flashed by, on and on and on and on. They were entranced at the beautiful sight. It was a sign, they said, of God's joy.

Then they talked on for one more hour. They talked of his burial. He requested a funeral pyre. His wish was to burn with the bodies of his sons. He told her also how to dispose of his last worldly possessions. To each child he gave some valuable thing, his books, his surveying tools, his watch, his rifle, his Bible.

And then the guard returned and said she must leave. She begged for more time but he could do not more, rules were rules. They kissed and she wept. John cried as well, not wanting to let her go.

"You be brave my John. Do not let them see you cry. Do you hear me? Do not show that you care a whit for this world."

"I do not care a whit only for you."

But you must be strong for the cause; the cause will go on now stronger and stronger. They march the streets of Boston. There are rallies in New York. All of the newspapers write about you. You have done it, John. Slavery is in their sights. The world knows. Now finish the deed. Be strong my love, as I will."

"Do not come to see me. Promise me. Promise me."

"I will dream of you in better times, when we were young. Here, take this," and she handed him her locket which he grasped with all his might. "Carry it with you to the end. I love you my dearest." And she was escorted out by the guard.

John Brown's Gallows

The hanging day was mild for winter. Few people yet alive in all America will ever forget it. So much had happened in just two short months it overwhelmed all. Brown's crime, capture and trial had raced bold print across papers everywhere.

Attack on Federal Armory!
Incitement of Slave Revolt!
Sentenced to Hang!

These words circled the globe. The ensuing speeches in the North, the gatherings, the church services, the marches, all infused with pious anger and recrimination, added to a whirlpool of unimaginable strength, sucking the nation to its vortex.

The sun stood cool in the gray blue December sky. Hazy clouds combed into slender tongs rinsed the sun's rays, giving gentle hints of many colors. But there was no rainbow, no ethereal light. But a sense of something great and momentous was at hand.

Spectators were kept at a distance, I among them. The Virginia Regiment assigned to this duty, Robert E. Lee at its head, leading some from the Virginia Military Institute, stood with military precision, at attention, ready for orders. Virginia soldiers smartly dressed, bayonets sharp, boots polished, stood in a large rectangle around the gallows, to protect from any who may seek to disrupt, to stage an escape or take revenge.

I stood far away, at some distance with all the curious, the angry, the inspired. Negroes stood in the crowd with their children so they could see with their own eyes the man who wanted to save them.

Brown left his jail cell and was led out in shackles past the onlookers. A Negro woman held her baby up to him and he kissed the child, saying he prayed she would walk free some day. He climbed into the back of a wagon and sat upon his own casket as he rode out. Slaves worked in the fields and they paused for a moment and took off their hats as he rode past. He smiled at them. Once out in the field he was led off the wagon and out toward the gallows.

A soldier with a smart beard and a jaunty self important bearing stood at attention striking a most dramatic pose as Brown walked by. The crowd's hush for the doomed man whisked through the air like a solemn broom sweeping the onlookers. There were a few tears and a few curses as Brown walked through the gap between the parallel lines of soldiers. As he walked past the soldier with the self important bearing and smart beard, the man called out boldly, "You'll burn in hell Brown."

Captain J.E.B. Stuart called out, "Hold your tongue Private Booth."

———◆———

I would see him again, this Booth. He'd find his fame for killing Abe Lincoln, shooting him dead in Ford's Theatre, jumping to the stage, yelling something in Latin about a tyrant. I can hear him to this day. But that was yet years away.

———◆———

Then I was pulled along by the surging crowd. We moved as one to get a closer look as Brown approached his final place. But we were blocked by the soldiers, who stood firm. I thought in a glance I saw among the faces in the crowd the dead woman from the massacre, her pallid skin, her empty eyes accusing and looking toward me. But I must have imagined her, as I have many times. I did not see her again that day.

Brown stepped up the stairs of his gallows, this wooden ship sailing to death, afloat above the dormant grass. His last stop this side of the veil, his thin place. He was straight, relaxed, with a luminous glow in his eyes, controlled, incredibly so. He knew he was going to meet Jesus, he would soon stand before God. His dead children would be there, his wife Dianthe. His father, his mother, and all his ancestors would be there. He would be reunited, blessed with a fine room in the mansion, with angels and archangels and all the glory of heaven.

He was at peace with himself, even glad. He looked around with his odd crooked smile to few friendly faces, too far off for his old eyes to see. He saw only the rigid looks of the soldiers at attention around his pulpit, the officer of the guard who held the black hood, Thomas Jackson, someday to be renamed Stonewall, and the minister, a withered drawn man to whom Brown said, "You may go sir. I would rather you were a poor black slave than a sinning southern preacher. I do not need your prayers. I am already consecrated."

And the minister bowed his head, walked down the stairs sheepishly.

The hood was placed over Brown's head; he was moved to the trap door, stood over it waiting for its release. For his release. But there was a delay. The guard was not properly organized, some detail of discipline raised by a persnickety young officer. And a full ten minutes was spent sorting the men. Brown had to wait. Not a sound except the wind; the crow's mocking call was his only companion. The rustling of the black cloth over his head, the rough tug and scratch of the rope round his neck and on his wrists was all he could feel.

Then the signal was given.

The trap door sprung open and he dropped, jerked, lurched, a sway then a shudder. Then still, dead still.

John Brown passed to glory.

———◆———

I looked at Brown's black hooded head, its unnatural tilt, the tight rope swinging in a morbid rhythm, a low creaking sound delayed by the wind and the distance. All about were silent for a time. Then some cheered, others stared, the Negroes cried and I stood mutely feeling so alone, having reached my goal but feeling hollowed out. It did not feel like an end but a beginning. I did not know why.

So as the crowd dispersed I stood for some time as they dropped the body, dumped it on a wagon and rode away as if hauling a slaughtered hog to a roast. The soldiers marched off with final boot cadence, justice done, now completed, as cold December gusts rose, shrugging off the unusual warmth of that day. I then rose on my mare, which might have been Beersheba, and rode away to the west, to the gold setting sun, to return to my home.

Missouri

Reuben sat dourly in a straight backed church pew in Uncle Esau's House of God. His trouser leg was folded up under his aching thigh. He knew his leg was gone forever, though at night he dreamed he could still feel his toes and walk. It was amputated neatly by Doc Hyssop above his right knee. When he stood on his crutches and tried to walk like a man the empty space from the ground to his swinging thigh was stared at like a body at a funeral viewing. The loss was seen as a wide gap in his soul.

Drawn in face, shrunk in body, his life had drained from within him; it seemed to have seeped out the protruding bone on his stump. He wanted to worship with the whole congregation but his faith was challenged by the loss of his limb and his father's abandonment.

Pastor Esau stood praying at the altar, arms raised up in awe of the power and the glory. The people rose and sang 'Hallelujah', their hands clapped and praises rang out in joy to the worship of the Lord, but Reuben could not rise with them. His crutches had fallen to the floor.

To the side of the altar, a hymn inspired woman named Mariah played the keys of the organ as she swayed and sang and rolled her eyes upward. Behind the instrument the pump plunged regularly, sucking and blowing vital air to the instrument, to the very hymn. The life of the tune was breathed from its lungs; the hymns humble harmonies were lifted up by the organ feeding the congregation the mystical eucharist of song.

At the organ's pump handle, hard working, the little slave girl worked grimly, the Christmas gift at her labor on that bright Sunday morn.

Atlantic Ocean

Zebulan leaned over the rail of the clipper ship Ariel, polished by sea storms too numerous to count. The sails, chests full of gusts, drove the schooner through feathered gray swells, rising and diving, digging in, falling, stalling, then climbing out, pulled upward, pushed forward, the ocean's splash sang out an eternal song.

His face sprayed wet and stinging, his soul cleansed by salt. Wind dried his eyelids as he blissfully beamed and yelled through sea salted lips at the top of his lungs at the thrill of the forces engaging, though no one could hear. His joy overtaking, his grip slipped so slightly, his shoes lost the deck top and he tumbled overboard. As the ship moved on past him, his calls of distress went unheard by anyone.

He looked at the ship, shrinking as it moved on, then at the wasteland of sea he floated in. Above him flew a bent neck albatross and alongside him rose a grey dorsal fin.

Jacob's Homestead

Zephaniah's sons glared at each other with growing dissension among them, each with the knowledge of the destruction they'd wrought and returned twofold and ten on their miserable lives. Cursed by plotting, by hatred, by jealousies growing, they fought and were spiteful and spoke words of no meaning and only those used as a tool to sting, to dig, to harm.

Eyes hollow, hands idle, Simeon and Dan and Isachar and Levi and Judah looked down at their shadows seeking answers in dust. The fields scorched hard and stubborn, no crop would grow this season, lost to the unbreakable evil of drought. The well, dried and unyielding, hid water like a secret it could not or would not ever reveal. Their beards in a tangle, their necks bent from looking, their teeth gnashed in anguish, curses spit through their lips. Ribs sagging in horse flesh, sheep bleating gone silent, geese long past consumed, the sons of Zephaniah barely existed, their lives were just tattered memories of good days gone by.

And in a crater collapsed over Diana's gravesite, lie the colorful feathers of the peacock's proud fan. Rustled dry by the hot wind, its black empty sockets, God's eyes now blinded by greed and lack of love.

Springfield

oseph followed the Colonel down the main street of Springfield, Capitol of Illinois, riding toward Washington. He would stay here for a few days and visit a friend of the Colonel at a party in a clapboard house of plain distinction. Simple in furnishings, no statement of fashion, this house of a lawyer and his wife was the home of the Lincoln's, Mary and Abe. He, the doting husband, lean in body and temper. Her nature was high strung, her emotions overpowering. She was a mystic, a patron of the black arts. She looked to the past and the future for meaning in séances, palm readings, astrology and such.

The gathering was a fine affair made even more remarkable for one simple reason.

Joseph spoke his first words there in the midst of the assembly; to the surprise of everyone, this mute beautiful valet said something extraordinary, a remarkable pronouncement.

Out of the blue aired gathering of Illinois society he said quite innocently, "From Springfield will spring a great leader of the nation. Sometime in the future, he will split more than rails."

This curious blonde boy, now noticed by Mary Lincoln, her eyes lit and widening; she sensed a power in his foretelling spirit. So they sat down to tea the day after the party and she looked into his eyes and questioned him quietly. She brushed back his blonde tresses and gazed a long inspired stare, hoping he could tell her secrets of the afterlife. Then she took out a deck of cards and picked one card, the ten of hearts. And she asked him to tell her which card it was she held.

So he did. And she gasped.

This boy was a sign, a gift, a blessing, perhaps even an otherworldly visitation.

This boy in their midst, this prophet so young, had something about him. She hoped he might sense her aspirations, read her future, put her in touch with those on the other side. She looked to the Colonel and queried Joseph's origins, his lineage, his name. The Colonel told her the full story of the daring rescue from savages, sure as well to illustrate his valiant command.

Mary thought for a second then asked the Colonel his plans. When she heard that Washington was their destination, she asked them to promise to visit again soon. He could be of use.

Along the Missouri

Rachel walked holding her tiny granddaughter along the banks of the sweeping Missouri. A figure far distant, a horse rider loping, his mind in a vision, an unspoken question absorbing his being, approached them. In a time the two came close and their eyes met. Each recognized the other. They stood in silence with unspoken feelings released through the frozen air of their glances, captured and exchanged and sent back consoling. Their eyes rose up then fell in modest awareness of the sin in their hearts.

Rachel took his horse's bridle and he then dismounted, looked first at the child then fell in her arms. She cried as he smothered himself in the warmth of her fire, the thing he most missed, the woman he'd longed for in the cold nights gone by.

They stood there for some time, talking, explaining all that had befallen in this fleeting expiration of God's earthly time. They then turned again eastward, hand in hand and heads down, horse trailing submissive, Helen in his arms.

There was no clear answer to anything in life, that was the truth, but only one thing they both knew for sure, God loved them and they must go on together.

Manassas

Zephaniah entered Manassas where Joseph had foretold John Brown would be and where the Great War that would challenge God's order would begin. As he rode in to this place he'd so long sought, he questioned what the order would be like.

His heart was changed; he was confused by his understanding of Brown. He saw the slave's faces and they looked to him as never before. They looked human. He could read their emotions from the expressions they bore; resigned, cowering, empty, feigning submission above roaring souls. Zephaniah knew that he had been wrong about so many things. But he had done his best to try to discern God's will. He had driven himself harder, given up more than most men would have. And the journey that had brought him to the place called Manassas had many hardships. He was not the same man.

Now he must wait for God to speak to him again. He did not have Joseph to rely on, he must listen to his own inner voice. Zephaniah would wait in this pastoral village for the sign, a thought, a vision, a dream. He knew that his fate was in God's hands. He prayed for God's will to be revealed. For he trusted the Lord and knew that this journey was not in vain and he knew he was meant to experience all of this, to see all of it; the Indians, the dead woman, the abominations of Dr. Sunderland, Reuben's wounding, his children's rebellion, the Shining Man, Job's lynching.

He went into the saloon in the only hotel, ordered a whiskey and waited for his future by God to unfold.

There was a card game at a table near a statue of the god Ares, the Roman god of war. Zephaniah walked over and asked the men, deep in concentration of their cards, if he might join the game. They were playing five card stud around a green felt table. He sat and put his money down as a new hand was dealt, five cards all face down. And they then began to go around the table, each player turning a card at a time, betting with each view of the hand they held.

Zephaniah was last and turned a black ace of spades on the first round. The bet, two bits.

Just then a man ran in holding a newspaper saying to all who could hear, "John Brown has been hung in Charles Town today. The bastard's dead and gone to hell."

The men at the table rose at once and hurried to see these words in print. So as Zephaniah sat alone at the table, he realized killing Brown was not the reason for this journey to Manassas. God wanted something else of him. But he did not yet know what it was.

He looked about the decorative bar, at the zaftig cupids carved into the columns, at the painting of naked nymphs lounging near a green pool and centaurs on the hills, at Ares the god of war, at the large mirrors behind the liquor bottles, and finally he looked out the window to the still working slaves and pondered this life.

He said in a whisper, "Thank you, God."

. When the men returned, the game proceeded. And Zephaniah felt hopeful knowing more of his life was yet to unfold. He was far from done. Zephaniah revealed his remaining cards, one at a time in his turn, until finally the last card, a jack of spades, could be seen. He looked about at his fellow players who gazed on his royal straight flush with envy.

The pot was his. His luck had changed.

THE END